Praise for the novels of Kaki Warner

"A truly original new voice in historical fiction."
—*New York Times* bestselling author Jodi Thomas

"[An] emotionally compelling, subtly nuanced tale of revenge, redemption, and romance. . . . This flawlessly written book is worth every tear." —*Chicago Tribune*

"Romance, passion, and thrilling adventure fill the pages."
—*New York Times* bestselling author Rosemary Rogers

"A romance you won't soon forget."
—International bestselling author Sara Donati

"Draws readers into the romance and often unvarnished reality of life in nineteenth-century America." —*Library Journal*

"Kaki Warner's warm, witty, and lovable characters shine."
—*USA Today*

"Halfway between Penelope Williamson's and Jodi Thomas's gritty, powerful novels and LaVyrle Spencer's small-town stories lie Warner's realistic, atmospheric romances."
—*RT Book Reviews*

WARRANTY.

Home to Texas

Kaki Warner

JOVE
New York

A JOVE BOOK
Published by Berkley
An imprint of Penguin Random House LLC
penguinrandomhouse.com

ISBN: 9781984806215

First Edition: June 2021

Printed in the United States of America
1 3 5 7 9 10 8 6 4 2

Book design by Gaelyn Galbreath

*To all those in uniform who have sacrificed so much
to keep this great country safe, I thank you.*

Stay strong. Stay safe. Come home.

PROLOGUE

Landstuhl Regional Medical Center
Landstuhl, Germany
April 2018

Army Second Lieutenant KD Whitcomb drifted on a cold dark sea, lulled by the steady hum and beep of the machines that surrounded her bed. She knew she was in a hospital, in a room with a big window looking out onto the nurses' station. But she didn't know why or how long she'd been there. Nothing made sense and thinking was too hard.

Occasionally nausea or deep, throbbing pain in her abdomen and back and hip would pull her toward the light. She would become groggily aware of noise beyond the window or movement around her, people touching her while voices spoke in soft, hushed tones. Then a warm rush, and she would sink back into the safety of the uncaring, unfeeling drift.

The room was never dark. Sometimes the light was so bright, it hurt to open her eyes. But occasionally, during the hush of night when the halls were quiet and the overhead lights were dimmed, she could keep her eyes open for brief periods. During one of those times, she saw a man standing in the hall, watching her through the window.

He was tall, with a stern, unsmiling face. Not in an army uniform. Black shirt, black ball cap with writing above the bill. No scrubs or white coat or stethoscope, so not a nurse or a doctor. She didn't know who he was, or why he was there, or why he watched her so intently. It worried her, the not knowing. Even with all the pain meds dripping from the IV line into her arm, she felt a spark of fear. But all she could do was close her eyes and hope he went away.

Later—an hour, a day?—she felt hands touching her. Movement by her bed. Voices again. Bright light against her closed lids told her it must be day. That awareness awakened the pain and she grew anxious, waiting for the warm rush that promised oblivion and forgetfulness in the gentle, peaceful drift.

Instead, the footfalls receded.

Then silence.

But she wasn't alone.

She could sense a presence nearby. Heard breathing, the rustle of cloth.

An image of the figure at the window burst into her mind. Fear shot through her body, and with a gasp, she forced open her eyes.

The man in the black shirt stood beside her bed, looking down at her.

She blinked up at him, her thoughts in disarray, not sure if he was real, or why he was there, or what he wanted. She heard him breathe, watched his cold blue eyes lock on to hers, and knew he expected something from her. *But what? Why?*

She slid shaking fingers toward the red call button, then froze when she saw the holstered gun on his belt and the badge beside it. In an instant, everything came rushing back. Fear clutched at her throat. She sucked in air, her head reeling as terror flooded her mind.

Farid smiling. Gunshots. Pain. Blood. I shouldn't have left her. I should have looked for a gun. I should have gone back as soon as they started shouting.

The beeping of the machines grew louder, faster. Voices intruded, jerked her back to her hospital bed. The man was talking to her nurse, but all she could hear was the pounding of her heart. Vomit burned in the back of her throat. It was an effort to swallow, to think. But before she could bring her thoughts in focus, the nurse hurried away and she was alone with the dark man again.

She struggled to speak, finally managed a raspy whisper. "Captain."

The man stepped closer. "Say again?"

She licked her lips, tried again. "Captain . . . Mouton . . ."

He shook his head. "I'm sorry. She didn't make it. Neither did Farid."

No! KD clenched her eyes against an onslaught of pain. Her stomach rolled. She grappled for the pink bowl wedged between her pillow and the bed rail, and vomited up dark, bitter bile.

A hand supported her until the retching stopped, then it took the bowl away. Trembling with exhaustion, she slumped back against the pillows. A cool, damp cloth pressed against her forehead.

"What can I do, Lieutenant?" a deep voice asked. His voice. The man with the gun and the badge. "Should I get the nurse?"

She was afraid to move her head or open her eyes. Every time she did, it felt like her brains had liquefied and were sloshing around inside her skull.

"Can I get you anything? Water?"

"No." The spinning slowed enough that she opened her eyes.

This time, her vision was clearer. A beard-stubbled face hung over her. Tired blue eyes. A squarish face. More worried now, not as grim or threatening as when she'd first seen him. No black ball cap to keep the dark hair from sliding down his forehead. But she knew who he was now, and why he had come.

"Farid . . . shot her?" she asked.

"We're still investigating."

"I should . . . have checked. He . . . had on a robe. I didn't see a gun." Every word was an effort.

"He who?"

"Farid . . . Captain Farid." KD closed her eyes and fought back another wave of nausea. The whirling in her head slowed but didn't go away.

"If you're up for it, Lieutenant, I have a few questions."

Of course he did. He had a badge and a gun. He would want to know it all.

She opened her eyes. "You're . . . criminal investigations. CID."

He nodded. "Warrant Officer Murdock."

"Here to . . . arrest me?"

"CID investigates. We can't make arrests or file charges. We leave that to the board of inquiry."

"Am I . . . in trouble?"

"Should you be?"

Tears welled up. "I shouldn't have . . . left her."

"Why did you?"

"The boy . . ."

"What boy?"

"She sent me . . . to find the boy."

He said something, but she was so weary, she could barely form a thought. "I didn't see . . . the gun." She was dying. Sinking. Her lids felt heavy as stone. "I should have . . . checked. . . ."

He spoke again, but the drone of his voice faded into the hum and beep of the machines as darkness sucked her down.

When next she opened her eyes, he was gone. It was dark and a nurse was fiddling with her IV bag.

"How're you feeling?" the nurse asked.

"Like . . . I'm dying."

"You're not." The nurse gave a practiced smile. "The

doctor will be by in the morning to give you a full report. And Warrant Officer Murdock said to tell you he'd be back in a day or two. Still nauseated?"

"Whenever I . . . move . . . my head."

"That's the pain meds. I'll see if I can get you something to settle your stomach. From one to ten, how bad is the pain?"

More pain meant more meds, which meant more vomiting. "Five . . . maybe six," KD lied. She was willing to suffer a little pain to clear the fog in her brain and stop the churning in her stomach. She was a soldier, after all. And when Murdock came back with his questions, she had to be ready. Because he would want her to relive that bloody, terrifying day when everything fell apart.

CHAPTER 1

Forward Operating Base Hickock
Northern Afghanistan
Three days earlier

The seven o'clock supper rush was over and the mess hall in the inner compound of the FOB was almost empty, except for two Special Forces guys bent over a map spread across a corner table. KD and Captain Mouton were the only diners, enjoying their first real meal in four days.

Mouton, a battle-hardened veteran on her third tour in Afghanistan, led the base's Female Engagement Team and was KD's next-in-command. Raised in southern Louisiana, Nataleah had clawed her way out of the swamps to earn a track scholarship at LSU. After graduation, not wanting to go back to the bayou country she'd left behind, she had enlisted in the army, which was about as colorblind as any place could be. Her harsh upbringing had prepared her well for the hardships of an active combat zone in inhospitable terrain, but it was her rich Cajun background and quirky sense of humor that got her through the worst days. In the short time KD had been in Afghanistan, she had learned a lot from the captain, especially how to laugh in dismal situations. Like the fruitless and frustrating patrol they had just concluded.

But now, after four days in the field with a Special Forces unit that never seemed to rest, the two women had shed their heavy armor, taken real showers, put on clean ACUs, and hurried to the mess for hot food on an actual plate. It wasn't great, but it sure beat MREs gobbled down in a dust storm.

"Ever eat gator?" Nataleah asked, forking up another bite of chicken.

KD shook her head.

"Tastes like quail, but chewier. Kinda fishy. I prefer nutria."

"What's that?"

"Swamp rat."

Never quite sure when Nataleah was joking, KD kept eating, hoping the captain wasn't going to launch into another of her roadkill recipes. Not knowing when they'd be sent out again, she focused on her meal, eating as much as she could, as fast as she could. She might pay for it later, but at least she'd go to bed with a full stomach.

Although Female Engagement Teams had been officially disbanded several years earlier, there were still remnants in rural, tribal areas of the mountain provinces. Since Afghan women were forbidden to speak to men not of their families, female soldiers were invaluable in bridging that communication gap. Their purpose was to gain the trust of female villagers who might be able to provide intel on insurgent activities in the area, distribute health information and humanitarian supplies, and offer help where needed.

KD enjoyed doing it. Her teammates were tough women. Fully trained and combat-ready, they had to be fit enough to keep up with the SF units to which they were attached, and calm enough to make sound decisions under fire. KD was proud to be a part of it, and thought she was holding up well, despite the harsh conditions. She might be small and wiry compared to most of her team members, but she had great endurance and was able to carry the weaponry, armor, and thirty-five-pound pack as easily and for as many miles as the other women. Still, she was glad to be rid of it after four days of carting it around.

In the distance, the *whup whup* of rotor blades indicated another helicopter was landing at the helo pad in the outer compound. KD stopped chewing and listened for the *boom* of mortar rounds or staccato bursts of gunfire. When she heard nothing unusual, she resumed eating.

"Maybe it's supplies," Nataleah said, starting on her pudding. "We run out of toilet paper, you see some real fighting, yeah."

They were low on laundry soap, too. The only clean clothes KD had were the ones on her back. Since they were within the relative security of the inner circle of the FOB, both women wore stripped-down versions of their ACUs— Army Combat Uniforms. Baggy multi-cam-patterned pants tucked into their lace-up boots, and the standard padded, long-sleeved combat shirt, designed to minimize hot spots and chaffing when worn under the tactical vest and armor.

It helped. Most of the time.

They had left their vests, helmets, and rifles in their quarters, although each woman wore a Beretta M9 sidearm in a drop holster attached to her thigh, and carried extra ammo, combat knives, and radios on their belts. And like their SF counterparts, who rarely followed army regs, KD and Nataleah wore ball caps rather than the usual goofy camo patrol caps.

Hardly an outfit a Gunther County debutante from Rough Creek, Texas would have sported, but KD was okay with that. Having been raised in wealth on a sprawling Texas ranch, she was proud to be making her own way rather than relying on the family trust fund and connections.

But she wouldn't mind a manicure now and then. Maybe even a pedicure and facial. Or an overnight trip to a Dallas spa with her three sisters.

Static crackled on Nataleah's radio. A voice said, "Captain, you back? This is MP Specialist Rogers at Com."

Frowning, Mouton unhooked the radio from her belt. "Yeah, I'm back. And this better be good, Rogers, or your ass is grass and I'm the lawn mower."

"There's two women at the inner gate looking for you. One's in ACUs, but unarmed. Says she's your Afghan interpreter. The other is local. At least, I think she's a woman. Hard to tell under all those clothes. Seems upset. The dog didn't detect explosives, but the women won't come inside the gate."

"On my way." With a weary sigh, Nataleah hooked the radio back to her belt. "Probably another complaint about a guy beating on a woman. Assholes."

"Shouldn't that be a job for the army MPs?" If the captain was called away, KD would have to go, too. No woman left the inner compound alone.

"It would be, if the complaint was on one of ours." Mouton pushed back her chair and stood.

KD stood, too. "You don't think it's on us?"

"Better not be. Our guys know better than to interfere in local issues."

Local issues, KD thought in disgust. Like the beatings of women, honor killings, abuse of children. She hated that part of her job.

As they walked across the mess hall, the SF guys, ever-vigilant, studied them for a moment, then went back to their map.

"Then if it's local," KD went on to Nataleah as they stepped outside, "shouldn't the ANP take care of it?" There was a sizable contingent of the Afghan National Police stationed in the outer ring of the FOB. Usually, they handled village or tribal issues. KD didn't want to suit up and go out again. She just wanted an uninterrupted night's sleep on a real cot.

"Unless the complaint is on one of them."

"On the ANP?" KD hadn't noticed any issues between the Afghan police and army personnel. But then, she'd only been in Afghanistan a short while.

Mouton nodded. "If it's local, and we report it to the ANP, they just tattle to the husband or father or brother or fifth cousin twice removed, and the woman gets beat up worse. Happens a lot. It's a fucked-up system, and not kind to women."

KD studied the stern profile of the woman beside her. "Yet you keep coming back. Why?" KD wasn't sure she wanted another tour in Afghanistan after this one ended. As a cultural support team member, she would be stationed here for a year. But after that, she wouldn't mind rounding out her service résumé elsewhere. Like most other West Point graduates, she dreamed of ending her career in the Pentagon with a chest full of metals and laurel leaves on her cap.

"Like my daddy say when our pirogue get caught in a fast-moving current," Mouton said in answer to KD's question. "'Trow out de anc.' 'Anc got no twine on it,' I tell him. He say, 'Trow it out anyway. Might do some good.' That's all we can do here, Lieutenant. Keep tossing out the anc and hope someday it'll do some good."

KD didn't know what to think of that. Not all of the captain's colorful stories were easily understood, especially when told in a Cajun accent.

Gravel crunched under their boots as they left the mess and followed the bright lights toward the inner gate. Since it was early spring, the breeze sweeping down from the mountains was still cool and not too dry. But in two months, they'd be sweating under their gear and choking on dust. A lot like northwest Texas.

But tonight, it was cool and quiet except for the moan of wind gusts along the eaves of the concrete buildings and the flap of canvas on the soft-sided structures. Occasionally a scrap of tune, low laughter, or voices drifted past, but mostly everything was tucked in for the night.

Hickock had once been a Soviet stronghold, well forti-fied and almost medieval in appearance with its concrete watchtowers and sturdy fencing. Like most FOBs, it was built in two concentric circles, each fenced and gated.

The outer circle contained a helicopter pad, a munitions and fuel depot, vehicle parking, barracks for the Afghan National Police, and a local bazaar that sold trinkets, ques-tionable dried meats, local wares, and a variety of illicit drugs such as hashish, valium, uppers, downers, pain meds, cocaine, and anything derived from the poppy. Afghanistan produced over 80 percent of the world's heroin.

The inner circle contained living quarters for American soldiers and contractors, various offices and meeting areas, the mess hall, a small detention center connected to the MP barracks, a communications center, and a medical facility. Any unauthorized person coming through the inner gate was thoroughly checked for firearms and explosives before being escorted by two heavily armed soldiers to their stated destination. The local translator, or terp, for their team, Samira, often came through the inner gate, but she was never armed and had to be escorted, as well. That she hadn't requested entrance but had asked for the captain, instead, was curious to KD.

As they neared the grim-looking tower by the inner gate, an MP pointed to where Samira and the local woman were waiting.

"I am sorry to get you out again," Samira said as they walked up. "This is Azyan." She nodded to the woman be-side her, draped head to toe in black cloth except for the open area around her eyes. Samira wore a *hijab*, or scarf around her head, but didn't cover her face. "Azyan's son, Tajamul, was taken from her home. She wants him back."

"Taken by who?" Nataleah asked.

"Captain Asef Farid."

"The commander of the ANP unit?"

Samira nodded.

"You fucking with me?"

"No, ma'am."

Mouton looked at KD. They'd both been briefed about Asef Farid. Volatile, cruel, violent, and also the son of a powerful local poppy grower and suspected Taliban sympathizer, Khalil Farid, a vengeful bastard if there ever was one. The villagers were terrified of him. "Shit." The captain turned back to Samira. "Can't she just go get him?"

"She tried. Farid hit her. Many times." At a nod from Samira, Azyan pulled aside her scarf to show a split lip and a bruised cheek. She pushed up her sleeve to show more bruises. When she started to lift her hem, Mouton waved her to stop.

"I get it. The guy's an asshole. But it's a local matter. We can't interfere."

The Afghan women looked at each other then back to Nataleah.

"*Lutfan*," Azyan whispered in Dari, the language spoken by most of the villagers. It was one of the two-dozen words and phrases KD knew. *Please*.

A long pause, then Nataleah asked, "Why did Farid take the boy? He is a boy, right? Not a grown man?"

Samira and Azyan spoke for a moment, then Samira said to the captain, "Taj has eight years. Farid is using him for *jensiyat*. Sex."

"Shit."

KD was horrified. Pederasty had always been a problem in Afghanistan. When the Taliban was in power, they had forbidden it. But now that their control had slipped, the practice was growing in popularity again, especially in rural and mountainous areas among powerful tribal leaders and the Afghan police. They even had a term for it. *Bacha bazi*. Boy play.

At the mandatory cultural briefing KD had attended when she'd first arrived, she was told to look the other way, since *bacha bazi* was considered a local cultural issue. The Afghan Minister of Interior Affairs, who oversaw the ANP, had attempted to crack down on the abusive practice, but because of bribery and the villagers' fears of police retaliation, charges were never brought. Afghanistan was one of the most corrupt nations in the world, and KD often wondered if the place was worth all the blood and treasure lost trying to bring it out of the dark ages.

"I can talk to him," Mouton finally agreed. "But that's all. I can't force him to give up the boy. Make sure Azyan understands that."

Samira translated, then nodded to Nataleah. "She understands."

Mouton told her to take the woman close to the ANP barracks and wait while she found a couple of SF guys to go with them. "If we get the boy out, she and her son should disappear for a while," she warned Samira. "There could be payback."

After the two Afghan women left, the captain and KD headed back to the women's barracks in the inner FOB. "We really doing this?" KD asked, worried about the look-the-other-way directive.

"I got to try. Somebody's got to stand up for the kid. But you shouldn't go with me. No use fucking up your career, too."

"You're not going without me, ma'am," KD said firmly.

Nataleah gave her a small but grateful smile. "Okay, but keep your mouth shut. You're just there to witness. We don't want to look like we're hunting for trouble, so we won't suit up, either."

Outside the female barracks, she stopped. "No rifles or armor. Just our sidearms and Kevlar vests. And headscarves, instead of helmets. No use showing disrespect even if he is an asshole. Get my vest and scarf, too, while I round up a couple of bored SF guys to go with us."

"Yes, ma'am."

Minutes later, in *hijabs* and vests, KD and Captain Mouton walked through the inner gate again, this time trailed by two Special Forces soldiers in full combat gear. KD hadn't been on patrol with either of them, but she'd seen them around. They seemed like okay guys.

As they passed the ANP quarters, Samira stepped out of an alley. "Farid's hut is two past the barracks," she said in a low voice. "Down there, on the right."

Mouton looked where Samira pointed, then back at the ANP barracks. They were standing halfway between the two on a dark, deserted street.

She turned to the SF guys. "Good line of sight to both the hut and the barracks. One of you could stay here with the women, while the other covers the back of the hut. What do you think?"

"You sure you don't want us to go inside with you?" the older soldier asked.

Mouton shook her head. "I don't want it to look like a confrontation. If this goes south, the less you know the better. Just cover us if something goes wrong."

The soldier nodded in agreement, waved the Afghan women to follow him, then the three of them slipped noiselessly into the darkness of the alley.

Trailed by the other soldier, a short, wiry Hispanic, KD followed her captain toward the hut. On reflex, she rested her hand on the butt of her handgun and scanned the shadows. This would be a great place for an ambush. The soldier with them must have sensed it, too. She could feel the tension in him. No scuffling or small talk. Just silent, watchful movement, loaded rifle held at the ready across his chest. She was grateful he had her back.

Farther down at the end of the street, the booths at the bazaar were draped and shuttered for the night. An insurgent could be watching and waiting behind any one of them, but KD saw no movement or signs of life.

Lamplight shone through the half-closed front shutters of Farid's concrete hut. From the rear of the building came the sound of a child talking in a high, panicky voice. Maybe crying.

At Mouton's nod, the Hispanic soldier silently peeled off and disappeared into the shadowed gap between buildings. After allowing him time to set his position behind the hut, the captain stepped up to the wooden door and knocked.

A short wait, then a dark, bearded man wearing a robe and sandals yanked open the door. He said something in Dari, then saw they were American. "What do you want?" he demanded in a barely civil tone.

"We'd like to talk to you for a moment, Captain Farid," Mouton said politely.

The Afghan hesitated, leaned out to study the empty street, then reluctantly motioned them inside. Turning away, he walked over to a desk in front of the back wall. "I am surprised to see two unescorted females out at night," he said in a contemptuous voice as he filled a glass with water from a dented metal pitcher. "Why have you come?"

Mouton planted herself directly across the desk from him. He didn't appear to be armed, but she was wise to stand out of arm's reach of a man who thought nothing of brutalizing women. And children.

KD moved up behind her and to the right so her gun arm was free and she could watch both Farid and a curtained doorway on the side wall. Since she didn't see the boy in the front room, she assumed he was somewhere in the back. She hoped he could speak enough English to hear them through the thin drape and understand why they were there.

"I've received a request, Captain Farid," Mouton said. "The mother of the boy you are holding wants him back. He is needed at home."

The police officer's face twisted with fury. "What boy?" He threw the arm not holding his glass wide, the sleeve of his robe whipping like a wing. "I see no boy."

Something about the man seemed off to KD. He acted anxious. Hyper. His eyes were so black she couldn't tell pupil from iris. Maybe he was high on drugs. It was a problem with some of the local police.

"I thought I heard someone crying," Captain Mouton said. "Perhaps he's in the back room. Lieutenant Whitcomb, go check. He might need help."

"*Ne!* No!" the Afghan ordered. "You have no right!"

But KD was already pushing aside the drape.

Voices rose behind her.

She ignored them and scanned the room.

A heavy square table beside the drape. On another wall, a cabinet with a tarnished mirror above it. In the center of the room, a rumpled bed with a length of chain around one leg, and beside it, wall-mounted hooks from which hung an ANP uniform, various clothing, and lengths of rope. No rear exit, only a single small window with open shutters six feet up on the rear wall. No boy.

Then she heard movement inside the cabinet.

She moved toward it. "Taj," she whispered. "*Aya suma englisi yad daren?* Do you speak English?"

She opened the cabinet door.

A boy with tear tracks down his dirty cheeks shrank away. He was bruised, his face battered, dried blood at the corner of his mouth and around his wrists.

"Tajamul," KD said, trying not to frighten him more than he already was. "Your mother—*maadar*—waits out back." She pointed to the window. "*Watan.* You go now. *Raftan watan.* Go home."

Voices in the front room rose to shouts, threats.

The boy began to cry.

Desperate to get the child away before Farid came looking for her, KD pulled Tajamul from the cabinet and carried him, kicking and crying, to the window on the back wall.

Glass shattered on the other side of the drape.

Shit! Arms straining, KD lifted the struggling boy toward the narrow opening.

Suddenly the top of a helmet appeared just above the sill. "What the fuck's going on?" the Hispanic SF soldier whispered up to her.

"Take him!" KD flinched when a gun went off in the front room.

"Fuck! What was that?" The soldier tried to peer over the sill into the room behind KD and the boy. "I don't have a shot!"

"Just take him!" KD cried and shoved the boy out the window just as the sound of a second gunshot bounced off the walls of the concrete hut. Grabbing her Beretta, she started to turn.

A deafening *boom* and she slammed face-first against the wall. Fire exploded low in her back. Her left leg gave way. She slid down, rolled onto her left side, and lay gasping in pain and terror.

Farid stood in the doorway, smiling.

"No," she said. But no sound came out.

Vibrations in the plank floor as he walked toward her. *God please no.*

He stopped two feet away, pointed his gun down at her. "Infidel," he said, his eyes dark and gleaming above his beaked nose and black beard.

The Beretta was still in her hand. With all the strength she had left, KD raised it and squeezed the trigger. Two gun blasts in close succession.

A spray of warm blood.

Then she sank into darkness.

CHAPTER 2

Richard was so weary after leaving the hospital in Germany, he dozed on and off through most of the flight from LRMC to Bagram Airfield, Afghanistan, arriving just after noon, local time. Despite wearing earplugs and drinking four bottles of water, after traveling nearly twenty of the last twenty-four hours aboard noisy transports, he had a pounding headache and felt like he'd lost half his hearing. But he'd managed to sleep some, so he was good to go. And hungry.

After a quick meal in the Bagram Airfield officer's lounge, he showered and changed into his ACUs, then donned the armor and weaponry required when entering a combat zone—armored vest, SIG M11 handgun in a drop holster on his right thigh, K-pot helmet, rifle strapped over his shoulder. Making sure the lanyard holding his CID badge was in place, he picked up his duffle and hurried out to the helicopter waiting to take him on to FOB Hickock.

Another noisy, jostling ride, which would undoubtedly add a queasy stomach to his pounding head and ringing ears. But at least he would be back on solid ground. For a while.

God, he hated flying. Almost as much as he hated this latest assignment. There was something fishy about it. Not the least of which was the timing . . . coming a day after his request for leave.

He was almost thirty years old. He'd been in the army since he'd graduated from Washington State University eight years earlier, and had been in CID for the last six. He liked the investigative aspect of the job and was good at it—collecting and analyzing criminal intelligence. What he didn't like was having to fly all over the world to do it.

It was time for a change. Either within the army, or in a new direction altogether. And with his re-enlistment date coming up, now was the time to make his move.

He reached into the duffle at his feet and pulled out his copy of the DA 31 Request for Leave Form, the original of which Chief Warrant Officer Stranton should have approved several days ago. The delay troubled Richard. He didn't like Stranton and sensed the feeling was mutual. The chief was new to his post and determined to prove himself at CENTCOM. Richard wouldn't put it past the prick to deny leave just because Richard had forgotten to cross a *T* on the request. After scanning the form for errors and finding none, Richard slipped it back into the pouch on his duffle.

He'd requested a month. Four weeks to figure out if he was ready to commit to another tour of service, or if he should cut the cord and leave the army for good.

And do what?

He'd considered and rejected joining the FBI. Too political. Same with big metro police departments, especially with the intense media scrutiny lately and the open season on cops. Homeland Security would require too much time in DC or New York. Not his favorite cities. He was more of a small-town guy.

He had no reason to go back to his hometown in Washington state. His parents had sold their home and hardware store to move into a retirement community in Tucson. They rarely communicated anymore anyway. What separated them couldn't be undone, and he had given up trying. He was on his own to do whatever he wanted, wherever he wanted to do it.

Maybe somewhere west of humid Alabama and east of bankrupt California. Something with a state CID or county sheriff's department. Maybe the US Marshals Service or the Texas Rangers. Not that he knew anything about Texas or Rangers. But it sounded interesting. A good change of pace. And not much flying. He was tired of chasing down scared, battle-weary soldiers.

But first, he had to complete this latest assignment, one that was shaping up to be a lot more complicated than the usual drug, suspicious death, missing armaments, or AWOL situations. One American officer dead, another critically wounded—both female—and a captain in the Afghan National Police shot to death in his own quarters. No apparent motive.

Why had two female army officers gone at night to the residence of the commander of the local unit of the Afghan National Police? Drugs? Sex? Bartering stolen weapons? And who shot whom?

He'd have to fly all over hell and down the sides to find out. In addition, he'd been ordered to complete his investigation ASAP and he was already behind.

Since the body of Army Captain Nataleah Mouton was already on its way to Dover, Delaware for a detailed autopsy, he'd have to wait for their findings before he could complete his report. Plus, the wounded officer, Whitcomb, was in no condition for a comprehensive interview at this time, so he'd have to make a return trip to Landstuhl within a day or so. Either delay could be costly, and Stranton, his next-in-command, expected his final report in a week. All

Richard could do for now was go to FOB Hickock, where the crime had occurred, and start from there.

He'd have to move fast. Cultural traditions stipulated that the Afghan officer's body should be washed by his male relatives, wrapped in a white shroud, and buried within two days of death. No autopsy. Already the captain's father, a local poppy grower, was raising hell about the delay, as well as the circumstances of his only son's death.

But with the fourteen-hour flight from the United States, the eight-and-a-half-hour time difference, plus the short stopover in Germany to interview Whitcomb, by the time Richard arrived at Hickock, he would have only a few hours before he had to release Farid's body to his family. He'd never had to work so fast. But Richard was beginning to understand why.

Damage control. DOD had CENTCOM scrambling, and Chief Warrant Officer Stranton was desperate to end the investigation before it escalated into an international scandal. The military was already facing enough backlash from other PR problems. They wouldn't welcome more.

A political shitstorm, with Richard caught in the middle. If he didn't do this right, he was fucked.

Knowing his leave couldn't begin until he'd finished his part of the investigation, Richard had already e-mailed the FOB medical officer, asking him to draw blood from the dead Afghan, take DNA samples, make dental impressions, and provide detailed descriptions and photographs of the body and wounds. He'd also alerted the base's MP commander, Captain Vocek, of his arrival. They hated when CID showed up out of the blue.

Pulling a pen and small notebook from his pocket, he jotted down the hoops he would have to jump through as soon as he landed. Check in with Captain Vocek, set up witness interviews, talk to the medical officer, study the ballistics report, examine then release Farid's body, report his progress to Stranton. After tracking down and talking to the witnesses, he would have to return to Germany to reinterview Lieutenant Whitcomb, give Stranton another progress report, then head back to Florida and CENTCOM, where, hopefully, Captain Mouton's autopsy report would be waiting. And finally, he would write up his report, turn in his findings and recommendations, and start his leave, assuming Stranton had approved it. Richard figured by then he'd be happy to move on to something less politically charged. Like rescuing cats, arresting cattle rustlers, ticketing speeders, or stopping bar fights.

And no flying, he vowed, as he watched the fortress that was FOB Hickock grow bigger as the copter descended. He really hated flying.

Landstuhl Regional Medical Center
Landstuhl, Germany

Dr. Hwang was a civilian doctor with MEDCOM, specializing in traumatic injury and orthopedic surgery. He was young, brisk, and spoke in short, clipped sentences with an accent. Korean or maybe Chinese. KD wasn't sure.

He spared no details.

"When you were shot," he began, "the bullet traveled in a downward path through the ilium on the left side of the pelvic cradle, where it caused damage to the left ovary and fallopian tube and uterus before deflecting into your left hip joint. If you do not reinjure it, the ilium will heal in eight weeks without surgical intervention. We were not able to save your left ovary and fallopian tube, but have repaired the uterus, and have replaced the joint of your left hip with a polyethylene socket and a metal femoral head. Neither the abdominal aorta nor the left iliac artery were injured, and all of the components of the broad ligament remain intact. Nerve function was not compromised, and the muscles of the pelvis appear minimally damaged. You were very lucky."

Lucky?

"You have questions?"

Hell, yeah, she had questions. If she could even figure out what he was talking about. A hole in her pelvis, one ovary gone, and a metal and plastic hip joint? What did that mean? "Will I still be able to walk and do normal things?" she asked.

"Such as? You have specific concerns?"

"Such as go to the bathroom like a regular person, have sex, bear children, dance, ride a horse, live a real life?"

"I anticipate no lasting problems," he assured her. "Bowel and bladder function will return to normal within a few days. Once initial healing is complete, sexual intercourse can resume. Conceiving might be problematic with only one functioning ovary, but you are young, healthy, and fit. You must limit alcohol and follow diet and exercise guidelines for a while, but once your physical therapy is complete, you should recover nicely. I suggest you do not fall down or attempt to run or dance vigorously for a while. Or ride a horse," he added with a smile at the absurdity of such an idea, as if no woman as small and delicate-appearing as KD would even contemplate such a thing.

She was accustomed to the attitude. No matter that she had finished boot with high marks, or had played sports all her life, or had been riding horses since she could walk, people always underestimated her because of her size and small frame.

Especially men. Until she beat them at their own games.

Dr. Hwang flipped through the pages on his clipboard, then went on with his report. "Your labs are good. We will continue hydration for another day. And the Foley catheter, as well. You should be able to eat solids later today, once bowel function is established. At your nurse's request, I am reducing pain medication and prescribing something for nausea. A physical therapist will be by later to determine when you can get out of bed for short periods and explain your exercises. For at least another week, you will remain here in the hospital, then you will be transferred to the States for rehabilitation and further assessment." He straightened the pages of the clipboard and looked up. "Any other concerns, Lieutenant?"

"When can I go back on active duty?"

The question seemed to surprise him. Apparently, he'd underestimated her commitment to the army, too. "We will have to see."

See what? Didn't he just say she would recover? "What does that mean?"

Impatience flashed. "It means there is a process, Lieutenant Whitcomb. Many factors must be taken into consideration."

She could sense his unwillingness to give her a full answer, but pressed on anyway. "What factors, Doctor? What do I have to do to get your permission to return to active duty?"

"It is not up to me. There is a medical board that evaluates such things."

"What things?"

"The degree of mobility you achieve, for one. Whether you can pass the active duty physical training requirements, and what your psychological test reveals. Based upon those findings, the board will decide if you remain in the army or receive a medical separation. That is all I can say for now. Anything else?"

She was too stunned to respond. How could she pass the APFT with a plastic hip and a hole in her pelvis?

"Then I wish you an excellent recovery." And off he went.

KD didn't dwell on her situation long; as the day passed, her pain increased. She tried to ignore it but panic hovered in the corners of her mind. *No kids? No army? No career? How could her life go to hell so fast?*

I shouldn't have left her. I should have looked for a gun. I should have gone back as soon as they started shouting.

Tears threatened—for her, for her captain, for the innocent little boy who had suffered at Farid's hands. She didn't even know if Taj had made it back to his mother. How could good intentions have gone so wrong?

The physical therapist came, poked and prodded, helped her put on compression hose to prevent blood clots, told KD she was doing great, and left. No walk today, *thank God*. Then dinner came—warm broth, juice, a soft-boiled egg, runny custard, and weak tea. After finishing off the custard, she was exhausted enough to nap.

By the time she awoke, the meds had worn off and pain encased her left side, radiating from her back and hip around to the thick bandages stretching over her abdomen. But her stomach had settled enough that she could turn her head without vomiting, and the pain was tolerable if she didn't move. Later, after they removed the catheter and took the IV out of her arm, she would try to lie on her right side, maybe walk a bit, ask for real food.

She would get through this. She would be strong again. Next week she'd go home and explain to her family what had happened and how her failure had cost her captain her life. Then, hopefully, the nightmares would stop and the real healing would begin.

But first, she had to face Warrant Officer Murdock and answer all his questions. She wasn't looking forward to that.

FOB Hickock
Northern Afghanistan

A young MP jumped out of a waiting Humvee and hurried to meet Richard when he hopped down from the helicopter. "Warrant Officer Murdock?"

When Richard nodded, the soldier saluted smartly, despite protocol that salutes weren't exchanged in combat zones, gave his name as Private First Class Jamison, and offered to take Richard's rifle and heavy duffle.

Richard handed them over—one of the privileges of rank, minor though his was—and climbed into the Humvee. A few minutes later, they stopped before a gate attached to a concrete watchtower. After another MP checked them through to the inner FOB, Richard exchanged the K-pot and armor for a patrol cap with the CID badge on the front and his name on the back, stuffed the helmet and vest into his duffle, and left it in the Humvee with his rifle. Making sure his ID was visible, he followed the private into a building adjacent to the tower.

Another check-in, this time with a female MP sergeant at a desk in the entry, then they continued down the hall to a closed door. Stenciled at eye level—for normal-size people— was MILITARY POLICE, and below it, CAPTAIN VOCEK, CO.

A single knock and the private opened the door.

The office was small, and felt even more so when Richard stepped inside. He fought the urge to duck his head, the ceilings were so low. The walls were concrete. On one was a single sand-pitted window, on another, a gray metal file cabinet. In front of the rear wall and facing the door stood a battered army-issue gray metal desk, and behind it sat a fit-looking middle-aged man with thinning hair and the stub of an unlit cigar clamped in his teeth.

"Captain Vocek, sir," the private said and saluted the man at the desk, which earned him a glare in return, since salutes weren't exchanged indoors, either. "CID Warrant Officer Murdock is here, sir." Then, because the doorway was too narrow to comfortably accommodate him, as well as Richard's six-foot-three frame, he stepped back into the hall, promised to send the duffle and rifle to Richard's quarters, saluted again, and closed the door.

"He's new." Captain Vocek sighed and shook his head in disgust. "Probably salutes the head before he takes a dump."

Waving Richard to the straight-backed gray metal chair in front of the desk, he said, "Welcome to my coffin."

After a few minutes of small talk about Richard's flight, the weather, and what foods to avoid in the mess, the captain set the unlit, soggy cigar in a dented metal ashtray on his desk and sat back. "We've got a hell of a mess with this ANP killing. I'm already getting calls from reporters in Kabul and Bagram."

"What are you telling them?"

"That it's under investigation."

Richard nodded. "I read the initial report. Sounds like he might have been shot by one of ours."

"I doubt it was self-inflicted, although there's no way to know for sure, considering his wound. Up through the neck and out the back of the head. Instantaneous. Whoever did it should get a medal."

Richard preferred talking directly to the medical officer and examining the wound himself before he made any determinations. "Any idea why our soldiers were in the Afghan's quarters?"

"The MP at the gate on the night of the shooting said one of our female terps and a local woman asked to speak to Captain Mouton. He figured it was a complaint. We get a lot of them, mostly on the police. He didn't hear what was said. Later, the two Afghan women left with Captain Mouton and Second Lieutenant Whitcomb and two suited-up SF guys."

"On foot?"

"They didn't ask for a vehicle, and neither of the women wore battle gear. It didn't look like they were expecting trouble."

"You have a lot of female soldiers here?"

"A few. Part of the cultural support team. Mouton was their CO, Whitcomb her second. They'll be missed."

"I saw Whitcomb in Germany. She wasn't doing well."

"She's tougher than she looks. Check out her service file."

Richard had. But he still couldn't reconcile the stats on paper with the frail, broken woman he'd seen at Landstuhl.

Female combat casualties in Afghanistan were rare. That a female army officer had been killed under questionable circumstances only made it worse. And then there was the dead Afghan captain. No surprise CENTCOM was worked up.

"You're assuming they walked to this Afghan officer's quarters, where they got into a gunfight?" Richard asked. "Over what?"

"Like the gate guard said, probably a complaint."

"Does that normally lead to violence?"

"Not usually. But this one might have involved the guy they went to see. We've had several complaints on Captain Farid. He didn't handle them well."

"The man who was killed."

Vocek nodded. "Can't say it's a huge loss. He was an arrogant son-of-a-bitch. Corrupt as hell. Hard on his men and cruel to the locals. The kind of CO that gets accidentally shot by friendly fire, if you know what I mean. We sent complaints to the office of Afghan Interior Affairs, but all they do is reassign these assholes to other posts. That's how we got Farid in the first place. Like we were running low on assholes around here."

Richard thought for a moment, fitting the few pieces he had into a rough sketch. "You're thinking the interpreter and a local woman came to Captain Mouton with a complaint—possibly about Farid himself. Then Mouton and Whitcomb went with two SF soldiers to Farid's quarters, where they got into a firefight that ended with the ANP CO dead, Captain Mouton dead, and Lieutenant Whitcomb critically wounded."

"That's about it."

"Where were the SF guys during all this?"

"Outside. As ordered by Mouton. By the time they got inside, it was over. Luckily, they had IFAKs, or the lieutenant wouldn't have made it." The captain shoved a folder across the desk toward Richard. "It's in their report. Such as it is."

Richard picked up the folder and opened it. Two pages. "This is all of it?"

Vocek shrugged. "You know SF. They'd rather have their fingernails torn out than give you the time of day just to show how tough they are." Vocek reached for his cigar butt, hesitated, then dropped his hand back to the desk.

Richard could see why. The stub, being brown, with the unlit end slightly rounded, and the soggy end chewed to a point, looked like a fresh dog turd. He wouldn't have put it in his mouth, either. "Do you have their names?" he asked. "And the name of the MP at the gate that night? I need to interview all of them."

Vocek wrote on a sheet of paper, shoved it across to Richard, and sat back. "The sergeant out front can arrange it. Just tell her when and where."

Richard dropped the paper into his pocket. "Lieutenant Whitcomb mentioned a boy that Farid might have been abusing. Know anything about that?"

"We think he's the Afghan woman's son. We're not sure what happened to him or where he is now."

"What do the terp and his mother say?"

"Can't find either. Which is a worry. The interpreter is committed to her team. Very loyal. Wants to emigrate to America. If she's missing, there's a damn good reason why. As far as the local woman goes, she and the boy might have headed into the hills. If word got out that she had complained about one of the ANP, especially Farid, there might be retaliation. The Farid family is notoriously brutal."

"So. No motive, no witnesses, and no clear reason why two female army officers went to talk to Farid in the first place."

"That about sums it up."

Not much to go on.

"And then there's the father of the ANP captain," Vocek added. "Khalil Farid. He's like his son on PCP. Rich. Big poppy grower. Lots of political pull. The family patriarch, and totally devoted to his son. We've had to put a special watch on him in case he tries to come through the gate with a truckload of explosives to exact retribution against the American infidels. Bat-shit crazy. Bad enough that his only son was killed, but he's also pissed that Asef's remains haven't been turned over to the family for burial." When he saw Richard check his watch, he added, "You're okay. We figure Farid died around eight P.M., night before last, so you've got a few more hours before you have to release the body."

"Has the medical officer completed his report?"

Vocek lifted another folder off his desk and passed it to Richard. "Here's the abbreviated version. Not much you can do without an actual autopsy. We sent the guns found at the scene and the bullets extracted from all three victims to the Bagram firearm and ballistics lab yesterday."

Richard pulled his notepad and pen from his pocket. "Call me when you hear more. Here's my cell number. You do have satellite cell service, right?"

"Most of the time."

After they'd exchanged contact information, Richard put his pen and notebook away. "I'd best examine Farid and talk to the medical officer so we can release the body." Richard would rather get something to eat, but knew better than to go into a morgue on a full stomach. "I appreciate your help, Captain." He started to rise.

"There's more."

Shit. Richard sat back down, fingertips pressed against his throbbing temple.

"Ever heard of *bacha bazi*?"

Taking his hand away, Richard looked up. "Is that what this is about?"

"Could be. Sometimes at night, we hear kids crying at the ANP barracks. Our men hate it. But all we can do is send complaints to Kabul."

"Shit." Richard shared the captain's obvious disgust at the barbaric practice of powerful Afghan men using young boys as sex slaves. *Dancing boys*, they were often called, because they were trained to put on makeup and women's clothing and dance at all-male parties where they were expected to perform sex acts with the guests. In many Muslim cultures, homosexuality and sodomy were punishable by death. But in remote tribal areas of Afghanistan, the saying went, *Women are for childbearing, boys are for pleasure.* Pedophilia was acceptable.

Richard didn't try to make sense of it. This country was so fucked up, he wouldn't know where to start. But if the confrontation between Mouton and Farid had been about *bacha bazi*, then Richard could understand why it might have escalated into a gunfight. Despite the DOD policy that American personnel were to ignore the sexual abuse of Afghan children because it was considered a "local cultural issue," most soldiers found the practice repugnant.

Was he supposed to look the other way, too?

"If there's nothing else," Vocek said by way of dismissal, "I'll let Dr. Erickson know you're coming."

Richard stood. "Thank you for your help, Captain."

"Good luck. You'll need it."

On his way out, Richard stopped at the MP sergeant's desk and gave her the list of names Captain Vocek had provided. "If these guys are on base," he told her, "have them report to me in the mess at eighteen hundred hours. I'll be the one eating alone."

As he headed across the inner compound to his temporary quarters, Richard battled a growing sense of unease. He was beginning to suspect that no matter what his findings were, the DOD would figure out a way to blame this fiasco on the only survivor of the incident, Second Lieutenant KD Whitcomb. And Richard's report would be the weapon used against her.

Shit. It made perfect sense—why Stranton was so anxious to send his lead investigator—a man he neither liked or trusted—into a no-win situation.

The DOD couldn't let it be known that it was unable or unwilling to control the ANP—a police force trained and weaponized by the United States—a force whose members routinely engaged in sexual abuse of kids without consequence. The army had been down this road before. After stripping a decorated Special Forces officer of his command for trying to intervene in a similar incident, the public and political fallout had been horrific. The pentagon would do anything to avoid another major international scandal.

This was more than simple damage control. It was a full-blown cover-up. And they were using Richard to find a way to incriminate a soldier who had only been trying to do the moral thing. If his report exonerated the lieutenant, his career was over. But if he defused the situation by dumping all the blame on Whitcomb, his career would be safe, the chief would look like the golden boy, the army would be blameless, and the political hacks in the DOD could avoid further scrutiny of a despicable practice and their controversial policy toward it. A win for everyone.

Except Second Lieutenant KD Whitcomb.

The idea made Richard furious. He was trapped. Either fall in line and lie, or tell the truth and end his career.

Fuck that. The army had the UCMJ—Uniform Code of Military Justice. Richard had a code, too. He wouldn't lie, not to protect Lieutenant Whitcomb or the army. She might have made a misstep, but he wouldn't spin the facts so that she carried all the blame. The rot had started well before KD Whitcomb arrived, and Richard was determined not to add to it. He'd just have to figure a way to do the right thing without ending his military career along with hers.

CHAPTER 3

Major Erickson, the Hickock FOB medical officer, was a white-haired short-timer counting the days until retirement. He even had a short-timer's stick hanging on the wall—a tradition dating back to the Vietnam War when soldiers would notch off the last sixty days until their release from service.

As Richard settled in the only chair not loaded with medical books and dogeared folders, he studied the array of dated photographs pinned to the wall behind the doctor's cluttered desk.

The major was obviously a man of vast experience throughout the Middle East. Iraq, Syria, Yemen, Afghanistan, even one dated 2005 taken in the Kashmir Mountains of Pakistan. It was all there in the smiling faces staring back at him. Different backdrops, same giant cross on army green tents and trucks. It was a chronology of the doctor's life that showed little change except in the face he presented to the camera. That he had stayed in the army all these years said a lot about the doctor's sense of commitment. That he was ending his long career as a major told Richard that, at some point during all that time, the doctor had done something to piss off the army. Richard hoped it wasn't alcoholism, drugs, or general incompetence.

"I see you studying my gallery," the major said with an over-the-shoulder gesture at the wall behind him. "And I'm guessing you're wondering why I'll be terminal at major instead of a higher rank."

Luckily, he didn't wait for Richard to respond.

"The fact is, son, I'm not a good enough bootlicker to make it through the promotion boards. Even went backwards a time or two. But since I'm damned good at my job, the army keeps me around." He gave a bark of a laugh, and waved a hand in dismissal. "I prefer being where the action is anyway, rather than hanging out with the REMFs in the Pentagon, getting rich off kickbacks, and having my ass kissed by those lobbying leeches in Washington."

Richard hid his surprise. *Rear Echelon Mother Fuckers?* Harsh maybe, but accurate. Not many officers dared refer to the Pentagon's military elite as REMFs. Which could explain why the doctor might be terminal at major.

Richard could really like this guy.

"I had hoped to walk out of here with my pension intact," Erickson went on, "but that might be questionable if I'm expected to shade my findings in this Farid mess." His smile faded. Age-dimmed blue eyes studied Richard over the rim of his wire glasses. "And if you don't watch your words, Murdock, it could be the same for you, too."

Richard sensed he might get the truth from this man, rather than a honey-coated version of events the army could easily swallow. Investigations were always harder when the story presented to him was less fact than whitewashed bullshit. Seeing in this crusty old man a possible ally, rather than an adversary, Richard tested the waters. "I'll admit, Major, I have concerns about where this investigation is headed."

"You should be concerned, boy. A clusterfuck is what it is. Totally FUBAR. But I suspect you're already figuring that out." There was a slyness to the older man's grin that made Richard wary. "I looked you up. Lots of investigations. All clean. In fact, you're considered a bit of a hotshot, Warrant Officer Murdock. But there were also a couple of subtle hints that you don't always play by the army's rules. Makes me wonder why they sent you to run this investigation and not some mealy-mouthed ass-wipe. Credibility, maybe?" Grinning, Erickson pushed back his chair and rose. "Come on. I'll take you to Farid's body so you can do what you need to do and we can get him out of here. Bastard's starting to stink up the place." He headed down the hall with long, purposeful strides.

Richard hurried to catch up. Despite his age, the man could move. "You've finished examining him?"

"I've finished examining them all, and completed the tasks you so graciously listed in your e-mail." Erickson gave him a sarcastic smirk. "Thanks for the reminders . . . Warrant Officer Murdock."

Richard took the gentle reprimand in stride. "Anything stand out?"

"Toxicology indicates Farid was a habitual cocaine user and had taken a substantial amount before his death."

"And your ruling?"

"Other than him being an addict and a pederast with a bad case of clap?"

"I was thinking cause of death."

"GSW. Gunshot wound. All three, if the lieutenant dies of her injuries. Hold your nose." Erickson pushed open a door marked EXAM 1. "Gloves and mask on the table to your right."

Asef Farid's body was unremarkable except that it was covered in black hair, carried at least forty pounds too many for its five-foot-nine frame, and was missing the back of its head. In addition, there were several gouges and cuts on the face and the side of the head, but they hadn't bled much, so were possibly made during transport after he was dead.

The small hole below his chin was consistent with the entry wound of a 9mm bullet, but the extensive damage at the back of Farid's head might indicate an expanding round, maybe a hollow point—which the army normally didn't issue.

Holding the mask over his nose and mouth, Richard bent closer to look at the entry and exit wounds and the facial lacerations. "One bullet did all this?"

"'Course not. When he fell backward, he hit the edge of a table and knocked out a chunk of his skull. The round wasn't hot. Standard army issue—124 grain full metal jacket. The damage to his face was probably postmortem. I also ran trajectory. The bullet traveled from low to high at a fairly severe angle. The shooter either fired from the hip, or while lying on the ground."

"Already injured when he fired the kill shot?"

"She," the doctor corrected. "Second Lieutenant Whitcomb killed him."

Erickson stepped over to a counter loaded with medical equipment, boxes of medical supplies, and stacks of papers. He pulled out a thick folder and handed it to Richard. "Here's your copy of my report. Take your time."

Richard opened the folder. On top were drawings of the crime scene.

Two rooms, the outline of a body in the front room, the outlines of two bodies in the second room. There were also photographs of the rooms and bodies from several angles. Richard studied them for a long time as the doctor filled in the gaps.

"The body in the first room was that of Captain Mouton, a thirty-three-year-old African-American woman. The first round hit her in the upper torso, which threw her backward. We dug a 9mm bullet out of her vest. She took the second round in her forehead while she was down. We dug that bullet out of the floorboards. Her sidearm was still holstered. Notice anything else?"

Richard took his time, mentally cataloging all the details he could see and making suppositions about those he couldn't. "There's an open drawer on the desk. Probably where Farid kept his gun. Mouton was facing the desk when his first shot hit her. There's also a damp stain on the upper left quadrant of the door and broken glass below it. A few damp spots on her vest. I'm guessing there was more glass under her body."

"There was. Farid threw a glass of water at her. What else?"

"The way her arms are thrown wide makes me think she had the breath knocked out of her by the first bullet, which was why she didn't draw her gun. Were there any other marks on the body?"

"Nothing recent."

"Any blood spatter besides on the floor and around her body?"

"None. And no other blood present anywhere in the room. First thoughts?"

"Mouton confronted Farid. He was high on cocaine. In the heat of argument, he threw a glass at her to distract her and grabbed his gun from the drawer. Before she could draw her own weapon, he shot her in the chest, which knocked her down. While she lay stunned, he walked over and shot her in the head, execution-style. No indication he was harmed in any way."

Erickson smiled. "Homicide. Very good. And in the second room?"

Richard felt like he was back in a classroom being schooled by his professor.

A drape separated the two rooms. The second room was smaller in size, maybe ten feet by twelve. An unmade bed, a small, high window with open shutters, clothes hanging on hooks, an overturned table near the entrance into the room, and a small cabinet with a mirror above it. The doors of the cabinet were open and there was a chain attached to the leg of the bed.

Richard grimaced in disgust.

Farid lay on his back, his feet just past the middle of the room, his head a couple of feet or so from the draped opening into the front room. He wore a robe and sandals. The overturned table by his right shoulder was what had probably split his head open when he fell backward. Near his right hand was a handgun. Looked like a Russian-made Makarov 9mm.

There were mostly drawings, rather than photographs, of Lieutenant Whitcomb, since she'd been treated on site before the crime scene was processed. The few photos included were poorly framed, probably taken in a hurry with a cell phone. Which meant Richard would have to rely more heavily on eyewitness observations than he would have liked.

The drawings indicated that Farid's bullet had thrown her against the wall opposite the door and below the window. There was a blood smear down to where she had fallen. She lay on her left side, her right arm across her body, an army standard-issue Beretta M9 held loosely in her slack right hand. The amount of blood near her abdomen was probably from an exit wound, which told him she had been shot in the back. Had she been trying to escape through the window when Farid came in?

She was a small woman. Caucasian. Young. Surprisingly delicate, for a soldier. But he knew all that. Had seen it firsthand. "She was shot in the back?"

Erickson nodded. "Low. Below her vest. Through the pelvic bone and out by her hip. Shattered the hip joint. Some internal damage. All I could do here was get her stabilized and send her on to Landstuhl with a critical care team."

Richard thought of her pain-stricken eyes filling with tears when he told her Mouton was dead. Too young and pretty to die. "What are her chances?"

"Good. She survived transport and surgery. She's small but tough."

"Was she conscious? Did she say anything?"

The doctor shook his head. "She was intubated and put into a medical coma. Easier if they're out during transport." He nodded toward the file in Richard's hands. "So? What happened in the back room?"

Richard slid the drawings and photographs back into the folder and closed it. "The lieutenant was facing the window when Farid came in. Since Farid's death was instantaneous, and there was no way she could have shot herself in the back, that means Farid fired first, wounding her. She went down. Then he walked to within a few feet of where she fell, probably to make sure she was dead. Instead, she fired a single shot, which killed him."

"Actually, she fired twice. Missed him with the first shot. We found the bullet in the ceiling and ballistics confirmed it. They faxed their report an hour ago. It's in the file. Your deductions?"

Richard saw it play out in his head. "Farid shot Captain Mouton in the front room—murder. Then he went to the bedroom, where he shot and wounded Second Lieutenant Whitcomb—attempted murder. Then before he could finish her off, Whitcomb shot and killed Captain Farid in self-defense."

"Exactly!" The doctor all but patted Richard on the back. "So there's no way Lieutenant Whitcomb can be charged for Farid's death, even though she fired the round that killed him."

Richard felt a rush of relief. Immediately, it faded. "Except for one thing. The reason why she and Captain Mouton were where they shouldn't have been, confronting a coked-up ANP captain they had no authority to confront, about an is-

sue they had been told by DOD to ignore. It's called disobeying a direct order."

"Semantics, son. But that's not my problem. I've done
my part." Erickson took the file from Richard, slipped it
into an oversized courier envelope, and handed it back.
"You're smart. You know your way around all the bullshit
legalities. Study this report well, then find a way to shape it
into a narrative that we can all live with. Especially that
pretty little lieutenant."

Pretty? Maybe when she wasn't vomiting or crying.

He and Erickson were discussing the protocol for releasing Farid's remains, when Richard's cell phone buzzed.

Vocek.

"Khalil Farid is on his way to Medical," the MP captain
said. "Worked up, as usual. Two MPs are escorting him.
They're to remain with him until he exits the inner gate."

"Understood. The doctor and I were trying to figure out
the procedure for releasing his son's body. We're done
with him."

"I'll send over a vehicle. The MPs can help load him and
transport him to where he needs to go."

"Yes, sir." As they exited the exam room, Richard told
Erickson that Farid's father was on his way and Captain
Vocek was sending a vehicle to deliver Farid's body to his
family. "Since I may have dealings with the father, I'll stay
to meet him. But this is your show."

"It always is."

Khalil Farid was everything that had been advertised,
and then some. Early sixties, short, heavy, bearded like his
son, but much louder. But then, anyone would be, considering Asef Farid's condition. As soon as he saw Erickson and
Richard in the hall, the Afghan charged toward them, yelling in a thick accent. Richard didn't need to speak Dari or
Pashto to know the guy was pissed, and judging by the
puckered scar that sliced through one dark eyebrow and
across the bridge of his nose, he had violence in his past.

He was also high. Excitable and jittery, his small, dark eyes never still. Cocaine, Richard guessed.

As soon as the outraged Afghan paused for breath, Erickson calmly cut in. "I'm glad you're here, Mr. Farid. We've completed our examination of your son. You may retrieve his remains whenever it's convenient."

That set Khalil back. It was apparent he had expected another delay and was primed to yell about it. "Who are you?" he demanded, shifting his indignation to Richard.

"CID Warrant Officer Murdock. I'm here to ask questions and determine the circumstances of your son's death."

"He was attacked and killed in his own home! By your countrymen!"

"Countrymen?" Richard lifted his brows. "I was told it was a *woman* who killed him," he needled.

"If so, it was unprovoked! Questions about my son? What questions?"

"Well . . . like, was Captain Farid always a pederast? Or was that something he got into after he became an addict?"

Erickson covered his laugh with a cough.

Khalil Farid's mouth opened, closed, and opened again before any words came out. Interesting to watch. "My son was not a sodomizer and he was not an addict! He was a hero! A decorated officer in the Afghan National Police!"

"Come, Mr. Farid." With a warning glance at Richard, Erickson stepped between the two and smoothly steered the irate Afghan back the way he had come. "The vehicle sent to carry your son to his family is probably waiting. These soldiers"—he nodded to the two escorts—"will follow with the captain's body. He's already prepared for transport." Which meant he was still on the gurney, covered with a stained autopsy sheet. Nothing fancy for good ol' Farid.

The MPs continued to block the narrow hallway. "Our orders are to stay with Mr. Farid until he exits the inner gate," one of them said.

Richard stepped up. "I'll be happy to wheel Captain Farid out," he offered. "If that's okay with you, Mr. Farid."

It wasn't, but the furious Afghan limited his response to an acid glare before turning his back on Richard and retracing his steps down the hall with Major Erickson.

A few minutes later, Richard arrived with the remains and helped the MPs load Farid's body into the back of a Humvee. Before Khalil climbed into the passenger seat, he turned to Richard and said, "I will remember you, CID Warrant Officer Murdock. No matter what your investigation says, my son will be avenged. And be assured," he added with a sneer, "I will personally see to it that the woman who killed him is severely punished, as well as those who dared to cast doubt on his name and the honor of my family." Then he climbed into the vehicle, shut the door, and the Humvee drove away.

"Was I just threatened?" Richard asked Erickson.

"Seems so." The doctor gave him a smile that brought a twinkle to his faded blue eyes. "I see now why the army picked you for this investigation. You don't mince words, do you? Too bad. If that pretty little lieutenant dies and they're still looking for a scapegoat, you may have just given them a reason to pick you."

At 1730 hours, Richard was sitting at a table for four in a back corner of the mess, enjoying baked chicken, cottage fries, overcooked peas and carrots, a fruit cup, and a biscuit. Not bad, and the servings were large. He studied the other diners and found most of them studying him. Apparently, word of his arrival had spread. There were no nods of welcome or open signs of friendliness. Only cautious, wary eyes, quickly averted when Richard glanced their way. Understandable. Anyone wearing a CID badge was considered an adversary sent to find fault or lay blame. And few were blameless in this war.

At exactly 1800 hours, two SF guys came in—a white guy in his thirties, and a wiry young Hispanic. Rainor and Gonzales, their files said, aka Rainman and Chico. They were trailed by a huge Black MP specialist, who was probably the enforcer for his unit. He made the smaller, more agile SF soldiers look underweight and insubstantial. Stopping beside Richard's table, the older Special Forces soldier, Rainor, looked down at him and said, "Reporting as ordered."

No salute—as expected—but a "sir" would have been acceptable, since Richard outranked all of them. He let it pass and instead made them wait while he finished chewing a bite of potato, swallowed, got out his pen and pulled a legal pad from the courier pouch the doctor had given him, then said, "Sit."

Having established that they wouldn't allow themselves to be pushed around, the three soldiers pulled out chairs.

"Not you two," Richard said to Rainman and Chico. "Go get yourselves coffee if you'd like, but don't leave the mess. I'll let you know when I'm ready to talk to you."

Richard wouldn't be pushed around, either.

"Let's start with you," he said to the MP warily taking a seat as the other two wandered off. Richard hoped the chair didn't collapse. After writing down on the yellow pad the MP's name—Reggie Hargrove—his rank, unit, and military ID number, Richard asked the gate guard to tell him what he saw and heard on the night of the killings.

Everything Hargrove related, Richard already knew, but he wrote it down anyway. If there was one thing that gave the army a hard-on faster than big budgets, it was paperwork. After the MP read over and verified the account as written, Richard had him sign it and dismissed him. He turned to a fresh, clean page, finished his coffee, then nodded to the SF guys.

This time, they looked more cautious than belligerent,

and took their seats without initiating another pissing contest. After getting the particulars on each soldier, Richard decided to start with an unexpected question. "Tell me about Captain Mouton."

The men looked at each other, then the older one—Rainman—said, "She was a good soldier. Kept up, followed orders, wasn't afraid to take risks when necessary. You could count on her." He glanced at the Hispanic for corroboration.

Chico nodded. "Smart, too. And funny. Always cracking Cajun jokes."

"Respected?"

"Absolutely," Rainman said. "Never played the gender card. Just one of the guys. We trusted her. If she had a reason to be at Farid's quarters, it was a good one. Although she didn't say anything about that to us."

Richard wrote *trusted* and *respected* on the legal pad. "What about the terp and local woman?"

"We didn't know anything about them," Rainman said, "until they showed up outside Farid's hut. I think the terp's name is Samira. The other woman was in traditional dress. Her eyes were all we could see. Didn't get her name."

Richard noted that, then asked him why Mouton had asked them to go with her to Farid's.

"Said there was a complaint she'd been asked to check out and she needed two escorts. None of our female soldiers leave the inner FOB without armed backup."

"We didn't expect no trouble," Chico added. "She didn't even want us going inside Farid's quarters. Thought it might look too confrontational."

Richard asked each where they were when the shooting started.

"Where the captain wanted us," Rainman told him. "She had me stay with the two Afghan women. I was to watch both the house and the ANP barracks from a covert position halfway between the two."

Chico said, "She told me to wait at the back of the house. I don't know why. There was no door, just a small, high window."

"What did she tell you about the boy?"

The two soldiers looked at each other, then back at Richard. "The boy?" Chico asked.

"The one the lieutenant passed out to you, Chico, through the rear window."

"Oh. That boy."

"Yeah, that boy."

It was just a guess. But after Lieutenant Whitcomb mentioned a boy, and considering what Vocek and the doctor had said about Farid's perversions and the earlier complaints about the ANP captain, Richard figured Mouton and Whitcomb had gone to the Afghan's quarters that night to rescue a boy. He was hoping these SF soldiers could confirm it.

Chico let out a deep breath. "The captain didn't mention no boy. We had no idea he was there. Then suddenly I hear two gunshots and the lieutenant is shoving a kid through the window and yelling for me to take him."

"What did you do?"

"I couldn't let him fall, so I took him. Soon as I do, the Afghan woman runs up, yanks him out of my hands, then she and the terp run off. I'm guessing she was his mother."

"Then what?" Richard prodded.

"I'm pissed, you know? I don't know what the fuck's going on. I can't get through the window and it's too high for me to get off a shot. Then I hear three more gunshots. *Pop*, a pause, then *pop pop*. A handgun, maybe two. The last two shots closer to the window and really loud because of the concrete walls. I run around to the front, and by then, Rainman is already inside."

"That's five gunshots. How long between the first one and the last two?"

"Total?" Chico looked at Rainman and shrugged. "Nine,

ten seconds. The first two sounded farther away, three, four seconds apart. The third one was closer, maybe four seconds later. The last two came close together. A double tap."

"What happened when you first heard the shots?" Richard asked Rainman.

"The women scattered. I radioed for backup and ran to the hut. As soon as I got inside, I saw Captain Mouton was dead, so I went to the back room, where I found both Farid and the lieutenant down. I could see Farid was dead, but the lieutenant was still alive."

"Then what?"

"I heard Chico come in behind me. I told him to make sure Farid was neutralized, while I did what I could for Lieutenant Whitcomb."

Richard wrote that down, then asked Chico how he determined that Farid was dead. Usually you thump an eyeball. If there's no reaction, the victim is dead.

The Hispanic looked sheepish. "I may have kicked him around some."

Probably didn't want any evidence found on Farid to be traced back to him. Special Forces were great at covering their tracks. The kicking also explained the postmortem lacerations on the Afghan's head and face.

"When he didn't react," Chico continued, "I knew for sure he was dead. Especially since the back of his head was gone. So I went back to the front room and secured the entrance until backup came."

Richard asked Rainman if the lieutenant had said anything while he'd been administering first aid.

"She mumbled something about the captain and if Farid was dead. I told her everything was fine and to stop moving. Then she went into shock and passed out."

"That's it?"

"That's it. By that time, the sirens were going off and I could hear backup pouring into the front room and a medic took over for me."

Richard finished writing up their interviews, had the soldiers read and sign them, then slipped them inside the courier pouch with the gate guard's witness account and Erickson's medical report.

He sat back and studied the men across the table. Good soldiers. Not geniuses, but not stupid, either. Confident and forthcoming, showing no signs of misdirection in their behavior or words. As relaxed as any innocent soldier would be when questioned by CID about their involvement in a murder investigation. Richard believed they were telling the truth.

"Look, guys, I'm not trying to fuck anyone up. I advise you to remember everything you just told me. If you're ever questioned about it, do not vary in a single detail. That's really important for both you and the lieutenant. Understood?"

The soldiers nodded. "Understood, sir."

"You're dismissed."

Neither moved. "Is this about *bacha bazi*?" Rainor asked. "Sometimes we hear kids crying inside the ANP barracks. Was Farid using the boy for sex?"

"Fucking *pendejo*," the Hispanic muttered.

"I can't comment. It's an ongoing investigation."

Rainman ignored Richard's stock response. "If he was, I might know why Captain Mouton went to his quarters."

"Why?"

"Off the record?"

Richard didn't answer.

Rainman went on anyway. "I think there may have been an incident in Mouton's past. She never said anything, and I'm not hinting she was gay. But she definitely kept her distance from the male soldiers. Didn't even want them touching her. I heard that in boot, a guy tried and she put him on the ground. No one's touched her since."

Richard filed that away in his head. It could explain why a by-the-book soldier might feel driven to confront a man who was sexually abusing a child. "Thanks for telling me. I won't mention it unless I have to. And by the way, Rainor, what you did for the lieutenant probably saved her life."

The soldier gave a small, tight smile. "I'm glad. She just got here a while back, so I don't know much about her, but what I've heard is all good."

"She's a helluva looker, too," Chico added, then saw the way the other two men looked at him. "What? I didn't do nothing. I wouldn't. None of us would. I'm just saying she's too damn pretty for the army, that's all."

Richard silently agreed. Ever since he'd seen the photo of Whitcomb lying broken on the dirty floor with blood-soaked IFAK pressure bandages stuck to her slim body, he'd hadn't been able to get the image out of his mind.

After Rainor and Gonzales had left, Richard refilled his coffee cup, got a piece of pecan pie, and returned to his seat to mull over all he'd learned since he'd landed at the Hickock helo pad earlier that afternoon.

The investigation was beginning to take shape. But he wasn't encouraged by what he'd seen and heard. The incident had all the elements of a nasty international scandal. If word got out, it would create a feeding frenzy, which the media—often reluctant to take the side of the military and the soldiers protecting its right to say or print whatever it wanted, true or not—would keep going for months. And through it all, the ones who would suffer most would be those least at fault. Richard just hoped the Department of Defense had the balls to do the right thing this time. Otherwise, that "pretty little lieutenant" might lose not only her career, but her freedom, as well.

But for now, until the Afghan interpreter, Samira, showed up so he could interview her, or the mother of the boy returned from hiding, he'd done all he could at FOB Hickock. Tomorrow, he'd go back to Bagram, then on to the medical center in Germany to try to talk to Lieutenant Whitcomb again.

He hoped she was still alive and was as smart as her entry scores indicated, because there were only two ways the lieutenant might survive this fiasco with her career intact. To have no memory of what happened that night—which often happened in traumatic injury cases. Or to be clever enough to *say* she didn't remember. That way, since she was the only survivor, and with no apparent motive and no other eyewitnesses, the army would be free to spin the incident any way it chose. Drugs. An insurgent ambush. A Taliban attack on Farid that our soldiers stumbled into.

But for any of those scenarios to work, unless Whitcomb truly didn't remember, she had two choices: lie about it or die of her injuries. And for some irrational and confusing reason, Richard would be really pissed if she did either.

At 0530 hours the next morning, Richard was showered, dressed, packed, and heading back to the mess with his duffle and rifle. The sun was already up and the base was bustling. Several groups of fully armored soldiers were heading past the watchtower toward Humvees rumbling impatiently outside the inner gate.

A lot more activity than when Richard had arrived. Something was up. He hoped whatever it was wouldn't delay his departure to Germany. He needed to interview Lieutenant Whitcomb as soon as possible. Chief Stranton at CENTCOM would be expecting his preliminary report that afternoon.

Two messages were waiting for him when he arrived at the mess. The first confirmed that he was scheduled to depart Hickock at 0700 hours. The second was that Captain Vocek wanted to talk to him before he left. Hopefully, he had found the terp, Samira, and learned the identities of the local Afghan woman and the boy. Richard was running low on witnesses.

He ate fast, then headed to Vocek's office.

The MP CO didn't look happy. Before Richard could ask why, Captain Vocek said, "We found the terp. Throat cut. She'd been worked over good then dumped beside the road like trash."

Damn. One less witness. "And the local woman?"

"No idea who she is. Or the boy. And nobody's talking. Can't blame them. They're afraid of payback. Farid's father, Khalil, is big on honor killings."

"You think he killed the terp?"

"If not him, then I'd bet it was on his orders. He's a real piece of work."

"I know. I met him." Richard tipped his head in the direction of the gate. "Is that what all the troop movement is about?"

Vocek nodded. "Mostly for show. To let the locals know we care. And we do care. Samira was a good terp. The female support team is really worked up. First their captain and the lieutenant, and now their interpreter. A real shitstorm." Vocek pushed back his chair and rose.

Richard stood, too.

"You better get going," the captain said. "Your chopper's warming up. You can catch a ride to the helo pad on one of the Humvees." He held out his hand. "Good luck, Murdock. Sounds like we'll all need hip boots before this is over."

"Thank you for your help, sir."

Richard was walking past the watchtower's inner gate when his phone buzzed. Stranton. *Shit.* The chief better not have canceled his leave.

"Good morning, sir. Warrant Officer Murdock speaking."

"Progress report."

Richard stuck to the facts, answering "Not yet determined" to questions he couldn't answer. The chief listened until Richard finished, then said, "We have a problem, Murdock. DOD is all over me, and now there are whisperings in Congress. We have to put an end to this. And soon."

"Yes, sir. I'm on my way to LRMC right now to interview Lieutenant Whitcomb again. The evidence so far indicates she shot Captain Farid in self-defense. But I'll need to hear her account before I put anything in writing."

There was a pause, then Stranton said, "Go back through her file. Find something we can use. Something that'll stick. This has to be old news by tomorrow."

Richard's steps slowed. "Farid shot her in the back, Chief. The medical officer agrees he shot first and the lieutenant returned fire in self-defense."

No response.

Coming to a dead stop, Richard chose his words carefully. "But you still feel she's at fault, sir?"

Stranton's voice boomed through the cell phone. "I don't care whose fault it is, Murdock! I'm saying both our asses are in the wringer here, so clean up this mess any way you can, whatever it takes! Am I clear?"

"Yes, sir," Richard said, and ended the call. Apparently, Stranton had forgotten about Richard's leave or the chief would have thrown that at him, too. *Asshole.*

CHAPTER 4

Landstuhl Regional Medical Center
Landstuhl, Germany

Even though his head ached and his ears still rang from the
seven-hour flight from Bagram, Richard tried to sound
cheery when he walked into Lieutenant Whitcomb's hospital room. "Afternoon, Lieutenant. You're looking better."

Actually, she looked like death. Yet if he studied her
hard enough, despite the dark circles around her eyes—
brown or black, he couldn't tell—and the pinched tightness
of her mouth—pain, probably—and the rat's nest in her
brown hair, the beauty he hadn't noticed when she'd been
vomiting was obvious. With her delicate features and slight
frame, she should never have made it in the army. Yet she
had overcome the odds, graduating with a top rank from
West Point then sailing through boot camp and officer
training to earn her right to be a soldier. From everything
he'd read in her service file, she was determined and committed, headed for the top. He hated that he might be the
tool used to bring her down.

He'd done a lot of thinking since he'd last spoken to
her—about this case, his future, how far he might go to

cover the army's ass, and whether or not he'd be willing to
ruin this soldier's career to keep his job. Which would happen if he turned in the report Stranton wanted, regardless
of the truth. Another reason for him to get out before he lost
all respect for the army and himself.

"Ready for a few questions?" he asked, anxious to get
down to business.

"Ready as I'll ever be."

And totally lacking in enthusiasm, it seemed. No one
liked being interrogated. He pulled his pen and yellow
notepad out of the courier pouch, nodded toward the chair
beside the bed, and asked if he could sit.

"Suit yourself."

He sat. Hoping to put her more at ease, he said, "Again,
I'm sorry about Captain Mouton. From everything I've
heard, she was a fine officer."

"And friend," she added, blinking hard.

To give her a chance to pull herself together—he hated
when they cried—Richard leafed through the notepad a bit.
When he figured she'd had enough time, he started with,
"When did Captain Mouton decide to go to Farid's quarters? Start from the beginning and try not to leave anything out."

"We had just returned from a four-day patrol and were
at mess," she said, her voice stronger than when he'd first
interviewed her. He picked up a hint of Texas twang, but
softer and more refined than some he'd heard. It suited her.
"COM radioed that two women were at the gate asking
for her."

"That would be your interpreter, Samira, and a local
woman?"

"Yes. Azyan. I don't know her last name."

Richard jotted that down. "And what did they say to the
captain?"

"That Farid had taken Azyan's eight-year-old son and
she wanted him back."

"Mouton agreed to go get him?"

"Not after she learned it was the CO of the ANP who had taken him. She explained that we couldn't interfere in local matters and asked why Azyan couldn't get her son herself. Samira told us she'd tried but Farid had hit her. Azyan showed us cuts and bruises on her face and arms."

"And that's when the captain decided to go to Farid's?"

"Not until Azyan told us why Farid had taken her son. For sex." Disgust twisted Whitcomb's features. Nice features, with a few freckles across the nose and cheeks, a wide mouth, and watchful, intelligent eyes. He wondered what her smile was like. "Captain Mouton made it clear she could only ask Farid to return the boy. If he refused, there was nothing more we could do."

Richard started a new page, and reminded himself to get more batteries for his recorder. "Did she order you to go with her?"

"No."

"But you went anyway."

"Yes."

"Despite the noninterference policy."

A look came over her face that made her seem older, less vulnerable. And definitely not broken. "She was my captain. I had her back. That was my job."

Instead of responding, Richard sat quietly and waited. After two years with the 8th Psychological Operations Group and six with CID, he'd found that silence often worked better than questions to keep a conversation going.

Which it did now. "Actually, she didn't want me going," Whitcomb finally admitted. "She knew the risks and didn't want me to damage my career."

"So both of you knowingly disobeyed army policy."

Emotion flashed in her eyes. Brown eyes, he saw now, showing flecks of yellow when she was mad. She studied him for a long time, her mouth set, her hands fisted against the sheets. She gave off an impregnable aura of strength, as if showing weakness was the same as dying. Dr. Erickson was right; she might be small, but she was tough. Richard admired that.

"I see where this is going, Warrant Officer Murdock." She spoke calmly, precisely, every word carefully enunciated. "The army is worried about PR so they've sent you to find a way to spin it so Captain Mouton takes the blame." She smiled. It wasn't a pleasant smile and did nothing to bank the fire in those amazing eyes. "You'll get no help from me. Captain Mouton was an excellent soldier. Honest, fair, courageous. And I will *never* let anyone paint her differently."

"I wasn't trying to. I only want the truth."

"Oh, really? Then, here's the truth. We went to Farid's as a courtesy to a desperate mother. That's why we're in Afghanistan. To offer help to the Afghan women wherever, and however, we can. Captain Mouton had no intention of violating the DOD policy, and she didn't order me to go with her. The only thing she asked of me was that we both wear headscarves to show respect."

Richard wrote furiously, intent on getting down every word. The woman should have been in JAG. She would have made a hell of a lawyer. When he'd finally finished, he shook a cramp out of his hand and looked up.

The hard-faced resolve was gone, replaced by one of those looks women did so well—a cross between a smirk and bored impatience, one of those *Why do I have to do all the thinking?* looks. "Do you have a cell phone, Officer Murdock?"

He blinked, caught off guard by the question. "Yes."

"Most of them have an app for that."

"For what?"

"Notes, dictation, videoing conversations, or in your case, recording interrogations. You don't have to write it all down. Your phone can do it for you."

"Really?" Playing along, he pulled out his cell, studied

it, then looked innocently back at her. "Wow." And there was that eye roll he'd expected.

Richard didn't much trust technology, but he did know how to use a phone. He just preferred to rely on hard copies, rather than battery-dependent cells or recorders. Plus, paper files were harder for him to lose since they all ended up in the same place. His duffle. He wasn't a total fucktard.

"Let me make it easy for you," she went on in a snarky tone. "Jot this down. *Talk to Samira.* She'll verify my account of our conversation at the gate."

"I can't."

Her expression changed again, alarm eroding the smirk. "Why not?"

"Samira's dead. Her body was found last night in the hills outside the FOB."

He said it harsher than he should have. She made a sound—part cry, part moan. It raised the hairs on the back of his neck. Then she did that vomiting thing again, and one of her machines started beeping, and nurses rushed into the room.

And that was the end of the interview.

He escaped as quickly as he could. With nowhere to go until his overnight flight to CENTCOM, he headed to the hospital cafeteria. Loading up a tray, he took it to a table near the windows. He was still unnerved by what had happened. And by KD Whitcomb. And especially his reaction to her. He shouldn't have cared when she'd blown up at him. Or felt so relieved when she'd calmed back down. Or been so abrupt about Samira. This was no different from any other interrogation. Except for the vomiting. That had never happened before.

He took a bite of chicken and looked out the window as he chewed. The woman was complicated. Truthful, but unpredictable. Fearless, even lying wounded in a hospital bed. And so beautiful, it made him forget why he was there. She was also probably on pain meds, he reminded himself. He doubted she'd remember much of the interview. But he sure as hell would.

He took another bite of chicken and wished he'd been nicer. It disturbed him that every time they talked, she ended up vomiting. He'd try to do better next time.

KD didn't want it, but they gave her a sedative and another dose of the pain meds. Once they kicked in, she was able to stop crying, her stomach settled, and she finally drifted into a deep, dreamless sleep.

Four hours later, she awoke to see another semiliquid dinner on the rolling table thing, and Warrant Officer Murdock dozing in the chair, head back, mouth open, long legs stretched past the end of the bed. His big hands were clasped over his belt and he was snoring. The picture of relaxation.

She wanted to hit him. Wake him and ask him why he'd told her about Samira in such a cruel, heartless way. But she had known, even before he had said the words. The regret had shown on his face. He hadn't liked telling her that Samira was dead any more than she'd liked hearing it.

Another death, another loss. Soldiers were supposed to accept losing friends and brothers. Casualties of war. Maybe she wasn't such a good soldier, after all.

Blocking that thought, she studied the man in the chair.

He wasn't as old as she had originally thought. Early thirties, maybe. But she guessed in his job he had heard so many lies and seen so many terrible things it had prematurely aged him and put that weary, cynical look in his eyes. She hadn't seen him smile and wondered if he found anything worth the effort. He might be more approachable if he did. Another casualty of war, the capacity for joy. That's what she had admired most about Nataleah—her ability to bring a smile to those around her and make them feel a little less alone and afraid.

Irritated at where her thoughts had taken her, KD reached to pull the rolling table with her dinner tray closer, and accidentally knocked the pink barf bowl off the nightstand. It was clean. But it landed on the floor with a clatter.

"What?" Murdock jerked upright and looked around. When he saw her leaning over the side of the bed and the bowl upended on the floor, he bolted to his feet with such a look of horror, it was almost comical.

"Are you sick again? Should I call the nurse? I'll call the nurse."

"Don't. I'm okay. I accidentally knocked it off when I reached for my dinner tray." And even that simple effort had been exhausting. Fearing another bout of light-headedness, KD slumped back against the pillows. "I'm okay."

Warily, he picked up the bowl, saw it was clean and set it back on the nightstand, then positioned her rolling table so that it crossed her lap.

He frowned at the items on the tray. "That's all you get?"

Unwilling to go into an explanation of postsurgical bowel function, she simply said, "For now," and punched the button on her bed to raise the back so she could sit up. Which didn't work as well as she'd hoped, since she'd slid down in her sleep so that the bend in the mattress hit just below her shoulder blades. She tried to scoot up, then inhaled sharply when a jolt of pain hit her back.

"Here. Let me help." And before she could stop him, he grabbed her under the arms and bodily lifted her higher. His hands were so big, his thumbs reached past her collarbones. Pain stole her breath away or she might have started shouting at him. Once he'd pulled the covers up, he pushed the edge of the table into her chest and stood back, a pleased look on his unshaven face. "Better?"

"Much," she gasped, terrified he might do something else to hurt her.

He started to open her various juice and fruit containers, but when she saw his struggle with the tiny tabs on the seals, she feared those big hands would make a mess of it and she waved him away. "I can do that. Thanks anyway."

"Okay." He looked around for something else to do, spotted the pink plastic water pitcher on the night stand, grabbed a paper cup, and started pouring. "Anything else?" he asked, spilling only a little of it when he put it on her tray.

"You've done more than enough."

"Well. Okay, then. Feel up to a few more questions? I'd like to get this over with as soon as possible."

KD took a sip of lukewarm broth. "Get what over with? My career?" She said it as a joke, but he didn't smile. Probably accustomed to being snarked at.

He let out a deep breath and rested one of those farmer's hands on the butt of the pistol holstered at his hip. She wondered how he got his big index finger through the trigger guard. "I'm not trying to jam you up, Lieutenant. I see no fault in what you did. But you were right in thinking CENTCOM is looking for a way to make this go away as soon as possible."

She moved on to the cranberry juice. "And they figure to use me?"

"I already told them you killed Farid in self-defense."

"Then what's the problem?"

"Some might think you going to Farid's was a violation of DOD policy."

She set the cup down so hard, juice sloshed over the side. "But I explained that. We went as a courtesy to a distraught mother."

"Let's start there." He sat, retrieved his notepad and pen from the courier pouch on the floor by his chair, turned to a fresh page, and said, "Whose idea was it to go? Yours, or the captain's?"

"The captain's. But I backed her." KD wiped the spilled juice from her fingers then slapped the napkin back onto the tray. "This is unbelievable! You know what Farid had planned for the kid, don't you? An eight-year-old boy. It's disgusting!"

"If Mouton hadn't already decided on going, would you have suggested it?"

KD was the one who had made the biggest mistakes—not checking Farid for a weapon, not going back to the front room when the argument escalated to shouts. Why did he keep asking about Nataleah? "I'll admit, I was worried about the policy of looking the other way in such matters. But Farid was an animal. He needed to be stopped. It was the moral thing to do."

Murdock wrote for a minute, then looked up and studied her, his blue eyes as cold as a November wind. "Can you think of a reason Captain Mouton might have been more motivated than most to stop him? Maybe something in her past that compelled her to save the boy?"

It was an effort for KD to keep her voice even. "What are you implying?"

"I heard rumors that she might have been abused herself. Could that have triggered her decision to go to Farid's despite being told not to intervene?"

Anger erupted. "She was a good soldier!"

"I'm not disputing that."

"Then why are you trying to drag her reputation through the mud?" KD's voice shook with fury. "I will never say anything against Captain Mouton! No matter what you throw at me!"

"Oh, for the love of God!" Murdock slapped his pen down on the notepad. "Mouton doesn't need you to defend her," he said in a tight voice. "She did what she felt she had to do. I respect that. But now it's time for *you* to do the right thing and tell the truth."

"I *am* telling the truth!"

"Then try telling it with less emotion!"

Sexist pig. KD pressed a hand against the throbbing in her side and reminded herself to stop shouting.

A nurse came to the window, a worried look on her face. KD waved her away.

Obviously trying to tamp down his own irritation, Murdock picked up his pen again and smoothed the page in his notepad. "If you're ever called for an Article 32 hearing, Lieutenant Whitcomb," he said with strained patience, "I advise you to get some coaching. A lot of coaching."

"Go to hell. I'm done talking to—"

Patience snapped. "Then how about you shut up and listen for once. I'm trying to help you! Don't you get that? You go ballistic like this before a judge or an Article 32 panel, you not only risk a big blot on your record, but you could be dismissed from service altogether. Is that what you want?"

The words knocked the breath out of her. Dismissal from service was the officer equivalent of a bad conduct discharge. Would the army really do that to her?

Murdock took a deep breath and let it out in a rush. His anger seemed to go with it. "Look. I'm not trying to throw blame on you or your captain. I'm only looking for a mitigating reason why she decided to go to Farid's. If something in her past compelled her to rescue the boy from Farid, I need to know that. It would certainly read better than reporting she willfully disregarded a DOD directive."

Oh, God. Murdock was right. To disregard a direct order was military suicide. "I don't know anything about her being abused," she admitted. "I'd heard rumors that she'd decked a guy for being grabby at boot. But we never talked about it." She could see it wasn't the answer he wanted. "Is it that important?"

"Maybe. Maybe not." He rubbed a hand across the back of his neck. "But what is important—since you're the only witness to what happened that night—is that you understand the kind of scrutiny you'll face. You need to be ready."

"To lie?"

"Hell, no. Never lie. I'm just saying when you're questioned—and you will be, I'm afraid—don't give out more information than necessary. Stay on point and give simple answers. Don't sidestep anything, don't get defensive, and don't lose your temper. Just tell the truth."

The fight went out of her. He was right again. If she didn't get ahold of herself, she could ruin everything. "You really think they'll convene an Article 32 hearing?"

He shrugged. "I doubt they'll like my report of the facts, so yeah. They'll probably want to ask you the pertinent questions themselves."

"But we only went there to talk to him. He fired first."

He didn't respond.

"If you report what I've told you," she rushed on, "and they still convene a hearing, doesn't that mean they've already decided I've done something wrong?"

He shook his head. "An Article 32 isn't a court-martial. It's an inquiry into the facts to decide if any charges should be brought. Like what a civilian grand jury does, except in this case, you can have a lawyer with you and you can question witnesses. If you don't lose your cool, and answer the panel's questions calmly, with short, truthful responses, they'll probably decide not to charge you."

Charge me? Oh, God. Suddenly it was hard to breathe. Her heart beat so fast, she could hear blood *shushing* past her ear, and the ache in her hip grew worse no matter how hard she pressed against it. "Questions like what? And how do I stay calm when I'm being accused of something I didn't do?"

"See? You're getting worked up again. You should try not to do that."

Was he afraid she would start vomiting? *Condescending prick.* She felt the panic build and struggled to slow her breathing, but nothing seemed to work. She could feel her chest pumping, yet no air seemed to get in.

"Not accused. Questioned," he corrected, oblivious to

how badly she wanted to punch his heart out, or how hard it was for her to draw a full breath, or how much she felt like everything was slipping out of her control.

"Questions like, *Whose idea was it to go to Farid's?* Captain Mouton's. *Did the captain order you to go?* No. *Then why did you?* Female soldiers aren't supposed to leave the inner FOB alone at night."

He went on and on, asking and answering his own questions, but his words grew muffled by her struggle to breathe. Why didn't he shut up? Couldn't he see something was wrong? *Why can't I breathe!*

"Lieutenant?" His voice sounded distant, even though he had moved closer to the side of the bed. "Lieutenant, are you okay?"

I can't breathe! Help me!

"Step aside," a new voice said. The nurse. She would know what to do.

Murdock didn't move. "What happened? Is she okay?"

"She'll be fine. Just give me some room." KD was dimly aware of the nurse stroking her arm. "You're okay, Lieutenant," she said in a calm voice. "You're safe. These are just feelings. There's no danger. I'm with you. Just breathe easy."

"I . . . can't . . ." KD gasped.

"You can. You're talking, so you're breathing. You're okay. Everything's fine. Just slow it down a little. That's right. Nice and easy. Good."

The nurse's calm assurances slowly reached through the fog of terror. The tightness in KD's chest began to ease. Her heart stopped racing. The tingling in her arms and legs faded and she could feel air flowing into her lungs.

"Wh-what happened?" she asked once she felt strong enough to speak.

"You had an anxiety attack. They're common in people who've had a traumatic experience. You're okay. Nothing is wrong with your lungs. Take a deep breath, hold it to a count of four, now let it out as slowly as you can. Good. Again."

KD concentrated on her breathing, on staying calm and clearing her mind of fear. Slowly she came back into herself. For a few terrifying moments she'd felt like she was drowning. Dying. But now, with the nurse's touch and voice, she felt anchored again. She gave her a shaky smile. "Th-thank you. That was scary."

"It can be. But you're fine now."

"Will it . . . happen again?"

"Talk to Dr. Hwang when he comes in. He might prescribe something."

More meds. Just what she needed. But if drugs kept that choking terror away, KD was all for them. She saw movement behind the nurse and realized Murdock was still in the room, staring at her from a shadowed corner, dark brows drawn low over his deep-set eyes. How humiliating that he had witnessed her freaking out. No telling what he would put in his report now. *Unfit for duty. A total nut ball.*

With a final pat, the nurse promised to check on her later, then headed to the station across the hall. Probably to reserve KD a rubber room in the mental ward.

As soon as she'd left, Murdock came hesitantly toward the bed. KD could barely look at him, she was so disgusted with herself. The last thing she needed was to see pity and disgust on his face, too.

"You okay?"

The absurdity of that question brought out the meanness in her. "You mean am I okay other than having a bullet hole in my pelvis, a missing ovary, an after-market hip joint, the threat of a court-martial hanging over my head, and a raging panic attack? Yeah, I'm just peachy. Thanks for asking."

He studied her, an odd expression on his rugged face. "That's amazing," he said after a moment. "After all you've been through, and you're still ready to pick a fight."

"I wasn't picking a fight. I was subtly letting you know

that considering my situation, 'You okay?' was a stupid question."

"It was an expression of concern." He was laughing at her. She could see it in his eyes. "You scared the shit out of me, Lieutenant."

"I scared the shit out of myself, so we're even." She looked away, embarrassed to admit how terrified she had been. Especially in front of a man who had the power to end her career. Soldiers were taught to control their fears, not turn into gasping neurotics.

"Look at me," he said after a long silence.

She did, chin high, hoping he didn't see how afraid she still was.

"I'm not here to hurt you, Lieutenant. I can't do anything about your medical problems, but I might be able to help you with the military issues. If you let me."

"Why would you?"

"Because I don't believe you're totally at fault here. Because you're a good soldier and I don't want the army using you as a scapegoat for their bad policy. But mostly, because I might have done the same thing."

She doubted he would have made the mistakes she had that had cost Nataleah her life. But he did seem sincere, and that was reassuring. She tried to smile, despite the pain hammering at her back and hip and everywhere in between. Too much yelling. Too much anger and fear. "Thank you for that, Officer Murdock. And for telling me what I'm up against. I appreciate your honesty."

He shrugged and looked away. Not comfortable with compliments, she guessed. Probably didn't get many in his job. Moving on to more practical concerns, she asked how long until she found out what the army planned to do.

"Once I present my findings, CENTCOM will probably request an Article 32 to cover their asses. After the hearing, they'll have a hundred and twenty days to decide whether to bring charges or not."

Four months. July. Would she even be well enough by then to withstand such an ordeal? "If they do bring charges, will you testify on my behalf?"

The question seemed to rattle him. She was sorry she'd asked it when she saw the blush inch up his neck. "Never mind. I was out of line to ask."

"No. It's okay." He busied himself retrieving his notepad and pen from the floor, where he'd dropped them. "Sure. If I'm called, I'll be there. Absolutely."

He was making her request into a personal thing, which wasn't her intent. She just thought it might help if he was at the hearing. "Thank you," and seeing a way to ease the awkwardness, she smiled and added, "But clean up first."

His dark brows rose. "Pardon?"

"You could use a shave, Warrant Officer Murdock. And a haircut."

For a moment, he looked surprised. Then a laugh burst out of him, surprising them both. A real laugh, which showed a flash of white teeth, and crinkled the corners of his blue eyes, and changed a grim face into one that had a lot of appeal. "And you could use a hairbrush, Second Lieutenant Whitcomb."

She resisted the urge to check her hair. "I'll try to rustle one up." KD liked this side of Warrant Officer Murdock. She liked the sound of his laughter, the way a smile took away the sternness in his face and warmed the chill in his beautiful blue eyes. It felt like they could almost be friends. "Is my interview over?"

"Just a few more questions, if you're up for it."

"Fire away. I'll try not to lose my temper or vomit."

"I'd be grateful."

That grin again, but replaced immediately by his stern CID face. KD sensed it was half real and half façade. Not as threatening as it had been when she'd first met him. Was that just two days ago?

"The forensics are straightforward," he said, regaining

her attention. "Ballistics backs it up. I interviewed the SF guys who went with you, but I need you to tell me what happened inside Farid's hut. Start with when you arrived."

This was the part KD had dreaded. Taking a moment to gather her thoughts, she began. "He definitely wasn't happy to see us. I think he was high on drugs."

Murdock nodded. "Cocaine. He was a habitual user. Was he armed?"

"He was wearing a robe without pockets. I didn't see a gun."

"Once you were inside, what did you do?"

She replayed it in her mind. "Captain Mouton explained we'd come about the boy. Farid got angry, denied he was there. She said she thought she heard someone crying and told me to check in the other room, see if he needed help. Farid objected, but I went anyway. I found the boy hiding in a cabinet."

The image of Taj's battered face made her chest hurt, but KD forced herself to go on. "He didn't speak English and I know very little Dari. He didn't understand I was trying to help. He fought me when I pulled him out of the cabinet."

She wasn't aware she was sweating until Murdock filled a cup with water and held it out, then passed her a tissue. She drank, wiped her face, then drank again.

"Take your time, Lieutenant. I know this is hard, but we're almost done."

She took a deep breath, counted to four, exhaled, took another. "Mouton and Farid were still arguing in the front room. I heard glass breaking, then a gunshot. I should have gone back. I should have helped her. But I didn't." She glanced at Murdock, hoping to see understanding, validation . . . something.

Instead, he just shrugged. "You made a split-second decision. Save the boy or help your captain. You chose the boy. Why?"

She looked away, irritated by his indifferent response. "I

thought if I could get Taj out the back window, I could go back and tell Mouton that there was no boy. Then we could walk away and forget it. But that didn't happen."

She saw that she had torn the tissue to shreds, and balled it in her fist. "When I was pushing Taj out the window, I heard a second gunshot. Seconds later, Farid came in. I realized then that Mouton was hurt. Or worse." She struggled to calm her breathing and keep her voice steady, but everything was jumbling up in her head. "I remember being shot. Falling to the floor. Watching him come toward me, with a gun in his hand. I think he said something. But after that, it's all a blank." She felt something touch her hand and drew back, startled, to see Murdock holding out another tissue. "What are you doing?"

"You were crying."

The sympathy she had wanted from him earlier was evident now. She hated it. Hated showing weakness. "You're wrong. I never cry." Soldiers didn't.

He studied her for a moment, then dropped the tissue in the trash can by her bed. "My mistake." Glancing at his watch, he suddenly became all business again. "I have to go. The transport to CENTCOM leaves in an hour." He slipped the notepad and pen back into the courier pouch. "I'll let you know if there's a hearing. Just remember what I told you. Hold your temper, stay calm, and tell the truth. And don't vomit." He walked to the door, calling over his shoulder as he stepped into the hall, "Probably see you stateside before this is over. Don't forget your hairbrush." Then, laughter floating behind him, he was gone.

KD stared at the empty doorway and wondered if she would ever see Warrant Officer Murdock again. The room seemed bigger without him. And quieter. But that laugh echoed through her mind for a long time.

CHAPTER 5

Whitcomb Four Star Ranch
Rough Creek, Texas
Late May 2018

"You can't hide forever, you know," a deep voice said. "Even if you close your eyes and don't see me, I can still see you."

KD cracked open an eye. Dalton Cardwell, her sister Raney's husband and partner in running the ranch, sat in the upholstered patio chair beside hers, two frosty Lone Star longnecks in his hands. Big hands, she noted. As big as Murdock's, but more work-worn. He held out one of the longnecks. "Nightcap?"

Only in Texas would a longneck be considered a nightcap. Especially while the sun was still up. But since it was Saturday, rules were more relaxed.

KD hesitated—she was still on a lot of meds—then thought, *What the hell*, and took it anyway. "Thanks." Maybe it would help. She hadn't slept through the night even once since she got home.

It was late afternoon. Hot and muggy, which meant it would probably rain overnight. She and Dalton were on the veranda—Mama's word for an unscreened, covered back porch. Raney was in the office, going over invoices, Mama was headed to a girls' evening out with the menopause set, and KD's next-in-age sister, Josslyn, sat with her husband, Grady, on the long sloping back lawn to the creek, watching their adorable baby, Lyric, do infant calisthenics on a blanket.

KD felt bad she wasn't out there playing the besotted auntie, but she didn't have the energy. She had missed Lyric's birth as well as her two sisters' double December wedding, and the doting parents had only stopped for the night before heading on to Fort Worth and Joss's next concert.

Not that Joss was the headliner—yet—but under Grady's careful management, she was on her way. From family dream chaser and wild child to country singer, songwriter, and now adored wife and adoring mother, crazy, harebrained Joss had it all. While KD, the hotshot college graduate and army officer, might soon be out of a job. Who would have guessed?

Anger blazed in KD's mind, igniting the shame she could never seem to outrun. Disgusted with herself, she took a sip of beer, flinching when the cold liquid hit her empty stomach. "Why do you think I'm hiding?" she asked Dalton, setting the beer on the end table between their chairs.

He gave her a look that warned another lecture was on the way. Not that Dalton actually lectured. Or fussed. Or hovered, like Mama and her sisters did. The worry in his green eyes said it all. "You missed supper again."

"Don't scold, Ma. I'm fine."

She could tell he didn't believe her, and that added to her sense of helplessness and alienation. She was sick of the worried looks. Of the hovering. Of being angry all the time. Everyone wanted her to be fine, to be a tough little soldier. But she wasn't, and nothing seemed to help.

The self-pity added to KD's irritation. Why couldn't she be happy to be home, safe and surrounded by family, rather than letting her thoughts keep circling back to those she had left behind? Why couldn't she let that go?

At least Dalton seemed to understand. He didn't push or question, and allowed her the space she needed. She gave him a weary smile. "Marry me."

"Too late."

"Bummer."

"I know. It's the muscles. Everybody wants me now I've got muscles."

KD laughed, and it lightened her dark mood. Bless Dalton. He always knew the perfect thing to say.

Even though he was older than KD by several years, and had attended schools on the other side of the county, she had heard about "Beanpole" Cardwell throughout her childhood. Mainly because of his amazing athletic abilities. He even had his high school football picture on City Hall's wall of local notables. Football is king in Texas, and anyone who stands out at the state level becomes a minor celebrity.

But that was a long time ago and they had both changed. After two tours in Iraq right out of high school, and later, eighteen months lifting weights in the exercise yard at the state prison in Huntsville, Beanpole had "filled out nicely," as Mama put it. Easygoing, big, and muscular, yet still gentle-hearted despite his experiences, he was a perfect match for her workaholic, managing, second-oldest sister. Now he was a standout as a highly respected cutting horse trainer, and had taken some of the burden of running Whitcomb Four Star off Raney's shoulders so she could concentrate on living a normal life. He had blended seamlessly into the family, becoming the son Mama had never had, and the big brother KD had wished for ever since Daddy had died of a heart attack when she was ten.

And strangely—although she was just getting to know her brother-in-law since she'd come home—of all of her family, KD felt the strongest bond with the ex-con and horse trainer. Probably because he was an ex-soldier, too.

"I wasn't hiding," she lied, ending the long silence. "I was dozing. I didn't sleep very well last night."

"The hip bothering you?"

"Some."

"Or maybe it was the nightmares that kept you pacing all night."

KD glanced at him in surprise. He had heard her? He and Raney were using Raney's bedroom upstairs until the house they were building was finished. Because of KD's hip, and since her old bedroom was now Lyric's nursery, Mama had insisted KD stay in the downstairs guest suite between the office and the kitchen.

The nightmares had started soon after they'd taken her off the heavy pain meds and sent her home. KD hadn't realized how much those pills had dulled her mind and kept her safely insulated from the dark thoughts that haunted her now. She often awoke in panic, her heart kicking against her ribs, her body shaking and wet with sweat. It embarrassed her that her sister and her brother-in-law might have heard her. She decided when she went to Fort Hood next week, she would ask Dr. Prescott to up her anti-anxiety meds. Maybe then she'd be able to sleep.

Somewhere inside the house, the ranch phone rang. It sounded out-of-date in this age of cell phones. But comforting. KD liked that some things hadn't changed while she'd been gone. She gave Dalton a weary smile. "Sorry I woke you."

"You didn't. I went to the kitchen for a snack and heard you walking around."

How could she admit to him what she hadn't even told her family? That every night seemed harder than the last and the guilt never stopped. They were all so supportive. So worried. And so justifiably confused. She wasn't the same person who had marched off to defend the world. And the broken person who had come back was as much a stranger to them as she was to KD.

But Dalton knew. He understood. He'd been to hell, too.

"How's the house coming?" she asked.

"Too slow." He grinned. "Not that I mind staying here under your mama's watchful eye. Day in and day out. At every meal."

"I feel your pain." Soon after they'd married, Raney and Dalton had started construction on a house out past the married workers' duplex, close to the creek but far enough away to give them privacy. Not that Mama was nosey, bless her heart. KD was feeling smothered, too. She loved her family, but between four years at West Point, boot camp, officer training, and her brief time in Afghanistan, she'd lived away from home for the last five years. The weight of their solicitous attentions was starting to crush her. Maybe it was time she had a break from all that unbridled motherly concern.

"Monday morning, when I go back to Hood," she said, "I may stay over a few days. Not on base. It's overcrowded as it is. Maybe a hotel in Killeen. Or a short-term rental. The long drives are hard on my hip."

"I could take you," Dalton offered. "I know the boss pretty well. I bet she'd give me a day off."

KD met his grin with a weak smile. "She'd give you the moon if you asked."

"Which is why I don't ask."

"Smart man. Thanks for the offer," she went on, "but I'll need a car while I'm down there." Twice a week, she had to report for physical therapy, strength training to prepare her for the active duty fitness test, and group therapy, a requirement for soldiers who had sustained traumatic combat injuries. The physical therapy and training sessions were helping. The visits to the nut factory, not so much. Which was partly KD's fault. She'd spilled her guts—literally—in Afghanistan. She wasn't interested in doing it again in front of strangers.

As the sun slipped behind the trees along Rough Creek, the sky exploded in bands of fiery color. Because of dust storms, sunsets in Afghanistan were beautiful, too. But instead of the chirp of crickets and frogs croaking down by the creek, those in Afghanistan were often accompanied by the rumble of distant explosions, gunfire, or the *whup* and howl of helicopters carrying the wounded back to base.

"Is the group therapy helping?" Dalton asked, regaining her attention. "Some vets don't like putting their business out there for everyone to see."

"It's hard," KD admitted. "We're supposed to be tough, stoic warriors. And yet . . ." *When bad thoughts come, there's no armor in the world that can protect us.*

Dalton leaned over and patted her shoulder. "You'll get there, KD. You're not in this alone. You've got a lot of people pulling for you."

"I know." Which was part of the problem. The hovering wasn't helping.

Maria, their housekeeper and cook, and a gentle, kind-hearted woman with the patience of Job, stepped out onto the veranda. "There is a phone call for you, KD."

Great. Probably another barely remembered high school BFF calling to ask how she was doing and to get all the grisly details of her injury. Other than a couple of hunting mishaps, and that time one of the Higgins boys peppered his brother's butt with buckshot over some girl, not that many people in Rough Creek had ever been shot. KD was big news, it seemed.

"Take a number, could you, Maria? Tell her I'll call back later."

"It is a him," the housekeeper said. "Calling from Florida."

CENTCOM. KD came instantly alert. She'd been expecting—and dreading—a call from Central Command informing her that she was being called before an Article 32 panel. She had hoped she would have a little more time.

"You will talk to him?" Maria pressed. At KD's nod, she said, "I will bring the phone to you," and went back into the house.

KD was aware of Dalton studying her. She hadn't told

any of her family about the investigation, or the possibility that she might be facing charges. She said nothing about it now, either. The call might be about something else altogether.

Maria came back with the phone, handed it to KD, and went back inside.

"Lieutenant Whitcomb speaking." KD said.

"Do you have any idea how many Whitcombs there are in the United States Army?" a familiar deep voice said.

Odd, how the sound of that voice could be so welcome.

"Too many," he went on. "Twelve in Texas alone. And since you never gave me your cell number, I had to dig up your 'next-of-kin' notification, which, incidentally, isn't filed under KD, but Katherine Diane Whitcomb. This is Warrant Officer Murdock, by the way."

She had to laugh. "I guessed. Who else would call up a superior officer and rant at her about her name?"

"I don't think of you as a superior." He sounded amused.

"Clearly." An image of him flashed through her mind. Dark stubble, dark hair sliding down his forehead, that wide grin brightening his blue eyes.

"What's your cell number?" he asked.

She gave it to him, imagined him writing it down in that notepad of his.

"And I wasn't ranting," he said after a moment. "I was expressing my irritation at having to sit at this damned computer for two hours trying to track you down. Why don't you use your real name?"

"KD is my real name. I just haven't changed it legally yet. Are you a Luddite?"

"A what?"

"Luddite. They distrust technology, too."

He made a snorting noise. Then she heard the rustle of movement, the creak of a chair, and a deep sigh. She pictured him leaning back in a beat-up swivel chair before a bank of outdated computers in some windowless records basement, his long legs outstretched, heels propped on a gray metal desk.

"So how's it going, Lieutenant Whitcomb?"

"Same as always. Doing the Lord's work as best I can. But I doubt you called to fuss at me about my name or inquire about my health. You have news?"

"I do." He no longer sounded amused. "There's a panel hearing scheduled Monday after next. I got them to hold it at Hood, rather than here at CENTCOM, so you won't have so far to travel. You are able to travel, aren't you?"

"I have to report to medical in Hood twice a week." *Ten days.* A weight seemed to press against KD's chest, making it hard to breathe. "I was hoping they wouldn't convene an Article 32."

"Probably just for show. A CYA thing. When will you be at the base?"

It took her a moment to catch her breath. "This coming Monday. I have a final medical checkup and strength training." She didn't mention group therapy. She didn't think she needed it and was embarrassed to admit that Hwang had recommended it after that one panic attack at Landstuhl. She wasn't crazy, just a little anxious, and she knew how to control it now, so she was fine. "I'll stay either on base or in town until the hearing's over. How long do you think it'll last?"

"A week. Unless there are a lot of witnesses. Which there aren't."

Her heart started to pound. Her throat felt stuffed with cotton. In ten days, she might not be a soldier, or belong to the greatest army in the world, or see Murdock again.

That last thought shocked her. Why would she care if she never saw Warrant Officer Murdock again? Yet she did care. Except for the poor damaged souls in her therapy group, Murdock was her only link to the person—the soldier—she had been. Other than a get-well card or two, the women in the cultural support team at Hickock hadn't contacted her. It was as if after that day, she had ceased to exist to the soldiers she had lived with for that short time in Afghanistan. Probably for the best. She didn't want to have to tell them what happened. How Nataleah had died. It was too shameful and would only remind her of what she'd done.

"Will you be there, too?" It disgusted her how badly she wanted him to say yes. She hated feeling this needy.

"They haven't called me, but I'll be there. I've got paperwork to do." There was a pause. KD could hear him breathing, and an image of him dozing in the chair at the hospital filled her mind. "You sure you're up for this, Lieutenant? Your recovery going okay? I can postpone it a couple more weeks if you need me to."

"No. I'll be there." She needed this hearing behind her so she could move on.

"I'll text you the name of a good JAG lawyer to represent you at the hearing. You'll have to request him," he added. "I can't. But I'll try to come in early to help you prep."

That news was so welcome, for a moment KD couldn't respond. Suddenly, she didn't feel quite so outnumbered and alone. Suddenly, she had something to hang on to. "Thanks. And bring a hairbrush in case I forget mine." He was chuckling when she ended the call, afraid she might say something even stupider.

"Who was that?" Dalton asked. "And what's this about an Article 32 hearing? And why are you sharing a hairbrush with him?"

"He's a CID warrant officer, and we're not sharing a hairbrush. That was a joke. He's investigating what happened in Afghanistan. And the Article 32 is only a formality. No big deal."

"Bullshit." Dalton leaned forward, elbows on his thighs, and studied her, his dark brows drawn in a hard, straight line. "An Article 32 is a very big deal. And they're not convened as a formality. What's going on, KD?"

She didn't want to talk about it and risk bursting the tiny

bubble of joy that talking to Murdock had brought. Hearing his voice, his laugh, the low, rolling timbre of his voice had lifted her spirits higher than they had been in days. Weeks. She knew that bubble would burst eventually—she hardly knew the man—but it was precious to her now. Yet Dalton had a point. In the event she didn't—or couldn't—come back, her family would need to know why.

"I'll explain it all before I leave for Hood," she told him. "I promise. Okay?"

He studied her for a long time, then sat back, a speculative gleam in his eyes. "You like him, don't you? This CID guy."

She waved the notion away. "I barely know him."

"He made you laugh. You haven't done that since you came home."

"You're dreaming." Afraid of where this was headed, KD rose. "Enjoy my beer. I'm for bed."

"It's not even eight thirty."

"Late enough."

She'd almost made her escape when he called after her, "If you see the CID guy in your dreams, tell him to call me. I need to know where this thing y'all have going is headed."

"It's not a thing."

"Sounds like a thing."

"Bite me."

Richard was disappointed. He had hoped to talk longer to KD. He liked that sexy Texas drawl and her odd sense of humor. For a guy who'd spent years perfecting his ability to read people, her unpredictability was a turn-on. Maybe he should arrange his schedule to be at Fort Hood earlier in the week. That would give him plenty of time to complete his paperwork and prep her for the hearing. He smiled, liking that idea. But those happy thoughts faded when a call came in and he saw it was Stranton. *Shit*.

It was 2200 hours in Florida. If his CO was calling this late, he must be pissed about something. Richard was officially on leave, although Stranton could still cancel it any time. Or the chief could be calling about his case report on Farid. Wanting to avoid making waves before his leave started, Richard had asked the sergeant who handled the CID paperwork—a guy he'd known for years—to put his report at the bottom of the pile. Hopefully, Stranton hadn't seen it yet.

"Evening, sir. Murdock speaking."

"Who is this Khalil Farid who keeps calling me? Man's driving me insane."

Richard let out a breath. Nothing about his case report or his leave. "He's Asef Farid's father, sir. The ANP captain who was killed in Afghanistan."

"He wants to come to the Article 32 hearing. How did he even hear about it?"

"Maybe he heard talk at the FOB."

"Says he wants to testify. Some crap about defending his son's honor. As usual, State is caving, afraid if they refuse his visa request, it'll bring even more scrutiny. Christ! You said this was cut-and-dried. How did it get so fucked up?"

"I don't know, sir. But Khalil Farid is an addict and unstable. Local poppy grower, very rich. A suspected Taliban sympathizer and big on honor killings. The villagers at Hickock are terrified of him. There's even been speculation he might have been behind the murder of the FET interpreter, Samira."

"Great." Stranton let out a deep breath that sounded like a wind storm through the phone. "What's your schedule?"

"I'm heading to Fort Hood, sir. That's where the Article 32 is being held." Richard didn't want to tell him he was still on base in Florida.

"Texas? Who moved it over there?"

"I did, sir. That's where Lieutenant Whitcomb is. She

isn't fully recovered, and rather than wait any longer, I thought—"

"Okay! Whatever."

Stranton was obviously stressing. Worried about his promotion, no doubt. If the man wasn't such an ass-wipe, Richard might have felt sorry for him.

"Warn the Hood MPs about this Farid guy," the chief ordered. "And alert the preliminary hearing officer, major-what's-his-name."

"Major Phillip Hendricks, sir. I have his number if you want it."

"Text it to me."

"Yes, sir."

"How damaging will Khalil Farid's testimony be?"

"Not very. He's mostly bluster and threats." Richard hoped.

"Threats against whom?"

"Me, Lieutenant Whitcomb, the Hickock medical officer, just about everyone involved in his son's case."

"Are the threats credible?"

"I didn't think so." *But if Khalil came to Hood . . .*

Richard decided he would warn the MPs to keep an eye on KD Whitcomb, too. Fort Hood didn't need another fiasco like that mass shooting back in 2009.

"Anything you can do to counter Khalil's testimony?" Stranton asked, steering Richard back on track.

"I'll check with the FOB medical officer. He might have some insights or names." Best case would be if Erickson had ever treated another boy Asef Farid had exploited. Or knew of a villager who had firsthand knowledge of the ANP captain's drug use and sexual abuse. A long shot, but worth a try.

"They ever find the boy he took, or his mother?"

"No, sir. Not likely to, either."

"Christ." The chief was still cussing when he ended the call.

Richard sent him a text with Hendricks's contact info, then punched in Captain William Breslin's number. Dr. Erickson was right. This was turning into a real clusterfuck. Hell of a way to start his leave.

"Hey, Bill," he said, recognizing the voice that answered. "Murdock here. Hope I'm not calling too late."

"Mudlark!" Bill said, using Richard's nickname from boot camp. Bill had been called Opie because of his red hair and boyish face. He'd hated it. And since Richard was calling for a favor, he refrained from using it now.

"It's not even dark yet," Bill went on. "What am I? Seventy? How's it hanging, buddy?"

"About a foot."

"You wish." Their standard joke from those early days.

After a few minutes of small talk, Richard told Bill he needed the name of a good JAG lawyer. "Best criminal defender you've got."

"Shit, man. What'd you do?"

"Not for me." Richard gave a brief explanation of the shooting. "Since it involves an ANP captain, my CO is trying to cover his ass by convening an Article 32. But I ran the investigation, Bill, and I can tell you she didn't do anything wrong."

"She?" Bill laughed. "About time you started looking at women again."

"I look all the time. I'm just not a horndog like you."

Richard's divorced status was probably in his service file, but Bill was the only one Richard had ever talked to about his short, bitter marriage. Since then, whenever they got together for a beer, Bill tried to hook him up with every bar hog they saw. "This hearing is bogus," Richard insisted, hoping to get Bill back on subject. "The shooting was self-defense. Forensics backs it up."

"Then what's the problem?"

"Remember that SF officer in Afghanistan who had his command jerked for body-slamming a pedophile?"

"Shit."

"Yeah. A PR disaster. CENTCOM doesn't want another one. Phillip Hendricks is PHO. Know anything about him?"

"Phil's a good guy. He'll do you right. When's the hearing?"

Richard told him, adding that he would be heading to Hood in a day or two.

There was a pause, the sound of papers flipping, then Bill said, "I can be there Thursday. That's next week, right?"

"Right. Thanks, man. I was hoping you'd take it on."

Bill chuckled. "You wanted the best, didn't you? Besides, I need to meet the lady who made tight-assed, by-the-book Mudlark break protocol by arranging her counsel himself. Just make sure she makes the request, not you."

"Thanks, Bill. I owe you."

Richard texted Bill's contact info to KD, told her not to worry, then punched in Vocek's cell number. "Evening, sir. This is CID Warrant Officer Murdock."

"I don't give a rat's hairy ass if you're the Pope. You know what time it is?"

Richard grimaced. All these different time zones were getting him confused. "Sorry, sir. I forgot about the time difference. Should I call back later?"

"Hell, I'm awake now. But this better be good."

"I need a solid, sir."

Vocek's laugh turned into a smoker's cough. "A warrant officer asking a favor from a captain not in his chain of command. Gimme a minute to jot that down in my Book of Memories."

Richard let him have his fun. He really needed the guy's help.

"So ask," Vocek said once he'd quit laughing. "I'll decide if it's worth you waking me up at this ungodly hour on another balmy summer day in beautiful Goat Hump, Afghanistan."

The guy was a real card. "I need you to make a call, sir. That's all."

After Vocek had agreed to contact the CO of the Hood MPs and request a watch on both Khalil Farid and Lieutenant Whitcomb, Richard thanked him profusely and hung up. Wisely, he waited almost two hours before making his next call.

"I need to speak to the major," he told the sergeant at the Hickock medical desk. "This is CID Warrant Officer Murdock."

"I thought I was done with you, Murdock," Dr. Erickson said as soon as the call went through. "What's the status on that pretty little lieutenant?"

"Still alive, but facing an Article 32."

In a testament to the doctor's long service in various foreign lands, he let loose a highly imaginative and uniquely structured string of foreign and medical words. The only one Richard made out was *syphilitic*, which Erickson made sound like a four-star cuss word. Impressive. "So what are you doing to get her through this mess unscathed?" the major demanded after he'd calmed down.

"Right now, I'm calling to see if you would testify in her defense."

"All the pertinent findings are in my medical report."

"Yes, sir. But what I'm looking for is information that wasn't in the report."

"Like what?"

"Like did you ever treat a boy that Farid might have sexually abused?"

When the doctor didn't answer right away, Richard hurriedly explained about Khalil Farid coming to the hearing. "He's still making threats and insisting on clearing his son's name. If you have information that might prove Asef Farid was a pederast and drug user, it would help a lot."

"His drug use is fully documented in my report."

"Yes, sir." Richard waited.

After a long pause, Erickson said in a thoughtful voice, "So what you're really asking, Warrant Officer Murdock, is will I violate confidentiality by giving you the name of any other boy that I may, or may not, have treated who was allegedly abused by Captain Farid?"

Richard felt his hopes dwindle. "Yes, sir."

"I'll see what I can do."

Bingo. "Thank you, sir. I really appreciate it."

His final call would have to wait. It was almost midnight in Texas. Richard didn't want to wake her only to deliver the news she might have a target on her back.

After a restless night thinking inappropriate thoughts about Lieutenant Whitcomb, Richard punched in her cell number. "It's me again."

"You stalking me, Warrant Officer Murdock?" As soon as he heard that sexy drawl, he had to smile.

"Of course not. Unless you want me to stalk you. I'm a really good stalker. Not in a creepy way, of course," he quickly added. "Although some of the soldiers I've had to track down might disagree." *Shit.* That sounded even worse. Determined to stay on script before he made an even bigger ass of himself, Richard cleared his throat and said in his professional voice, "Actually, Lieutenant, I called to see if you got my text about the JAG lawyer. You should call him as soon as you can. And also, I wanted to warn you that Captain Farid's father will probably be at the hearing."

"I just called Breslin, and why do I need to be warned about Farid's father?"

"For one thing, he's nuts. You should stay away from him."

"And the other?"

"Other what?"

"You said, 'for one thing.' What's the other thing?"

"Oh. Right. Well, he may have made some threats."

"*May* have?" Her voice rose a notch. "Against *me*?"

"Against anyone involved in his son's death, or the investigation, or who had ever insulted his family. Which probably means anyone who's ever met him."

"Is that supposed to be reassuring?"

He could almost feel the energy seep out of her. He hated adding this new burden to someone who must already feel overwhelmed. "Don't worry about it, Lieutenant. He won't get anywhere near you." Richard tried to sound positive, but he was worried, too. Khalil was a very disturbed man. "The MPs at Hood are being alerted to keep an eye on him. And you. And because he's considered high risk, his visa will be flagged. Plus, I'll be there. You'll be safe enough."

"You signing on as my personal bodyguard?"

Good idea. "I'm on leave for a month," he explained. "I've got nothing better to do than cater to your every whim."

He finally got the chuckle he'd hoped for. "Sounds fun."

Richard thought so, too. He wondered what was wrong with him. He hardly knew the woman. But he had to admit that spending time with Lieutenant Whitcomb wouldn't be a hardship. "Maybe we could have dinner. Or a beer. Or something." *God*, he was out of practice.

"Maybe."

"Okay then. I'll hunt you up as soon as I get to Hood."

"Hunt me up how?"

"I'm a highly trained investigator, Lieutenant. If I want to find you, I will. Although I'll admit it would be a hell of a lot easier if you just told me where you'll be."

This time the chuckle built into a laugh that made him grin. "Do your best, Murdock. Think of it as a bodyguard audition. But just to be fair, I'll give you a hint. I'll be the one with a limp. See you next week."

CHAPTER 6

Sunday morning, KD awoke with a feeling of dread.

Other than when she was battling a nightmare and had no choice, she tried not to think about what happened in Afghanistan, much less talk about it. She had told her family as little as possible about the circumstances of her injury, and for once, they hadn't pried. They knew she'd been shot, but not why or under what circumstances. But today, with the hearing coming up, a madman threatening her, and an extended stay in Fort Hood until the matter was resolved, she had to bring them up to date.

Her stomach hurt just thinking about it. It seemed her entire life revolved around that one terrible night. She couldn't sleep, had little appetite, and was so mired in anger and shame she couldn't find her way out. The one time she'd talked about it in group therapy had made her feel worse because most of the other soldiers had sacrificed a lot more than she had. It wasn't just the shooting that haunted her, but also the things she could have done differently that might have saved Nataleah's life. Now, she would have to admit all that to her family and they would know how utterly she had failed by making the wrong choice.

Luckily, Josslyn, Grady, and baby Lyric had left for the concert in Fort Worth early that morning, and KD's oldest sister, Lennox—or Len—was on an end-of-the-school-year Caribbean cruise with her surgeon husband and two teenaged children. She would only have to talk to Raney and Dalton. And of course, Mama.

Now in her early sixties, Coralee Lennox Whitcomb was still a beautiful, vivacious, energetic woman . . . as well as a master manipulator and relentless manager. She had been the driving force that had built the Lennox family farm into the Whitcomb Four Star Ranch, while at the same time molding a smart, likable, well-respected young lawyer into a highly successful businessman and behind-the-scenes player in Texas politics. Mama was the backbone of the family, and KD was proud to be her daughter.

But it came with a price.

Being the youngest of four daughters, KD had been in a unique position to see Mama work hard to build her older sisters into the strong, compassionate, dynamic women she wanted them to be. For the most part, she'd been successful—although Joss was still a work in progress. KD had never doubted her mother's good intentions, or faulted her for her efforts, but from the time she'd learned to walk, she'd been driven to find her own way. After witnessing her mother's tireless efforts firsthand, she'd decided early on to stay as far away from Mama's manipulations as possible.

Now that Raney and Dalton were married and shared management of the ranch—something Raney said Mama had angled for since the day Dalton had come looking for a job fresh out of prison—and Len was a busy Dallas socialite—every Texas Mama's dream—and Joss was out of reach on her concert tour—a blessing for all—KD could see that her mother was looking for fresh raw material to mold. Up to now, KD had felt relatively safe. Years ago, realizing the only things Mama couldn't boss were God and the United States government, KD had set her sights on West Point and the US Army. But now . . .

Now she had to involve Mama in something she wouldn't be able to fix, or manipulate, or understand. KD would have to tell her family the truth about what happened in Afghanistan. There would be questions she would have to answer. Pain she would have to relive. But what choice did she have? They were her family, and they deserved to know that a shitstorm was headed their way.

As was the custom on many ranches, the ranch foreman, Glenn Hicks, and their head wrangler, Alejandro, ate their evening meals and Sunday lunch at the main house. That Sunday, as soon as they'd finished their meals and excused themselves, KD turned to the three lingering over dessert— Raney, Dalton, and Mama—and said, "We need to talk."

Worried faces all around, but no argument. A good omen.

At her mother's suggestion, they went out onto the back veranda and the four overstuffed chairs grouped around a huge ottoman in front of the unlit outdoor fireplace—Mama's favorite place for the heart-to-heart chats her daughters always dreaded. Once seated, they looked at KD with varying degrees of concern and wariness, but waited patiently for her to begin. Another good omen.

Still, it was hard to find the words. So she started with an explanation of *bacha bazi* and the DOD policy of non-interference in local cultural matters.

As expected, her mother was outraged. "Our own government condoned such a thing?"

"No one condoned it, Mama. We were just told to look the other way, to 'refrain from cultural bias.' But I'll admit it was awful, hearing the crying, knowing what was happening on the other side of the watchtower gate. Especially when one of the worst offenders was the commander of the local unit of the Afghan National Police. A man we had trained." KD shuddered, disgusted all over again that such a thing was allowed to happen. "And he wasn't the only one."

"That's horrible!" Raney turned to Dalton. "Did that happen in Iraq, too?"

He shrugged. "It's a different culture. Luckily, I didn't have to deal with the darker aspects of it. But it was one of the reasons I mustered out as soon as my second tour ended."

"Well, I'm flabbergasted," Mama said, and looked it. "I had no idea. Was that why you were shot, KD? Was someone doing that to a child and you tried to stop him? Why didn't you tell us?"

"I'm trying to," KD said, sending her mother a warning look. Immediately, she regretted it. None of this was their fault. Taking a deep breath, she began at the beginning. "A local woman told me and Nataleah Mouton, the captain of our team, that the Afghan police commander, Captain Farid, had taken her son. She asked us to try to get him to release the boy. Which we did."

KD paused to draw in another deep breath. Whenever she talked about that night, her lungs seemed to constrict.

"Things went bad right away." She told them about Farid's denials, his argument with Nataleah, and that her captain had sent her into the other room to look for the boy. "I found him hiding in a cabinet, beaten and terrified. Then I heard a gunshot in the front room . . ."

Images flashed through KD's mind. She tried to block them, wiped her sweating palms on her jeans, took another deep breath. But her heart kept speeding up. Panic sent her into a free fall, spinning her backward in time, back to the hut, the shouting, the gunshot, the boy crying and fighting—

"Lieutenant." Dalton's voice snapped her back. "You're in no danger here. No one can hurt you. You're safe."

She focused on his voice, reminded herself this was Texas, not Afghanistan. She was alive and Farid was dead. *Breathe in, breathe out. Count to four. Do it again.* The spinning slowed. The ground steadied. *I'm okay. I'm home.* That choking sensation faded and she drew a full breath.

KD was furious she had let it happen again. She hated showing weakness. She had always been the strong one. The one who managed and never needed coddling. But since she'd come home, every day had become a balancing act between gasping terror and brittle normalcy and convincing everyone she was okay.

But she wasn't okay. And now, seeing the way her mother and sister stared at her, their faces stricken, she knew they realized it, too. She couldn't bear that. So she continued to lie and deny and pretend . . . as she always had . . . as soldiers were trained to do. "Don't look so worried. I'm all right," she told them with a shaky laugh. "It's just hard to talk about, is all."

Thank God they didn't offer sympathy. It would have crushed her if they had.

"Anyway," she went on in a steadier voice, "while I was getting the boy out the back window, I heard shooting in the other room. Then Farid came in and shot me. I don't remember what happened next. They told me later that I had shot and killed him, and that Nataleah had died of her wounds."

She looked down at her clenched hands.

"I realize I should have checked him for a gun. Or gone back to help her when I heard them arguing. But I wanted to get the boy away, and I didn't think—"

"It's on her," Dalton cut in. "Not you. She was in charge."

In the chair beside KD's, Mama cried softly. KD couldn't look at her. Couldn't look at any of them, afraid of what she might see. Condemnation? Pity? She couldn't bear that. Instead, she watched birds flitting through shrubs bordering the back lawn. Oblivious. Unconcerned. Just doing their thing. If only her own life could be that carefree and simple.

"I'm sorry you had to do it," Raney, her no-nonsense, gun-toting sister said fiercely. "But I'm glad he's dead."

KD was, too. It was Nataleah, not Farid, who haunted her.

Mama reached over and took KD's hand in hers. "Dearest . . . I'm so sorry." Her blue eyes were swollen with tears, her mouth wobbly with grief. But her grip was strong and steady, as if by force of will her mother could take away all of KD's pain and draw it into herself.

KD clung to it like a lifeline, wishing that were true, and Mama really could make everything right again. But she couldn't. And after a moment, KD pulled herself together and forced herself to let go, afraid if she didn't, she would never find her own strength again.

"I'm okay. I promise." She brushed a hand over her face, as if that might wipe away the senselessness of it, the waste and guilt, then forged on, intent on saying it all. "Because an Afghan police captain died, and an American officer was killed, the army wanted a full investigation."

"I should hope so!" Mama swiped tears from her own cheeks. "Such disgusting behavior should never have been allowed to happen!"

KD didn't tell her that *she* was the focus of the investigation, not Farid's sexual abuse. Mama was strictly black-and-white, regardless of cultural traditions.

"That's where the CID guy comes in?" Dalton asked.

KD nodded. To Mama and Raney, she explained that CID was the army's Criminal Investigation Division. "Both the CID investigator and the base's medical officer are aware Farid shot first and I returned fire in self-defense. But to make sure everything is done properly, there's to be an Article 32 hearing."

"Damage control," Dalton muttered.

"What's an Article 32 hearing?" Raney glanced from KD to her husband. "Is that bad?"

"It's a preliminary hearing to determine if charges should be brought," Dalton explained.

"Charges against KD?" Mama was aghast. "For what?"

"She hasn't been charged with anything," Dalton assured her. "It's like an inquest. That's all."

"I don't understand," Mama said. "What do they think you did, KD, other than protect an abused child?"

KD explained that they were trying to determine if she and the captain willfully violated the look-the-other-way policy by confronting Farid. "That wasn't our intent, of course. We only went there to talk to him. But it got out of control so fast."

"This is bullshit!" Raney turned to Dalton, blue eyes flashing with outrage. "We have to do something! We can't let them railroad my little sister!"

"They won't." Dalton cupped his big hand against his wife's cheek and looked into her eyes. "Stop worrying, sweetheart. I've got this."

"But—"

"Trust me." He smiled.

Amazing, the cooling effect that smile had on her sister.

Turning back to KD, he asked if they'd assigned someone from JAG to her case yet.

"The CID guy texted me a name. Said he's the best. I already called him and requested him as my counsel."

"Well, I don't understand any of it," Mama broke in. "Why would they put you through all this, KD? You were protecting an innocent child!"

KD tried to explain, even though she was confused, too. "There have been similar incidents before, although no one was killed. Warrant Officer Murdock thinks the brass is only pursuing it because they're afraid of a PR problem. Or maybe because Khalil Farid, the father of the dead Afghan officer, is determined to clear his son's name. He's even insisted on coming to the hearing."

"Then I'm coming, too," Dalton said.

"We all are!" Mama shot from her chair.

KD tried to pull her back, but she was already out of reach. The last thing she needed was Mama getting involved. "That's not necessary, Mama. Really."

"Of course it is. When is it? And where?"

"I'm serious, Mama. There's no need for you to come."

"Don't be silly. Dalton can drive me."

"What about me?" Raney demanded. "I'm going, too."

"You shouldn't wear yourself out, dear." Mama gave her an indulgent smile. "And who would look after the ranch? Dalton, convince her. I'll make arrangements for rooms in Killeen. When did you say the hearing was, KD?"

KD sighed in defeat. Although it would add to the confusion with Mama and Dalton there, she wouldn't mind their support, as long as Mama didn't cause a scene. "A week from tomorrow. I'll find out the time from my JAG lawyer next week. In any case, I'll be staying in Killeen until the hearing is over."

"Be sure to tell him we're coming, too," Mama said, already in planning mode. "And that we'll be happy to testify to whatever he wants us to. Now if you'll excuse me, I have some calls to make."

As soon as Mama had disappeared into the kitchen, KD rounded on her sister and brother-in-law. "None of you should come. I doubt I could talk Mama out of it, but you definitely shouldn't come, Raney. Especially now."

"What's that supposed to mean?"

"Oh, please. I may not know Dalton all that well, but I know you, big sister. All those solicitous glances and 'Be careful, sweethearts' he gives you? You hate being babied as much as I do. And the food you've been putting away—gag! Since when do you eat fried bologna sandwiches?"

"So?"

"So you either have worms or you're pregnant."

Raney frowned at Dalton. "I told you she'd figure it out. She's the smart one."

KD threw her hands up in exasperation. "Everybody's figured it out, Raney! Mama, most of all. Can't you tell you're her new favorite daughter?"

"Crap. After seeing the way she hovered over Joss when

she was pregnant, I wanted to wait at least until I was showing."

"Now that *our* secret is out," Dalton said, studying KD in that intrusive way he had. "Why don't you tell us yours?"

KD tried to signal him to drop it with a sidewise glance at Raney.

He didn't buy it. "No secrets, KD. Your sister and I made a pact before we got married—no matter what, there would be no more secrets between us."

"More?" KD asked, hoping to get him off track.

"What's really going on, KD?"

She slumped back in her chair. "I was afraid this would happen. If I tell you, you can't say anything to Mama. Promise." She waited for them to nod, then told them about Khalil Farid's threats and his insistence on coming to the hearing.

Raney grabbed her husband's arm. "We have to do something, Dalton!"

"No, you don't," KD cut in. "Murdock texted me that he's already arranging for the MPs at Hood to keep an eye on Khalil Farid and me during the hearing. But just to be safe, I don't want that lunatic knowing anything about my family, who you are, where you live, anything. That's why you shouldn't come to the hearing, Dalton. I need you here to watch over Raney and Mama. Okay?"

"Not okay," Dalton said. "I want to talk to this Murdock. Have him call me. Meanwhile, we can hire people for both here and Fort Hood."

"See?" KD waved a hand in exasperation. "This is exactly what I was afraid of. It's not me I'm worried about. I'll be on a base surrounded by thousands of highly trained soldiers. But y'all are stuck out here with only a few workers and some old hunting rifles."

"And my Glock," Raney put in.

KD ignored that. "You're the ones at risk! You have no protection out here. You'd be sitting ducks."

"No protection?" Dalton smiled at his wife. "I think she just insulted me."

"She did," Raney agreed. "I'm shocked she would do such a thing."

"Oh, stop, you two. I'm serious."

"So am I." No longer smiling, Dalton said in clipped tones, "You're forgetting I did two tours in Iraq, KD. I know how to protect your mother and Raney and the ranch. And don't sell our workers short. Old man Harvey was a marine sniper. He's still got the eyes for it. And Alejandro is handy with a rifle, too. As are the others. They're family. All our people are. And nobody comes after our family. End of discussion."

"I love it when he's forceful," Raney told KD with a dreamy smile at her husband.

"I think I may hurl," KD muttered.

Raney bounded to her feet. "Now that we've finished *the talk*, why don't we check out the leftovers. I'm starved." At KD's look of disbelief, since they had only finished Sunday lunch two hours earlier, Raney patted her still-flat stomach. "I may not show it, but I am eating for two, you know."

"And doing a damned fine job of it, sweetheart," Dalton assured her as he followed her toward the kitchen. "C'mon, KD, before she eats it all."

Exhausted from the emotional afternoon, KD was too tired to make the five-hour drive to Killeen that evening, so she went to bed early and slept surprisingly well. By dawn, Monday morning, she was making the turn at Gunther, heading south toward Fort Hood. By late morning, she had checked into the Barkley Suites in Killeen, and was driving through the main gate at the Fort Hood army base on her way to her final appointment with the surgeon.

It didn't take long. Apparently, her body was healing faster than her mind.

Thirty minutes later, when she'd left the Carl R. Darnall Army Medical Center—or CRDAMC, the military acronym—she stepped into a day as dry and blindingly bright as any she had seen in Afghanistan. Squinting into the glare, she walked as briskly as her hip would allow toward the parking area.

"Hey, Lieutenant," a voice called. "Wait up."

A familiar voice. Low and slightly husky, like a smoker's, but without the roughness. She hadn't expected to hear it so soon, and the sound of it gave her whole body a jolt. She thought he wasn't due at Hood until later in the week.

Turning carefully so she didn't pull herself off balance, she watched Murdock walk toward her, an army duffle over his shoulder. He was dressed in what he'd worn the first time she'd seen him at the hospital in Germany. Black ball cap with CID above the bill, black polo, khakis, gun and badge on his belt. This time he also wore mirrored aviators so she couldn't see his dark blue eyes, but that broad, white-toothed grin she definitely remembered. It made her a little short of breath, but not in a panicky way.

As he drew closer, she resisted stepping back, a bit intimidated by his size. She had never stood next to him and hadn't realized he was so big. Not quite as tall as Dalton, but every bit as broad.

"You found me," she said, wondering how he'd done it so quickly. She hadn't been on base for more than an hour.

"I told you I would."

She smiled, not sure how to respond. For all that she was one of the privileged Whitcomb girls and a debutante of Gunther County, she wasn't as socially adept as her sisters were. Probably from lack of interest. "When did you get in?"

"This morning on an early transport. Since you said you were seeing the doctor, I came straight here. Do I get the job?"

"I'll need a character reference. And not one from your parents," she warned.

"I doubt they'd give me one anyway. Where you headed?"

"My car."

"I'll walk with you. I hope it's air-conditioned. It's hotter than the hinges of hell out here."

"Welcome to summer in Texas."

He didn't rush her, but kept pace with her slower progress. "You're moving well," he observed. "The hip must be healing."

"So the doctor says. He released me to begin the next phase of physical fitness training." She wasn't looking forward to it. After losing weight and muscle mass from three weeks of inactivity, she had a long way to go. The APFT—Army Physical Fitness Test—had been grueling enough when she'd been whole and in shape.

"I heard they're coming up with an alternative test for soldiers with permanent injuries. Maybe they'll let you take that."

She shook her head. "Won't be available until the end of 2020. Until then, they're sticking with the deploy-or-out policy. I have a year to pass, or go before the Medical Evaluation Board."

"You're tough. If you want it, you'll pass."

"Maybe." *But do I want it?*

The thought shocked her. It was the first time KD had ever considered being anything but an army officer since her first day of high school when she'd seen the ROTC notice on the bulletin board outside the registrar's office. She wanted to stay in the army. But doing what? Even if she retained active status, she might be posted to a desk job somewhere. A dead-end desk job. And that was assuming she got past the Article 32 hearing. With a black mark like that against her, she would have limited promotion options. For sure, no Pentagon or laurel leaves.

When they reached the Camry, she unlocked it and tossed her bag in back.

"Nice car," Murdock said as she closed the rear door.

"My sister's. She's letting me use it while she's on tour."

Seeing his look of surprise, she clarified. "Musical tour. Not military. She's an almost nearly semifamous country singer and songwriter."

"Ah. Any good?"

That grin was addictive. Good thing he didn't use it often. "Very much so. But it's a tough business. Can I give you a lift somewhere?"

"Not sure where I'm staying. You staying on base?"

"I rented a room with a kitchen in Killeen." With her sleep disruptions, KD didn't want to stay in the crowded visiting officers' quarters. Or explain to people why she was at Hood.

It was hot, standing by the car. She could feel sweat forming on her back, and saw beads of it gathering on Murdock's neck. It was a nice neck.

She should probably go. And do what? Sit in an empty room, staring at the walls and feeling sorry for herself? She'd done too much of that lately. "You want to get lunch?" she asked on impulse.

"It's barely ten o'clock."

"Whatever." She reached for the driver's side door handle.

"But I know a quiet little diner that serves great pie and coffee," he said before she could open the door. "We could go over notes for the hearing."

Not something she wanted to do. But at least she wouldn't be alone. "You drive."

He tossed his duffle in back, then followed her to the other side of the car. Reaching around her, he opened the passenger door. "Need help?"

"Sitting down? No, I think I can manage."

"Smartass." But he said it with that grin. Which made her grin, too.

As they pulled out of the parking lot, he glanced over at her with a smile tugging at one side of his mouth. "So is this like . . . a date?"

"You don't have to pay my way, if that's what you're worried about."

"I'm more worried about what to do. I haven't been on a date in a long time."

"People don't go on dates anymore." At least, she didn't. She got together with friends, met up with a fellow officer for coffee or a movie every now and then, had a poignant goodbye hookup with a guy she'd gone out with during her last year at West Point. But living in close quarters with hundreds of other soldiers didn't leave much time for "dating" in the traditional sense. "And anyway," she added, "I never go on a date unless I know the guy's first name, at least."

He surprised her, like he had in the hospital, by laughing out loud. A warm, appealing, masculine chuckle that brought a clench to her chest.

"Richard. Richard Milton Murdock. The Third."

"Impressive."

"Pretentious."

He stopped at the gate. They showed their active duty IDs to the gate guard, who waved them through, then he turned toward Copperas Cove, rather than Killeen. "Why do you call yourself KD? What's wrong with Katherine Diane?"

"Not pretentious enough," she said. "I changed it to KD after I signed up for Army ROTC. Sounded more decisive. Less girly."

"I like girly."

"Of course you do. You're a guy. But I'd prefer to be admired for my skill set, rather than my ass."

"Too bad. You're admired for both."

The diner was a quaint little family eatery with a retro feel to it. Formica-topped tables, soda fountain, booths and chairs with plastic-covered seats and chrome legs. There were even checkered gingham café curtains at the front windows. Like stepping through a time warp. KD and Richard were the youngest customers, but instead of a *Happy Days* look-alike, their waitress was a gum-popping, purple-haired high school kid wearing more makeup than KD had bought in the last year. Overall, a nice change from institutional furniture, gray walls, and camo BDUs. The pie was homemade and delicious, and in deference to the temperature on the other side of the window by their booth, they both opted for iced tea, instead of coffee. Which was freshly brewed and also delicious.

Having gotten past the initial awkwardness and moving beyond rank to first names, KD found Richard Murdock surprisingly good company. Smart, funny, confident, and easy to talk to. Until he asked how she was doing and if the group therapy was helping.

CHAPTER 7

Richard knew immediately he had overstepped. He could feel her backing away. Not physically, although she did put down her fork and push aside the plate with her unfinished pie. But he knew the signs, saw it in the way her mouth tightened and her eyes narrowed. He was a trained observer, after all.

"How did you know about the group therapy?" she asked in a voice as warm as sunlight on snow. "You've seen my medical file, as well as my service file? What else have you been checking up on?"

"I don't have access to your medical file. And I haven't been checking up on you. I assumed. Therapy is customary for soldiers who've been shot."

She turned her head and looked out the window. "I don't have PTSD, if that's what you're wondering about."

"I wasn't. But it's nothing to be ashamed of if you do."

"I don't." She continued to watch the traffic passing by, her jaw so tight he could see the pulse beat in her temple.

He waited.

After a long silence, she turned back to him and said, "The doctor said my symptoms are inconsistent with a PTSD diagnosis. I have acute anxiety disorder, instead. But I'm coping."

He heard the sharp edge of challenge in her voice and thought again how easy . . . and foolish . . . it would be to underestimate this woman.

He lifted his glass. "Then here's to coping." He waited her out, his glass raised between them, until she finally raised hers.

"To coping," she said and tapped the edge of her glass against his.

Richard understood people fairly well, partly due to his training, but also through observation. He could usually tell when they were lying, or being evasive, or when they were afraid. When he was in PsyOps, he'd learned about body language, autonomic responses, and a host of other "tells." He'd spent countless hours in interrogation, studying eye movements and hand gestures and voice inflection. And based on what he'd learned and what instinct told him, he realized now that he'd made a lot of incorrect assumptions about Second Lieutenant KD Whitcomb.

She was an angry woman. Yet he sensed it wasn't her normal outlook.

Taking into account her lack of visible ink or piercings, her attention to personal hygiene and appearance, and her level of education, he'd assumed she'd been raised in a stable, two-parent, conservative, middle-class home. Probably went to church on Sunday. Followed the rules and stayed out of trouble. Grew up as either an only child or the oldest of several, falling in line with her parents' expectations, and primed to succeed. He doubted she made her bed every day or ironed her socks, but she performed as expected. Her West Point ranking and officer training evaluation put her in the upper percentile. Overall, a nice person—highly motivated, hardworking, predictable, and maybe a little boring.

She was anything but boring or predictable. And really pretty. And the more time he spent with her, the more he realized how off his other assumptions had been, too.

Happy to listen, he let her do the talking, enjoying the play of emotions across her expressive face while he built a whole different file in his head.

She was the youngest of four sisters. Loved her family, but valued her time away from them. Her father had died of a heart attack when she was ten, yet she didn't seem to be trying to replace him by seeking out older men. She certainly wasn't playing up to him, and he was at least eight years older than she was.

Independent, capable, decisive. All outstanding traits. But the thing he admired most was her dry sense of humor. Almost sarcastic, but in a funny way. She could be serious but didn't take herself too seriously, and that she had chosen a life of service indicated a strength of character he couldn't help but admire.

Which is why he was surprised she had anxiety issues. Anxiety is most often based in fear, but he didn't sense fear in KD. She didn't appear overly upset that she'd taken a life, and seemed more disturbed about her captain's death than the injury to herself. Denial? Survivor's guilt?

She was a puzzle he couldn't figure out. Which only made him more determined to do just that.

The waitress came with their bill just as Richard's phone buzzed. He checked caller ID. Stranton. *Shit.* The chief either had seen Richard's final report on the Farid case, or had remembered approving Richard's request for leave. Neither would put him in a good mood. But rather than have his ass chewed in front of KD, Richard let the call go to voice mail and put away his phone. "Now that we've had dessert," he said after checking his watch, "how about lunch?"

They ordered—a BLT for him, a salad for her—and stayed another hour-and-a-half. Mostly they talked, although there were periods of companionable silence, as well. Richard appreciated that. Despite being surrounded by thousands of soldiers every day and dealing with new people and new circumstances on a regular basis, he considered himself a solitary person. Being a CID investigator only reinforced that. No one liked Big Brother analyzing his or her decisions and actions. Yet spending time with KD was surprisingly easy and comfortable. And watching her across the table was an added bonus. She was seriously sexy.

When the waitress headed their way for the third time, KD checked her phone. "Damn! I didn't realize it was so late. My group session is about to start."

Richard offered to pay the tab. "You provided the transportation."

"Okay. Then thanks for lunch."

She let him drive again. Probably easier on her hip. When he pulled into the parking lot outside the medical center, their earlier awkwardness returned. Richard wasn't ready to walk away without finding out if he could see her again. Even though she was running late for her session, she seemed hesitant, too. He hoped for the same reason.

After he'd handed her the keys, he took a chance. "We never talked about the hearing. If you're free later, maybe we could try again."

She fought a smile. "Like a real date?"

He shrugged. "More like dinner."

She handed the keys back to him. "My session is over at four."

"I'll meet you here."

As soon as she'd disappeared into the building, Richard checked his voice mail. "No further action?" Stranton shouted in his message. "That's your recommendation on the Farid case? Bullshit! We talked about this, Murdock! You know what you're supposed to do, so do it! I want a revised report on my desk by tomorrow morning! Are we clear?"

Apparently, Chief Warrant Officer Stranton had finally checked his in-basket.

The Monday and Friday group therapy sessions were always hard on KD. She didn't feel right sharing her personal business with strangers, especially strangers who had much bigger problems than she did. There were six patients in the group, three men, three women. Tommy was working through a TBI—traumatic brain injury—and was still struggling with neurological and physical issues. When he wasn't heavily medicated.

Shirley, a petite female medic who had lost her right leg below the knee when an IED exploded beneath the ambulance she was driving, was waiting for a high-end prosthetic and anxious to get back to the front. Apparently, after-market limbs were less problematic than plastic and metal joints. A young Hispanic—KD didn't remember his name but mentally thought of him as Drummer Boy—couldn't sit still and tapped out drumbeats on his knees throughout each session. The third woman, Laura, might have been pretty, if not for the burn scar that covered half of her face. She tried to hide it by wearing hoodies and sitting with her head down while she silently cried for the hour she was there.

And then there was Rayfield, a big Black sergeant with no visible injuries. He sat sullenly through the meetings, stewing in rage and giving some of the other members nicknames—a common practice in the military. In boot camp, KD had been called Pocket Pal because of her small stature. But Sergeant Rayfield went for a racial approach and called her Snow White. Shirley, also small, but highly energetic and more talkative, was Mighty Mouse, and he'd given Dr. Prescott, a small, timid man with thick glasses and a mild voice, the name Conan because of his meek, nonconfrontational approach to the group dynamic. Every patient in the group suffered some form of anxiety or PTSD, and each expressed it in varying degrees of anger, fear, frustration, and grief.

Other than to offer a brief explanation of her injury when she attended her first session, KD rarely contributed. Like Sergeant Rayfield, none of her scars were visible. After her panic attack at Landstuhl, Dr. Hwang said that although she didn't display the usual signs of PTSD—jitteriness, hypervigilance, flashbacks, depression, or any of the other dozens of ways the brain fucked with people who had suffered terrible, traumatic events—she still had unresolved issues, and he felt she might benefit from group therapy. So here she sat twice a week. And since she didn't talk much or show any outward symptoms, the others in the group largely ignored her.

Except for Sergeant Rayfield. He had been on KD's case from the beginning, harassing her for not speaking up more and saying there were already too many pussies in the army without having to recruit women, too. She did her best to ignore him.

But when she walked into the meeting after her lunch with Murdock, she saw that the sergeant was in an especially bad mood and looking for a fight. With her, it seemed.

"Why you even show up, Snow White?" he demanded as soon as the others had settled into their chairs. "You never say nothing. Never do nothing. Just sit with that smug look on your face. You too good to share with the likes of us?"

KD met his belligerence with a bland smile. "What would you like for me to say, Sergeant? I've told you how I was injured." She didn't mention that he'd never told her why he was there, either. Not that she particularly wanted to know.

"Yeah, but that ain't why you're here, is it? Getting shot don't seem to be what's bothering you. It's something else. Something worse. You got shame written all over your lily-white face. What'd you do, Snow White?"

He had asked the question before, and KD had managed to steer him off the subject. But today, his wasn't the only questioning face turned her way.

"Why won't you talk?" Tommy TBI asked in a slurred voice.

"Yeah. Everybody else does," Drummer Boy added.

"If you ain't gonna participate, then get the hell out," the sergeant said, nodding to the others. "We trying to work here."

"Now, Rayfield," murmured Dr. Prescott.

"I ain't talking to you, Conan. I'm talking to her."

Afraid things would devolve into a shouting match, KD said, "I'm here because my doctor thinks I have acute anxiety disorder."

"Anxiety about what?" Shirley, the female amputee, asked.

The past. The future. Failing again. Having another anxiety attack and making an ass of myself. "The death of my captain."

"You killed her?"

"No. But I might have caused her death." Knowing they would keep at her until she said it all, KD went through the whole ordeal, focusing on her mistakes in not looking for a gun and not going back to help when she'd heard the first gunshot. It took a while, but they listened without interruption.

By the time she'd finished, she felt wrung out. Sweat dampened the back of her shirt, and her fingers were numb from being clasped together so hard. *I'm okay*, she told herself. *There's no danger. Breathe.* She did, but it still took effort to keep her voice steady. "I feel like I let my captain down. Like I let myself down. That's all."

Rayfield asked how long the captain had been in the army.

Apprehension built, making her heart beat too fast, but KD forced herself to take another long, deep breath. "I'm not sure. At least a decade. Maybe more."

"Combat?"

"This was her third tour in Afghanistan."

"You?"

"My first. I just finished officer training school." *Please, don't let it happen again. Not in front of all these people. I'm okay. I'm safe. It's just my mind playing tricks on me.*

"Shit!" The big sergeant rocked back in his chair, a deep laugh rumbling out of his barrel chest. "Damn! You sure full of yourself, ain't you, Snow White?"

KD wasn't sure how to respond. Or if she was able to.

"Now, Sergeant," Dr. Prescott said.

Rayfield ignored him. "You whining about not protecting *her*? You? An undersized, know-nothing, still-wet-behind-the-ears, green-ass lieutenant? Hell, she should have been watching out for *you*."

"Maybe she was," Shirley cut in. "Maybe she saw the situation was going bad, and to protect the lieutenant, she sent her out of the room to look for the boy."

"Then the captain damn sure should have checked for a gun herself. Just like a woman to forget the important stuff." Sarge turned back to KD. "As for not running in when the shooting started, she sent you to find the boy and see if he needed help. You supposed to disobey that order, forget the kid, and dive into the middle of a firefight? That's stupid, even for a white woman."

"Go to hell, Sarge," Shirley snapped.

"See you there, Mighty Mouse!"

Abruptly, Dr. Prescott stood and looked at his wristwatch. "Time's up. Enough for today, people. Excellent progress. See you on Friday."

Before he'd finished speaking, the room had emptied. Except for KD.

She sat frozen, her mind reeling. Had she been wrong all this time about her part in her captain's death? But what should she have done? Help the boy, as ordered? Or disobey that order and go back to help her captain? Or do nothing, as per DOD policy, and leave the boy to his abuser? It was a no-win situation.

"Are you all right, Lieutenant?"

KD looked up to see Dr. Prescott standing over her with a look of concern. "Wh-what? No—I mean yes, I'm fine." Aware of the doctor still staring at her, she rose unsteadily and walked toward the exit. But once the door had closed behind her, she stumbled to a stop, Rayfield's words still careening through her mind. Was he right? Should she have disobeyed her captain and run back to help? Or should she have disobeyed the DOD policy of noninterference and stayed to save Taj? Either way, she was screwed.

It was that simple. And that complicated. And as everything suddenly fell into place, the implications of what she had done took her breath away.

The moral choice was clear—help the boy—even if that was in direct conflict with DOD policy. That's what she'd done. Would do again if she had to. And once the Article 32 panel heard that, it would all be over. Her career. Her future. Everything she had worked for.

But at least Taj would be safe.

"Wait up," a voice called.

Her thoughts in turmoil, KD looked over to see Shirley swinging out of the restroom on her crutches.

"Sarge might be an asshole," she said when she fell in beside KD. "But he's right. Your captain's death isn't on you."

KD wanted so badly to believe that was true. But she was so confused she didn't know what to think anymore.

"Sarge is mad at the world right now," Shirley went on as KD moved automatically to open the exit door for her. "But he's not a bad guy. And he's got more experience than you and your captain combined, so he knows what's what."

KD nodded numbly.

"And it's not just you he's mad at," Shirley continued as she started awkwardly down the steps. "It's all women. He's old-school. Thinks the army should never have allowed us in." When she reached the sidewalk, she paused to catch her breath.

KD stopped beside her. She looked out over the parking lot, saw the Camry and a tall, dark-clad figure leaning against it, scrolling through his phone. Calm, capable Murdock. Suddenly, the need to go to him almost overwhelmed her. He would know what to do. How to make sense of this.

"Sarge lost someone dear to him, too," Shirley said. "He told us before you joined the group."

KD forced her attention back to the woman beside her. "Sarge lost someone? In combat?"

"Fool fell in love. Hooked up with a woman in his unit. Told us they were going to get married soon as her tour was up. Then one day she goes out on patrol and never comes back."

"What happened?"

"Ambush." Shirley let out a long, deep sigh. "Taliban got them all. Except for her. Her, they kept for a while. And when they were done, they left pieces of her scattered where the others had died. Except for her head. Never found that. But Sarge recognized what was left and went crazy. He's still crazy. Blames himself. Blames God. Blames the army for letting women in, in the first place." She gave KD a small, sad smile. "But he doesn't hate you, Snow White. He's just afraid it'll happen again. To you, or me, or some other woman." Shaking her head, she started toward the side lot. "Thinks we should all stay home in the kitchen," she called back over her shoulder as she swung along. "Barefoot and pregnant and out of harm's way. Yeah, right. Like that'll happen." She laughed. "See you Friday."

Richard saw KD coming and knew right off something was wrong. By the time she reached him, she was gulping at air and her eyes were frantic. "Drive," she said in a choked voice. "I have to get out of here."

He opened her door, closed it after she got in, then went around to the driver's side. "Where to?" he asked, punching the ignition button.

"I don't care. I don't know. Shit." Leaning forward, she pressed her hands to her face.

He could hear ragged breathing and wondered if she was crying or having another panic attack. *What happened?* Needing something to do, he buckled his seat belt, fiddled with the air-conditioning, adjusted his seat. "What can I do?"

She shook her head.

He'd seen a lot of soldiers with PTSD and anxiety issues. He knew to wait them out. But it was hard to sit and do nothing when she was hurting this bad.

After a few minutes, her breathing slowed. The shaking stopped. When she took her hands from her face and sat up, he saw her eyes were red and her cheeks were wet. He didn't know if it was from tears or sweat, but she seemed to be calming down.

"Where are you staying?" he asked.

"Killeen. Barkley Suites." She fumbled in her purse, took out a hotel key card, and clutched it in both hands like a lifeline. "A mile or so outside the gates."

He drove out of the lot. A few minutes later, they passed through the main gate and turned toward Killeen.

"Take a left at the Shell station," she said. "Around back. One fourteen."

Whatever had happened in her therapy session had sucked the life right out of her. She moved like an old woman when she got out of the car. Richard stayed close behind her in case she crumbled, but she made it on her own. Once inside, she stumbled over to the couch and almost fell into it. Tipping her head back, she closed her eyes and swallowed hard. "Thanks."

"No problem." Afraid to leave until he was sure she was okay, Richard wandered around, getting his bearings.

It was a nice suite. A small but well-appointed kitchen with all the necessary appliances, cookware, and dishes, separated from the living area by a long, high counter. The main part of the room held the couch she was on, an end table, a small dining table with two chairs, an upholstered chair and footrest, a credenza with a flat-screen on top and drawers below, and a small corner desk with a chair.

A door across from the kitchen opened into a bedroom with a queen bed and nightstand, a chest of drawers with a TV on top, a small closet, and a chair with a floor lamp beside it. Another door led to a sizable bathroom with an oversized shower, a separate room for the head, and double sinks. Both the main room and the bedroom overlooked an interior courtyard with a pool, two barbecue grills, a couple of tables and chairs, and several chaise lounges. A nice place. Not cheap. Safe for a woman traveling alone.

He returned to the main room. She hadn't moved. Her eyes were still closed.

He checked the refrigerator—nothing. The cabinets—nothing but dishes and glasses and cooking stuff. Going back to the couch, he sat across from her on the coffee table and said, "Hey."

She opened her eyes. Seemed disoriented for a moment, then focused on him.

"No need to go out to dinner," he told her. "Why don't you take a nap, and I'll run to the store and get something for us to eat later. Any suggestions?"

"Hemlock."

At least she still had her weird sense of humor. "Would that go better with chicken or steak? They have grills in the courtyard."

"Salad."

He nodded. "I'll get something for breakfast, too." As soon as the words were out, he realized how they sounded. "Not that I'll still be here," he hurriedly added. "But you need to eat."

"You're welcome to stay. This couch makes into a bed."

"We'll see." Richard rose and pulled a small blanket from the back of the couch. "Stretch out."

He waited while she got comfortable, then covered her with the blanket. "Want me to get a pillow from the bedroom?"

"I'm fine." She reached out and touched his hand. Looking up at him with watery eyes and a wobbly smile, she said, "Thank you," then tucked her hand beneath her chin, took a deep breath, and closed her eyes.

Richard watched her breathing settle into a sleep rhythm and wondered what had brought this fiercely determined woman so low. It was more than the injury. Something else was going on. He wanted to help, but knew if he pushed, she might withdraw even more, then he'd never know what had happened in the group session to set her off. Resisting the urge to brush a fall of dark brown hair off her cheek, he picked up the car keys and the room key card he'd left on the kitchen counter, and slipped quietly out the door.

Two minutes later, he was cruising the main drag and hunting for a grocery store while all sorts of inappropriate thoughts circled in his mind.

CHAPTER 8

When KD stepped out of the shower at ten after six, she smelled grilled beef and felt a surge of relief. Richard had come back.

When she'd awoken on the couch fifteen minutes earlier and had seen the car keys on the kitchen bar, but no Richard, she'd assumed he'd dropped off the keys and a few groceries and had left for good.

She wouldn't have blamed him. Not after her freak-out in the car. How embarrassing. Why did her panic attacks come whenever he was around? Yet he had come back, and she was glad he had. Knowing she wasn't alone gave her battered spirits a much-needed lift. Smiling, she quickly pulled on lightweight sweatpants and a tee, grabbed a comb, and went to thank him. Again.

He was sitting at the small dining table, watching the local news and cutting into a huge steak.

"You came back," she said.

He looked over, saw her in the doorway, stared for a moment, then switched off the TV with the remote beside his plate. "I figured it would be impolite to steal your car, so I brought food instead. And beer." His gaze dropped to the comb in her hand. "Forget your brush?"

"A brush doesn't work on wet hair."

"It does on mine."

She glanced at the army duffel beside the door.

"You told me I could stay," he said.

"And I meant it." She walked over and looked down at his plate. "Looks good. Where's mine?"

"You said you wanted salad." At her look of disappointment, he grinned. "Luckily there's enough here for two. I would have waited, but I was really hungry." Rising, he motioned to the place setting across from his. "Sit. I'll get the salad. Hope you like blue cheese dressing."

"I do." She sat down and began working the comb through her hair as she watched him bustle around in the kitchen. She liked having him there, having his male energy fill the sterile emptiness of the small room. Liked not being alone.

"Thanks for fixing supper," she said. "And for staying."

He walked out of the kitchen area carrying two bowls of salad, his blue eyes dancing with amusement. "This isn't a hookup, is it? I just want to be sure before I accidentally put moves on you."

"Accidentally?" She tried to look stern, but felt the smile building. "No worries. I never hook up with a guy before going on at least one date with him."

He set a bowl of salad and the bottle of dressing beside her plate. "You said people don't date anymore."

"I know. It's a conundrum."

"Still, I did buy you dinner." He cut off a chunk of his porterhouse and put it on her plate. "Cooked it, too. Plus, I brought beer. That's got to get me something."

"My heartfelt gratitude."

"Guess that's a start. Eat slow. The potatoes won't be ready for half an hour."

* * *

Richard liked hanging out with KD. She didn't play games and there was no meaningless small talk or forced conversation. He was a little bothered that she'd offered no explanation for what had upset her earlier, but decided all he could do was hope if he didn't pry, she might confide in him. In his experience, women hated silence and, if left to it too long, felt driven to fill it.

As it turned out, KD was no exception. "I need your help."

Finally. He watched her as he chewed, then swallowed. "With what?"

She gave him a thoughtful look, like she was still trying to think it through. Richard realized he could dive headfirst into those caramel brown eyes and never remember to come up for air.

"I'm thinking I shouldn't blame myself for Nataleah's death."

"You're right. You shouldn't." He cut a bite of steak. "What changed your mind?"

"It's not a what, but a who." She gave a wry smile and poked at her salad. "A big Black sergeant with strong opinions about women in the military. Calls me Snow White."

He watched her take a bite of lettuce, her lips pursing as she chewed. It was strangely arousing. Just watching her eat was getting him worked up.

"Farid was wearing a robe," she said, jerking him back on track. "No pockets. If he'd had a gun in his hand, we would have seen it. You said it was probably on his desk or in a drawer?"

Richard nodded and cut into his steak. "In the crime scene photos, one of the drawers on his desk was open."

She waved her fork. "That's it, then. He must have gotten the gun from his desk." Her shoulders slumped. "But surely Nataleah would have noticed when he reached for it."

"Not if she was distracted."

"By what?"

"There was evidence Farid had thrown a glass of water at her. Her clothes weren't that wet, so it didn't hit her. But while she was ducking, he could have pulled a gun from the drawer and fired."

"Why didn't she shoot back?"

"Couldn't." Richard took a sip of beer and sat back, the bottle cold and wet against his palm. "You've obviously never been shot in the chest at nearly point-blank range. Even wearing a vest, it feels like being kicked by a mule. Probably knocked her down. For sure, knocked the wind out of her. I'm guessing before she could recover, he walked over and shot her in the head."

She shivered. "Like he was going to do to me."

"But you got him first."

She frowned and looked away.

Richard studied her. KD had an expressive face. It didn't hide much of what she was thinking. And he was beginning to learn how to read her moods. "I hope you don't feel bad about killing him."

"I probably should. But I don't. He deserved it. If you'd seen that poor, battered little boy . . ." She pressed her lips together, as if biting back words describing an image she didn't want in her head. "But I did make a bad mistake."

He resumed eating. "What's that?"

"I shouldn't have pushed the boy out the window. That was a clear violation of the noninterference policy. But what if I was ordered to violate that policy? Which am I supposed to obey if they're in conflict?"

He studied her, confused. She'd never mentioned this conflict before. "You're saying the captain *ordered* you to rescue the boy?"

"Not exactly."

Richard set down his fork and sat back again. "Then

what exactly did she say?" Was she changing her story after he'd already turned in his report?

"When Farid told us there was no boy, Nataleah said she heard crying, that maybe he was in the back room, and for me to go see if he needed help."

"And you thought she was ordering you to get him out of the hut?"

"She didn't order me to do it. More like implied. But that would still be against the DOD policy."

He didn't respond.

"You see my problem, don't you?"

He nodded, but didn't know what she wanted him to do about it. The army was pretty clear about policy violations. But if she truly thought her captain had given her a direct order . . . that might be open to interpretation. He'd ask Bill.

"So here's what I'm thinking." Pushing aside her plate, she folded her arms on top of the table and leaned in, all business. "Maybe we should try a different approach."

"Like what?"

"Isn't it written in the UCMJ that a soldier can't be prosecuted for disobeying an illegal order?"

"You think the noninterference policy is illegal?"

"Shouldn't it be? Shouldn't it be unlawful to *not* stop the abuse of a civilian by military personnel? Military personnel trained and funded by us?"

Now that he saw where she was headed, Richard was both relieved that she hadn't been lying to him in the earlier interviews, and regretful that he'd have to shoot down her idea. "Morally, maybe. But legally? A DOD policy is not a direct order. It's a strongly worded suggestion that you ignore at your peril. And even though we trained them, the ANP are not army personnel. They're Afghan police and therefore not subject to US laws." He could tell she didn't like his answer. But other soldiers had argued this point, and lost. He didn't want to see it happen to her, too. "I find the look-the-other-way thing as repugnant as you do, KD. But it's not a direct order telling you to commit a crime. It's a policy, advising you to refrain from cultural bias by looking the other way, rather than reacting to local practices you don't like. It's not illegal or unlawful."

"But it's wrong. It's disgusting!"

"I agree. But there's a fine line between helping a different culture and forcing it to become like ours. The East and West have been walking that line for a thousand years, and it'll probably go on for a thousand more."

"Then which takes precedence? A strongly worded suggestion from DOD, or an implied order from your superior officer?"

"An implied order isn't a direct order."

She slumped back in the chair with a sigh of defeat. "So it won't work."

"I don't think so."

"Then I'm screwed. No way I can survive this with my career intact."

"Maybe we can come up with a different angle." He wasn't hopeful, but it bothered him to see her so discouraged.

They tossed other ideas around while they finished the meal and cleaned up. Then they sat on the couch and talked about it some more. Nothing jumped out at Richard. A violation was a violation, and the army was hard on those who ignored policy. Her clean record and West Point creds might buy her leniency. Might not. There were other soldiers who had ignored the look-the-other-way policy and had paid the price. That she had killed an ANP officer, even in self-defense, only complicated things.

When he saw KD struggling to hold back a yawn for the third time, he decided to call it a night. "When your JAG lawyer gets here, we'll talk to him and see what he suggests. Bill Breslin is an old friend. Crafty as hell and a great lawyer. Maybe he can figure it out."

"I hope so." Yawning, she rose from the couch. For a

moment, she stood looking down at him, a sleepy look in her eyes and a half smile softening her face.

Those earlier inappropriate thoughts roared back to life. "What?" he asked.

"Have I told you how much I appreciate all you're doing for me?"

"Several times." He finished his beer and considered another. He didn't want it to go to waste. Or maybe he should go for a swim. A run. Something.

"I know you have other things you could be doing, Richard, but I—"

"I'm on a month's leave," he cut in, embarrassed to be thanked for something he was enjoying doing. Enjoying too much, he realized, and shifted the hand holding the nearly empty beer bottle to his lap to hide evidence of it.

"Thanks anyway." She patted his knee, told him good night, then headed toward the bedroom.

Richard watched her, admiring the way her butt moved as she walked away. Getting worked up over a woman in sweatpants. He had to be the sorriest bastard there ever was.

"You coming?" she called back as she opened the bedroom door.

He almost choked on a swallow of beer. "Wh-what?"

"The linens are in the closet. I'll brush my teeth while you make up the hide-a-bed, then the bathroom's all yours."

KD awoke Tuesday morning to the aromas of frying bacon and coffee, and the low rumble of Richard's voice in the main room. She heard no other voices and assumed he was on the phone. By the time she'd dressed in shorts and a tank top and left the bedroom, he was at the stove scrambling eggs.

He looked over as she came in, gave her that thorough, masculine once-over, then went back to the eggs, which were starting to burn. "Sleep okay?"

"Better than okay." Which was odd. She'd rarely slept

through the night since she'd left the hospital. She'd even forgotten to take her meds, yet it didn't seem to have made a difference. No dreams, no wakeful restlessness, and no dismal thoughts lingering in her head. Maybe it was true, that if you talked through your problems, they didn't seem so big. "Smells good. Anything I can do?"

"Squeeze oranges."

Several minutes later, they sat down before glasses of fresh orange juice, mugs of steaming coffee, and plates heaped with eggs, bacon, toast, and jelly. It all looked delicious. Richard, too. KD liked his rumpled, bristly-jawed look, and the way his dark hair stuck out in all directions. And she especially liked the way his well-washed army green tee hugged his muscular frame.

"Was that Breslin on the phone?" she asked, shaking Tabasco on her eggs.

He watched her as he chewed. "He's coming in tomorrow afternoon."

"So soon?" KD didn't think her lawyer was due until Thursday or Friday.

"Says he needs to talk to us. That's a lot of hot sauce."

"I like spice." She grinned at him and winked.

He froze, blue eyes wide, a forkful of eggs halfway to his mouth.

Had the man never been winked at? "Talk to us about what?" she asked.

He resumed eating. "Didn't say. He was hurrying to get to a deposition."

KD's appetite dwindled. "He didn't tell you anything?"

"Only that the two of you have a meeting Thursday morning with Major Hendricks, the PHO—preliminary hearing officer."

"That doesn't sound good."

Putting down his fork, he braced his elbows on the table and studied her over his clasped hands. "Stop worrying, KD. Bill's the best. He wasn't concerned, so you shouldn't be, either." He picked up his fork again. "Now stop flirting with me while I eat. You'll make me choke."

"Flirting with you? Why would you think I'm flirting with you?"

"Wishful thinking. Eat your eggs before they get cold."

Had she flirted? Or was he worried she would have another anxiety attack over what Breslin said, and he was trying to distract her? She wasn't. But she was definitely distracted. Or maybe he was flirting with her? And when had watching a man eat become so unsettling?

Actually, she felt fairly calm. Possibly because she'd had a good night's sleep. Or because she wasn't facing this alone. Or because at this point, it was all out of her hands anyway. *Focus on the here and now,* Dr. Hwang had told her when he'd prescribed her anti-anxiety medication. *Forget the what-ifs.* Good advice.

She started eating again. "By the way, my family's coming."

He looked up. "Here? Today?"

"To the hearing. I don't know when. And they want to talk to you. Especially my sister's husband, Dalton. He's an Iraq vet."

"Talk to me about what?"

"He's worried about Farid's father. I told them not to come. I don't want Khalil Farid to find out anything about my family or where they live."

"That info is probably not classified. Are any of your sisters on social media?"

KD shrugged, not wanting to think it would be that easy to track them down.

He frowned at her. "You think he's a threat to them?"

"Why wouldn't he be?" And why did Richard look so surprised? Hadn't he been threatened, too? "He's clearly unstable. And if he killed Samira, like you say, he'll apparently do anything to avenge his son." It made her sick to think about it. "Our place is in a remote area. It would be vulnerable to ambush."

"You're thinking like a soldier."

"I am a soldier. Or was. And I don't want my family at risk for something I did." Surely Farid wouldn't come half-way around the world just for revenge.

"Don't you have any law enforcement nearby?"

"Not really." Deputy Toby Langers was less than use-less, and hardly a friend to the Whitcombs. His boss, Sher-iff Ford, was almost retired and lived in Gunther, which was even farther away from the ranch than Rough Creek was.

"Nothing's going to happen," Richard insisted. "I'll talk to your brother-in-law if you want, but this is hardly worth getting your family worked up about."

KD hoped he was right. But he didn't know her mother. If Mama found out a terrorist and suspected murderer might be after her daughter, she would stir up enough trou-ble to set the whole county on fire.

After cleaning up from breakfast, and with a free day ahead of them, they packed a picnic lunch and went to nearby Belton Lake, where the Army Corps of Engineers maintained several parks, trails, and recreational facilities.

They hiked, they ate, they talked and laughed. They even rented paddle boards. But with KD's limited flexibil-ity since her surgery, she spent most of the time falling off, while Richard paddled circles around her, laughing and taunting her to try again. Instead, she just smiled and watched the way water on his long, strong back glistened in the sunlight as his arms worked the paddle.

It was the best day KD had had in a long time.

That night, they went out for Tex-Mex, then came back to the hotel suite and ate popcorn and binge-watched the first season of *Game of Thrones*, which they'd both heard about but hadn't had time to watch. It was okay. Richard's commentary throughout all the racy parts was a lot better. KD sensed they were both edging toward something deeper than movie night on the couch. But she valued his companionship too much to jeopardize their growing friendship with a quick, meaningless hookup.

After breakfast Wednesday morning, since Breslin wouldn't be in until later that afternoon, KD suggested they go to Waco and check out the Magnolia Market at the Silos. Richard was more interested in visiting the Texas Ranger Hall of Fame and Museum. They ended up doing both. Museum first, then Magnolia, then lunch from one of the food trucks parked outside the silos, followed by a long stroll on the grounds of the Mammoth National Monument.

KD was getting stronger every day, although her hip still tired easily and her stamina was somewhat decreased. But Richard didn't push her, and slowed his pace to match hers, so she was able to make her goal of two miles without stopping to rest.

It was another great day, marred only by having to dodge around a drugged-out addict, lurching along the path and mumbling to invisible people.

Richard scowled at him as they passed by. KD was afraid he might say something to the guy and was relieved when he didn't. Yet as they continued their walk, she could see he was still upset.

"My brother was an addict," he said a few minutes later. "Started using after I left for college."

Surprised by the abrupt revelation. she looked over, saw the set look of his mouth, and sensed he was lost in a painful memory he didn't often share. That he trusted her enough to tell her about it made her want to offer the comfort she had so often received from him. But she didn't know how. She wasn't the "there-there" type. Emotional scenes made her feel inept and desperate to escape because she was never sure how to react or what to say. Usually she just stood in awkward silence, hoping her unspoken support would bring comfort enough. She doubted Richard wanted comfort or sympathy anyway. He was too self-assured for that. But at least she could show interest and give him a listening ear. "Marijuana?" she asked, not knowing what else to say.

"At first. Then crack, meth, heroin, fentanyl. Whatever he could get."

"That's awful." On impulse, KD slipped her arm through his. "Is he okay now?"

"He's not an addict anymore, if that's what you mean."

There was a hard edge in his voice that KD didn't understand. Not wanting to blunder or say the wrong thing, she remained silent as they continued to walk.

"I tried to help him," he said after a lengthy silence. "But I was a lot older, a senior in college two hundred miles away, and gone most of the time."

"What about your parents?"

He let out a huff of air. "They were in denial at first. Thought it was just a phase. When we realized Kenny was definitely hooked, I started making the trip home every weekend to play big brother and try to talk sense into him. Even got him into rehab."

"How'd that go?"

"Not good." He kicked a rock out of the path. "The day he got out, I caught him taking money from my wallet. Within a month, he was stealing from my parents' hardware store."

"They couldn't do anything?"

"He wouldn't listen to them, either. After months of hell, they turned to me. Wanted me to quit college and stay home, where I could keep an eye on him. Figured if I dogged him twenty-four seven, he might turn himself around."

"Did you?"

He shook his head. "Couldn't. Didn't want to. He wasn't my little brother anymore. I thought if I quit coddling him, he'd straighten up. I was wrong."

"You're not thinking his problems were your fault, are you?" Odd how those words echoed back to what Sarge had said to her about Nataleah.

"I probably could have tried harder. But . . ." His steps slowed to a stop. He stared into the distance, his dark brows drawn low, his mouth tense. "Some things can't be fixed. Addiction is one of them." He started walking again.

"Families can be difficult," KD admitted.

He looked down at her. "Is yours?"

She thought for a moment. "In some ways, yes. After my dad died, it was five women in the same house. It could definitely get crazy sometimes. Too much estrogen, I think."

"You don't get along with your sisters?"

"I do. And I love them dearly. But I never fit comfortably into the family mold. Too different. Too aloof maybe." *Or too determined not to get sucked into the vortex of family drama.* "They were happy at the ranch, but I was driven to rush out and save the world. Yet now . . . here I am, back in the nest."

"I doubt you were ever that comfortable in the nest anyway."

Surprised by his insight, she saw that his grim expression was now softened with amusement. Without thinking about it, she slid her hand down his arm and laced her fingers through his. His hand was broad and a little rough. But it cradled hers in a warm, gentle grip that made her feel safe and protected and accepted.

"I like you, Warrant Officer Murdock," she told him with a smile. "And I'm very glad you came to the base early to keep me company."

A slow grin spread across his chiseled face, crinkling the corners of his eyes, and revealing again the handsome man lurking beneath the stern expression. "Any time, Lieutenant."

They walked on without speaking. But there was no awkwardness now. No rush to fill the silence. Just the quiet, calm enjoyment of each other's company. With a sigh of contentment, KD rested her temple against his arm, needing the contact, the assurance his presence always gave.

She didn't question it. Didn't try to analyze what she was feeling. Just accepted that Richard was fast becoming her own addiction. Being with him was so easy. She hadn't felt this happy or relaxed in months . . . as long as she ignored that voice in her head reminding her this was only temporary. After the hearing was over and his leave was up, they would each go their separate ways.

But until then, she resolved to enjoy his company as long as she could.

Several hours later, as they pulled in outside Room 114 at the Barkley Suites, Richard got a text from Bill, saying he'd arrived on base and was checking into the VBOQ—Visiting Bachelor Officers' Quarters.

Richard texted back that they would pick him up outside the barracks at 1800 hours, adding, "Hope you like barbecue. Wear civvies."

He and Bill Breslin had immediately hit it off in boot camp. Bill, being smaller in stature, had appreciated having a buddy who could take on three men at once if necessary. Richard, for his part, was glad to have someone tutor him through all the boring briefings and classes. Not that he wasn't smart enough to hack it, but back then, he was more physical than cerebral. Probably a reaction to his failed marriage. Rage creates an energy all its own.

By the time he and Bill had graduated boot, what had started as a symbiotic relationship had evolved into a deep, unshakable friendship. Over the years, they'd been sent to different postings and didn't cross paths very often, but they'd always managed to stay in touch. If either of them ever needed anything, he knew the other was ready to help. Like now.

"You'll like him," Richard told KD later, when they pulled up outside the VBOQ. No sign of Bill so he powered down the windows so they wouldn't cook while they waited. "He's small and fierce, like you. But not near as pretty."

"He'd better not be."

Seeing the way KD kept picking at her nails, and hoping she wasn't building up to another anxiety attack, Richard reached over and took her hand in his. "Don't be nervous, babe. Bill knows what happened. You won't have to go through all that again. I'm sure he's read your service file and seen your army record, so he knows you're the kind of soldier the army wants to retain. He'll make sure the panel knows it, too. Stop worrying."

"I'm not worried. I'm just wondering what he needs to talk to us about." She looked over at him, a frown bunching above her lightly freckled nose. "They can't convene a court-martial without first going through an Article 32, can they?"

"No. And whatever Bill wants to talk to you about can't be anything bad, or I would have heard from Chief Stranton. He's an even bigger worrier than you."

"He's the one who sent you to investigate?"

Richard nodded and explained that Stranton was his next at CENTCOM, the command that was responsible for a huge swath of Northeast Africa, the Middle East, and Asia. "He's terrified of getting caught in an international scandal. Calling for an Article 32 is his version of damage control."

"Let's hope." She looked down their hands.

He thought she might pull away. Instead, she put her other hand on top of both of theirs and gave a gentle squeeze. Other than in the hospital when he'd held her shoulder while she vomited—which Richard didn't count—and earlier today when she'd taken his hand in sympathy after he'd told her about his brother, this was only the second time he and KD had had meaningful contact. In fact, it was the first meaningful contact Richard had had with any

woman in longer than he wanted to admit. It opened a
warm spot inside his chest.

"Thanks, Richard."

"If you start that gratitude crap again, I'll quit cooking
for you."

"Then can I tell you I had a wonderful day?"

"Sure." He grinned over at her. "Ditto."

"You're such a romantic." She gave him the smile he was
hoping for, which sent that warmth pulsing throughout his
body.

"You're not in this alone, babe. I've got your back. Bill,
too." Looking past her, he saw Bill coming toward the car.
"Speak of the devil." Letting go of KD's hand, he stepped
out and called over the roof of the Camry, "Looking for a
good time, sailor?"

"Not with you, *Dick*. But I wouldn't mind having a go
with the pretty lady." Ignoring Richard's scowl, he bent beside KD's open window. "You must be Lieutenant Whitcomb. You do know you're too good-looking to be riding
around with this Gomer, don't you?"

KD laughed, taking an instant liking to Richard's friend.

A few minutes later, they were heading out the gate to
what Richard had been assured was the best barbecue joint
in Texas. For some reason, KD thought that was funny. "It's
not?" he asked her.

"Could be. This is Texas." She explained that there were
probably a thousand places that considered themselves the
best. "But not to worry. If it's done right, the brisket will
melt in your mouth and the ribs will fall off the bone. If not,
it'll still be pretty damn good. This is beef country. Our
standards are high."

CHAPTER 9

The Longhorn Smokehouse smelled right and was already so crowded when they arrived that there were only two booths left. Plus, within two minutes they had ice-cold drinks in their hands.

"What more can you ask?" Richard raised his bottle high. "To friends, here and gone," he said, clinking the neck of his Lone Star against Bill's Tecate and KD's glass of sweet tea. "And to those who love peace enough to fight for it."

"OO-rah!" Two men with military haircuts at a nearby table raised their beers and grinned at them.

"Friendly place," Richard observed, and nodded back.

KD laughed. "Of course. You're in Texas."

And one of the best things about a good Texas barbecue joint was the service. Since the meat had been in the smoker since dawn, little time was spent waiting for your food to arrive. Within ten minutes of placing their order, platters of ribs and brisket and bowls filled with all the fixings covered their table.

It wasn't until they'd taken the edge off their appetites that KD asked Bill if he knew why Major Hendricks wanted to talk to her.

"It's not that unusual," he told her. "Most PHOs meet with the defendant and counsel before a hearing to go over motions, evidentiary rules, protocols, and so on. Mostly it's to make certain you're adequately represented and both sides are ready to proceed. Any more slaw?"

Richard passed it over. "When will the hearing start?"

"Zero nine hundred Monday morning. We have plenty of time to go over testimony this weekend. And you were right, KD. This brisket is amazing."

She smiled. "Texas beef. Maybe even Whitcomb Four Star beef."

"Your family raises cattle?" Bill asked.

"Until recently. Now we focus more on Angus bulls for breeding. We also raise and train cutting horses. My brother-in-law is a very successful trainer."

Richard looked at her in surprise. Another assumption shot down. He'd figured her for a small-town girl, not one raised on a ranch. "I thought you lived in Rough Creek."

"In the suburbs, more or less. What about you two? Where are y'all from?"

Despite all that he and KD had talked about earlier, Richard hadn't told her where he was from. He didn't like talking about his family.

"Wisconsin," Bill answered, wiping sauce off his fingers. "Dairy farmers."

"Washington state," Richard said. "Hardware store. But after retiring, my family moved down South. Now, I'm from wherever the army sends me. But maybe not for long," he added, hoping to stop any more family questions.

Both KD and Bill looked at him. "What's that supposed to mean?" Bill asked.

"My re-enlistment date is coming up."

"You're not re-upping?" Bill asked.

"You're leaving the army?" KD's eyes were round with surprise.

"Maybe. I'm taking a month's leave to think it over."

Bill set down his beer. "Damn, Richard. I thought we'd retire together. If you're tired of CID, come to JAG. We always need good investigators."

"It's the investigations I'm tired of," Richard admitted. "Hunting down scared soldiers, rooting out the badness in others. Not a lot of upside to this job. And I'm sick of the traveling." This was the first time he'd revealed to anyone his doubts about re-upping. But hearing the words spoken aloud told him he might be closer to leaving the army than staying.

"Then pick another MOS. The army's got dozens of occupational specialties."

"I'm tired of the army, too."

It felt odd, putting all these feelings into words. Richard had battled discontent for a while now, and even more so lately. Verbalizing it only seemed to reinforce his need to do something else. Something more positive. When he'd enlisted years ago, he'd been running from a broken marriage, a shattered family, and a lot of anger. But he was past all that now. Maybe it was time to build a real future. He looked at the two confused faces staring back at him and had to grin. "What? Don't you think it'd be fun to rescue a cat from a tree?"

"You want to be a fireman?" Bill asked.

"Cops do that, too."

"You want to be a cop?"

Richard shrugged. "Like I said, I've got a month before I have to decide." And right now, to show he was done talking about it, he pushed back his empty plate. "If you two are through, there's a line of hungry people waiting outside."

It was still early when they returned to the car, but Bill had notes to go over before meeting with the PHO in the morning. He was ready to head back to base.

"Is there anything I can do to prepare for tomorrow's meeting?" KD asked Bill as they drove through the main gate.

"Just show up on time and in dress blues. I'll do the rest."

"Have you decided on a defense?" KD still thought the "unlawful order" angle might work.

"I have some ideas."

When they pulled up outside the VBOQ, Bill got out, then bent down by the open passenger window. "Don't worry about tomorrow, Lieutenant," he said. "Your role is simply to be there. And to admire my brilliance, of course." To Richard, he added, "Don't you worry, either, buddy. I'll take good care of her." Then with a thump on the roof of the Camry, he waved them off.

As they drove through the Hood main gate, Richard asked if KD wanted to go back to the hotel or do something else.

"It's been a long day. And I need to make sure my uniform is pressed."

"Barclay it is, then."

They drove back without speaking. Richard parked in their usual spot and shut down the motor. But neither of them moved to get out of the car. Taking that as his cue, Richard said, "If this is getting awkward for you, KD, I can stay on base."

She studied him, that frown between her eyes. "Is it awkward for you?"

She was deflecting. But he ignored that and told her the truth. "Not yet. But unless you do something to completely turn me off, it will be."

"What do you mean?"

"You know exactly what I mean, babe." He smiled, enjoying the way color rose up her neck. "You're an amazing, beautiful, sexy woman, KD. The kind of woman men in the service dream about. Hell, the kind of woman *I've* dreamed about. How can I not be attracted to you?"

The blush deepened. With an embarrassed laugh, she looked out the window. "Flattering words. Why?"

"Because I want to get into your pants, why else?"

Her head whipped toward him, eyes snapping. "Seriously?"

"Oh, I'm definitely serious, babe. But not hopeful." He decided to quit kidding around and just say what had been on his mind. "Look. I know you're struggling right now, and the last thing you're looking for is any kind of relationship. I get that. So if you want me to go, I'll go. But if you want me to stay, I'll stay. No strings either way. For now." He let go a deep breath, a little unnerved by the intense way she watched him. "But at some point, that'll change. Because the more time I spend with you, the more time I want. That's just the way it is. If that idea bothers you, I can leave now."

She continued to study him, her beautiful brown eyes reflecting back his own uncertainty. And maybe something else. Something that gave him hope. He waited, transfixed by the way the last rays of sunlight slanting through her window brought out a hint of red in her brown hair and highlighted the downy fuzz on her cheek.

He wanted to touch her, brush his fingers through that mane of glossy hair, find a way to bridge the space between them.

"I don't want you to leave, Richard," she finally said. "But I can't promise anything else. Not right now." She hesitated, then added, "But given time, that might change for me, too. I'm just not there yet."

It felt like an anvil had been lifted off his chest. Suddenly, Richard could let out the breath he wasn't aware he'd been holding. "Well. Okay, then. You go press your uniform while I get my swim trunks and go for a long swim in a short pool."

* * *

As dusk crept in on the tails of another fiery Texas sunset, KD stood at the window overlooking the courtyard, towel drying her hair and watching Richard do laps in the small hotel pool. He moved with effortless grace, long arms cutting cleanly through the water, no splash on his kicks. He was a superb athlete. But probably not as quick as she was. She considered challenging him to one-on-one hoops, then realized with his height and those long arms, she'd never get off a shot.

The more time I spend with you, the more time I want. What did that mean?

Her phone buzzed. She checked caller ID and saw it was her sister. "Hey, Raney, what's happening? How's Cletus the Fetus?"

"Cletus is fine and a lot's been happening. Mama's on a tear."

"What is it this time?"

KD watched Richard pull himself out of the pool, water sluicing down his shoulders and chest, making his swim trunks sag even lower.

"I don't know. Did she show up there?"

"What? Here?" KD swung from the window. "She's at Hood?" Mama was the last thing KD needed. She could imagine how her mother would react if she found her baby daughter sharing a hotel room with a man she'd never met nor approved, innocent though it might be. Mama could be pretty old-fashioned when it suited her. "Why would she come here?"

"I'm not sure she did. All I know is she flew out of Gunther yesterday morning and was back in time for supper."

Gunther's small six-passenger shuttle only made the round trip to the Dallas–Fort Worth Airport on Mondays and Fridays. Since yesterday was Wednesday, she must have flown private. "Did you check with Len?"

"They don't get back from Florida until Sunday. And Joss is heading to the next concert. That's why I'm checking with you. When I asked her where she went, she said, 'Shopping.' But she didn't bring home any packages."

"Maybe it's a guy." KD turned back to the window, but the only sign of Richard was wet footprints leading away from the pool.

"Like a date? Ha! She swore off dating after we nagged her into giving Esterbrook another try. Apparently, it didn't work out. She even changed churches to avoid him. The sheriff's been coming around. Maybe I should check with him."

"Sheriff Ford? Isn't he retiring?"

"He's only a year older than Mama. And in great shape. I think he likes her."

Everybody liked Mama. Especially men. "Well, she didn't show up here."

"Yet."

"Hush your mouth. Are Mama and Dalton still coming to the hearing?"

"She hasn't mentioned it. I don't think she's made hotel reservations, either."

KD heard the key card slide into the slot on the door. "Then don't remind her. Look, I've got to go. I just got out of the shower. Call me if she runs off again."

Richard came in, towel over his shoulders. "Who ran off?" he asked, rubbing the towel over his wet hair.

"Mama. My sister says she's on a tear. Thought she might have come here."

He lowered the towel. "Your mother's missing? For how long?"

"She's not missing," KD assured him. "She just took a day trip. But Raney's pregnant and tends to overreact and thinks Mama lied about where she went because she came home empty-handed."

"Where did your mother say she went?"

"Shopping."

Richard stared at her for a moment then shook his head. "I can see why you're worried. A woman going shopping. The audacity. Call out the troops."

"You don't know Mama."

"That bad, huh?" He bent to dig clean clothes out of his duffle by the door. Which made the muscles in his back do amazing things.

"You'll see," she said once she'd curtailed her errant thoughts. "Besides, Mama never comes back from shopping without a dozen bags." To distract herself, KD walked over to the couch and picked up the remote. "How was your swim?"

"Short." He straightened, a wad of clothing tucked under his arm. "You done with the bathroom for a while? I want to wash off the chlorine."

KD clicked on the TV. "Go for it. Just don't use my loofah."

"I won't use whatever that is if you don't use my razor."

A few minutes later, he came out in shorts and a tee and went into the kitchen. She heard him rummaging through the refrigerator, then he came out with a beer and plopped down next to her on the couch, propped his crossed ankles and bare feet on the coffee table, took two big swigs of the beer, bit back a burp, and asked what she was watching. Like they had been together for years rather than days. How quickly the need to impress fades.

She clicked off the TV. "Rerun number two hundred twenty-nine of *Law & Order*. Trying to get in the mood for tomorrow."

"You'll do fine. Bill's a great lawyer."

KD asked how they met, and he told her about boot camp and a few scrapes they had gotten into. She watched more than she listened, enjoying the animation in his face and that wide, toothy grin when he talked about his friend. Richard was a different man when he was relaxed. Not so intense or guarded. Easy to be with. Which wouldn't be for long, she reminded herself. *Best not get too attached.*

When he wound down, she asked if he was serious about leaving the army.

His mood abruptly sobered. No longer smiling, he thought for a moment then said, "It gets to me, you know? All the broken promises, broken lives, the drugs, the lies, the fear." He took a swallow of beer before continuing. "I once cornered a guy with PTSD. Had it bad. The shakes, the twitches, off somewhere else in his head and definitely self-medicated. He'd deserted and had left a trail of blood behind him. Civilian, Taliban, he didn't care. He just wanted to go home. To make it stop." With his thumbnail, Richard scraped a line of label off the beer bottle. "When I caught up to him, he looked at me, his eyes as empty of hope as any I'd ever seen. I'll never forget it. Then before I could stop him, he put his gun in his mouth and pulled the trigger."

Silence. KD didn't know how to fill it, or if she should even try. If she'd learned anything in group therapy, it was the value of listening.

After a minute, he gave a sad, weary smile. "So to answer your question, yeah, I'm thinking of leaving the army. I love my country. The army, too. But I don't want to do this anymore. I don't want to invest more of myself in this endless war." He looked over at her, his gaze flat and shuttered. "What about you, KD? How bad do you want to stay in the army after all you've been through?"

"I'm not ready to quit. And I sure as hell don't want to be dismissed from service."

"But if you're given a choice," he persisted, "between getting out now or being on permanent disability in some administrative position for the rest of your career, what would you choose?"

Doubts nagged at her. Would that be her future—assuming the Article 32 panel didn't charge her and she passed the army fitness tests? Would she spend the rest of her career on the sidelines, watching her chance at the Pentagon slip away? But if she left the army, what would she do? And where would she do it? Rough Creek didn't offer many opportunities. "I don't know," she admitted. "I've been focused on the military since I was a kid. I never thought of doing anything else."

He picked up her hand, idly watching as he laced his fingers through hers. His palm was almost twice as broad as hers, his fingers a fourth again as long. A strong, capable hand. "I get it. I can't figure out what I want to do, either."

"I thought you wanted to rescue cats."

"Maybe."

"We're a pair, aren't we? Muddled in indecision with no clear path ahead."

"Maybe in some things." He looked up. His gaze paused on her mouth, then slowly rose to meet hers. "But not in everything." That intense look was back. She knew what it meant and waited to see what he would do.

"Come here," he finally said and gently tugged her hand to pull her closer.

She didn't resist.

It was a slow, lingering kiss. No rush. No demands. Just a tender exploration with his lips, the tip of his tongue, the hand he moved to her cheek. She tasted beer, felt the slight roughness of his evening beard, smelled soap and a hint of chlorine. It moved her that a man so much bigger than she could touch her so gently.

He pulled back first. She didn't want him to. But if he didn't, this would inevitably lead to places she wasn't ready yet to go.

With a crooked smile, he tucked a lock of hair behind her ear. "Get some sleep, babe. Tomorrow's a big day."

She liked the way he said her name, putting emphasis on the first letter, then blending the two together so it sounded more like *Kady* than KD. And she especially liked it when he called her babe.

"You're right." On impulse, she leaned in, gave him a short good-night kiss, then rose and left the room.

At 0700 hours Thursday morning, KD stepped out of the bathroom to the smell of bacon frying. Again. She smiled. Bless a man who knew his way around a kitchen. Her family had always depended on Maria—the wife of one of their workers, as well as their housekeeper—to cook their meals. Consequently, neither KD nor any of her three sisters were very adept in the kitchen.

She dressed carefully in her dress uniform, white shirt, neck tab, blue jacket, opting for the skirt, rather than the slacks, and low-heeled, high-gloss pumps. She pinned up her hair, put on her cap, and checked the mirror. She had been so proud the first time she'd put on the officer's uniform with all its bright shiny buttons, shoulder straps, insignia badges, ribbons, and braid. Would she ever wear it again?

Richard looked over when she came in, gave her that careful appraisal, and nodded in approval. "You're a credit to the uniform, Lieutenant Whitcomb."

KD smoothed a hand down her tailored skirt. "Let's hope I'm still allowed to wear it after all this is over."

"Bill will do you right. How do you want your eggs?"

After they'd eaten and cleaned up, Richard drove them to Fort Hood while KD texted Bill they were on the way.

"Bill or I will text you when we're done," she told Richard as they turned onto the base. "Maybe we can get lunch." Although right then, KD was so nervous her stomach felt like it was filled with broken glass.

Bill was coming through the doors of the VBOQ when they drove up. He looked a little intimidating in his uniform, and KD reminded herself he was no longer Bill, but Captain Breslin. After telling Richard to look for their text, she got out of the car and walked to meet him.

Ten minutes later, she and Captain Breslin were sitting at a conference table across from the government counsel, Captain McCready, a middle-aged man with a buzz cut and a fat folder in front of him. The preliminary hearing officer, Major Hendricks, took the chair at the head of the table, and behind him sat a woman ready to transcribe the proceedings on an outdated stenotype. Some things were slow to change in the army. For all the advances in ordnance and military hardware, administrative improvements lagged years behind.

After the introductions were made, Major Hendricks turned to the government's lawyer and said, "Since you called this meeting, Captain McCready, you may begin."

The prosecutor rested his forearms on the table and clasped his hands atop the folder. He wore a stern expression, made even more forbidding by pale gray eyes as cold as any she had ever seen. "We have recently come into new evidence pertinent to the case involving Second Lieutenant Whitcomb and the death of Captain Asef Farid at FOB Hickock."

Bill leaned forward. "What evidence?"

"That's classified. All I can say is that it's medical in nature. To say more would violate doctor-patient privilege."

KD frowned. *What doctor? What patient?*

Bill asked how McCready had come by this evidence.

"Down the chain of command through CENTCOM to me."

"Chief Warrant Officer Stranton?"

McCready didn't respond.

When Bill started to press him, McCready held up a hand. "If you'll be patient, I'll answer what questions I can when I'm finished."

Bill sat back, one hand resting on the table, fingers tapping impatiently. "Go ahead, Captain."

McCready opened the folder and studied the top paper. It looked like a document of some kind, with places for signatures at the bottom. Something official. "After careful review of this new information," he said in a flat voice, as if reading from a script, "we find it raises sufficient cause to forgo the Article 32 hearing."

Bill seemed as confused as KD was. "You're canceling the hearing?"

McCready nodded.

"With prejudice?"

Again, McCready nodded.

"You're saying the issue is closed?" Bill persisted. "There will be no forthcoming charges or hearings relating to the death of ANP Captain Farid or Lieutenant Whitcomb's alleged part in it?"

The counselor nodded a third time.

It's over? Really over? KD blinked at Bill, then at the prosecutor. Sudden relief almost made her light-headed. "So that's it? We're done?"

"Once you agree to a couple of stipulations."

Bill frowned. "You mean conditions."

Ignoring that, McCready studied the form in the folder. "First, Lieutenant Whitcomb must sign a Form SF-312, a Classified Information Nondisclosure agreement prohibiting her from discussing any meetings, findings, or decisions relative to events leading up to and including the night Captain Farid was killed at FOB Hickock. It is now classified." He pierced KD with those cold eyes. "In other words, Lieutenant, if you are questioned about this matter by any persons or media outlets, including print, radio, TV, Internet, or whatever, you are to answer, 'That's classified.' Period. Do you understand?"

The three men looked expectantly at KD.

Behind the PHO, the stenographer waited, fingers poised above the keys.

KD's relief turned to dread. "But I've already told my family what happened. And the people in my therapy group know how I was injured."

"Then they must sign nondisclosure agreements, as well. I can send the forms to your group moderator. Will your family be a problem?"

She shook her head. "No, sir." KD would make sure of it.

McCready nodded and flipped to the next paper in the folder. Another official-looking document. "Secondly, in view of Lieutenant Whitcomb's prosthetic hip and related injuries—which combined, qualify as a permanent injury—and taking into account her doctor's assessment that she has a less than fifty percent chance of meeting the army's physical fitness requirements, we further stipulate that she accept a medical separation from the army."

KD stared at him, not sure she'd heard right. She was being released from service? Without even having a chance to pass the tests? "But I think I can pass the APFT, sir. I have a year to try, don't I?"

McCready shook his head. "The separation would be effective immediately."

Immediately? Today?

"Honorable?" Bill asked before KD could catch her breath.

"Of course. With full VA benefits, along with a Purple Heart and the army's gratitude for her service." McCready must have sensed KD's shock and outrage. That cold gaze swung her way again. "Unless, of course, Lieutenant Whitcomb would prefer to state her case at an Article 32 hearing and risk charges."

The bastard! He was blackmailing her! Get out and shut up, or stay in and risk losing everything. KD was stunned. How could this be happening?

"Lieutenant Whitcomb." The PHO's voice broke through her spiraling panic. "It's a fair resolution to a difficult situation. I suggest you consider Captain McCready's offer and the stipulations."

"When would she have to decide?" Bill asked.

"Today."

"Then please excuse us, gentlemen, I'd like to talk to the lieutenant in private."

Richard had finished filling the Camry at the PX service station closest to where he'd dropped off KD and Bill, when his cell phone buzzed. Caller ID said it was Chief Stranton. Muttering under his breath, he punched *Accept* and said, "Warrant Officer Murdock speaking."

Stranton's voice burst through the phone, "I've been getting calls from the Pentagon, the *Wall Street Journal*, the *New York Times*, even the *Dallas Morning News*, *Fort Worth Star-Telegram*, and *Houston Chronicle*, for God's sake! You know why? Because of that fuck-up at FOB Hickock! The one you were supposed to take care of!"

"I don't understand, sir."

"I don't give a damn, Murdock! Ever heard of the SASC?"

"The Senate Armed Services Committee? Yes, sir."

"How about Senator Roy Bob Tomlinson? Heard of him?" Before Richard could answer, he said, "He's the senior senator from the state of Texas and a sitting member of that committee. Know what else he does? He writes letters of recommendation to West Point for deserving applicants. And guess who one of his biggest donors is."

Richard was beginning to understand. "The Whitcomb family?"

"You're a damn genius, Sherlock! He's been rattling chains in the Pentagon, and now I'm getting calls from everybody and their grandmother. Well, shit flows downhill, Murdock, and it flows especially fast down the chain of command. I just got a face full of it and now it's headed your way. I hear your reenlistment date has come up. You signed your separation papers yet?"

"I'm thinking about—"

"Quit thinking, Murdock! Just sign the damn papers and

pack your bags! You're better off leaving the service after the way you've handled this investigation. Any hope of future advancement in this army is deader than Osama bin Laden. Am I clear?" The call ended.

Richard stared at his cell. *Fuck was that about?*

Before he could put the phone away, it buzzed again. This time it was a text from Bill saying that they were finished and telling Richard where to meet them.

Richard left the gas station, hoping Bill could tell him what was going on. When he pulled up, he saw Bill and KD talking on a bench under a shade tree in a small grassy area between two buildings. As he walked toward them, he guessed by the slump of KD's shoulders that things hadn't gone well.

"What happened?" He stopped before them, his gaze pinned on KD. Her expression was similar to the one she'd worn after her group session days ago. Not quite as bleak, but still anxious and rattled. By contrast, Bill was smiling.

"It's over. Done."

"What is?"

"Everything. The hearing, the investigation—"

"My career," KD cut in. Her eyes were suspiciously shiny, but no tears were falling. Yet. "I've been ordered to get out and shut up. Either that, or face a possible court-martial."

"They're also giving you a Purple Heart," Bill reminded her.

"Whoop-de-do."

Richard stood over them, feet spread, arms crossed over his chest, jaw clamped against rising anger as Bill explained that new evidence had come to light that convinced the army to cancel the hearing.

"What evidence?"

"Opposing counsel said it was classified. All he could tell us was that it was medical in nature and to say more would violate doctor-patient privacy."

"This is the army," Richard argued. "They own us. We have no privacy."

"I know. Weird, isn't it? They also attached two stipulations. KD and everybody she's talked to about the shooting have to sign classified nondisclosures. As added incentive, she'll be given a medical separation, along with full veteran benefits and a Purple Heart."

"It's blackmail!" KD burst out.

She was breathing fast again, that frantic look in her eyes. Richard wondered if she was having another anxiety attack, and what he could do to help her. Yet this time seemed different than before. Less anxiety and more fury. He didn't know if that was an improvement or not.

"They wouldn't even give me a chance to pass the fitness tests. Damn them!"

"They want her out and fast," Bill said. "I'm not sure why."

Richard thought of his last conversation with Dr. Erickson, and his earlier one with Chief Stranton. It was beginning to make sense. Maybe Erickson had found evidence of other victims of Farid's pederasty, which would mean it had been going on for a while and right under the army's nose. A PR nightmare. The big brains in the Pentagon must have decided that the best way to control the damage and cover their asses would be to classify the entire incident, cut KD out of the picture, and make everyone involved sign a nondisclosure agreement. "They're afraid."

"Of what?"

"Exposure." Richard shook his head in disgust. "Politicians and bureaucrats, including those REMFs in the Pentagon, are like roaches. As soon as you shine a light on them, they run for cover. Their shortsighted look-the-other-way policy has created a PR nightmare, and now they're trying to get out from under it."

Richard told them about the heat Stranton had been getting from the press and Pentagon. "Apparently, even the

SASC is involved. And a senator named Roy Bob Tomlinson." He gave KD a thoughtful look. "Know anything about that, KD?"

She blinked up at him, a frown furrowing her brow. Then her eyes widened as understanding dawned. "Shit!" The frown gave way to baffled astonishment, which built into a full-throated laugh that held more despair than amusement. "Son of a bitch," she cried, rocking on the bench, hands clasped to her head. "I was wrong. Mama really can boss everything."

CHAPTER 10

Bill left that afternoon. KD was at her final appointment with the physical therapist, so Richard stood alone at the terminal window, watching his buddy's westbound transport lift off the runway.

Now that Richard had decided to leave the service, they both knew they might never see each other again. The transient nature of military life didn't encourage long friendships, and without that bond holding them together, it was easy for soldiers to drift apart once they separated from service.

Richard hoped that wouldn't happen to him and Bill. He wasn't close to many people, and being more solitary than social in nature, he didn't collect friends as easily as others did. It hit him hard to see Bill go.

His mood was somber as he left the airport and drove to the Fort Hood Transition Center to start the long process of separating from the army. It wasn't that he was second-guessing his decision to leave. Richard knew it was time. But by not re-upping, he would be walking away from a job he'd been good at, a rank he'd worked hard for, and a nice re-enlistment bonus. Not that the bonus was a deal maker or deal breaker. He wasn't much of a spender or barfly, and without the expenses of a car, a house, or dependents for the last eight years, most of his pay had gone into the bank. But now he'd have to dip into those savings. Transitioning to civilian life would be costly.

Costly, but also exciting. Driving KD's Camry these last few days had reminded him how much he enjoyed being behind the wheel. He was looking forward to picking his own destinations, going when and where he chose, maybe even taking a road trip through someplace he wanted to know better. Like Texas.

There was a word for that.

Oh, yeah. Freedom.

He soon learned that separating from the army was more complicated than joining it had been. Luckily, he'd had his annual medical and dental exams before he went to Afghanistan, so he could cross that off. And since he'd been undecided about re-upping, he'd already gone through pre-separation counseling, too. All he had left to do was fill out a pile of forms, then fly back to CENTCOM to complete the process, relinquish his badge and army-issue SIG M11 handgun, turn in his tactical gear, exchange his CID identification for a veteran ID card, then pack up his personal belongings. His last chore would be the discharge interview with his next-in-command, Chief Warrant Officer Stranton.

He wasn't looking forward to that. Hopefully, Stranton would release him with minimal fuss and an honorable discharge. Then the separation process would slide beyond Richard's reach into the shadowy, slow-moving realms of army bureaucracy. And that would be the end of his army career.

The finality of it panicked him a little. He would be on his own. No room and board. No military safety net. But no one breathing down his neck all the time, either. And assuming Stranton didn't cancel his leave, Richard would depart with almost a month's terminal leave pay in his pocket.

Several hours later, he left the Transition Center with a thick pouch of discharge paperwork, a confirmed seat on tomorrow's early transport to MacDill Air Force Base in Tampa, and a confirmed commercial return ticket to Killeen. In twenty-four hours, he'd be a free man with no home, no car, no job, but limitless options to go anywhere, do anything, or be whatever he wanted.

At 1530 hours—or 3:30 P.M., now that he was practicing to be a civilian—he was sitting in the CRDAMC parking lot, waiting for KD to finish her final appointment, and wondering if he'd soon be saying goodbye to her, too. He hoped not. His attraction to KD grew stronger every day, and the thought of her drifting out of his life forever bothered him a lot. More than a lot. But he didn't know what to do about it.

She was a complicated lady. Tough, smart, capable. And as different from his ex-wife as a woman could be. But she was also suffering from the blow the army had dealt her that morning. He'd like to help but wasn't sure how. Not that he wanted to be her rescuer. She wouldn't allow that anyway. But what was he supposed to do with all these feelings he couldn't act on? How was he supposed to break through all that armor she wore? Or should he even try?

A sudden thought bounced through his head and made him smile. KD hadn't been in the army long enough to make many friends, and the person she'd felt closest to, Captain Mouton, had died. She probably felt as isolated as Richard did. Why else would she share a hotel suite with a man she barely knew? Maybe she needed him as much as he needed her.

His smile grew. Now *that* was something he could work with.

A few minutes later, she climbed into the car. "Lord, it's hot. Quick, turn on the AC. Bill make his flight?"

Richard nodded and started the car. As soon as the AC came on, she leaned forward and held her collar open to the blast of air coming from the vent.

"How'd your appointment with PT go?" he asked as he pulled out of the lot.

"Good." After adjusting the temp and fan speeds, she sat back with a deep sigh. "He said I'm done with rehab, as long as I walk two miles a day and don't fall on my hip. Since McCready made me sign all the separation papers at the meeting yesterday—that jerk—all I have left is my therapy group tomorrow. I'll have to come back later to pick up my Purple Heart and a copy of the completed DD 214, then I'm done. How about you?"

"Signed, sealed, and delivered, except to turn in my equipment and have my discharge interview with Stranton at CENTCOM tomorrow."

"You have to go to Florida?"

Was that regret in her voice? Richard hoped so. "It's a turnaround trip. I fly back into Killeen tomorrow night." He wanted to ask if she'd still be here but was reluctant. He might not like the answer. "The army must be anxious to get rid of us. I never heard of separations happening so fast."

She looked out the window as a squad trotted by, shouting out the *Bravo on the Go* marching cadence that was burned into every army recruit's heart. "It's sad," she said in a wistful tone, "knowing we'll never be a part of it again. I really loved being a soldier."

Change was never easy. And for KD, leaving the army was more than just a change of career. It was also the loss of a dream. Reaching over the console, he took her hand in his. "So what do you want to do, babe?"

"I'm not hungry. You?"

"I mean what do you want to do now that you're footloose and fancy free until you come back next month to get your Purple Heart."

She thought for a moment. "After my group session tomorrow, I'd better go home to Rough Creek and tell my family I'm no longer in the service. That's the bad news. The good news"—she shot him a weak imitation of the saucy grin that kept him awake at night—"is I'm hoping you'll go with me."

He grinned. *Progress.*

While Richard did laps in the hotel pool, KD changed into shorts and a tank top. As she packed her uniform into her suitcase, she realized when she returned to Hood in a month to get her Purple Heart, she would probably wear her dress blues for the last time. Next month might also be the last time she would hear "Reveille" blasting over the huge base speaker system, signaling the beginning of the duty day, or hear "Taps" played as the flag was lowered in the evening. Never again would she fall asleep to the distant *whump* of rounds exploding on the artillery range, or hear a troop leader call out the cadence as recruits trotted across the drill field. She had been so pumped to be a part of all that, so proud to wear the uniform. She had felt that she was making a difference being a part of something bigger than herself.

What was she to do now? And what was she to do about Richard? It surprised her to realize that separating from him might be harder than leaving the army.

With a sigh, she sank onto the foot of the bed and texted Mama that the Article 32 had been canceled and she would be coming home sometime this weekend. I'll text you when. Since Warrant Officer Murdock is on leave, and Dalton wanted to talk to him, I'll see if he wants to come with me. No texting shortcuts for Mama. Proper punctuation expected.

KD paused, wondering if now would be the time to tell

her mother she was no longer in the military. She decided against it. She was still too angry. It had been a bad enough day without opening herself up to dozens of questions she wasn't yet sure how to answer. So she ended with a simple Text you later. KD.

She was rummaging in the refrigerator, deciding what could be eaten and what should be tossed, when Richard came in, wearing trunks and a towel.

"I'm starved," he said, tossing the key card on the counter and bending over the duffle by the door. "What's for supper?"

"There's a pack of chicken breasts left." She turned to watch as he dug through his duffel, enjoying the play of muscles across his shoulders. Amazing how many muscles it took to accomplish such a simple task. When he straightened, clean shorts and a T-shirt in his hands, she shifted her attention back to the refrigerator. "Think they're still good?"

"You'll know when you open the package. I'll get changed, then cook them on the grill by the pool."

A few minutes later, after a thorough sniff test on the chicken breasts, Richard took them to the courtyard while KD put together a side dish containing everything that was still edible. Sort of a cross between a cold casserole and a salad. Strange but filling—if you were hungry enough and swallowed fast. That was something you learned in the military: Eat when you can, whatever you can, because you never know when you'll have the chance again. She wouldn't miss that.

They didn't talk while they ate. Perhaps the day had been as hard on Richard as it had been on her since he'd invested a lot more years into the army than she had. It had to bother him to walk away. Or maybe he was worried what her spontaneous invite to Rough Creek might mean. Introducing him to her family would push whatever was going on between them to a whole new level.

She felt like everything was changing around her and within her. She needed to adapt. Reinvent herself. Lieutenant KD Whitcomb was no more. So who was she now?

She looked over at Richard, head bent, totally focused on his meal. Maybe she could take her cue from him. He didn't think of her as a soldier, or as Lieutenant Whitcomb, or Katherine Diane. To him, she was simply KD.

So from now on, that's who she'd be. Simply KD Whitcomb.

Richard watched KD toy with her food and wondered why she was so quiet. Probably still upset about being forced out of service. Or maybe she was regretting that off-the-cuff invitation for him to come with her to Rough Creek.

He had concerns about that himself. Showing up at her home would bring questions he wasn't sure how to answer. They weren't a couple. And they certainly weren't lovers. Not yet anyway, although he had high hopes. Buddies? Not on his part. He'd never felt about a buddy the way he felt about KD. But having whatever was happening between them play out in front of her family? That would be awkward as hell. Or it could be fun. He'd never know if they didn't talk about it.

"So." He pushed away his empty plate and leaned back in the chair. "Were you serious about me going with you to Rough Creek?"

She studied him for a moment. "Having second thoughts?"

Why did she always answer a touchy question with another question? "More like first thoughts, since you didn't actually invite me and I didn't actually accept."

"Oh. Well, then." Moving her own plate aside, she folded her arms on the tabletop and said in solemn tones, "Will you please come with me to my home in Rough Creek, Richard-something-Murdock-the-Third?"

"Milton." He watched her beautiful eyes crinkle as her

lips spread in a crooked, teasing smile that made him forget what they were talking about. "I'm sorry. Say again?"

"Smartass."

He shook his head. "I'm pretty sure that wasn't it. Besides, you're the smartass. I'm . . . just . . ."

"Really good-looking."

He laughed. "Come sit on my lap, soldier, and say that like you mean it."

Her smile faltered. "Ex-soldier."

"Come sit on my lap anyway," he dared her.

Eyes locked on his, she pushed back her chair and came around the table. But instead of sitting primly across his thighs, she threw her good leg over both of his and straddled him. "How's this?" she asked in a low, throaty voice as she wiggled to get comfortable.

Which made him very uncomfortable.

"Perfect," he managed, keeping his arms at his sides, watching to see what she would do next.

"You're really good-looking," she repeated, as ordered, while running her hands through his hair.

He almost shivered as her nails gently raked over his scalp.

"And you have great hair, and I really want you to come with me."

"Patience, babe." He looped his arms around her, more to steady himself, than her. "I'm halfway there."

She leaned in to nip his earlobe. "Don't be nasty."

No one had ever nipped Richard's earlobe before. Not even his dog.

"I meant come with me to Rough Creek," she clarified, sitting back and fiddling with his hair again. Thankfully, he was overdue for a haircut so she had plenty to fiddle with. Or maybe all the playing around was because she was nervous about where this lap dance was headed.

He was, too. A knockout like her probably had guys chasing after her all the time. He wondered how he would measure up. Guess they'd know soon—she was sitting on his lap, after all.

Maybe she was feeling vulnerable. There was an element of shyness in KD, he'd come to realize. She might be the bravest, most straightforward woman he knew, but she didn't like showing her emotions. They were alike in that.

"I'm sure Mama will love you," she said, finger-combing his hair into this style or that. "She's partial to muscular young men. But not in a creepy way. And you and Dalton will really hit it off. He's a big, handsome vet, too. Not as handsome as you, of course."

A wink instead of a nip this time.

What the hell was she up to? Richard didn't know—with KD he often didn't—but he was content to wait and see.

"Raney will worry that we're moving too fast," she rattled on, "but don't take it personally. Worrying is what she does. Luckily Joss won't be there. She's easily impressed by big muscles, and I wouldn't want her reaction to yours to upset her new husband. Since my oldest sister, Len, is off God-knows-where in the Caribbean, she won't even be there. You'll only have to deal with Raney and Dalton and Mama."

Sounded doable, although he would have to keep an eye on Mama. "No second thoughts about taking me to meet them?"

"Of course not, Richard. I'll be proud and delighted to show—"

He kissed her. Couldn't help himself. When she didn't resist, he wrapped his arms around her slender body, pulled her closer and kissed her again. Maybe three or four more times, so lost in the newness of her, he didn't question the rightness of it. It was pure joy having her body pressed up against his, her arms locked around his neck, her tongue dueling with his. But through it all, the part of his brain that could still reason kept warning him to slow down and think about what he was doing. When KD had first climbed into his lap, he'd been stunned—and grateful—for her enthusiasm. But now he sensed a hint of desperation in the way she clung to him. And that surprised him.

KD was a unique blend of all the best female traits—definitely not clingy or desperate. She could be everything he'd ever wanted. But he'd been badly burned in his marriage, and had learned to listen to his instincts. And right now, his instincts were telling him something was off. "Hey," he said. "Wait."

She immediately stiffened and pulled back. "What?"

Not trusting that wary look and afraid she might bolt, he moved his hands up to her shoulders. "What's going on, KD?"

"What do you mean?"

"Yesterday you tell me 'not yet.' Now you're giving me a lap dance."

"This is a lap dance? I thought lap dances were more . . . involved."

"You're dodging the question. What's going on? Is this you wanting a distraction from all the upheaval you've just suffered through? Or something more?" He'd been conned once. Never again.

Her eyes narrowed. He felt a subtle stiffening in her posture. "You think I'm using you?" When he didn't answer, she pulled out of his hands and slid off his lap. "You're right. Maybe this isn't the time."

"I didn't say that, KD."

She turned toward the bedroom, pulling off her top as she went. "I'm taking a shower. I'll clean up the dishes when I'm done."

Richard stared after her. *Fuck was that about?* The closing of the bathroom door jangled along his nerves and set off an explosion in his head. *No. Hell, no.* He couldn't let her get away with that. And the thought of bringing her to heel—or trying to anyway—almost made him laugh out loud.

He dug through his duffle, grabbed what he needed, took care of business, then headed for the bedroom. She was already in the shower when he yanked aside the shower curtain a few minutes later.

With a startled sound, she whirled, turning her back to him, a dripping washcloth clutched to her breasts. Thankfully, it didn't cover much. "What are you doing?"

"Let's not play these games, KD."

"Games?" She glared back at him over her shoulder, strands of wet hair clinging to her face and neck. "You're the one playing games! Telling me to get on your lap then pushing me away. I don't know what to do anymore."

He watched water pour onto her head, run over her shoulders, and down the dip of her spine to the red puckered hollow low on her hip where the bullet had gone in.

The fight went out of him. He'd been so wrong. About everything. This definitely wasn't a game for either of them.

Still wearing his shorts and T-shirt, he stepped into the shower behind her and drew the curtain closed. Wrapping his arms around her, he pulled her back against his chest and out from under the spray. "You know I want you," he murmured into her wet hair. He pressed against her, letting her feel the evidence of it. "I want you more than you could believe. But I don't want to mess this up."

She twisted to look back at him. "Mess it up, how?"

"Look what you've been through, KD. You were shot, lost a good friend, had major surgery, and just a few hours ago you had to sign away your career and a lifelong dream. Are you really ready to take on a guy with no job and no idea where he's headed? Or do you just need a temporary distraction?"

She stiffened. A shiver ran through her wet body. Anger? Hurt? A chill?

Not wanting her to misinterpret his words, he took her by the shoulders and turned her to face him. "I can be either. Whatever you want from me, KD. Whatever you need, I'm here. But I need to know where we're headed. And why."

Tears pooled in her beautiful eyes. He watched them spill over and mingle with the water on her cheeks. It sapped his strength. "Babe, don't cry. I'm sorry. I didn't mean to fuck this up so bad. What can I do to fix it?"

She ducked her head and wiped at her cheeks. Still trying to be tough. Still afraid to let him see her cry. Hell, he'd seen her vomit, for God's sake. A few tears wouldn't break him.

"There's nothing you can fix, Richard. That's all on me." She hiked her chin and met his gaze with that unshakable resolve he'd noticed in the hospital in Germany. "I'll get through this on my own. I don't need to be coddled or rescued."

Pride in her made him smile. He adored this warrior woman. "I know, babe. I have no doubt of it."

That took some of her anger away. "But I'm at loose ends, too, Richard," she went on in a gentler tone. "I don't know where I'm headed, either, or what I'll do when I get there. Right now, all I'm certain of is that being with you keeps the bad dreams away. You make me feel safe. I don't know if that's fair to you, or what it means, or how long it will last. But I want to find out." She tried to smile, her eyes red and brimming. "Maybe together, we can make sense of it. Maybe not. But I'm willing to try. Are you?"

"God, yes." His relief was so great, he pulled her against his chest before she saw the emotion he couldn't hide. They *would* get through this. Together, they would make this work. "Then how about tomorrow," he said in a rough voice, "we get away from here. Put all this bullshit behind us and start again. Just you and me. What do you say?"

"I'd like that. But . . ."

Fuck. There was always a *but.* "But what?"

She pulled back far enough to see his face. "But I still want you to go with me to Rough Creek."

"Oh. Sure." He could do that.

Her smile hit every nerve in his body. "And I want you to take off those wet clothes."

He could do that, too, and quickly pulled down his soaked shorts, kicked them aside, and looked up to find her staring at his manly parts with what he hoped was awe.

"You're wearing a condom."

"Better safe than sorry, I always say."

"But . . . when did you put it on?"

"Earlier. Luckily the water in the pool is heated."

"Earlier? *How much earlier?* But that's . . . it's not . . . you can't be serious."

He struggled to get his soaked T-shirt off his wet back, then dropped it on top of his shorts and away from the drain. "Never hurts to be prepared. Turn around so I can wash your back."

She continued to stare. Part fascination. Part shock. Not so much awe. "That can't be right."

"I know. Impressive, isn't it? Forget the back. We'll start directly on the front. I'll go first." He cupped her breasts. "These are amazing. What are they called?"

She lifted her head. That dumbfounded look again. "Breasts. What's wrong with you?"

"Sorry. I've been living with men so long, I forgot."

The expression on her face would have made him laugh out loud if he hadn't been so distracted by the most beautiful breasts he'd ever held.

"Tell me you're kidding about all of this," she said.

"I'm kidding about all of this." Grinning, he slid his hands down her ribcage to her hips. "Where's the soap, Miss Gullible?"

"I knew you were kidding!" She punched his shoulder. "Jerk!"

It was the longest foreplay Richard had ever endured, and might have gone on even longer if the hot water hadn't run out. After quickly drying off each other—another excruciating assault on Richard's fraying control—they finally made it to the bed.

And to the quickest, most explosive climax in the history of the Western World. He felt like he might have had a stroke. For a minute or two he could hardly move. "Good thing I'm not a pig," he panted as he lay staring up at the ceiling, so spent he was still a little dizzy. "I'd be dead by now."

Breathing hard, she brushed hair out of her face and looked over at him. "What's a pig got to do with it?"

"Their orgasms last thirty minutes. My heart would have burst."

"Thirty minutes? No wonder there's so many baby pigs running around."

"Piglets." Looping an arm around her to pull her against his side, Richard gave her a kiss. "You're amazing," he murmured into the damp hair at her temple. "Next time, I'll do better. I'll light you up and watch you burn, I promise."

"Sounds painful. But interesting. Make sure I'm awake." And within seconds she was asleep.

It took him at least a minute longer.

As it happened, she woke him up. And what a wake-up it was. This time, he took it slow and easy, exploring, teasing, learning what set her body quivering, and how to keep her going until he couldn't hold off anymore. It sickened him to see the scars left by Farid's attack and the surgery. She deserved more than a Purple Heart for what she'd gone through.

And he'd see that she got it.

Later. After a short nap.

CHAPTER 11

They overslept Friday morning. KD had barely enough time to shower and dress, grab their last two energy bars, and herd a sleepy-eyed Richard into the car.

This time, she drove. They made it to the Hood airfield for his flight to MacDill Air Force Base just as the plane was warming up. As soon as she stopped the car, Richard leaned over the console and gave her a hard, possessive kiss. When he drew back, she saw worry in his eyes. "Promise me you'll still be here when I get back," he said.

"If you promise me to come back. I still need a body-guard."

"I mean it, KD."

Did he truly think she could walk away after the night they just had? But something had him upset. Which upset her. Leaning over, she pressed her lips to his, putting into the kiss all the emotion she felt for this remarkable man and how desperately she needed him to come back to her. "You're my guy, Richard Milton Murdock the Third," she told him. "And I'll be waiting for your text when you land in Killeen. No matter what time it is."

Another quick kiss and he was out and sprinting to the plane just before the ground crew rolled away the stairs. KD waited until the plane lifted off, then battled tears all the way to the Friday morning group session.

She was utterly exhausted, her emotions in turmoil, still riding high on a cloud of euphoria, yet terrified she'd never see him again. Which was disturbing. She'd never gotten this wound up over a guy before. What lingering anger she felt about being run out of the army seemed unimportant now. That part of her life was over. It was time to move on. And hopefully, with Richard by her side.

The group session started on a solemn note. Tommy TBI had suffered seizures since their meeting on Monday, and had been admitted to the neuro center at the hospital. Laura, the woman with the burn scars, was on suicide watch and being counseled privately, and would be absent from the group for a while, as well.

"So," Dr. Prescott concluded, blinking rapidly behind his thick glasses, "until new people are assigned to our little group, it's just us five chickens."

A poor attempt to make light of their diminished numbers, KD thought.

For a moment it looked like Sarge might kick over the mild-mannered psychologist's chair. "I ain't your chicken, Conan."

While the timid man tried to soothe the sergeant's feathers, KD studied her fellow group members. Shirley-the-amputee, big angry Sarge, and the fidgety, overmedicated finger drummer. With people like that around her, she almost felt sane.

"Who would like to share first," the doctor asked cheerfully, once Sarge had settled down.

KD raised a hand.

All eyes turned her way.

It moved her that they actually seemed interested in what she might say. Or maybe they always had, but she'd been so filled with self-pity she hadn't noticed. She felt her eyes burning again and blinked hard, realizing she would actually miss them. "I'm leaving, too."

Sarge smirked at her. "We too mean to you last Monday, Snow White? Hurt your tender feelings, did we?"

"Not at all, Sarge. In fact"—she smiled directly at him—"you told me exactly what I needed to hear. And it really helped."

The smirk wavered. His dark eyes narrowed. "You fucking with me, Snow White?"

"I would never fuck with you, Sergeant," she said with sweet innocence. "That's a promise."

Shirley coughed into her fist. The drummer stopped fidgeting. Dr. Prescott blinked faster, watching the big sergeant for signs of eruption.

Instead, Sarge relaxed back in his chair. "You sassy, ain't you?"

"Maybe a little."

"Maybe a lot. Why you quitting group? We not sick enough for you?"

"Oh, you're plenty sick," she said with a smile. "And I'm not quitting. I was forced out." Not bothering to hide her bitterness, she told them she'd been threatened with charges unless she kept her mouth shut about what had happened in Afghanistan and accepted a medical separation. "They were so desperate to avoid a scandal, they even tossed in a shiny new Purple Heart to sweeten the deal. And now that you know all of it, you'll each have to sign nondisclosures since everything I've told you is now classified."

"I have the SF-312 forms," the doctor told her. "I'll see that they sign them before they leave today."

"Bastards," Sarge muttered.

Shirley nodded. "CYA. Happens all the time. I'd be pissed, too."

"I'm more sad than pissed," KD admitted. "I wanted to be a soldier since my first day of high school. It's hard giving that up." Yet today, it didn't seem to matter to her as much as it had yesterday . . . pre–sex with Richard.

"Women don't belong in the military anyway," Sarge muttered.

KD whipped toward him. "There's a difference, Sarge, between *having* a pussy and *being* a pussy. I was a good soldier. I would have made a difference. Given the chance, I might even have been able to convince a hardheaded asshole like you that the army is better off with women in the ranks."

"Watch yourself, Snow White," he warned.

"You can still make a difference, Lieutenant Whitcomb," Dr. Prescott cut in before tempers ignited.

"I no longer have rank," KD reminded him, still glaring at Sarge.

"Yes, well." The psychologist rummaged through the thick zipper pouch he always brought to sessions. "There are ways to stay connected to the military without being in uniform. Ah, here it is." He pulled a pamphlet out of the pouch, blinked at it for a moment, then nodded. "You've heard of the Wounded Warrior charitable organization?" he asked her.

"Of course."

"This is different. Revolutionary, I'd say. And it seems to be working. Do you know anything about equine therapy?"

"Horse therapy?"

"It's not therapy *for* horses, but *through* horses. Here." Holding the open pouch to his chest, he half rose and leaned toward her, the pamphlet in his outstretched hand. "Read about it. The program is showing amazing results. And you're familiar with horses, I believe."

With reluctance, she took the pamphlet and studied the photograph on the front; a man with a prosthetic leg standing beside a horse. The man was grinning. The horse looked bored.

"What she know about horses?" Sarge asked.

"I grew up on a ranch," KD said as she opened the pamphlet and scanned the inside page. *Healing through horses. A unique approach to PTSD.*

"I love horses," Shirley said in a wistful tone. "But I doubt I'll ever be able to ride again with this leg."

KD wondered the same thing about her hip.

"I don't trust them," Sarge announced. "I ain't putting my life in the hands of a dumb animal."

"Hooves," KD said absently, still scanning. "Horses don't have hands, they have hooves. Four of them." She looked at Shirley. "From what it says here, you don't have to ride to get benefit. Just being around horses, grooming, feeding, and taking care of them is also helpful."

She closed the pamphlet. This might actually work.

"I knew a girl who suffered a TBI when she and her horse fell down a slope," she told them. "They were both badly hurt. Her parents wanted to put the horse down, but the girl insisted on trying to save him. Once she focused on taking care of the horse, she recovered fast."

"I think I'm going to cry," Sarge muttered sarcastically.

"Not to worry, big guy. They both pulled through just fine."

Actually, the more KD thought about it, the more she thought horse therapy might help both Sarge and Shirley. Get their minds off their troubles. Give them something to think about other than their losses. It wouldn't help the drummer. Too nervous. All that fidgeting and jerking around would drive a horse crazy. Maybe a sloth would work better for him.

"You serious about doing this horse thing?" Shirley asked.

"I'll have to read up on it. Talk to people who've done it.

But if it really does work, we've got the horses and the space."
She grinned, an idea taking shape. "Maybe I'll do a test run
with you guys and put you to work currying our horses."

"I'd do it," Shirley said.

Sarge shook his head. "Not none of me."

"You're not afraid, are you, Sarge?" KD challenged. "If
you are, I could always find a little pony for you."

"Fuck that."

An hour later, as the therapy session wound down, KD
thanked Dr. Prescott for the information and the pamphlet,
and reminded him to send the signed nondisclosure agreements to the JAG office. "I'll let you know if I decide to do
anything about the horse therapy." To the others, she said,
"I have to be back at Hood in a month. Maybe I'll see you
then. Unless you've been classified, too."

"Fucking bureaucrats," Sarge muttered.

*Half a world away, on a hot, starlit night, three vehicles in
close formation crossed the Afghan-Pakistan border. They
moved fast, without lights, half-hidden by the dust kicked
up by the spinning tires. The first and last vehicles were
Toyota Hilux pickup trucks, referred to as technicals. Both
had men in the back, armed with AKs and RPGs—portable
rocket-propelled grenade launchers—and each truck had
a PKM—light machine gun—hard-mounted to the bed.*

*The middle car was an older, dark Mercedes sedan with
black-tinted one-inch-thick Lexan windows, steel plates in
the door panels, and more plates welded to the frame.
None of the passengers were armed, and on the rear floor-
board at the feet of the middle passenger—a heavyset,
late-middle-aged man with feral eyes and an old knife
wound that cut across the bridge of his nose, down his
cheek, and into his black beard—sat a worn leather valise.
Neither the driver nor his three passengers spoke as the car
bounced and lurched over the rough mountain track.*

They were on a holy mission of vengeance and were assured of Allah's blessing.

Friday afternoon, Richard sat in the CID headquarters at CENTCOM, waiting for his appointment with Chief Stranton. He'd already turned in his armor and firearms and cleaned out his locker. Since he owned two other registered handguns and couldn't take them on a civilian airplane, he used his parents' return address and shipped them directly to KD Whitcomb, Whitcomb Four Star Ranch, Rough Creek, Texas. Hopefully, they would get there. He doubted he would need them while he was visiting but liked having them handy. After carrying a firearm for the last eight years, being without one made him feel half-dressed.

While he waited for Stranton to condescend to see him, he made calls to people he thought should know about his separation from the army. Since Bill was aware he'd been considering it, he was more disappointed than surprised by the news. After he ragged Richard about KD and insisted he be invited to the wedding, they told each other they'd stay in touch, although they both knew they would eventually drift apart.

When he called his folks, they sounded more confused than concerned by his decision. He told them he'd come for a visit as soon as he could, which was an empty promise, since things were still tense between them, even after eight years.

Next, he called FOB Hickock. Dr. Erickson, having had his run-ins with army brass, guessed the reason for Richard's sudden departure. "Using you to cover their butts, are they? Thought you were smart enough to avoid that."

"That's not it," Richard said. "I've been thinking about leaving for a while."

"Well, good luck with that. And how's that pretty little lieutenant?"

"They cut her loose. Apparently, someone sent counsel for the army some new evidence of a medical nature."

"Is that so? Like what?"

"It's classified."

"That's convenient."

"I thought so, too. Whatever it was, it was enough to convince them to cancel the Article 32, but not enough to allow her to stay in the army. They made her sign an SF-312, tossed in a Purple Heart to make it look good, and forced her to take a medical separation."

Erickson sighed. "Probably just as well. From what I hear, she liked being in the thick of things. Wouldn't have been suited to a desk job. What's she doing now that she's a civilian?"

"Taking me to meet her family."

"You sly dog!" The old man laughed so hard, it sounded like he might have coughed up a lung. "So the two of you are off to tiptoe through the tulips," he said once he'd quit coughing.

"How's that?"

"Never mind. It's a Tiny Tim thing. Before your time."

Having run out of things to say, Richard told Erickson that if he ever heard who'd come up with that new medical evidence, to be sure and thank him.

The doctor chuckled and promised he would.

After the call had ended, Richard felt that sense of loss he'd experienced as he'd watched Bill's plane climb into the sky. He wished he'd gotten to know the major earlier. For every Stranton or political hack in the military, there were a thousand good servicemen and women, making the sacrifices and doing what needed to be done. He was proud that, for a while, he'd been a part of that.

His last call was to Vocek, to thank the captain for helping him with the investigation, and for alerting the MPs at Hood about Khalil Farid. Not every MP CO was so cooperative.

"I didn't do much," Vocek said, brushing off Richard's thanks. "Our MPs here are still watching for him. If we pick him up, or hear he's headed stateside, we'll let you know. I gave the MP CO your cell number. Assuming Khalil hasn't already slipped by us."

Richard felt a ripple of unease. "What do you mean? The Article 32 hearing has been canceled. Surely State revoked Farid's visa."

"They did, but he'd already left. You know how slow they are."

"Left for where?"

"Satan's hot tub, I hope. Or Pakistan. From there, who knows? And he's not alone. One of the locals told us two men left with him."

"How reliable is your informant?"

"Very. She was Samira's sister."

After hanging up, Richard fretted over what Khalil's disappearance might mean. Hopefully, the Afghan would be capped by one of his own, or by a competing poppy grower, or die from an overdose, or have his balls shot off by an outraged mother.

Barring that, the worst scenario—once Khalil learned the hearing had been canceled, along with his visa—would be if he took matters into his own hands. Assuming the guy had contacts within the ANP, he could probably find out that KD lived in Texas. And from there, he could easily cross the porous Texas-Mexico border undetected.

Suddenly, Richard was glad he was having his handguns shipped directly to Rough Creek. Hopefully, KD's brother-in-law, the Iraq vet, would know what other weapons were available at the ranch. He'd have to make sure KD was armed, too, unless she had her own guns. He smiled, re-membering the expert marksmanship medal he'd seen pinned to her dress blues. Hell of a warrior.

Had they only reconnected five days ago? Considering how much he cared about her, and after what had happened last night, five days seemed a really short time. Yet ever since their first meeting in Landstuhl weeks earlier, she had been pretty constantly in his thoughts. And now, after spending these last days with her, he couldn't imagine how empty his life would be without her in it. Knowing she might be in danger sent panic humming along his nerves and made him realize how important to him KD had become. He would do everything in his power to keep her safe.

A few minutes before five, eastern time, a private came to where Richard had been waiting for over an hour and told him the chief would see him now. *Jerk.*

Stranton's office was a stark contrast to Major Erickson's. No memorabilia, no treasured photos, no sense of the man behind the desk. Maybe because Stranton hadn't occupied the office long enough to put his stamp on it. Or maybe because his life was that sterile. The chief didn't seem the type of man who had a lot of friendships, but it might only be Richard who rubbed him the wrong way.

"Sit down," Stranton said without looking up from his paperwork as Richard walked in.

Richard sat.

Another wait, this time just long enough to reinforce who was top dog. Then Stranton put down his pen and sat back. He studied Richard through hazel eyes so yellow they reminded Richard of a predatory bird. Or a lizard.

"So you're not re-upping, Murdock?"

"No, sir."

"Why?"

Because of you, asshole. Although that wasn't strictly true. There were a lot of reasons Richard wanted to make a fresh start. "I'm looking to try something new," he said. "Maybe even get married." *Where did that come from?* After his divorce, Richard had vowed never to marry again. But after spending less than a week with KD, the idea wasn't nearly as repugnant to him. Not that he was ready to make any permanent commitments. Yet.

"Any employment opportunities?"

Richard decided to get creative. "I have a contact in a state CID up north. He said to drop by when I got out. I'll start there. See if I like it."

"How are you fixed financially?"

"Fine, sir. I'm not much of a spender so I have enough set aside."

Having dispensed with the required questions, Stranton leaned forward and rested his forearms on the desk. "Look, Murdock, I know I've been pretty hard on you lately—"

"No problem, sir." Richard didn't want to hear it. "The whole thing was a mess. Luckily, we got out of it as easily as we did."

Easy for Stranton. Not so easy for KD.

But Richard left it at that, not wanting to prolong this interview, or make waves that might swamp his chances of a quick, clean discharge. Intent on changing the subject, he asked if Stranton had heard anything more from the State Department about Khalil Farid. "The MP CO at Hickock told me they'd lost him several days ago," he added. "They think he and two other guys crossed the border into Pakistan. If they make their way stateside, they could cause a lot of trouble."

For all Richard knew, Khalil might be off humping a camel somewhere. But if he could light a small fire under Stranton, the chief might be able to pressure State or Homeland Security to keep Khalil in their sights.

Stranton shook his head. "I've already talked to State. They can't find him, either." He let out a gust of air like a deflating balloon. Probably seeing his short, ineffective career turn to shit. Richard was gratified to have had a part in that. "All they can do is flag his passport," the chief went on, "and let us know if he tries to come into the country through normal channels. If he comes in illegally . . ." He shrugged. "We're in trouble."

Not "we," *asshole.*

"Well," Stranton said, getting back to the business at hand. "You've turned in everything? Cleaned out your locker?"

"Yes, sir." Richard pulled his CID badge and active army ID from his pocket and set them on the desk.

With little more to say to each other, Stranton shuffled through papers, found Richard's discharge form and terminal pay envelope, added his signature to both items, then shoved them across the desk to Richard. "You'll get the official DD 214 in a month or so. Thank you for your service. Dismissed."

Thirty minutes later, Richard sat in a shuttle on the way to the Tampa Airport, once a decorated army CID warrant officer, now a free man with an honorable discharge, life-long veteran benefits, and money in his pocket.

It felt weird. But good.

Only the army flew direct from Tampa to Fort Hood, and since Richard was now a civilian, he had no access to military flights. When he'd gotten his commercial last-minute return ticket to Killeen the day before, he'd had to take what he could get. Which meant he'd be traveling back to Hood the long way—one stop in Pensacola, another in Dallas, then down to Killeen. Flight time, six hours and twenty minutes, which would put him in Killeen around midnight, Texas time. Too late for KD to be driving to the airport to get him.

He tried for standby on an earlier, shorter run, but couldn't get a seat, so he texted KD that he'd be late and would take an Uber to the hotel.

She texted back, Just as long as you get here. I miss you.

He smiled, relieved to know she would be waiting for him.

He spent the hour-and-a-half flight to Pensacola reliving the high points of the previous night—the first hundred of them anyway. But on the longer run to Dallas, exhaustion claimed him and he slept straight through.

It was hot and muggy when he deplaned in Killeen. By

the time he got an Uber to the hotel, he was sweating, even though it was the middle of the night.

As he cut across the courtyard from the lobby entrance, he saw the lights were off in KD's suite. Just as well. He was desperate for a shower. Relieved she hadn't used the privacy bolt and he still had a key card, he slipped quietly inside, dropped his duffle by the door, locked up, and moved silently to the bedroom.

She looked like a little kid scrunched in a tight ball in the middle of the bed, her hands tucked under her cheek. He stood for a moment, listening to her breathe, and thinking what a lucky man he was to have gotten this second chance. He was determined not to blow it.

Moving on to the bathroom, he stripped and turned on the shower as hot as he could take it. After he soaped down and rinsed, he turned it on cold—which wasn't all that cold compared to the well water in Washington. Then he toweled off, brushed his teeth, and padded, naked, into the bedroom.

She hadn't moved.

He slipped under the covers and lay quietly for a moment, breathing her in. Soap, warm woman, the strawberry shampoo she favored. He was pleased to note she was naked, too, and set to work waking her gently with slow strokes down her side and over her butt and hip until she rolled onto her back, arms thrown wide.

Then he really got to work.

She awoke with sighs and soft moans, until finally her arms came up and around his neck and she whispered his name in his ear. Then, "Condom."

He tended to that, then slipped in beside her again and found her awake and as eager as he was. Wanting it to last, they made slow, unhurried love now that that first rush of newness was behind him and they'd learned what each other liked. Afterward, still holding her in his arms, Richard drifted into deep, dreamless sleep.

CHAPTER 12

Since they were now free agents with nowhere to be, Richard let KD sleep in, then woke her for a Saturday morning romp, which ended in the shower. Which led to another romp. Which made them so late, by the time they had dressed and packed, it was time to check out of the hotel.

KD had already cleared the bill, so they took their stuff directly to the car.

Once they were in their seats, because he couldn't help himself, Richard put a hand on the back of her neck and pulled her in for a kiss. Not a long one. Just enough to let her know he'd been thinking about her during the entire half hour they'd been packing and loading the car. He was that hung up on her.

Which was why, suddenly, he was filled with a deep sense of dread. There were things he needed to tell her before whatever was going on between them went too much further. Painful things that he had already put off saying for too long. Things she needed to know.

He hated the thought of dredging up all that anger and

bitterness and dumping it on her. But if he didn't, the unspoken words would hang between them and might eventually ruin any chance they'd have to build something lasting.
Maybe this was the time to clear the air—away from her
family, stuck in a moving car in the middle of nowhere,
with all the time they needed to talk it through. But he
couldn't just blurt it out.

"Why so solemn?" KD asked as he started the car. "Sad
to leave our little love nest?"

"I am." He looked at the closed door of Room 114,
thought of all that had happened over the last few days, and
wondered if they'd ever recapture that magical joy of dis-
covering each other. "It was good, wasn't it?"

"You say that like you think it'll never be as good again."

He turned to find her studying him with a tentative smile
that didn't hide the puzzlement in her eyes, and he realized
now wasn't the time for confession. But if he saw an opening, he promised himself he'd take it. "I'm hoping it'll be
even better."

"Practice makes perfect." Grinning, she sat back and
snapped on her seat belt. "As my sister, Joss, says, 'What
say we blow this pop stand?'"

"Where to?"

"West to Lampasas, right onto US 183, and north toward
the panhandle."

After they drove past the Hood gates, she turned to
watch the sprawling base disappear behind them, then settled back in her seat with a deep sigh. "It's weird, not being
a part of that anymore. Not having the army be the total
focus of my life." She turned her head and looked at him,
that wrinkle of worry between her dark brows. "What do I
do now with the rest of my life?"

"What do you want to do?"

"I don't know. The army was everything. I've never
thought of doing anything else."

"Well, now you're free to be anything you want."

She gave him a sad, crooked smile. "Except be an army officer."

"It's overrated."

She was silent for a moment, then said, "Now that I think about it, I don't know if I've ever been truly free. Seemed there was always somebody chasing after me, waving a list of expectations. Mama, my teachers, coaches, the army. They were always there, telling me what to do next. Without them, I feel sort of . . . lost. Is it the same for you?"

"Yeah. It's called freedom. We'll adjust."

"We'll have to. By the way, I want to wait until tomorrow to tell the family I'm out of a job. I'd like at least one meal without the pitying looks."

"Up to you." Reaching into his shirt pocket, Richard pulled out a wad of bills. "Here's my half of the room charge," he said, holding it toward her.

She pushed his hand away. "I'd planned to stay there anyway."

"I thought you were a feminist. That cuts both ways, doesn't it?"

"I am a feminist. That's why I let you do all the cooking. But if it'll make you feel any better, you can pay for the gas."

"I already did. Twice."

"Then you can pay for the food, as well."

"I already did that, too."

"Sounds like I owe you."

"Damn, you're a hardheaded woman."

She grinned. "Yes, I am. Argue with me at your peril."

With reluctance, he stuffed the money back into his pocket. Seemed he had a lot to learn about the new non-dating rules.

When they reached the interchange, he merged onto US 183 North and accelerated to the posted speed limit. Since it was Saturday, traffic was heavy with soldiers out for the weekend. "How was group?" he asked, settling in for the long drive.

"Enlightening." She told him about the horse therapy idea the psychologist had mentioned. "I'll need to look into it, but it sounds interesting. Why are you driving so slow?"

He glanced at the odometer. "I'm going the speed limit."

She laughed. "This is Texas. We normally drive ten percent above the posted speed."

"That's allowed?"

"That's expected."

He adjusted the cruise. "Tell me about Rough Creek."

"Not much to tell. A dozen shops along Main Street, a feed and farm implement co-op out by the highway, two bars to keep the devil busy, and enough churches to keep God happy. Texas is in the Bible Belt, you know."

"How big is it?"

"Population-wise? Hard to tell, since it's difficult to get everybody in the hardware store at the same time to do a head count."

"You serious?"

"Oh, you want serious. Well, it's not as big as Dime Box, but bigger than Bug Tussle. Does that help?"

"Not at all."

KD laughed, and spent the next twenty minutes explaining the rural realities of wide-open cattle country.

She told him Rough Creek was situated in the southwestern part of the county with a sizable creek running through it and a state park on a lake outside of town. It catered mostly to ranchers and farmers and a few aging roughnecks left over from the oil drilling days. "Eventually it'll either wither and die," she added in a wistful tone, "or be eaten up by larger towns. But we love it."

She went on to say that although Gunther County covered a huge area in northwest Texas, it didn't have a large population. After the short-lived oil boom ended two decades ago, the population had shrunk even more. There was talk of putting in a wind farm nearby, but nothing had come of it so far.

"Not that many changes come to Rough Creek, good or bad," she said. "It's the kind of town where everybody knows everybody else, and gossip runs rampant. But overall, it's good people. In addition to the stores along Main Street, there's also a town square and, at last count, two rodeo arenas."

"Sounds . . . quaint."

"It is. A veritable hotbed of manure-scented, aw-shucks, God-fearing quaintness."

Richard hoped her smile meant she was joking.

"For serious shopping," she went on, "you can go to nearby Gunther, the county seat, or up to Lubbock, or east to Dallas and Fort Worth. Or you could do the save-the-planet thing and not add to all the cow-generated methane by driving four hundred miles to get a dress and, instead, just order one online, like everybody but Mama does."

"What's the ranch like?"

"They don't have ranches in Washington?"

"Sure. But I doubt they're as big or fancy as Texas ranches. Most of the open land east of the Cascade Mountains is tied up in orchards, wineries, wheat farming, forest service lands, and Indian reservations. What's your family's place like?"

"Grazing land, same as most ranches. Except the Whitcomb Four Star Ranch is named for the four precious Whitcomb daughters. It's smack-dab in the middle of the county and one of the bigger outfits in the area. Not *the* biggest," she assured him. "We're not *totally* decadent. Although I will say that the Whitcombs are easily the most prominent family in the area due to my daddy's shrewd investments before he died. Since then, Mama has maintained our prominence by keeping her finger in the proverbial town pie, changing churches twice a year to keep up social contacts and making generous donations to various deserving organizations and politicians."

"Like Senator Roy Bob Tomlinson?" Richard asked. "I

believe that was the name Stranton mentioned when he was advising me to seek other employment."

"The same. An old family friend. And another admirer of my mother. She does love to interfere. Sorry you had to find that out the hard way."

"Will she be okay with me showing up?"

"You mean you showing up with the intention of sleeping with me?"

"Yeah. That."

"Let's find out, shall we?" Pulling out her phone, she punched in a number. As soon as it rang through, she put it on speaker and winked at Richard. "Be strong. This won't hurt for long."

"KD, darling!" her mother cried, making KD wince. "Where are you? Are you on your way yet? I told Maria to cook your favorite baked chicken. When will you get here?"

"North of Lampasas—yes—yummy—in time for supper."

"What?"

"Yes, we're on our way, Mama, and we should be there by six or so."

"We?"

"Don't you remember? I'm bringing the CID guy, Richard Murdock, with me. You didn't forget, did you?" KD rolled her eyes at Richard.

"Of course not. We're delighted to have him."

"And don't worry about cleaning out Len's room for him; we can stay in the guest room downstairs."

"Together?"

"No, in shifts. Of course, together." This time she winked at him. "Will that be a problem, Mama?"

"Well—"

"If it is, we can stay at the motel out by the Roadhouse."

"Lord, no! That place is no better than a brothel. Of course he can stay here. With you. If that's what you want."

"Great." It was all KD could do not to bust out laughing. Richard almost felt sorry for her mama.

"Well. All right, then, dear. Drive safe. We'll see you soon."

After KD ended the call, she rocked back in the seat, unable to hold in her laughter. "Now you see what I have to put up with?"

Richard wondered if that would be his future, too. He gave her a scolding look. "You're mean."

"Yes, I am. I'm also old enough to have babies, vote, drink, and go to war. In addition, I've been shot, killed a man, and have already lost my first job. So I think it'll probably be okay if I have sex with you, too."

"Too? Who else have you been having sex with?"

"Oh, God! Men!" And she started laughing again, so hard Richard thought she might choke. She was still snorting and snickering a few minutes later when they stopped for lunch at a mom-and-pop diner in a little town south of Abilene.

Forty-five minutes later, they were back in the car. As they put Abilene and the last of the hill country behind them, the land flattened on high plains. Caliche outcrops covered with scrub cedar gave way to rolling hills with gnarly-branched oaks, pecans, and farmland. Which, in turn, gave way to wind farms, oil pump jacks—some still nodding, others rusted in place—and finally to endless vistas of prairie grass dotted with grazing cattle. And wind. Steady, constant wind pushing against the car. Reminded Richard of Afghanistan. Farm entrances soon became ranch gates with cattle guards. There were fewer dead deer by the road and more possums, skunks, and armadillos.

When they sped past a big black lump on the grassy shoulder, vultures exploded into the air. "What the hell was that?" Richard asked, twisting to stare back at it. "You don't have bears, do you?"

"Worse. Texas is overrun with feral hogs. They do hun-

dreds of millions in damages every year. We're even starting to get them at the ranch."

"What do you do about them?"

"Try to fence them out. Trap them if we can, or shoot
them if we have to. They're pretty wily. Do you hunt?" Another thing she didn't know about him. In so many ways,
Richard was a mystery to her. She didn't even know if he
had hobbies.

"Only lawbreakers," he answered. "But I like to fish."

Boring. But for Richard, she might give it another try.

In the distance, windmills churned in the steady wind,
dribbling water into huge round metal tanks or shallow
man-made ponds. Wide-open spaces grew even wider and
the cottony clouds hanging overhead stretched down to the
curve of the earth.

KD had never been to Washington state, but she'd heard
it rained all the time, and in addition to mountains and tall
fir and spruce trees, it had lots rivers, lakes, and waterfalls.
This flat, treeless landscape must seem like another world
to Richard.

"So what do you think?" She gestured to the prairie beyond the window.

"Where did the trees go?"

"Where the water is. What else?"

"It's flat. And windy. And a little boring. Except for the
variety of road kill."

"It certainly can be. It's the people in Texas that make it
a great place, not the topography. But if it makes you feel
any better, we have lots of trees on the ranch because
Rough Creek runs through the middle of it. And we have
outstanding people, too. What about Washington state?"

"The opposite. Outstanding topography, people okay."

"Probably cranky because there's not enough sun."

"On the west side there isn't. But east of the mountains
it's a lot like this. Hot, dry, rattlers, although winters can be
snowy and dip below zero. There's more farming than

grazing there, too. Orchards, wheat, hay, vegetables, dairy farms. And since they legalized it, marijuana farms, too."

She gave him a look. "Are you a hemp head?" As soon as the words were out, she wanted them back. She'd forgotten that his brother was an addict.

He shook his head. "I hate that stuff. I've seen up close the damage drugs can do." He looked at her, the question in his eyes. "You?"

"I tried cannabis once. Almost passed out, coughing. Then I vomited."

"Well . . . you're are a hell of a vomiter."

"I am. Yet lately, that only seems to happen when you're near. I wonder why?"

"Probably suppressed sexual arousal."

"Then, glory be! I'm cured!"

"Maybe. But I suspect you'll need several boosters. Luckily, I'm certified to give them."

As the landscape sped by, KD tried to see it with new eyes, even though it was country she had lived in since she was born. Like Afghanistan, there was a savage loneliness to it. But here, there was life and, in the limitless horizon, a sense of hope. She loved it with a fierceness she had never felt anywhere else. The openness. The wind that sent dust devils dancing along the dirt ranch roads. The vastness that diminished yet renewed her energy.

"I need to look around more often," she announced decisively. "Rather than looking backward at my regrets and mistakes."

"What regrets?"

"Too many to list, I'm afraid. What about you? Do you have regrets?"

"Sure. Lots of them."

"Like what? Tell me the worst."

It was a long time before he answered. "It's a long, sad story."

She could see he was hesitant, which only made her

more curious. She'd found Richard to be a straight-arrow guy. Not one to equivocate, or skirt an issue. If he was reluctant to tell her something, it must be because he thought she might not like hearing it. He'd already told her about his brother. What could be worse than that? "Go ahead. I'm listening."

"I'm divorced," he finally said.

Not what KD had expected him to say. She'd anticipated more sad revelations about his brother. But a previous marriage? A third of the people she knew had previous marriages. But judging by the tension in Richard's voice and his grim expression, she guessed there was more to it than just a previous marriage.

"You want to talk about it?"

"No. I want to forget it ever happened. But . . ." He took a long, deep breath, let it out in a rush, then glanced over at her. "But after these last days—and nights—and the way I'm starting to feel about you, KD, I think you should know."

"Okay." She waited, her heart pressing against the walls of her chest, her mind conjuring up terrible scenarios to prepare herself for what he might say.

Maybe his wife had died. Something prolonged and painful and devastating. Daddy's death had hit all of them hard, but it had been sudden, and more shocking than agonizing. Plus, they'd had Mama to get them through it. Hearing what Richard had gone through with his brother and parents had been an eye-opener. But now there was more?

Unsure how to react, or what to say, she reached over the console, took his free hand, and laced her fingers through his, hoping he would take comfort in the contact, even if she didn't know the words. The way his fingers gripped hers showed he did.

"What happened?" she asked.

"We met at Washington State in our senior year about the same time Kenny started using the hard stuff. Emery—

that's her name—was very consoling. Definitely took my mind off the troubles at home. By Christmas, she had moved into my apartment. By Valentine's Day, she was talking marriage. I had already started making my weekend trips home to try to help Kenny, which put a crimp on things, but we managed. She and WSU were my safety lines. As long as I was with her or in class, I could put Kenny's problems out of my mind. Not a great basis for a relationship."

And not that much different from what she and Richard were doing now, KD realized. But was that wrong? Weren't people supposed to help each other through the rough spots?

Out there, in the vastness beyond the car window, the fight for survival went on as it always did—coyotes chasing rabbits, hawks swooping down from the sky, a rattler striking at a curious calf. But inside the car, in air-conditioned safety, there was only the sound of Richard's deep voice and the warmth of his broad hand gripping hers. Here, they were safe. In no danger from anything.

Except the past.

"Go on," she prodded.

It took him a minute. "In spring, we started sending out résumés and going to job fairs and setting up interviews. I wasn't sure what I wanted to do after graduation. I'd started in pre-law, then switched to criminology. Emery was straight business, so her prospects were better than mine. But we kept at it. By March, she was getting calls for second interviews. Then she found out she was pregnant."

Shit. Kids, too? Could this get any worse? An hour ago, she'd felt she didn't know enough about Richard. Now she was learning too much. "That must have been a shock," she said in a neutral tone.

"It was. But I was happy about it. It's weird, but in a way, I saw it as a chance to make up for failing my little brother."

"Was Emery happy about it, too?"

"I thought she was. When I said we should get married right away, she was all for it. Neither of us had much money, so we had a civil ceremony at City Hall. Didn't even tell our families until it was a done deal." He fell silent for a moment. "I like kids. They're cute and funny and so damn innocent it can break your heart. And the more I thought about being a dad, the more I liked the idea. I even started googling cribs and car seats and how to set up a college account." He gave a bitter laugh. "I can't believe I was such an idiot."

It sounded pretty responsible to KD. And sweet. And not surprising. Richard had a strong protective streak.

"In early May," he went on, "Emery got a job offer. A good one. On the East Coast, starting right after graduation. She wanted to take it. I asked how she planned to manage a cross-country move and a new job with the baby due in the fall. She got defensive, said she'd figure it out, and since I wasn't getting any good offers, she needed to take this one. A real ball-buster. We had some nasty arguments about it. In the middle of one of the worst, my father called to tell me to come home, Kenny had overdosed and was in the hospital."

God, it really can get worse. KD didn't want to hear more. Yet if he was willing to tell her, she should be willing to listen.

"The EMTs had given him a Narcan injection," he said in a flat, emotionless voice. "It pulled him out of the overdose, but he was still a mess. I tried to get him to go to rehab again. He wasn't interested. I told my parents to commit him. They wouldn't do it." He shook his head and sighed. "It was bad, KD. Totally FUBAR. As bad as it gets. Emery calling me every hour, yelling at me to come home, she didn't want to make all these decisions alone, and my folks insisting I stay with them and help my brother. I felt like I was drowning. A pissed-off, pregnant wife, a drugged-out brother, desperate parents, no job, no money, no prospects. I was so messed up, I didn't know what to do."

"So you enlisted," KD guessed. She knew more than

one soldier who had opted for the disciplined predictability of the military over the mayhem they'd left behind.

"I had to. I needed the enlistment bonus, and a regular paycheck, and any spousal health benefits we could get."

"What did your parents and Emery say?"

"My folks were pissed. Thought I was bailing on Kenny. Which I was. But I was tired of fighting about it, so I left and went back to school. They still haven't forgiven me. Emery hated it, of course, but didn't stick around to fight about it. When I got back to our apartment, I found a note saying she'd accepted the job, had had an abortion, and for me to go to fuck myself."

An abortion? KD had seen it coming but was still shocked. "You were the baby's father. The doctor didn't notify you before the procedure?"

"She had emptied out our account, paid cash, and used a false name."

Oh my God. "What did you do?"

"What could I do? I filed divorce papers and went to basic. Kenny died of an overdose a month later. I haven't seen or heard from Emery since, and don't ever want to." He shook his head, as if still unable to fit all that misery into his mind. Then he looked over at her with an attempt at a smile. "So there you have it. All my dark secrets. I hope telling you wasn't a mistake."

"Never. I'm just sad you went through all that. I don't know how you can even talk about it." KD doubted she could have. She could still barely talk about Daddy and what it meant to have him gone from her life.

They made the turn at Gunther and headed down the road leading to the ranch. Their private time was running out. Yet KD felt there was more they needed to talk about. Mostly—and selfishly, she admitted to herself—how this awful family tragedy had impacted Richard. Would he ever consider marrying again? Having kids? Could he allow himself to trust after such a terrible betrayal? But most important . . . did she and Richard have any chance of a future together? Of course, right now they weren't ready to make any commitments. But if they were never going to be able to, she wanted to know now.

"So . . . to answer your question," Richard said after a moment. "Yeah, I have regrets. Emery was a bad chapter in a sorry story. We weren't ready for marriage. We definitely weren't good for each other. I regret marrying her, not divorcing her. As for Kenny, I was mad at him for a long time. Now I only see the waste of it. I did what I could, but it wasn't enough. With addicts, it never is. It's up to them to get better, not you. Maybe someday, my parents will accept that and forgive me. Maybe not. But my deepest regret is the abortion. I regret that a lot. I always will."

She heard the bewilderment in his voice, saw the pain in his eyes, and it brought tears to her own.

"That was my kid, KD. A son. I was supposed to protect and nurture him. Now he's dead, and I don't know if he's buried somewhere, or was used for spare parts, or stem cell research, or just thrown out with the trash. It's not right. It'll never be right." He let go a ragged breath. It sounded to KD that it carried with it all the sadness in his heart and the turmoil in his mind. "He was an innocent. He deserved better."

"You deserved better, too," KD told him, gripping his hand tight. Blinking against tears, she tipped her forehead against his shoulder, needing to touch him, hoping he could feel the sympathy she couldn't express. "I'm so sorry, Richard."

"People say since it's a woman's body," he went on, his voice taking on that hard edge, "she has the right to do with it whatever she wants. I get that. And in certain cases, like incest or rape, abortion might be the merciful option. But it wasn't just her body anymore. It was my son's, too. Killing your own baby as a form of birth control? Or just because it's inconvenient to let it live? That's what I can't get past. I don't know if I ever will."

KD felt a chill, wondering if there was a message for her in his words: *I won't marry again. I won't risk having kids. So don't expect that of me.*

A well of fury rose within her. She despised Emery for bringing such pain to this decent man, and in the process, maybe ruining KD's chance to build a life with him. She wanted to shout and cry out in protest. *I did nothing wrong!* Yet in her heart, KD knew she'd probably end up paying for Emery's choices.

Up until that moment, she had avoided thinking about abortions since she had never been faced with that decision. Mama had wisely put her daughters on birth control when they reached high school. Apparently, Joss had forgotten how to take a pill, but she'd never considered abortion. Instead, she and Grady had worked out their problems and were now happily married and disgustingly devoted to their beautiful baby.

As for KD . . . with only one ovary and a damaged uterus, she had a less than 50 percent chance of ever getting pregnant. She hadn't yet come to terms with what that loss might mean in the future. Did she want kids? Would she be a good mother? After hearing what Richard had gone through, she now had a new perspective and was even more confused. All she knew for certain was if she were ever lucky enough to get pregnant, she would definitely carry the baby to full term.

"Still want me to meet the family?" Before she could answer, Richard added, "I know I've dumped a lot on you all at once, KD. It's got to make a difference in the way you see me. So if you want me to bail, I can get out here. No strings."

Why did he keep trying to run away from her? Or was he running from the commitment? Either way, KD wasn't ready to give up on him. Or them. Forcing a smile, she lifted their clasped hands and kissed his knuckles. "No, I don't want you to bail. If anything, I admire you more."

Richard looked like he didn't entirely believe that, but before he could say anything, the GPS lady announced that they had reached their destination.

Slowing to a stop, Richard glanced past the cattle guard down the long graveled drive leading to a two-story white stone house. The gate was open. Hanging off a timber crossbar above it was a black metal sign that read WHIT-COMB FOUR STAR RANCH in tall laser-cut letters. "Do I turn here?"

KD released his hand and looked around. "We're here already?"

"Time flies . . ."

"Yes, this is it." When he started to turn in, she grabbed his forearm. "No matter what happens, Richard, I've got your back."

"You expecting trouble?"

"You're my man. Remember that."

"You're scaring me, babe."

Hearing him call her *babe* told her everything was all right. They could deal with the rest later. Laughing, she said, "I'm preparing you. So listen up. Standard rules of conduct: open doors for ladies, and stand when they enter the room. If Mama's around, no PDA, spitting, smoking, or use of profanity. Also, no burping or farting at the table, and chew with your mouth closed."

"In other words, I'm not in the army anymore."

"Exactly. Oh, and most important, call Mama *ma'am* or Mrs. Whitcomb until she tells you otherwise. Which may be never. Dalton still hasn't crossed that barrier and he's her favorite next to Raney, but only because she's pregnant."

Sounded ominous. But Richard saw the laughter in her caramel brown eyes and felt a sense of relief. After spewing out all the sleazy details of his wrecked marriage and shattered family, he had been prepared for questions, doubts, withdrawal. That KD had done none of those things only reinforced his feelings for her. Made them stronger. Made *him* stronger. And as they pulled into the drive that led to the imposing ranch house, he felt re-energized, hopeful again, and ready to take on the world.

Even if that world included a sharp-eyed mother standing guard on the front porch, teeth bared in a welcoming smile that would make any sane man shiver.

CHAPTER 13

As they pulled in behind a slightly worn sheriff's cruiser blocking the driveway along the side of the house, Richard noticed an older man in a uniform standing with Mrs. Whitcomb on the porch.

"This can't be good," KD muttered.

"Why?"

"That's Sheriff Ford's car. Wonder why he's here."

Richard felt a twinge of concern, too. Surely Mrs. Whitcomb wasn't so upset he was sleeping with her daughter that she'd called in the law.

"Hey, Mama," KD called, stepping out of the car. "Why's the sheriff here? Is everything's okay?"

"Everything's fine," she assured them as Richard got out, pulled their bags from the backseat, and headed up the porch steps. "Lewis just dropped by for dinner."

"Lewis?"

"Sheriff Ford. Hello, Richard," Mrs. Whitcomb added over her daughter's shoulder as she drew KD in for a hug. "Welcome to Four Star."

"Thank you, ma'am."

Despite KD's innuendoes and warnings, it looked to Richard like a loving mother-daughter homecoming. A lot better than what he got when he went home.

"KD, you remember Sheriff Ford, don't you?" Mrs. Whitcomb turned to the older man, who had a seamed face, a strong build, and the look of authority in his sharp gray eyes.

"I do. Nice to see you again, Sheriff." Reaching back, she pulled Richard to her side. "This is Richard Murdock, the CID warrant officer who investigated the incident in Afghanistan. I'm sure Mama told you all about it."

"Pleased to meet you, Richard." The strength in the older man's handshake let Richard know the sheriff might be twice his age, but he wasn't an old man. Richard hoped the lawman wasn't there in an official capacity.

Behind them, the front door opened and a younger version of Mrs. Whitcomb, wearing a skirt and an overlarge blouse, came onto the porch, followed by a linebacker in a western shirt, with green eyes and dark hair. Richard guessed from KD's earlier descriptions they were Dalton and Raney Cardwell, the Iraq War vet and KD's pregnant sister.

Another round of introductions and more big hugs. Richard wondered what kind of welcome KD would have gotten had she been gone an entire month, rather than a week.

Then all eyes focused on him. The new guy. The one sleeping with the youngest of the four Whitcomb stars. Yet the introductions were surprisingly friendly, although not quite warm enough to hide the hard stare by the vet and the sister's narrow-eyed appraisal.

Richard didn't mind. He was accustomed to people being wary around him.

The mother, though, was a bit more restrained about it. The word *elegant* came to mind. It was obvious where the sisters got their beauty. Even though she was showing some years, Mrs. Whitcomb was a fine-looking woman.

"Y'all come in out of this heat," Mrs. Whitcomb said,

leading the five of them through the entry into a room big enough to house two cars, and where more introductions awaited.

Motioning two other men forward, Mrs. Whitcomb introduced their head wrangler, Alejandro, a stocky Hispanic wearing a silver belt buckle the size of Richard's palm, and an older lanky white guy named Glenn Hicks, the ranch foreman. Both offered nods but no handshake. Neither spoke.

Earlier, KD had explained to Richard that the ranch foreman and the head wrangler took their evening meals and Sunday midday meal with the family at the main house. It was a common practice on most big ranches, and Mama wouldn't be outdone. Since this was Saturday, everyone would be on hand. KD had added that after having the two men around for so many years, they were considered part of the family anyway. Which probably accounted for the cool reception they gave Richard now. They were obviously loyal to the family and wary of strangers, which might come in handy if Khalil showed up.

Altogether, an intimidating group. But no worse than Richard's boot camp sergeants.

Since supper was waiting, they moved directly into a fancy dining room, dominated by a table that was at least sixteen feet long and loaded with silver and china. Richard wondered if this Saturday night display of finery was for his benefit, or was meant as a subtle reminder that he was reaching way above his pay grade. He had expected the family to be comfortably well off, but it appeared the Whitcombs were a lot more than comfortable. Another assumption shot down.

The meal was just as elaborate—green salad, fruit salad, roasted chicken, carrots, green beans, rice, gravy, and dinner rolls, prepared and served by two Hispanic women who were introduced as *las esposas*, Rita Santiago and Maria Morales, wives of the two married ranch hands. And outstanding cooks.

In case this was some sort of test, Richard minded his manners, careful not to tip over his crystal goblet or drop any of the sterling silver tableware on the thick patterned carpet. He wasn't a complete hick.

Yet despite the formality—which he began to think was nothing more than old-fashioned, over-the-top Texas hospitality—Richard liked the Whitcombs. And before the baked chicken went around the table for the second time, he felt they were warming up to him, too. The fact that KD often rested her hand on his thigh under the linen tablecloth definitely added to that warm sense of acceptance.

Then the interrogation began.

"Tell us about yourself, Richard," Mrs. Whitcomb ordered with a smile during the lull between dinner and dessert.

Richard stuck to the basics, answering their questions but omitting the stuff he'd told KD earlier, or any reference to both of them leaving the army. He'd leave that to her. He explained how they met, what Washington state was like, what he did in the army, where he grew up, and so on. The usual questions any family might ask. Questions *he* might ask in an attempt to put the person he was questioning at ease.

When the sheriff wasn't staring at Mrs. Whitcomb, he silently watched Richard. Richard wondered if he was taking mental notes. Neither of the ranch workers spoke during the meal, although Richard occasionally found Alejandro studying him with speculation in his dark eyes.

"KD said the hearing was canceled," Dalton Cardwell said. "Any idea why?"

Richard explained that new evidence had been found that convinced counsel for the army not to go forward. "He said it was classified and couldn't say what it was. Just that KD was off the hook."

"Since it's now classified," KD added, "y'all will have to sign nondisclosures. I'll give you the forms later. And there was help from another area, too." KD gave her mother a pointed look. "The Senate Armed Services Committee. Apparently, Senator Tomlinson called the CID commander at Central Command and convinced him that a hearing wouldn't be in the army's best interest. How he even found out about it, or knew who to call, is odd, don't you think, Mama?"

Mrs. Whitcomb smiled. "Roy Bob always was a crafty one. And a talker. But he thought the world of your father. Made quite a bit of money off his investment advice, too. Would anyone care for more chicken?"

Now who's being crafty? Richard almost laughed, but a pinch from KD stopped him in time.

The conversation moved on to other topics—how KD's final doctor appointments had gone, how the Cardwells' house was coming along, what cutting horse show was coming up next, and when the technicians would be by to check the cryotanks in the bovine artificial insemination lab. Glad to have the attention shift away from him, Richard was finally able to sit back and enjoy KD's tender attentions to his thigh.

As soon as the meal ended, Hicks and Alejandro left. The sheriff gave a last, longing glance at Mrs. Whitcomb, then left, too. As the door closed behind him, Mrs. Whitcomb proposed that the family—"and Richard, too, of course"— retire to the veranda, which KD whispered was what Mama called the unscreened back porch.

More questions, Richard thought wearily. But when Dalton Cardwell suggested he and "KD's friend" should take a quick tour of the ranch before it got too dark, Richard jumped at the offer. He'd been looking for an opportunity to warn the vet about Khalil Farid and the possibility of him showing up at the ranch. And he was anxious to know how well the ranch could protect itself—and KD—if that happened.

The sun was sliding into another spectacular evening display when he and Cardwell left the veranda and crossed a wide lawn sloping down to a line of trees that Dalton told him bordered Rough Creek.

"Not much water in it this time of year," he said, "unless it floods after a heavy rain. But it's enough to keep the stock watered and irrigate a couple of hay fields, so it suits our needs just fine. Except for the mosquitoes."

As they walked along the graveled drive that led to the working part of the ranch, Cardwell pointed out the different buildings and their purposes.

It was an impressive outfit. Miles of welded tube fencing, an open hay barn, a dozen paddocks, a stone walk-through livestock barn with a round working pen out back and a big covered arena nearby. The two married workers stayed in a duplex with a big fenced yard, while the three bachelors stayed above the ranch offices and artificial in-semination lab. The foreman, Glenn Higgs, had his own house up by the front gate. And all of it was painted white, even the stone on the barn. The black Angus bulls dozing in their paddocks behind the AI lab were a stark contrast. As were the horses, especially a big, friendly buckskin stallion that came trotting across a paddock when Dalton gave a high, sharp whistle.

"This is Rosco," the horse trainer said, stroking the horse's sleek neck. "He won us a third at the cutting horse futurity last year. Now he's making the rounds of the regional shows to build up his résumé. Hopefully, in a year or two, he'll be bringing in substantial stud fees."

"You have an insemination program for horses, too?"

"Hell, no. I'd never do that to a horse. Especially one like Rosco. Come on. I'll show you the house Raney and I are building."

When they walked past the barn, Richard met the three bachelor workers—Alejandro, the wrangler he'd met at supper; Chuy, a young Hispanic; and an old white guy with the bushiest mustache Richard had ever seen. Looked like a white wig growing out of his nose. The three were adding three-foot-wide rolls of hog wire at the bottom of the welded tube-railed fences bordering just about everything.

"Harvey, here, used to be a marine sniper," Dalton said, clapping a big hand on the old white guy's shoulder. "Says he can still shoot a gnat's ass off a poppy seed roll in a strong crosswind. Isn't that right, Harvey?"

Harvey shrugged and studied the toes of his dusty boots.

"He say he can, *jefe*," Chuy chided with a gap-toothed grin. "But I never see him do it. Most days, he takes a *siesta* in the feed room." Which earned him a cuff on the back of his head from the old man.

"Harvey's more of a cuffer than a talker," Dalton explained as they walked on toward the married workers' duplex. "But he's a damn good shot."

Richard took note. If Khalil showed up here, they might need a good sniper.

More white welded fencing with hog wire along the bottom stretched around a yard filled with toys. When the four kids digging in a big sandbox saw Dalton, they rushed over, chattering like magpies. Richard didn't speak Spanish, but apparently Cardwell did. As soon as the kids reached the fence, he leaned over and dropped a piece of peppermint into each outstretched hand.

"Don't tell Raney I give them candy," he warned Richard when they'd resumed walking. "She says it's bad for their teeth. Since she got pregnant, she's suddenly an expert on children's health."

As they neared a construction area, more rolls of hog wire lay stacked beside pallets of quarried white rock. "That's to keep out the wild pigs?" Richard asked.

Dalton gave a look of disgust. "Damn bastards are taking over. There's already a million and a half of them in Texas. The rate they breed, there'll soon be a million more. Even having open season on them and shooting from helicopters isn't having much of an effect."

"Are they a hazard to humans?"

Dalton nodded. "If provoked. There've been a few attacks, but only one death that I know of. They'll eat anything, dead or alive. I suppose if you're wounded or bleeding, they might go for you. But mostly, they're too smart to mess with people."

The Cardwells' unfinished house was typical of some of the rural homes Richard had seen on the drive from Killeen. Only bigger. A two-story rectangular building with a metal roof, balconies and porches, front and back, and shaded by a half-dozen trees. The interior was still under construction, except for some fancy beam work and a curved wrought iron staircase. Judging by the pallets of stone off to the side, the exterior would be finished with white limestone like the main house. "Planning on a big family?" Richard asked, eyeing the span of window openings behind the front balcony.

"You never know. How about you? You like kids?"

"I do."

"And KD?"

"Her, too," Richard answered, a little surprised by the question.

After a tour of the unfinished building, they turned back toward the main house, this time following the creek. "You know about her injury?" Cardwell asked after a few minutes.

"I've seen her file."

"Then you know she may not be able to have kids."

Richard shrugged, growing uncomfortable with the conversation. It didn't seem right to discuss KD's reproductive issues with another guy, even if he was her brother-in-law.

But Cardwell wouldn't let it drop. "Will that be a problem? Not having kids?"

Richard stopped and faced the other man. "Do we really need to talk about this?" Next thing, he'd be asking about their sex life.

Dalton's face reddened. "You're right. Sorry. Somehow,

I've been appointed the family watchdog. I figured you should know about her issues, in case it's a problem."

"It's not a problem."

"Sure. Okay, then. Good to know."

They walked on in silence for a time, then Richard stopped again. "Now can we talk about why you really dragged me out here?"

"What do you mean?"

"KD said you wanted to talk to me. I doubt she meant the condition of her ovaries."

"Hell, no." Cardwell ran a hand across the back of his neck and gave an embarrassed laugh. "She'd kill me if she knew I'd said anything."

And justifiably so, Richard thought. "Then what?"

No longer smiling, the other man said, "She told us a relative of the guy she killed has threatened her."

Richard nodded. "Khalil Farid, the dead man's father. He's threatened everyone involved with the investigation, including me. He's rabid about it." Richard hesitated, not sure he should say anything about Farid's disappearance, then decided Dalton should know. "I haven't told KD yet and would rather you didn't say anything, either. Farid is missing. He may have plans to come here."

"Here? To the ranch? Shit! Is the army doing anything about it?"

"Not really, other than sources keeping me informed if they find him. State canceled his visa and flagged his passport, but they can't find him, either. We're on our own. Can we protect KD and her family here? Or should they relocate?"

"We?" Cardwell's green eyes narrowed. "You planning on staying long?"

"Long as it takes, whatever it takes. I don't leave until Khalil Farid is on his way to Guantanamo or fed to the hogs."

Cardwell looked relieved. "We could use the help. As

for relocating, you've met these women. Do you really think you could get them to leave?"

"Then you plan to stay and stand your ground? No matter what?" If anyone was going to bail, Richard wanted it to be now, so he could see what they were up against.

"Damn straight," Cardwell said adamantly. "Our workers, too. Although if there's any real danger of Farid coming here, I'll send the married families clear."

"Understood. Now all we need is a defensive plan. Let's talk to the workers."

"Are you serious?" Raney finished zipping KD's suitcase closed and straightened, her electric blue eyes wide with surprise. "He's staying in here? With you? And Mama said it was okay?"

"I didn't ask her permission." KD stuffed socks and underwear into the bureau, then shut the drawer. "I'm well past the age of consent, even if I am the baby of the family. I just told her we'd be staying in the guest room."

"She didn't have a problem with that?"

KD grinned. "Not after I told her we could stay at the hotel out by the Roadhouse, if she'd prefer."

Laughing, Raney shoved the roller bag into the back of the closet. "You're devious. I wish I'd thought of that when Dalton was bunking in here. But you know how Mama is—her house, her rules."

KD sank down in the upholstered chair by the side window. "You always worried too much about getting into trouble. Mama's not near the hard-ass you think she is. Give her reasonable pushback and she folds. I figured that out in high school when I joined ROTC. Told her I was aiming for West Point, that I'd given it a lot of thought and wanted a career in the army. She didn't argue at all."

"Maybe not, but she cried about it."

"She did?"

Her sister settled on the foot of the king bed, one hand absently cradling her tiny baby bump. "I'd hear her at night sometimes. When I asked her what she was upset about, she said she was worried about you being a soldier and was afraid something terrible might happen. Prophetic, huh?"

"I didn't know that."

"She didn't want you to. She's a little intimidated by you, I think."

"You're kidding."

Raney shrugged. "You were always so self-sufficient and independent. Even as a kid, you didn't seem to need her as much as the rest of us did. You had already planned out your life while we were worrying about what to wear to homecoming."

"Then she ought to be happy now," KD muttered.

"Happy about what?"

KD battled an urge to confide in her big sister. She'd always looked up to Raney and, when growing up, had gone to her more often than Mama whenever she'd had a problem. But this was more than a problem. It was an admission of failure. Rising from the chair, she went to the bureau to find something to wear after her shower. With her back to her sister, she said, "You know that day trip Mama took when she said she went shopping?"

"What about it?"

"I think she went to Austin. Don't the US senators usually come home on break in late May or June?" KD stared into the open drawer. What was she going to do with all these army green tees? She wasn't ready to toss them out. Not yet anyway. Pulling out a tank top and pair of shorts, she closed the drawer and turned back to Raney. "I bet she went to Tomlinson's office in Austin and talked him into convincing the army to cancel my hearing."

"She did leave right after you did," Raney mused. "Pretty ballsy of her to confront a US senator."

After tossing the shorts and tank top on the bed, KD

bent to unbuckle her sandals. "Tomlinson is also a ranking member of the Senate Armed Services Committee, the group that handles military budgets."

"No shit!" Laughing, Raney flopped onto her back across the duvet, arms thrown wide. "I bet if I checked with our accountants, I'd find that she gave the senator a sizable campaign donation while she was in Austin, too. The woman is incorrigible! You going to call her on it?"

"It's a moot point now anyway." KD tossed the sandals into the closet.

Raney lifted her head. "Why?"

KD hesitated, then thought, *What the hell. They'll know soon enough.* She went over to sit on the bed beside her sister. "If I tell you something, you can tell Dalton, since I know you will anyway. But not Mama. Promise?"

Raney nodded.

"I'm not in the army anymore."

Raney jerked upright. "You're not? What happened? Are you all right?"

"I'm fine. But it's complicated, and I'd rather wait and tell everybody at the same time tomorrow morning."

"Did Richard quit, too?"

"He was leaving anyway. And I didn't quit."

"Oh my God! They kicked you out?"

"We negotiated an amicable separation," KD said, thinking that sounded better than admitting she'd been blackmailed into leaving. "And stop looking so stricken. It's all good. I'm even getting a Purple Heart."

"But you loved being a soldier."

"Not one chained to a desk." She explained the limitations of her injury, adding, "So it was either sit behind a desk all day, which I would have hated, or leave. So here I am." Seeing her big sister was about to start in with more questions, KD rose from the bed. "I'll explain it all in the morning. Right now, I'm heading to the shower."

"But what about Richard? What's he going to do?"

"He hasn't decided." Picking up the clothes she'd chosen, KD crossed to the bathroom. "But he'll probably need a shower, too," she added, grinning back at her sister. "If he gets back before I'm done, tell him to come on in."

"Stop! You're my sister. That's almost as creepy as thinking about Mama and Sheriff Ford together."

"Together?" KD turned in the doorway. "You mean *biblically*?" Mama's favorite euphemism for knocking boots. It was difficult to think of prim and proper Coralee Whitcomb and sex in the same sentence. And a little horrifying.

"Don't know—don't want to know. But he's been coming around a lot, and she's not complaining. They look kind of cute together."

"They're in their sixties." And this was Mama they were talking about.

"He's not so bad. And I have to say I haven't seen Mama this happy since Daddy died."

"I'm not calling him Daddy."

"I doubt he'd expect it. He's not looking for grown kids. It's Mama he wants."

The idea gave KD the creeps. "You like him?"

Raney thought for a moment. "I do. He seems a good guy, and since none of us has snagged a lawyer, she might as well take a sheriff."

KD didn't even try to follow that. "She can take whoever she wants, as long as she gets a signed prenup before she marries him." Seeing the way her newly married, deeply in love, pregnant sister's eyes narrowed, KD quickly added, "For her grandkids' sakes," which seemed to calm her down.

"So what's going on between you and Richard?" Raney called as KD continued into the bathroom.

"Mostly, really good sex," KD called back.

"Ew, KD! You keep talking like that and I won't ever be able to look him in the eye again."

CHAPTER 14

It was late when Richard and Dalton headed back to the house after talking to the ranch hands. They both felt the workers should be told there might be trouble headed their way. The family, too. Richard would have to tell KD that night.

Hicks, Alejandro, Chuy, and Harvey had readily agreed to help. Dalton didn't press the married men, suggesting, instead, that if necessary, they should be prepared to move their families elsewhere for a while. It was probably a long shot that the Afghan would come to the ranch, but Khalil's erratic and violent nature made anything possible.

After determining what kind of firepower they had on hand—which included seven long guns, Raney's Glock, whatever pistols KD, her mother, and the workers might have, along with the two handguns Richard was having mailed to the ranch—Dalton suggested that on Monday they should buy as much ammo as they could, then begin target practice the following afternoon. Meanwhile, he would tell his wife and Mrs. Whitcomb what was going on, and Richard would get KD's input on how they could best protect the ranch. After he told her about Khalil disappearing.

He didn't look forward to it. She might be a trained soldier who had seen combat, but she was also vulnerable right now, and although Richard hated to add to her worries, he didn't want to keep her in the dark any longer. He felt bad that he'd shielded her this long. She was tough and didn't appreciate being pampered.

As they approached the house, he was disappointed to see the light was off in the guest bedroom.

Dalton noticed, too. "Looks like KD's in for the night. Raney, too. Want a beer? Mrs. Whitcomb keeps a stash on the back porch."

Richard shot him a wry look. "You mean on the *veranda*?"

"Yeah. I know. She's a starchy lady. But threaten one of her girls and she'll tear your face off."

"You seem okay."

"It wasn't me she went after."

The porch was deserted. Dalton grabbed four Lone Star longnecks from a cabinet refrigerator along the back wall, handed two to Richard, and motioned to the patio chairs around the ottoman in front of the unlit fireplace. "Have a seat."

Richard sat. It was surprisingly cool for such a hot night. Probably because of the misters strung along the outside eaves of the porch roof. There were also sun shades, but they were up for now, and the full moon hanging above the trees along the creek cast a milky glow across the long, sloping lawn.

Dalton propped his boots on the ottoman and downed most of his first beer before he spoke. "Raney was engaged to a guy who worked for their accountants. When she found out he was looking through the ranch books and making plans to run the ranch after they married, she kicked him to the curb. Mama suggested he find work in some other county. He did, but still filed for bankruptcy last year."

"Damn," Richard muttered.

Dalton gave him an appraising glance. "I think you'll be okay. Everyone's a little cowed by KD, and the fact that she brought you home gives you a free pass. Unless you screw up like he did."

"Cowed in what way?"

"KD's self-reliant. Independent. Knows exactly what she wants and what she'll have to do to get it. You can't boss her around or intimidate her, and if she's settled on you, no one would dare question it." He grinned. "Not your usual Gunther County debutante. None of the sisters are."

"She was a debutante?" Were any of his assumptions right? But he couldn't really be blamed. The woman was a mass of contradictions. Smart, yet gullible. Fearless, but sometimes timid. Softhearted, but capable of killing. Richard appreciated all that. Kept him on his toes. Most of the women he'd spent much time with seemed boring by comparison. And not nearly as sexy.

"The Whitcombs are the prominent family around here," Dalton said, yanking Richard back from memories of his pleasant romp with KD the previous night. His knees were still sore. "And they know others look up to them and follow their example. I think KD suffered through it only because it was expected, then she hit the road. She's the only one to totally leave the nest."

And now she's back, Richard thought. *No career, no focus, no idea what to do next. How will her family react to that?*

They sat in silence for a time, finishing off one beer, then starting on the second. Richard settled back, feeling mellow and relaxed for the first time since he'd arrived, lulled by the chorus of frogs down by the creek and the gliding, swooping paths of night birds hunting in the moonlit sky. "Nice place," he said.

"It is," Dalton agreed.

Another long pause, then, "How long you staying?" Dalton asked.

"Not sure."

"When do you have to be back?"

"Never. I didn't re-up." Richard didn't say anything about KD's forced separation. She would explain that when she was ready.

"Any plans?"

"Not yet. Hopefully, I'll come up with something before my savings run out. Maybe something in law enforcement somewhere."

"Sheriff Ford is retiring soon."

Richard looked over at him. "Isn't that an elected position? And doesn't he have deputies who might want it?"

"Toby Langers is the only deputy. A total douche. Doubt he could get elected shit sweeper."

"Not a fan, I'm guessing."

Dalton snorted. "He and I have had run-ins going back to our high school days. But if you want, I could ask Sheriff Ford if he might be interested in taking on another deputy. That might buy you name recognition come election time."

Richard didn't feel he needed anyone to speak for him. But he wouldn't mind talking to the sheriff, if not about a deputy job then about added protection for the ranch. "Maybe I'll check with him next time he comes around."

Dalton chuckled. "That'll probably be tomorrow. Guy's got a real hard-on for Mrs. Whitcomb."

"How does she feel about that?"

"She's not running him off, if that's what you mean."

Out on the lawn, a coyote trotted by. On the other side of the creek, another barked and yodeled. Reminded Richard of the valley in Washington state where he grew up. They'd heard coyotes almost every night. Often, eagles floated by, or the occasional black bear, moose, or cougar might show up. And since the valley was a major migration

route, mule deer could always be spotted in the alfalfa
fields.

He wondered what it would be like to live here in Texas.
No real mountains, no orchards, no snow skiing, or sub-
zero winters. But he liked the people and the pace and the
openness of it. And it had KD, who was the strongest attraction of all.

KD was asleep when he entered the bedroom. Curled in a
tight ball again. Dreaming, it sounded like, the way her
breathing rose and fell in short bursts. He wondered if she
was reliving that night in Afghanistan, or worried about
something else. She'd had a lot of things crashing down on
her at once, including the shocking things he'd told her
about Kenny's death and his disastrous marriage. And now
he'd have to tell her the maniac who had threatened her was
on the loose. His chest hurt just thinking about it.

For a minute or two, he stood by the bed, watching her,
not sure if he should wake her. The soldiers he'd known
who battled PTSD didn't do well if awakened abruptly. KD
suffered from acute anxiety disorder, which wasn't the
same, but it would probably be best to let her come out of
her dream on her own.

When she didn't waken, he went into the bathroom, took
a quick shower, pulled on a T-shirt and boxers, then went
back to check on her.

Her breathing had evened out, but her body remained
tense. In the dim moonlight coming through the window,
he could see the crease between her brows and guessed she
was still dreaming. He didn't wake her, but in case she
needed him, he stretched out as best he could in the upholstered chair by the bed.

While he watched her sleep, he thought about his own
unsettled situation. That initial panicky feeling of leaving
the army had faded, but he still didn't know what he wanted

to do. Every time he tried to think about it, his thoughts kept circling back to woman on the bed. How did she fit into his life? Or was it too soon to even think about that?

As the moon sank lower and KD began to relax, all those disjointed thoughts in his head lulled him into dozing fantasies of him starting over, building a life and a family in this windy, flat, sparsely treed prairie with KD by his side.

"Richard?"

He jerked awake, confused and disoriented, not sure where he was. Then saw KD sitting up in bed, staring at him. "What's wrong?"

"Nothing's wrong. Except that you're sleeping in the chair. Why?"

He dragged a hand through his hair and tried to gather his thoughts. "You were dreaming. I didn't want to wake you."

"Well, now I'm awake." She threw the covers aside. "Come to bed."

He climbed in, wrapped his arms around her, and pulled her back against his chest. "What was bothering you?"

She looked around at him. "When?"

"When you were dreaming. It looked bad. Afghanistan?"

She settled back, her fingers idly stroking the forearm he'd tucked under her breasts. "I'm not sure. You were there, and Nataleah and Dalton and Raney. We were all running from something. I'm not sure what. I don't remember much of it now. What were you and Dalton doing out so late?"

"Talking to the ranch hands."

"About what?"

Now or never. "Khalil Farid."

He felt her tense. "What about him?"

"He's disappeared. Vocek at Hickock thinks he and two others might be headed here."

"Here? To the ranch?" She bolted upright and twisted to face him, saw the answer he couldn't hide, and let out an angry hiss. "That asshole! Do I have to kill the whole fucking family to be free of this shit?"

Richard held back a grin. His fierce little warrior. "Take a number, babe. There are six guys ahead of you, not counting married reserves, the law, and your sister. Which reminds me, do you have any handguns in the house?"

"Seriously? A shootout?"

"I know. Sounds fun, doesn't it?"

"You're ridiculous." With a huff, she lay back down, her cheek against his chest. "Other than Daddy's hunting rifles and shotguns, I have an S&W .357, Raney has a Glock 19, and Mama has a .38. We never let Joss have a gun, and I don't know if Len has any. Probably not, with kids at home. What about you?"

"Since I couldn't take them on my flight back to Killeen, I had my two handguns mailed to the ranch. Dalton and I may go to Rough Creek and Gunther on Monday to get all the ammo we can."

"I can't believe they'd let Khalil come here. Didn't State cancel his visa?"

"They tried. He was already gone. His ID has been flagged, but you know how porous the southern border is." Feeling the way tension rippled through her body again, he lifted her head up for a kiss. Then another. And another.

"He probably won't come to the ranch even if he gets into the country," he said a few minutes later. "But if he does, we want to be ready." As he spoke, he ran a hand under her T-shirt. "Hope for the best, prepare for the worst. Isn't that what they taught you in boot camp?"

She arched, her heartbeat fluttering against his palm like that of a trapped bird. "We'll have to tell Mama and Raney."

"Dalton's talking to them in the morning. How about

you climb on and give me a riding lesson like you did last night."

He almost shivered when she reached between them and tugged down the waistband of his boxers. Her fingers closed around him, gave a squeeze that had him bucking against her. "You do seem to be a slow learner."

"I'll do better this time. I promise."

With a low, sexy laugh, she sat up, swung a leg over, then eased down with excruciating slowness. "How's this?" she asked when he was fully inside her.

"Ah . . . perfect."

She began to move, slow and sweet. "This is called the walk. Just a simple rocking motion. After a while, we'll move on to the trot and canter."

"You can move on now if you'd like."

"I'm not sure you're ready."

"I'm ready. I swear it."

"You're sure?"

"God, yes."

"Then grab ahold, cowboy. This is going to get wild."

And Lord love her, she was right.

The next morning, Richard rolled out of bed just as dawn turned the sky into an opalescent pink dome.

"Where you going?" KD mumbled, still half-asleep. "It's Sunday."

"For a run. Sorry I woke you."

"You'll be back for breakfast?"

Hearing the anxious note in her voice, he leaned over and gave her a kiss. He knew she was planning to tell her family this morning about leaving the army, and she wanted him there for moral support. "Relax, babe," he whispered in her ear. "I'll be there. Now go back to sleep."

An hour later, he came up the veranda steps, winded and

sweating, then stopped when he saw Mrs. Whitcomb sitting in one of the chairs by the fireplace, watching him. "Morning," he said.

"Have a nice jog?" she asked, eyeing him over the rim of her coffee mug.

"Yes, ma'am, I did."

A tray on the ottoman in front of her held a coffee urn, another mug like the one she held, a pitcher of orange juice, two unused glasses, and a plate of croissants. Almost like she had been waiting for someone—probably him—to accidentally fall into her web.

"It's a beautiful morning, isn't it?"

"Yes, ma'am, it is," he said, blotting sweat from his brow with the sleeve of his damp shirt. He'd been prepared for the heat, but hadn't expected so much humidity. By the look of the thunderheads rolling in from the southwest, they might be in for a rain storm before the day was over.

Smiling, she motioned to the tray. "Join me?"

It was more of an order than an invitation. But he was thirsty, and that juice looked really good. "Thanks," he said. Wondering what kind of interrogation he was in for now, he sat in the chair across from hers. "Did I miss breakfast?"

"No. You and I are the early Sunday risers, it seems. Coffee, juice, or both?"

"Juice would be great."

She poured, then sat back and watched him gulp it down. When he returned the empty glass to the tray, she said, "I'm aware that KD is no longer in the army. Apparently, she told Raney yesterday, who told Dalton, who let it slip to me this morning when he tried to sneak past me to go to the lab. But I wasn't aware that you had quit, too."

Cagey of her, going for a frontal attack, an interrogational ploy he'd used many times himself. Sensing this was another test, he simply gave her the truth. "I didn't exactly quit, ma'am," he said. "I just didn't re-enlist for another tour."

"Because of KD?"

He shook his head. "I'd already started the separation process before Senator Tomlinson pressured the army to cancel the hearing and release her from service instead." He could be cagey, too.

She stared at him without expression for a full ten seconds, then her shoulders slumped on a sigh. Leaning forward, she set her coffee mug on the tray and sat back. "I didn't intend for them to force her to leave the army. Is she upset?"

"More like conflicted."

She looked past him out toward the lawn. "Sometimes, when we care deeply about someone, we're so driven to protect them, we do things we shouldn't."

Having made his own mistakes, Richard understood. And in a way, he owed this woman. If not for her interference, he and KD might not have connected as strongly as they had. "KD's a realist, ma'am. I think she knew her career would be adversely impacted by her injury. Leaving the service was the right thing to do."

"But the army was everything to her."

He shrugged. "Do you think she would have been happy spending the next twenty years behind a desk?"

Her eyes were the same blue as Raney's, although they were shimmering with unshed tears now, and showing less challenge than regret. "I pray you're right."

He could see she was hurting. "She's already thinking about another project," he told her, hoping to lessen her pain. "Something with horses. Ask her about it."

"Horses?" Interest sparked in her eyes. "Like what?"

"You'd best ask her about it. I don't know all the details." He looked down the hall toward the empty kitchen. "When did you say breakfast was?"

"I didn't." She rose and picked up the tray. "But now that we've had our little chat, it should be ready in about thirty minutes."

A truce. He was okay with that. "Then I'd best get cleaned up." He stood. "Thanks for the juice."

"And, Richard," she said before he could escape.

He stopped and turned back.

"Thank you for your honesty. And your loyalty to my daughter."

"I assure you, ma'am, it's no hardship."

Two packages were waiting on the counter when Richard walked through the kitchen. Both addressed to KD, one written in his handwriting. Scooping them up, he headed back to the guest suite.

"Hey," KD said, coming out of the bathroom as he tossed the packages on the bed. "What's that?"

He turned, then went still. As always, whenever he saw KD, even after a short absence, he was struck anew by how beautiful and sexy she was. Especially when she was wearing a skimpy tank top and running shorts.

"You're staring. What's wrong?" Her hand flew up to her hair. "Is something crawling on me? I saw a spider in the bathroom."

"Seriously? A combat vet and you're afraid of spiders?"

"You don't know Texas spiders. What's that?" She eyed the packages.

"You get mail delivery on Sundays?" Richard tossed her the one he hadn't addressed and picked up the larger one. By the weight of it, it held his handguns. In the nick of time.

"We don't get delivery at all. These must have come to our PO box late yesterday." KD opened hers and dumped several books and pamphlets onto the spread. "I had them overnighted."

Richard read the titles over her shoulder. "Horse therapy?"

"I thought I'd do some research." Gathering up the books, she stacked them on the table beside the bed. "Might as well do something constructive, right?" Her eyes flicked over him. "That was a long run, but you're not even sweaty. I'm impressed."

Richard pulled her in for a kiss. She even smelled sexy. A lot better than him. "The run was only about fifty minutes. The chat with your mother was another twenty." He went in for another kiss.

She pulled back. "Oh, Lord. What did she say now?"

Richard pulled off his shirt and tossed it in the corner, then sat down to unlace his running shoes. "She knows you've left the army."

"Damn. Secrets never last in this house."

"She's worried about you, is all."

"She should be. She set it all in motion."

He lifted his head. Had KD forgotten she and Captain Mouton had ignored orders? "You blame her for what the army did?"

"No. Not really." She had the good grace to blush and look away.

Richard went back to work on his laces.

"But she did interfere," she pointed out.

Richard set his runners aside, tugged off his socks, then rose from the chair. "It's a good thing she did. The army could have dragged it out for months, even years, before reaching the same conclusion. But take heart," he said over his shoulder as he walked into the bathroom. "She's about to interfere again."

"Oh, crap. What is she going to do?" KD followed behind him, then stood in the doorway, watching as he finished undressing. "And quit trying to distract me by taking off your clothes."

Pulling back the glass shower door, he turned on the water then grinned back at her. "You could always shower with me."

"I just fixed my hair."

"Fix it again. Or leave it wet."

"Right. Then everybody would know we showered together on a Sunday."

"What does that matter?"

"You don't know Mama. Now tell me what she's got her sights on this time."

"I may have mentioned you had a new project involving horses."

"And?"

Reaching under the spray, he tested the temperature. "And don't be surprised if she wants to help out." As he stepped into the shower, he looked back and waggled his dark eyebrows at her. "Last chance."

"Just hurry. Family breakfast meeting in fifteen minutes."

The dreaded breakfast revelations went better than KD had expected, possibly because Richard was sitting beside her, offering silent support. And eating like he was preparing to meet the enemy. Which he might be, if Farid was headed this way. Raney already knew KD was out of the army, and she had obviously told Dalton, since he didn't seem surprised when KD announced that the army had forced her to take a medical separation. Mama pretended shock, even though they all figured she knew, since Dalton was incapable of hiding anything from Mama. No chance for private conversations in this house.

Relieved to have that behind them, KD moved on to the horse therapy idea. They were immediately intrigued and delighted that KD was working through her recovery toward something more positive. Or maybe they were just tired of her moping around. She certainly was.

Mama, bless her heart, offered to finance housing, which meant she would pay for as many slabs as the patients would need—

"Attendees," KD corrected.

—plus, campaign-style tents to go on top of them, and would also add a tack tent, a shower tent, and maybe a large screened tent for meetings and meals. "Don't we still have that propane cook stove that was in the chuck wagon? That would work for now. And perhaps later," she added with a glaringly bright smile to KD, "if you decide to do this full-time, we can build something more permanent." A subtle inducement to keep KD tied to the ranch?

Raney was all in and knew immediately which horses would be best suited to the PTSD "attendees." Dalton said he and the workers would lend a hand, and Richard added that he could help, too, since he'd worked in construction as a kid and his parents had owned a hardware store, so he knew which tools they'd need. KD took that to mean he intended to stay around awhile, which brightened her day considerably.

In a way, she was a little suspicious of how quickly and happily they had all accepted the idea. She'd just learned of horse therapy and still had a lot of research to do. But her family's enthusiastic response was encouraging.

Then the talk shifted to Khalil Farid, and things turned somber.

Richard and Dalton did the talking. It was clear they had thought through what to do should the Afghan come to the ranch. Both had calm, precise ways of speaking that seemed to ease Mama's and Raney's fears. Although, to KD's ear, Dalton spoke in a monotone, while Richard injected a bit more animation into his husky voice. That, along with his compelling deep blue eyes, unassailable masculinity, and unshakable self-confidence, seemed to draw people in. Mama, most of all. She was all but fawning over him, the hussy. It seemed Sheriff Ford's attentions had awakened something long dormant in her menopausal mother. KD found the idea weirdly disturbing.

Surprisingly, Mama accepted without a fuss that the ranch might be attacked by a revenge-driven Afghan ped-erast and heroin addict. Since she avoided unpleasant news when it suited her, she doubted even a crazed Middle East-ern Taliban sympathizer and suspected murderer would come all this way just for vengeance.

Denial could be a wonderful thing.

Raney was a bit more realistic, insisting she would start carrying her Glock and hold target practice for everyone behind the hay barn, until Dalton convinced her to let him do it, since all that noise and the gunpowder fumes wouldn't be good for the baby.

All in all, the big family talk wasn't as bad as KD had expected. After breakfast was over, everybody scattered—Dalton to give Rosco his morning workout; Mama to whatever church she was gracing now; and Raney up to the nursery to replace all of Lyric's girly décor with something more masculine. She was convinced she would have a boy, the second one on Mama's side since her father was born back in the late 1920s.

Which left KD and Richard on their own as they headed out for her required two-mile walk and to scout potential locations for Tent City, should she decide to start the horse therapy program. There were several suitable spots close to electricity and water but far enough from the other ranch buildings to provide a degree of privacy. The more they talked about it, the more excited KD became. But what about Richard? How would he fit in? Assuming he even wanted to.

"I like this one best," he said later, glancing around a flat, grassy meadow bordered by cottonwoods and the gurgling water of nearby Rough Creek. "It has a relaxing feel to it."

"I don't know. The creek floods after a hard rain, although the bank here is pretty high. I guess we could put in a berm to make it higher. And it's shady, and there's plenty of room to rig temporary corrals for the horses. It might do."

He looped an arm around her shoulders and pulled her against his side. "So you think you're going to do it?"

She tipped her head back and studied his bristly chin, liking the scruffy look of it. "I've got to do something. What about you? What are you going to do?"

He shrugged. "I've got a month to decide before I start cutting into my savings. But right now I'm thinking something in law enforcement. Maybe Homeland Security. I have the right degree, experience, and security clearance. As long as it doesn't entail too much travel, that might work."

"What about all those cats that need rescuing?" She thought for a moment, then said, "Sheriff Ford is retiring soon. Maybe you could try for that." If Richard was elected county sheriff, his office would be in Gunther, which wasn't that far from the ranch. Or that close.

He grinned down at her. "Is this a conspiracy?"

"What do you mean?"

"Dalton suggested I look into the sheriff job, too. Wonder what Ford would say. I'm sure your mother has already had him run a check on me."

"Now's as good a time as any to ask him. His cruiser just turned into the drive. It must be lunchtime."

CHAPTER 15

Sheriff Ford was a lot friendlier this time, Richard noted, and gave him a clap on the shoulder instead of a suspicious stare. His background check must have turned out okay. Maybe he should volunteer a blood draw and urine sample to seal the deal.

"Glad I ran into you, Murdock," the sheriff said, like they hadn't seen each other on this exact spot less than twenty-four hours ago. "Wanted to talk to you about taking on the sheriff's job. With my endorsement and the Whitcombs backing you, you'd be a shoo-in for the job."

That was abrupt. Richard was about to ask him who had suggested him for the job, but KD jumped in ahead of him.

"Did Dalton put you up to this?" she asked with a smile.

The older man gave a sheepish grin. "Actually, KD, it was your mama who mentioned it. She thinks it would be nice having the law on her side, rather than against her."

KD pretended shock. "Sheriff Ford, you're not referring to Deputy Langers, are you?"

"Toby has nothing but respect for your family," the sheriff hedged.

"Except for Dalton."

Ford rubbed the back of his neck. "I'll admit he can sometimes be a bit too vigorous in his duties, but it's part of his job to keep an eye on any convicted felon in the area."

Convicted felon? Dalton? Richard looked at KD in confusion.

She ignored him. "Dalton served his time."

"Yes, he did," Ford said. "But—"

Seeing the thrust of KD's chin, Richard quickly broke in. "Wouldn't your deputy want to step up to the sheriff position?"

"He might. But I'd prefer you." Ford studied Richard, that probing look in his faded gray eyes. When he finally spoke, it was in the tone of a man long accustomed to authority, and with the charm of one who could be a great friend or the shrewdness of one who could be a terrible enemy. "I'll admit I checked you out, son, and I'm impressed with what I learned. With your training, education, and experience, you could take your pick of any of the state or federal law enforcement agencies."

Here comes the "but," Richard thought. And sure enough . . .

"But if you wanted to be your own boss," Ford went on, "with less interference and mostly local travel, then I'd be happy to endorse you for Gunther County sheriff. It's up to you."

"I'm flattered, sir. It sounds interesting and I'd definitely like to know more about it. But right now, we have a situation on our hands that could turn ugly, and we could sure use your help. If you have time, why don't we go to the veranda and talk about it over a pitcher of iced tea?" Richard could be charming, too.

"Lead the way."

"I'll get Dalton," KD offered. "He'll want to be in on this."

As soon as Richard and the sheriff sat down with their glasses of iced tea, Dalton and KD came up the veranda steps. After taking seats in the other two upholstered chairs, they went over it all again—Richard explaining about Khalil, his threats, and what little the army could do about it, and Dalton detailing how they planned to protect the ranch and how many of their workers would be available to help.

The sheriff held up a hand. "Wait. Hold on." He leaned forward in the chair, his expression showing disbelief. "You really think this Farid fellow will travel all the way from Afghanistan to Rough Creek just to avenge his son?"

"We do. My guess is he'll probably come in through Mexico."

"That's crazy."

"It is," Richard agreed. "But Khalil Farid is clearly unstable. Asef was his only son, and our investigation highlighted some pretty unsavory aspects of his character. To Khalil, it's a matter of honor to exact revenge for his son's death as well as the insult to his family name."

"Can he do it?"

Richard nodded. "He's highly motivated and rich enough to pull it off."

Frowning, Ford sat back, obviously still wrestling with the idea that a Taliban sympathizer would come into his jurisdiction to kill the most prominent family in the county he'd been elected to protect. "You got any proof of this?"

Richard battled frustration. He knew how farfetched it sounded. But he had seen the fanaticism in Khalil Farid's eyes, and he had spent enough time in Afghanistan to take such threats seriously. "He threatened me and KD in front of witnesses."

"That doesn't mean he'd carry them out," Ford argued.

"I didn't think so, either, Sheriff, until I got word from

Afghanistan that a female interpreter involved in his son's case had been murdered, and shortly after, Farid and two other men made a midnight run to Pakistan before dropping off the radar."

Ford studied the faces staring back at him with the bemused expression of a man who suspected he was being pranked but wasn't sure.

Richard pressed harder. "I talked to Farid face-to-face, Sheriff. And I saw a man with nothing left—no son, no legacy, nothing but hate. And hate is a hell of a motivator. Especially in tribal Afghanistan."

"You're really convinced he's coming here?"

"I'm convinced we need to be prepared in the event he does."

"Couldn't you make us temporary deputies?" KD suggested. "That way, if there is shooting, we would be in the clear."

"I don't know about that," the sheriff said.

"What about the Posse Comitatus Act?" Richard asked, vaguely remembering a rarely used statute from one of his pre-law classes. "Can't a Texas sheriff call up a posse if necessary?"

Ford gave him a sharp look. "It's not that simple, son."

"Then what would make it simple?" Richard's patience was wearing thin. "You don't have the manpower to sit out here in the hopes Khalil might show up. How are we supposed to protect ourselves?"

"If he's on the watch list and tries to cross, Homeland Security or the Border Patrol will get him."

"And if he comes in illegally?" Dalton asked. "Thousands do it every year."

"The feds have added more border agents," Ford pointed out.

"But they're still undermanned," KD countered.

"Are you willing to risk this family's safety on them catching Khalil?" Richard challenged. "Because I'm not."

Ford gave a deep sigh. "If I did call up a posse—which I'm not saying I will—I can't arm you."

"We have our own guns," KD told him.

"Lord 'a' mercy," Ford muttered. "I'm assuming along with rifles and shotguns, you have handguns. They all registered?"

"Of course," KD said. "We're not lawbreakers."

Ford's gaze shifted to Dalton.

Dalton stared back.

An interesting exchange. Richard would have to ask KD about it later. He was still having trouble accepting that the quiet horse trainer had been in prison.

"Are any of you legally licensed to carry a concealed weapon?" Ford asked.

KD said she was. "Raney and Mama, too."

"I have a Florida concealed carry permit," Richard added. "They have a reciprocal agreement with Texas."

The sheriff looked at Dalton.

The horse trainer gave a tight smile. "You know it's illegal for me to own a firearm, Sheriff. But I'll tell you this. If anyone comes onto this property and threatens my wife or her family, I'll do whatever is necessary to protect them."

Ford shifted tactics. "And your ranch hands? They have guns, too?"

"I don't know. But you're welcome to check."

They all fell silent when a car came up the drive. The parking area wasn't visible from the veranda, but the slamming of a car door indicated someone had pulled in. A moment later, high heels clacked along the walk between the parking area and the veranda.

"Mama," KD muttered.

"Hi-do," Mrs. Whitcomb called, coming up the veranda steps. "Having a party and you didn't invite me? Shame on you. Hello, Lewis."

"Coralee." The sheriff's entire countenance changed as he stood and smiled at Mrs. Whitcomb. She definitely had him by the short hairs. "Been trying to convince Murdock to run for sheriff so I can retire."

Mrs. Whitcomb beamed at Richard. "He can certainly count on my vote."

Apparently, Richard's little chat with KD's mother that morning had done the trick. Seems he'd moved from the suspicious list to the cheerfully accepted list.

"Does Mrs. Whitcomb know?" the sheriff asked Dalton.

"Know what?" Mrs. Whitcomb asked.

"We told her at breakfast."

"Oh, that." KD's mother made an offhand gesture. "You're talking about that Arab person."

"Afghan," Richard corrected.

She waved that away, too. "Of course I know, Lewis. But we're not worried. Not with all these big men watching over us and you on the job."

"They're like horny teenagers," KD muttered under her breath.

Fighting a smile, Dalton reached down and brushed dust off his boot.

Mrs. Whitcomb dropped her purse on the ottoman. "Y'all hungry? Maria is serving roast beef for lunch."

Before any of them could respond, she started snapping out orders like a drill sergeant. "Dalton, wake up Raney, if she's still sleeping. KD, tell Maria the six of us will be eating out here, plus Glenn and Alejandro. Lewis, you and Richard can let the sun shades down and turn on the misters while I set the table. It's Sunday, Richard, so white shirt and tie, please."

"Oops," KD whispered to Richard. "Forgot to mention the dress code."

Mrs. Whitcomb made it to the hall doorway, then turned back. "By the way, KD, while I was listening to the most boring sermon I've heard in years, I found ten-by-twelve wall tents online and ordered six of them. I thought we could have four sleeping tents, a shower tent, and tack tent."

"Who's this 'we'?" KD asked.

Ignoring her, Mrs. Whitcomb added, "I also ordered a big screened canopy tent for meals. I saw TJ after church and told him what we're doing and he said he'll deliver flooring, screws and whatnot for the floors next week, so y'all can get started as soon as you decide on a location. Won't that be fun?"

"What're you building?" Ford asked her.

"KD is going into the horse therapy business to help mental patients."

"Vets with PTSD," Richard clarified. He was beginning to understand why KD had chosen deployment to a combat zone rather than staying at home.

That evening, a weather front blew through, thundered and poured for an hour, then settled in with a slow, gentle drizzle that KD thought would be perfect for cuddling.

Sadly, Richard had other things on his mind. As soon they'd retired to the guest room for the night, he closed the door and said, "Why was your brother-in-law in prison?"

She should have known. The man could give an elephant memory lessons. "Vehicular homicide," she told him. "He probably could have gotten off, but to spare his family, he didn't contest the charges and ended up serving eighteen months of a two-year sentence. Lord, it's stuffy in here. Turn on the overhead fan, will you?"

Richard turned on the fan. "Didn't he have a lawyer? If there was any question of guilt, he shouldn't have taken a plea."

"You sound like a cop."

"I was a cop. More or less."

Plopping down on the foot of the bed, KD let go a deep sigh. "It's been a long, stressful day. Do we really have to go through this now?"

"Yeah, we do. And quit dodging the question with another question. What happened at the arraignment?"

"I'm not dodging. We just don't talk about it." She undid her ponytail and shook out her hair, hoping to distract him.

No luck. "Why don't you talk about it?"

"You're interrogating me now?"

Richard frowned down at her, feet spread, arms folded across his chest. KD thought of it as his "just the facts, ma'am" pose. It made him look spectacularly handsome. And sexy. And very irritated, it seemed.

"I'm not interrogating. I'm asking."

Muttering, KD bent down and unbuckled her sandals. "We don't talk about it because if County Commissioner Adkins found out what really happened, Dalton could get into a lot of trouble."

"Who's that?"

She straightened, the sandals in her hand. "The uncle of the college kid Dalton was supposed to have killed."

"If Dalton didn't kill him, why—"

"Oh my God!" KD threw the sandals through the open closet door so hard they hit the back wall with a thud.

Richard waited.

"Okay. But if I tell you, you have to promise you won't ever say anything about it. Not even to Dalton."

"I promise. What happened at the arraignment?"

She leaned back onto her elbows, hoping to draw his attention to her boobs and away from Dalton's allegedly criminal past. That didn't work, either. "Dalton pleaded guilty," she finally said. "Told the judge that on the night of the wreck, he was moving a tractor across the county road from one field to another. It was late. He was tired. He didn't look before crossing and didn't see the car until it slammed into the side of his tractor."

"Was he hurt?"

"No. But the driver of the car was killed. Jim Bob Adkins. A known speeder with two previous DUIs that his uncle had made go away. There was talk he might have been drunk the night of the wreck. But since Dalton didn't have a trial, and the autopsy report wasn't made public, we'll never know for sure."

"Did Dalton have a lawyer?"

"Didn't want one. Said that since he hadn't looked before crossing the road, the wreck was his fault."

"And that's what he told the judge?"

KD nodded. "Are we done talking about it now?"

"After you tell me what really happened. And the truth, this time."

"For the love of sweet baby Jesus! You're relentless! You know that?" When he just stared at her in silence, she gave up. "Okay. Okay. If you must know, Dalton wasn't the one driving the tractor."

Richard blinked in surprise. "Then who was?"

"His younger brother."

"Why did Dalton cover for him?"

"Because Timmy is mentally challenged. Dalton figured he'd be warehoused in some institution, which would have been a nightmare for poor Timmy, or he'd be sent to prison, which would have been worse. He couldn't do that to his little brother, especially since he was the one who had told Timmy to move the tractor, but had forgotten to remind him to stop and look both ways. And that's the whole story." She flopped back on the bed, arms thrown wide. "So let's drop it."

"Let's not." Richard leaned over, grabbed her hand, and pulled her upright again. "That doesn't make sense, KD. A good lawyer probably could have gotten Timmy off on diminished capacity, or could have brought in the driver's record of DUIs. Maybe his brother would have gotten off with probation."

KD threw her hands up in exasperation. "Probably. Maybe. Who knows? The fact is, Dalton's parents didn't have money for a good lawyer. And even if Timmy had managed to avoid criminal liability, Commissioner Adkins would have filed a wrongful death civil suit against his parents as his guardian. The Cardwells would have been wiped out financially, and they weren't well-off to start with."

"He could have sued Dalton just as easily," Richard pointed out.

"Why? At the time, Dalton didn't have anything for Adkins to take. The way Dalton saw it, eighteen months in prison was a small price to pay to keep his brother safe and his family solvent."

"Damn, KD." Shaking his head, Richard sank down onto the bed beside her. "That's crazy."

"Maybe. But Dalton is still convinced it was the right thing to do. And if the commissioner found out he lied about what happened, he'd come after Dalton, his brother, and his family with everything he's got." She gave Richard a warning look. "You can't say anything to anybody. Ever. Understood?"

"Yeah. But it's still crazy. Is Timmy okay?"

"Dalton's parents sold their place and moved to Plainview. Tim's in a group home and doing great. And that's the end of it."

Richard thought of how he'd walked away from his own brother, and felt again the shame that still haunted him. He admired Dalton for doing what he did, even though it came at a terrible price. Yet somehow, Cardwell had made it through a prison stint without the bitterness or anger Richard had seen in other cons. And now here he was, living the dream. "Are your other sisters as soft touches as you and Raney are?"

"Soft? Me and Raney?" KD laughed. "We're the hard-asses. Wait until you meet dream-chaser Joss and socialite Len. You'll see who's soft."

"Yet you're the ones who took broken guys and tried to make them whole again."

Her smile faded. "Do you really consider yourself broken, Richard? Not because of Emery, I hope."

"More because of my brother. Kenny needed me, and I walked away."

KD understood guilt. She had lived with it for months. It saddened her to see it now on Richard's face. "You tried to help him, Richard. If he wouldn't accept it, that's on him, not you. And I certainly don't think of you as broken. Dalton, either. You both dealt with awful situations, did what you thought was right, suffered for it, and came out stronger. You're amazing guys."

He looked at her in silence for a long time. She hoped he believed her, could see the truth in her eyes.

Finally, he gave that crooked half smile. "Maybe you and Raney are the amazing ones for taking chances on us."

She covered her relief with a smirk. "That goes without saying."

With a predatory grin, he gently pushed her down on her back, then lay across her, chest to breast, his weight on his elbows, his hands framing her face.

"A wise man," he said, "Mark Twain, I think it was, said the two most important days in your life"—he paused to dip down for a kiss—"are the day you're born"—another, longer kiss—"and the day you find out why." He ran the tip of his tongue across her bottom lip. "I think I'm beginning to figure out why I was born."

Her arms slid around his waist and held him tight against her. "Why?" she whispered, and lifted her mouth for another kiss.

"I'll tell you when I'm sure. Right now, I need to see you naked."

Work on Tent City began late the following week.

Within a few days, Hicks had completed the tractor work and put the septic system in, foundations and flooring

for the tents were level and in place, and the therapy horses
had been selected. While Dalton and Raney strung hot-wire
corrals, Alejandro brought in water troughs and began collecting all the tack and grooming supplies the horses would
need for the first session. KD ordered two honey buckets, a
refrigerator, and a thousand-gallon propane tank to be delivered ASAP.

By the end of the next week, the electrical and propane
conduit was in, the water lines had been laid, and the six
10-by-12 tents and the big screened canopy tent had arrived
and were soon set up.

When KD's mother wasn't supervising, she was ordering everything from hot water heaters, kitchen cabinets and
counters, to dinnerware and utensils and furniture for the
tents. Which, thankfully, kept her busy and off-site.

With Harvey's help, Richard put in plumbing for the
shower stalls and valves for the propane hot water heaters
and cookstove, put in a circuit box, wired each tent for an
overhead light, and installed a 220 line for the oversized
refrigerator that would soon be delivered. After a busy
weekend, they called in an electrician and plumber to in-
spect all the wiring and plumbing connections and got the
go-ahead from both, which was a huge relief to Richard.

On Wednesday of the third week, the cots, camp chairs,
and small tables Mrs. Whitcomb had ordered for each tent
arrived, and she and her two daughters stayed out of everybody's way adding decorative touches to make the canvas
residences less stark. Dalton and Alejandro finished a big
stone firepit in the center of the compound, put split log
benches around it, and laid in a generous supply of dry
firewood. And finally, on Thursday, the propane guy arrived, tested all the connections, gave Richard a thumbs-up,
and set the tank. After a site cleanup, the only things missing were the refrigerator, a supply of food, and the two
honey buckets.

Start to finish. Three weeks. Not bad.

Now all they needed were a few traumatized guinea pigs willing to submit to a week of therapeutic horse handling at the Rough Creek Second Chance Rehabilitation Center and a trained therapist to run the show.

"What do you think?" Dalton asked Richard as they walked through the finished tent compound later that afternoon.

"I like it. Has kind of a homey feel to it. Adding the center fire ring and log benches was a nice touch." *Homey? A nice touch?* He was starting to sound like Mrs. Whitcomb.

Dalton's phone buzzed. He checked it and grinned. "The little woman says to hurry home. Dinner's ready."

"She fix it herself?" Richard asked as they headed back to the main house. He couldn't remember seeing any of the Whitcomb women hanging around the kitchen, except to eat.

Dalton snorted. "Hell, no. Woman can hardly make a sandwich. Matter of fact, I don't think any Whitcomb female can cook. Including Mama."

Richard grinned over at him. "Luckily they have other talents."

"Damn straight."

When they walked past the paddocks beside the horse barn, Rosco trotted over to see what they were up to. He was a beautiful animal, and it was clear there was a strong bond between the trainer and the stallion.

"When's his next cutting show?" Richard asked.

"This Saturday. You and KD ought to come."

"KD has to be in Hood on Friday to get her Purple Heart."

Dalton gave the horse a final pat, and they continued toward the house. "She still doesn't want us coming to the ceremony?"

Richard shook his head. "She'd prefer you didn't. Says she might just have them mail the medal to her instead. Sees it as a payoff for keeping her mouth shut, rather than something she should be proud of."

"That's wrong."

"I tried to tell her that. But she's still struggling with the whole thing."

When they neared the house, Richard saw the sheriff's cruiser parked on the drive and wondered how much longer he could put Ford off about running for sheriff. He'd been so busy at Tent City, he hadn't given it much thought. He knew he'd have to make a decision soon or start looking at other jobs. He couldn't stay at the ranch forever. But leaving Four Star would mean leaving KD, too. He wasn't ready for that.

"Maybe while KD's at Hood," Dalton suggested, "she can find a therapist to run the rehab project."

"She plans to." And hopefully, the therapist could figure out why, after a month of mostly calm nights, KD was having anxiety issues again. "She also has an appointment with Wounded Warrior to see if they might cover some of the food costs or help with transportation. I'll be talking to the MPs there, too," he added. "See if they've heard any chatter about Khalil."

Dalton opened the gate onto the back lawn. "It's been almost two months since his son died. You still think he's coming?"

"I do." Richard stopped and faced the horse trainer. "Earlier, I talked to my MP contact in Afghanistan. Still no sign of Khalil, but he confirmed that he'd left the country with two other men. His nephew and a friend of his son."

"Does he still think they're coming here?"

Richard shrugged. "I wouldn't put it past them. These guys love an honor killing, and Khalil Farid is known for them."

The three men from Afghanistan had traveled for many weeks, but soon, with Allah's blessing, they would begin the next part of their journey. In Pakistan, after buying falsified travel papers and new IDs, they had begun the long, circuitous sea route that took them across the Arabian Sea to Mombasa, Kenya, then around the Cape of Good Hope and up the west coast of Africa. Now in Dakar, Senegal, they waited impatiently for the trawler that would carry them across the Atlantic Ocean to Matamoros, Mexico, a small seaport on the Gulf of Mexico, across the border from a place in the state of Texas called Brownsville.

Soon, they would be in the land of the infidels. Their daggers would taste the blood of the savages who had brought dishonor to the Khalil family. Only then could the soul of Asef Khalil rest in peace. It had been a difficult journey and there was still a long way to go. But they were patient men and knew Allah would keep them safe.

CHAPTER 16

Shortly after dawn on Friday, KD and Richard headed out on the five-hour drive to Fort Hood. This time, they took Dalton's blue truck on a test run, since Richard was thinking of buying it. Four Star had two ranch trucks, and Raney had her own truck, so Dalton no longer needed one of his own. Besides, he always drove Rosco to the cutting shows in the ranch truck and trailer with the Whitcomb Four Star logos on the sides. He said it was good advertising. Especially after the stud's fine showing at the Fort Worth Futurity last year, and Dalton had added Rosco's name across the back of the trailer in big, bold letters. KD hoped her brother-in-law would love his offspring as much as he loved that horse.

Having slept poorly the night before, she dozed most of the way to Waco. Nightmares again. Richard had tried to talk to her about it, but she'd put him off, saying it was probably just indigestion. He didn't look like he bought it, but he didn't press her.

KD wasn't sure what was wrong. Everything was going

well. Even though she was tired from all the Tent City prep-
arations, she was proud of the results and totally committed
to the horse therapy project. She even planned to put the
idea of a test run before the members of her former therapy
group when she was at Hood.

She had also found time to spend with the horses they
would use for the project. A bittersweet chore. Although
she wasn't as horse-crazy as Raney, KD had spent her
younger years around horses, and while she'd been away at
school and on active duty, she had missed them almost as
much as her family. The smell of them, the snuffling sounds
they made when she brought them treats, the feel of their
warm, satiny coats beneath her stroking hand, all evoked
so many happy memories.

But since she'd come home, not knowing when, or if, she
would ever be able to ride again, she had purposely stayed
away from the stables. It was hard for her to accept that she
might never feel the sting of wind in her eyes as she raced
across a pasture, or carry a flag in a rodeo procession, or
simply enjoy a quiet, relaxing outing with her favorite
horse. Horses gave so much, and asked for so little in return. But after spending time with them over the last few
weeks, she'd realized equine therapy might be helping her,
too. Her bitterness was starting to fade. Maybe she wouldn't
be able to ride again, but she could still love horses, and
take care of them, and teach others how to do that, too. She
could still stay connected.

Richard was doing well, too. He and Dalton were like
brothers. Even Mama was warming up to him—probably
thinking Richard was her best inducement to keep her
youngest fledgling from escaping the nest a second time.
And his hard work on Tent City had quickly earned him the
respect of the other ranch hands, even overly protective
Alejandro. KD was amazed at what he had accomplished.

Her oldest sister, Len, had made a short one-day trip to
the ranch several days ago—specifically to meet Richard,

Raney said, although she had arrived loaded with gifts from her travels through the Caribbean. Before she returned home, Len gave Richard her seal of approval, wrote the therapy project a check for five thousand tax-deductible dollars, and told KD to bring "her hunk" to Dallas for a visit before her kids decamped for the summer. The only sister Richard hadn't met was Joss. Which was okay with KD. She had enough drama in her life for now.

It was strange, but fun, having two vibrant, oversized, opinionated men around after living so many years in a female household. Card games on the veranda were intensely competitive, and video sessions of *Call of Duty* often lasted well into the evening.

Nights were wonderful. KD never knew sex could be such fun, and falling asleep with Richard by her side should have been all the assurance she needed.

But something was wrong. As construction on Tent City had wound down, her anxiety had increased. Even Richard seemed more restless and distracted. She didn't know if her nightmares were keeping him awake, or if it was his unspoken worry about what he would do after the project was completed. Whatever it was that had them both so wound up, she planned to ask Dr. Prescott to increase her medication again.

Since it was late morning when they arrived in Killeen, they went directly to the base rather than checking into the hotel. As they stopped at Hood's main gate, KD's feeling of alienation returned. That they no longer belonged here was made clear by the careful scrutiny the guard gave their newly issued Veterans' IDs and by the VISITOR PASS they had to display on the windshield. Troops marching past didn't spare them a glance. Even having to circle around to the back of the medical center to find the visitors' lot were all reminders to KD that they were no longer a part of this bustling military community.

"Weird, isn't it?" Richard said as he hunted for a parking space. "Being back, but not really *being* back."

KD didn't answer. That tightness was starting to squeeze her chest again, and she didn't want to worry him. She'd awakened him often enough lately with choking nightmares, and had seen the concern on his face when she'd struggled to catch her breath. Poor guy hadn't signed on to be her personal watchdog. In fact, he hadn't signed on for anything, and now that construction on Tent City was completed, her month with him was coming to an end. She could sense the impatience in him. Richard had lived a regimented, yet transient existence for the last eight years. This lack of direction must be wearing him down.

After he parked the truck and killed the motor, he sat for a moment, looking around as if imprinting on his memory the sights and sounds of the largest active-duty, armored military base in the United States. After a minute, he turned and asked, "You ready for your big day?"

"I've decided to skip the ceremony. Have them mail the medal to me instead."

He didn't hide his disappointment. "You earned that Purple Heart, KD. You should be proud, not ashamed."

She shrugged. If anyone deserved a medal, it was Nataleah. The more KD thought about it, the more convinced she was that Shirley might have been right—the captain had purposely sent KD into the back room of Farid's hut to protect her. Nataleah was the true hero.

Trying to inject enthusiasm into her voice, she asked what he would be doing while she was at her appointments.

"After I check us into the hotel, I'll go by the MP offices and see if they've heard anything new about Khalil." Reaching over the console, he took her hand in his. "The sooner we figure out what he's up to, the better all of us will feel."

It was kind of him to say *all of us*, rather than *you*. "I'm sorry to drag you through this mess, Richard. You're not my babysitter."

"I like being your babysitter. And he threatened me, too, remember."

"Because of what I did." And even more troubling . . . if he stayed, he'd be in danger. But if he left— *No.* She couldn't bear to think about that. "Maybe we should leave," she said on impulse. "Go somewhere he can't ever find us."

"Leave your family to deal with him? Always wondering if he's still out there, looking for us? No. Better we face him now and end it. Then we'll know we're safe."

"But—"

"Quit worrying, babe. You've got half a dozen guys watching out for you. There's nothing to be afraid of. Your mama said so herself."

"She was just putting on a show for the sheriff."

"Then how about you put on a show for me. Maybe later . . . say . . . in the shower." He did that waggly thing with his eyebrows. "The Barkley has really big showers, as I recall."

The man did know how to make her smile. Although she wasn't sure about his obsession with the shower. Breathing easier now, she opened the car door and stepped out, then bent down and blew him a kiss. "Later, smartass."

Her first stop was Dr. Prescott's office to ask if he had any recommendations for a psychologist to run the horse therapy program.

"I'm glad you've decided to do it." He motioned her to one of the chairs by his desk. "Are you intending to put the idea before the members of your old group?"

"Except for those you think might not be suitable candidates."

"Laura and Thomas are back now. I think both would benefit greatly. Laura is the burn victim," he reminded her, as if she would have forgotten in a month. "And Thomas had the TBI—traumatic brain injury. They're doing much better now."

"What about the fidgety one?" KD asked. "I don't remember his name."

"Roberto has moved to a detox facility. But Sarge and Shirley are still here. Perhaps they would be interested."

"Are they meeting today?" The group usually met on Fridays.

"They are." He checked his watch. "In half an hour to be exact."

She asked if she could drop in and see if anybody would be interested. He said she could, then he hesitated, studying her with eyes that appeared bug-like and huge behind his thick lenses. "If I may," he finally said. "I know these people. I've worked with several of them for almost a year. I know their weaknesses and strengths, and what might set them back or help them move forward. If you'd permit, and assuming they're interested in coming to the ranch, I'd like to be group leader for your initial therapy session."

KD was taken aback. Dr. Prescott barely seemed capable of handling the group as it was. And now he wanted to add horses and an unknown environment to the mix? How was that going to work?

"I can see you're hesitant, Miss Whitcomb," he said with a smile. "I know I might seem a bit passive in group. I find that works best when people are dealing with aggression and unfocused anxiety. One mustn't appear challenging or judgmental. But I assure you I am capable of handling these patients. And my being there would avoid the additional stress of having them adapt to a new therapist. What do you think? Shall we give it a try?"

She had definitely underestimated this guy. "Sure. Let's do it."

"Excellent." He pulled the familiar zippered pouch from the lower desk drawer and checked his watch again. "Is there anything else I can help you with?"

"Do you have a contact name for Wounded Warrior? And could you renew my anti-anxiety prescription? Maybe increase the dosage a little? I haven't slept well lately." She hoped she wouldn't have to go into a long explanation of her worries about Richard leaving soon and Khalil Farid showing up at the ranch.

He scribbled a name and number on a piece of paper and handed it to her. "Tell Marilyn I'll be involved with the horse project, too. I told her about it, and she sounded anxious to help. Meanwhile, I'll look over your medications and see about adjusting the dosage." He pushed back his chair and stood. "Check back with me when you drop by the group session."

"Thanks." KD crossed to the door, then hesitated. "By the way, what should we call you? Dr. Prescott seems pretty formal for such a relaxed setting."

"Conan will be fine."

She laughed. "Then I'll be Snow White. See you in group."

"I look forward to it."

Next, KD called the number Conan had given her and asked for Marilyn. When she told her about the horse therapy project she was starting at the ranch, and that Dr. Prescott would be involved, Marilyn said she would be glad to help but would need more information before she took it to the board.

"Why don't I talk to Dr. Prescott and see what he recommends," Marilyn suggested. "Meanwhile, if you could work up projected expenses, what kind of help you're looking for, and some sort of time frame, that will get us started."

KD told her what would help most for now was transportation for the patients from Fort Hood to the ranch and meal expenses while they were there. "We already have places for them to stay and a way to prepare meals. And suitable horses, of course."

After Marilyn said she'd check into it and consult with Dr. Prescott about the patients' needs, KD promised to let her know when their first session would be, then hurried on to the group session.

They seemed almost semi-pleased to see her.

Shirley, the amputee, smiled and welcomed her back. Tommy TBI gave her a goofy smile, although that might have been his new meds. The burn victim, Laura, wasn't crying for once and actually made brief eye contact, and Sergeant Rayfield asked why she wasn't wearing her shiny new medal.

"I'll pick it up later. But I want to talk to y'all about something else." She looked over at Dr. Prescott—Conan. "Is now a good time?"

He nodded.

"Is this about that horse thing?" Sarge asked with a labored sigh.

"It is. And all I ask is that you listen before you make a decision." She waited for nods, waited a little longer for Sarge's, then started in about her horse therapy project.

"Dr. Prescott, or Conan"—she smiled at the doctor—"will be attending, too. He can explain what he hopes to accomplish in the group sessions. I'm here to talk about the facility. I'll provide the horses you'll be using, the wranglers who will be there to help you, and a cook, unless you want to do your own cooking. You'll be living in a rustic tent compound in the middle of a working ranch—no TV, no Internet, spotty cell service—but with miles of trails to hike and billions of stars to contemplate. You may see deer, snakes, coyotes, frogs, or raccoons along the creek, or skunks, squirrels, wild turkeys, possibly a few feral hogs, and various other small critters when you're out and about. It's a beautiful, peaceful setting. I hope you'll enjoy being there. Have any of you spent time around horses?"

Only Shirley nodded.

"That's okay. We can teach you all you need to know."

Shirley asked what they would do with the horses, and KD explained that at first, they would mostly groom and feed the animals until they were comfortable enough to do more. No pressure.

"Sounds like summer camp," Shirley said.

"I ain't doing no crafts," Sarge stated.

KD laughed. "Good. We're not planning any. But you'll have books and cards and games on hand. And your horse. Are any of you interested in giving it a try?"

"I am," Shirley said.

Tommy TBI grinned and shrugged—unless it was a twitch from his medication.

Laura nodded.

Sarge smirked. "I told you I didn't like horses." He looked around at the others, probably checking to see if anyone would try to talk him into coming. When no one did, he shrugged. "But I ain't doing no cooking."

"I'll cook for you, Sarge," Shirley said with a shy smile. "I'm good at it and I love doing it." She looked at the others. "In fact, I'd be happy to cook for everybody, if that's okay."

No dissenters, so KD suggested the others could take turns helping with prep and cleanup. "Dr. Prescott— Conan—can figure out a work schedule."

"Does that mean all of you are attending?" Conan glanced at Sarge.

He shrugged.

The others nodded.

"Great! I have only two rules," KD went on. "The doctor may have others that he will discuss with you later. Rule one: Even though you'll be staying in a remote part of it, this ranch is my home. I ask that you treat it—and all the people who live and work there—with respect.

"The second rule is that you must not mistreat your horse. If you don't feel safe with it, another will be assigned, or we will work with you until you feel comfortable. These are well-trained, even-tempered, experienced horses—bulletproof. Like humans, they can sometimes be stubborn, playful, cranky, lazy, fearful, and have bad days. But unlike humans, their first response is not to immediately lash out when things don't go their way. They'll give you plenty of warning if they're distressed. We'll teach you how to recognize those signals and how to deal with them. But if you're calm and gentle when handling them, and patient if they're slow to respond, you'll easily earn their trust and cooperation."

She paused to look from one to the other. "Break either of these rules—showing disrespect to my home and workers, or using violence against the horses—will get you a quick trip back to Hood. Is that understood?"

Nods all around. Except Sarge, who said, "How long do we have to stay there?"

KD had to smile. "You don't *have* to stay there at all, Sarge. You *get* to stay there. We're thinking a week. But y'all can decide that when you talk to Dr. Prescott. Anything else?"

Blank faces.

Great." She turned to Conan. "Is my prescription ready?"

The doctor handed it over—same dosage, KD saw—and told her to drop by his office later and he would let her know the date they picked for the visit to the ranch.

KD nodded and turned back to the group. "Thanks for doing this test run. We'll have a great time." A final wave and she left.

Now to get her medal with as little fuss as possible. Maybe someone in the administration building could mail it to her. She checked her map of the base, located the building, and headed north. As she walked, she texted Richard, telling him to pick her up there.

A few minutes later, a vehicle pulled over to the curb on the other side of the street. A familiar voice called out the open window, "Hey, good-looking! I got a room and ten bucks. Wanna have a good time?"

Cars driving between them slowed. Walkers turned to look.

That smartass. KD considered ignoring him but figured he would just follow after her, yelling more enticements out the window. "Best bring a friend," she called back. "You don't look up to the task."

A driver passing by honked and gave her a thumbs-up.

Laughter and hoots from two soldiers walking on the other side of the street.

Richard grinned. "Oh, baby, you're breaking my heart!"

Defeated by laughter, KD gave up and crossed the street. "You're such a jerk," she choked out as she climbed into the truck and waved at another car honking as it drove by.

"But you love me anyway."

"Not anymore."

He shot her a questioning look.

Ignoring him, she pointed to the left as he pulled away from the curb. "The admin building is a block over. I'm hoping they'll tell me where to get my medal or will mail to it to me."

"No chance you'll change your mind about the ceremony?"

"Not a one. But on a happier note," she added before he could argue with her about it, "we now have four guinea pigs and a handler willing to come to the ranch for the first horse therapy session."

"Great. When?"

"Not sure yet. The doctor is talking to the group even as we speak."

As soon as Richard pulled into a visitor slot at the admin building, KD hopped out. "I'll be quick as I can."

By the time she found the right office, she had a fine excuse cooked up. But the corporal behind the desk didn't care why she wanted the medal without the ceremony and, after checking her ID, simply handed it over. Sort of anticlimactic. Yet oddly, the moment she had the small box containing the Purple Heart in her hand, she felt like crying. "Do you know if Captain Nataleah Mouton got a medal, too?" she asked.

He turned to his computer, typed, scrolled, typed some more, then sat back. "Yes, she did. Posthumously."

"Could I take it to her family?"

"Already mailed."

"Then can I have her family's address so I can write to them? The captain and I were wounded in the same skirmish. I'd like to tell her folks what a courageous leader she was."

He typed and scrolled some more, made a notation on a sticky note, peeled it off, and handed it to her. "Thanks for your service."

A few minutes later she was back outside, heading across the visitor lot.

"Now where to?" Richard asked when she hopped into the truck. "I'm hungry."

"Medical again to get my prescription filled and find out from Prescott when the group decided to come to the ranch. Then on to our diner to celebrate. And to say goodbye."

That questioning look again. "To me?"

"Yeah. And I get to keep your stuff." She gave him a look. "Of course not, Einstein. Goodbye to all this, and hello to new beginnings."

He started up the truck. "I'm for that. Who's Einstein?"

Their gum-popping, purple-haired waitress wasn't on duty that day—probably at home, slapping on another layer of makeup—but they managed to order anyway. Burgers with fries for him, BLT for her, two chocolate shakes.

"When did you say the group is coming to the ranch?" Richard asked after the waitress left.

"As soon as Prescott can get a van lined up. I hope it's not too soon. We still don't have a refrigerator."

"We can make do with coolers. Who all's coming?"

KD gave him a brief rundown on the group members and Conan. "They seem pretty interested."

Their order came. As soon as they took the edge off their appetites, KD asked what the MPs had learned.

"Nothing. No chatter, no suspicious movements, no cryptic messages coming out of Afghanistan, no bloated bodies baking in the desert."

KD made a face. "Way to kill a girl's appetite."

"The point is"—he waved a limp fry for emphasis—"I'm beginning to think Khalil Farid was all talk and no bite. A sniveling coward. I bet he's not even coming."

"Yeah? How much?"

He chewed and thought for a moment. "Two dollars."

"Not much of a bet."

"I'm not much of a gambler. You going to finish that sandwich?"

While he ate everything on his plate and hers, KD thought about what she should do. As long as Khalil was a threat, Richard would hang around. And then what? And what about the horse therapy? Would he want to stay for that? She could almost feel him slipping away and realized this might be the last time in a while they'd be alone, on their own, without her family looking on.

"Let's go camping," she said on impulse. "Just for the night. I know a great little park on the way back to the ranch. There's even a lake. You'll like it."

"We don't have a tent."

"We might not need one." She picked up her phone and scrolled through the weather app. "Low seventy-three, clear skies, not much moon. Perfect for stargazing. We can sleep in the bed of the truck and watch the Milky Way slide across the sky."

"More like rotating than sliding," he pointed out. "The Milky Way is anchored by the North Star."

"Whatever. We can pick up air mattresses and bug spray and lightweight blankets and picnic supplies on our way out of town. It'll be fun."

"But I already booked our suite. The one with the big shower."

"Why are you so obsessed with showering?" Seeing that

gleam in his blue eyes, she laughed. "Forget I asked. But we leave first thing in the morning."

"After our morning shower."

"I don't plan to get that dirty."

"I do. I'll show you how."

That night, Richard awoke to find KD's side of the bed empty. He listened, heard nothing from the bathroom, then tossed back the covers and rose. She was in the main room, sitting in the dark on the couch. The window drapes were open, and a floodlight in the courtyard highlighted the tears on her face. As he stepped closer, he saw the glint of medal in her hand. Her Purple Heart.

Oh, babe.

He walked over and sat next to her on the couch. Then he waited.

After a while, she said, "It keeps coming back, you know? Over and over. Until Farid shoots me and I wake up. Nothing changes. Until tonight."

"What was different tonight?"

"I fired back before I woke up."

A mile away, the giant speakers at Fort Hood blasted out "Reveille." The glow of the courtyard floodlight faded as the sky took on the pink tint of dawn. Minutes passed before she spoke again. "At West Point we were told our first mission is to stay alive. Dead soldiers can't fight, and the army with the most soldiers still standing wins the war. I survived. He didn't. Strategically speaking, I did the right thing. I deserve this medal."

She turned to him, her eyes shimmering with tears. "So why do I feel so bad?"

"Why would you? You did what you were trained to do." Despite being a good soldier, KD wasn't a cold killer. Emotionally, Farid's death had hit her hard. Intellectually, she knew she was right to defend herself, but she would still struggle with it for a long time. "You probably saved your life and the boy's."

"Maybe."

Unable to hold back any longer, he lifted her onto his lap and cradled her against his chest. "It'll get better, babe," he murmured into her hair. "You'll get better. Then you'll know you did the right thing."

"I hope so."

"I know so. Just give it time."

After a few moments, she slid her arms up around his neck. Lifting her face to his, she kissed him then whispered, "I don't want you to leave."

"I'm right here, babe. I'm not going anywhere."

"But I don't want you to stay, either."

He drew back to look at her. "Why?"

"I don't want to lose someone else I care about because of what I did."

Farid. Everything came back to that fucking asshole. "You think I can't protect you?" He said it more forcefully than he'd intended.

She tipped her forehead against his jaw. He heard the hitch in her voice and knew she was fighting tears again. "I know you can. And would. Even at the cost of your own life. That's why I'm afraid for you to stay."

"I'm not going to die, KD. I've got too much to live for." He wrapped his arms tightly around her, as if that might drive all the fear and worry from her body and into his. He would do anything for this woman. Including stay, whether she wanted him to or not.

Slowly, in tiny increments, she relaxed against him. Lifting her face to his, she whispered into his ear, "Take me to bed, lover."

"Seriously?" He drew back. "After you said earlier I wasn't up to the task? I'm not sure I should."

"Okay." As she spoke, she ran a hand up under his tee.

His breath caught, then escaped in a rush. "But then, you

do seem remorseful. And I'm a generous and forgiving man."

A gentle tug on his earlobe with her teeth. "Are you?"

"I am. Hopefully, you've learned your lesson."

"Teach me again," she whispered, gently raking her nails down his chest.

"If I must."

CHAPTER 17

After checking out of the suite the next morning, KD and Richard stopped for lunch at another "Best in Texas" rib joint near the Lampasas interchange. While they ate, they discussed what was needed to finish Tent City.

"Have I told you how much I appreciate all you've done?" KD told him.

"Talk is cheap. But you can show your appreciation later if you'd like."

She laughed and bounced a green bean off his shoulder. But in truth, she wouldn't have tackled such an involved undertaking without Richard's help. He'd been invaluable, and they worked so well together, she felt like she'd known him far longer than just a few weeks. Every day she was impressed anew by how well he got along with her family and the workers, and how much effort he put into a project that wasn't even his. There had to be a fault somewhere, but she'd yet to see it. Other than the shower obsession. Not that she was complaining.

"Tell me more about your guinea pigs," he said over his baby back rib.

"They're good people. Even Sarge. But they've been through a lot, so we'll have to go really slow at first." She would have to give a heads-up to the "staff" on each of the attendees so everybody would know what to expect. But she was still worried . . . for the patients, as well as herself. She'd invested so much hope into this project and was determined that nothing go wrong. If she failed at this, too . . .

She blocked that thought. "Do you have much experience with horses?"

"Some. I had a summer job with a local outfitter taking city folks on horse pack trips into the mountains. Hopefully these guys won't be as much trouble as they were. You finished with the slaw?"

KD nodded. "I always wanted to take a pack trip." It had been a lifelong dream she had shared with Daddy. But after he died, she'd buried it with him.

"Why didn't you?"

"Ran out of time, I guess." And now that she did have the time, her after-market hip probably wouldn't allow it. A sad thought. She'd loved riding. But at least with the therapy project, she could still be around horses.

A few minutes later, they were back on the road and KD put those dismal worries behind her. It was too pretty a day for sad thoughts.

The park was small by Texas standards. Because it was Saturday afternoon, and June was the beginning of the high season for meteor showers and stargazing, every campsite was taken. Luckily, since they didn't need a tent pad or firepit, and KD used her best smile on the gawky young park ranger, they were allowed to park overnight in the overflow area by the boat ramp at the lake.

KD thought it was better than a campsite, since their only neighbors were empty boat trailers and there were picnic tables and a shower house with flush toilets nearby.

They decided to hike first, and it was dusk when they returned to set up camp. Leaving Richard to inflate the air mattresses in the bed of the truck and unbag the blankets they'd bought at a discount store outside of Brownwood, KD took their cold cuts, cheeses, pints of various salads, and soft drinks to a picnic table by the dock. The evening was mild and clear, eerily quiet after the noise and bustle of Fort Hood. With not much moon overhead, it was ideal for watching stars—once they slathered on enough bug repellant to send the mosquitoes elsewhere.

After they'd eaten and cleaned up, they climbed into their makeshift beds in the back of the truck and KD snuggled up to Richard's shoulder to watch for meteors and satellites. "Bet they don't have this in Washington."

His deep voice rumbled through his chest into her ear. "Actually, they do, as long as you're east of the mountains. The western side is too cloudy and rainy, and there's too much ambient light for stargazing. But this is perfect."

She kissed his neck. "Yeah. Perfect."

Full dark settled around them. To the east, a family of coyotes called to one another. By the lake, crickets and frogs began their own serenades, and above them, the sky exploded with stars. It was an amazing display, and so peaceful and intimate, it felt as if the whole world slept and the light show overhead was just for them.

They lay on their backs, side by side, rarely speaking except to point out the tiny, faint trail of a satellite bobbing through the clusters of brighter pinpoints of light. The Milky Way was so strewn with stars, KD said it looked like silver glitter sprinkled across a black gauze scarf. Richard argued it looked more like a smoky trail of embers, until she pointed out that embers were yellow, not white, and he got tired of talking about it and kissed her into silence.

"Puts things in perspective, doesn't it?" KD said after a while.

Slipping an arm under her neck, he pulled her closer. "What things?"

"Life, loss, our small successes and petty failures. We're so insignificant in the grand scheme of things, and yet still part of something this vast and beautiful and unfathomable."

"Didn't know I was sleeping with a philosopher."

She poked his ribs. "What do you think when you look up there?"

"I think, at this moment, I'm the luckiest guy in the world."

"How so?"

"I've got you by my side."

"Aw, that's sweet." She stretched up and kissed him on the lips, then cuddled back against his side. She would miss this. Having him within reach. Feeling his heart beat against her cheek. "I feel lucky, too. And a little sad."

"Why sad?"

"You'll be moving on soon. I'll miss you. That makes me sad." *More than sad. Crushed.* KD was glad it was too dark for him to see that in her eyes.

It was several minutes before he responded. "Why do you think I'll be moving on soon?"

She struggled to keep her voice light. "You can't be my boy toy forever, although you're really good at it."

"What if I want to?"

"You won't. Before long, you'll want to start the next phase of your life. Find out what's waiting for you now that you've left the army. Finish figuring out why you were born." *And I'll be alone again.*

Another pause. "Maybe I already know why I was born and I'm just trying to work up the courage to do it."

"Do what?"

"Try marriage again."

Marriage? Not what KD had expected to hear. She didn't

know what to say. Or what *he* was saying. Was this some sort
of oblique proposal? The thought made her chest tight. Marriage had never been a priority with her. Maybe because there
hadn't been a man she had cared enough about to consider it.
Her career had always been her main focus. Marriage could
be difficult in the military, especially if the wife was the
soldier—being absent from her family for long periods, up-
rooting the children every time she got a new posting, putting
her career above her husband's. But that was all a moot point
now. KD was no longer a part of the military. So why did the
thought of marriage make her so nervous? "After Emery, I'm
surprised you would consider marrying again."

"I swore I never would. But lately, I've been thinking
about it a lot."

"What changed your mind?"

"You. This. Us. We're good together, KD. We understand one another and can speak the truth to each other."
His chuckle vibrated in her ear. "You make me laugh. And
think. And want to do better. And on a more practical level,
I get a hard-on just watching you walk by. Want to see?"

"Maybe later."

"It may be gone then."

"I'll try to think of a way to bring it back."

"I look forward to it."

When he said nothing more, her anxiety rose. Her feelings for Richard were stronger than any she'd ever felt
before . . . but marriage? It was too soon. Too final. Couldn't
they just go on like they were? Indecision was intolerable
to KD. She hated having things unsettled, not knowing
what to do or what to expect. But she made herself wait him
out. He'd brought it up—he should be the one to finish it.

Overhead, a satellite passed slowly by. A star fell. Distant
voices of other campers intruded. Her patience snapped.
She had to say something, even if it was a mistake. "So . . .
despite being good together and wanting to do better and
getting hard-ons, you never mentioned love." *There*. She'd

said it. Love should come before marriage. There was even a song about it.

Beside her, Richard went absolutely still. A long pause, then, "Do you need me to?"

"Hell, Richard. How can you propose marriage when you can't even admit to love? How's that going to work?"

"When did I propose?"

She tilted her head back to look at him. In the dimness, she couldn't read his expression, but she could feel the tension in the big body next to hers. "Didn't you just say that because of me you were considering marriage again?"

"Well . . . yeah. But I didn't mean right now. It's too soon. Don't you think it's too soon?"

"Oh my God." She started to laugh.

"What's so funny?"

"You scared the shit out of me. I thought you were proposing." She settled back against him, relieved to have that settled. But it still bothered her that neither of them had mentioned love.

"Would it be so bad if I did propose?" he asked after a while.

"No, but you'd have to love me first." And she wanted to be certain he'd gotten over his disastrous marriage to Emery. KD wanted no ghosts between them. She wouldn't be judged by his first wife's failings. If she could have, she would have wiped those memories from his mind forever.

"Maybe I already do love you."

Maybe? "You don't sound very sure."

"I'm not sure I even understand the concept."

"Of love?" She felt him nod. "What about your family?"

"You mean my toxic, drug-addicted, unforgiving family?"

"You must have loved them at one time, or you wouldn't still be so hurt."

He didn't respond. Afraid she'd overstepped, she put her arm around his waist. "I'm sorry. I shouldn't have said that. I wasn't there."

"But you're right. I did love them. I still do. I just don't understand them."

Time passed. In the trees along the shore, night birds chirped; out in the lake, something splashed, while overhead, the sky darkened from deep blue to velvety black and more stars appeared. Finally, as if he'd spent the long silence mulling it over, he said, "What I feel for you, KD, is stronger than anything I've ever felt for anyone. Including my family. You're on my mind first thing every morning and last thing at night. Thoughts of you circle in my head all through the day. Things you've said. Things that made you happy or sad or worried. Things I could do to make you smile, or keep you safe, or make you want me as much as I want you. Is that love? I don't know."

Her head slid off his arm as he rolled toward her until they were face-to-face. His big hand cupped her cheek. "But what I do know is that living a life without seeing you every morning and sleeping beside you every night isn't a life I want. I need you, babe. And I think we're stronger together than apart. More complete."

Emotion pressed against her throat. It was a moment before she could speak. "I agree. I think marriage would only make life better for both of us. But . . ." Richard deserved a second chance at fatherhood after what he'd been through. If she couldn't give him that, would he still want her? Was that what made her so afraid?

"But what?" He tapped her cheek. "Say something. Give me hope, at least."

"Full disclosure?"

"Always."

"Because of my injury, I may not be able to have children."

He let out a huff of air that fanned her eyelashes. It had the sound of relief. "I know. And I'm sorry. You'd make a wonderful mother. But it's not a deal breaker."

"It doesn't matter to you?"

"You're what matters to me, KD." He leaned in for a kiss, then drew back. "Eight years ago, I would have said there was absolutely no way I'd ever marry again. But you blindsided me, babe. I didn't see you coming until you knocked me off my feet."

Those words sang through her mind. Unable to stop herself, she pressed a kiss to the hollow of his throat, felt his pulse beat against her lips. Vital. Alive. Hers for the taking.

"Tell me you feel the same way, KD. Don't leave me hanging."

Reaching up, she brushed her fingertips across his bristly cheek. "I do feel the same way, Richard. You're my man. When I'm with you, I feel whole and safe and . . . happy. But let's give it a little more time. Get this Khalil thing behind us. Figure out what you're going to do. What I'm going to do. Whether the horse therapy idea is a go or not. No need to make any decisions now. We've got time to think it through."

And maybe by then, we can admit to love.

It wasn't the answer Richard expected. Or had hoped to hear. But it wasn't a brush-off, either. And it made sense.

If he took a job that sent him somewhere else, would KD be willing to leave the ranch and her family? And if she decided to go full-time on the horse therapy thing, would he be willing to stay at Four Star? It wouldn't be a hardship, living in the lap of luxury at the ranch. But for a solitary person like him, it might not be easy, either. The place already had a clannish feel to it, although he wasn't sure if that was a good thing or bad.

KD was right. No need to rush it. Take care of Khalil, see if the sheriff's job was something he might be interested in, then talk it over again. "Okay," he agreed, and pulled her in for a long, slow kiss. "Oh, look," he said a few minutes later. "That pesky hard-on is back. Whatever will we do?"

KD laughed. "I have an idea." She slid her hand down, gave him a gentle squeeze. "How's that?"

"I'm not sure. Do it again."

Dawn is a real eye-opener when you're sleeping in the bed of a pickup. One moment, Richard was dreaming of KD's breasts, and the next, he was blinded by sunlight hitting him full in the face and had a mosquito buzzing in his ear.

Or maybe that was KD's phone.

Or maybe the little boy sitting on their picnic table, staring at them, had said something. No, it was the phone, he realized, when he heard it buzz again.

Beside him, KD bolted upright, hair poking out every which way. "What the—" She looked around, saw the boy watching them, and flopped back down.

"Better answer that," Richard advised when her phone buzzed a third time.

She dug through the blankets, found her cell, punched *Accept*. "Yes? Oh. Hello, Dr. Prescott. No, I was up." Leaning up on one elbow, she shot Richard a *what the hell* look, saw the boy still staring at them, and yanked the blanket over her mostly bare chest. "You did? What did she say?" A pause. "That soon?" Now the look showed panic. "Of course it's not a problem. I'll alert our staff."

Dropping the phone onto the blanket, she quickly straightened her tank top so it covered her breasts. Much to Richard's disappointment. "That was Dr. Prescott."

"I heard. Scoot over. You're on my pants."

"Shh. Is he still there?"

"Prescott?"

"The boy."

As she tugged his jeans out from under her butt, KD peered over the side of the truck.

The boy was still there.

"How long has he been watching us?" she asked, lying back down and digging for her shorts.

"I don't know." Richard kicked and bucked, struggling to pull his jeans on under the blanket. "I just woke up."

"Where are my shorts? Do you have my shorts?"

"Why are you whispering?"

"Found them." More squirming and twisting. "We have to hurry."

"Why?"

"Wounded Warrior is loaning us a van. But it's only available next Friday."

"That's almost a week away."

"Five-and-a-half days. But we're not ready. The refrigerator hasn't been delivered, we haven't stocked the kitchen, and the honey buckets won't come until Tuesday or Wednesday. Is the boy still there?"

"No. But his parents are."

"Shit."

"You decent yet? I need to use the head."

"Race you."

When they turned onto the ranch drive two hours later, Richard saw Raney supervising two people who were pulling luggage from a BMW in the rear parking area. "Looks like you have company," Richard said.

"That's just Joss and Grady and baby Lyric. Brace yourself."

The last time KD had said that was before he'd met her mother. Richard wondered if this meeting would be as stressful. "Brace myself for what?"

"You'll see. Just don't encourage her. Joss can be a little dramatic sometimes. Especially when she sees a handsome guy."

He grinned over at her. "You think I'm handsome?"

"I think you're adorable."

"Sounds girly."

"You're anything but girly. And try not to smile. You're especially adorable when you do. Hey, Joss!" KD climbed out of the truck as soon as it stopped and walked toward a pretty woman wearing a fringed leather vest and a multi-colored clown wig. "How was the concert?"

"Great! I even got an encore. Grady, get Lyric. Raney, that's too heavy for you. Who's that in Dalton's truck?"

"Richard Murdock. An army guy I brought home."

Richard frowned. *An army guy?* That's all he was? *Bullshit.* Putting on his best smile, he came around the hood of the truck. "You must be the famous sister Joss. KD told me you're a star. I can see why."

Before she could respond, he pulled her into a bear hug. "Hope I'm not being forward," he said over her head with a wink at her gawking sisters. "But since KD and I are practically engaged, I feel like we're already family."

It wasn't a clown wig, he realized when she jerked back, almost knocking into Raney, curls bouncing.

"Engaged!" She whirled toward KD, bangles and bracelets clanking. "When? Why didn't you tell me? Oh my God! I can't believe it! Grady! Come meet KD's fiancé!"

"Fiancé?" Raney looked from one to the other, eyes round as blue marbles.

You'll pay, KD's scowl warned him.

Bring it, his grin said back.

While Joss and Grady loaded their luggage and baby upstairs to the half-redecorated nursery, Raney cornered KD and Richard. "Is it true? Y'all are engaged?"

"No," KD blurted out before Richard could say anything. "We've talked about it, but nothing is official yet." The acid glare she sent him told Richard she was working through various payback scenarios. But rather than antagonizing her more by pretending innocence, he simply asked where Dalton was.

"The techs are here, running labs on the bulls. His second most hated task."

"What's his first?"

"When they draw the semen."

He didn't ask any more questions.

From an upstairs window came Joss's yell. "Raney! What did you do to the nursery? Where's all Lyric's stuff? Mama!"

"Mama's on a date with the sheriff," Raney yelled back.

"Then you better come up here and straighten this out!"

"Coming." To KD and Richard she added, "I can't wait until our house is done."

The next few days were a mad dash to get Tent City ready for occupancy. The refrigerator finally came, the honey buckets were delivered and set up, and Maria made sure the kitchen was stocked. By the time Friday came, Mama had worked herself into a dither planning all sorts of social activities to entertain "her guests."

"These are VA patients with adjustment issues, not guests," KD had reminded her several times. "And most of them are on meds and not allowed alcohol, so they won't be in festive moods. Plus, they might be dangerous."

"Dangerous?" Mama would collect any stray that came along—sick, injured, lost, whatever. But if she thought any posed a danger, she kept her distance.

Before KD could answer, Richard cut in. "They're not armed, ma'am. But you might want to lock up at night."

"I can't even serve dessert on the veranda?"

"Best not, Mama. Sugar doesn't help."

"But we should do *something*." Mama took her hostess duties very seriously.

Dalton saved the day by convincing Sheriff Ford to take Mama to Fort Worth for a few days. KD didn't want to think about what they would be doing while they were there. But at least Mama would be gone when the guinea pigs arrived.

The Wounded Warrior van drove through the front gate just after lunch on Friday. Dr. Prescott felt it would be less stressful if the patients could avoid introductions upon arrival, so KD met them in Richard's pickup and led the van down to Tent City, all the while praying that she wasn't making a colossal mistake. But when the van stopped in the compound and she saw the faces looking through the windows with various expressions of worry, hope, and maybe a little excitement, she began to believe this project might actually work.

Dr. Prescott—Conan—hopped out first, armed with his blue zipper pouch and his self-effacing smile.

Shirley exited next, returning KD's greeting with a grin of excitement and her new prosthetic leg. "The doctor said I could ride! As long as I don't fall off."

"You won't," KD assured her, and hoped she was right.

When Tommy TBI climbed out, he seemed fairly lucid for once, and actually seemed to remember where he was and why he was there.

Sarge ignored KD altogether. Last out was Laura, wearing a timid smile and a scarf over the burned side of her face.

Except for Drummer Boy, they had all taken a leap of faith and made the trip. Suddenly, KD realized she was doing the right thing. She didn't know if she could help these troubled soldiers, but she desperately wanted to try.

"Welcome to Whitcomb Four Star," she said, determined to make this week a memorable one. She gave them their tent assignments, pointed out the dining tent, the shower tent, and the honey buckets, as well as the tack tent and hot-wired paddocks, which were empty for now. Conan told them he had a few announcements and for them to

meet back at the fire ring in the center of the compound
after they had settled in.

While the others wandered around, getting their bearings, Shirley dumped her duffle in her tent then went to
scout out the kitchen. KD went with her to explain where
everything was and how to work the ancient propane cookstove.

Fifteen minutes later, the group gathered on the log
benches around the firepit. During Conan's announcements
about medications, schedules for meals, cleanup, and group
meetings, KD texted Dalton to bring the horses.

As soon as Conan turned the meeting over to her, KD put
on her brightest smile. "Y'all ready to meet your horses?"

Varying degrees of enthusiasm. Then wariness turned to
interest when Richard, Dalton, Alejandro, and Chuy came
through the trees, leading the horses.

Each newly appointed wrangler had been thoroughly
prepped about his assigned rider, and the horses were chosen
to fit each participant's specific needs. No fast movements
around Tommy TBI, so Chuy handed him the lead rope of the
oldest and calmest horse on the ranch. Dandy wasn't a dead
head, but it took a major event to get a rise out of him, and he
hadn't spontaneously broken into a gallop in over five years.

Since Alejandro was a charmer with a strong protective
streak, he was to help Laura, and he assured her that Roy,
the handsome, sweet-tempered gelding assigned to her, was
the gentlest and friendliest horse on the ranch. Richard led
Bob, a lively, but well-mannered chestnut gelding, to Shirley, who was almost beside herself with excitement. KD
hoped it was because of the horse, not the gorgeous hunk
of human masculinity assigned to help her. Dalton, who
was accustomed to keeping his temper when dealing with
stubborn, headstrong animals, introduced Rocky, a big, experienced, trail-wise bay gelding, to Sarge. Hopefully they
wouldn't kill each other.

After the wranglers explained the likes and dislikes,

quirks and preferences of the horse assigned to each rider, they stepped back to let the horse and the pupil get to know each other.

Tommy TBI mostly grinned and stroked Dandy's neck. Dandy mostly dozed.

Roy didn't seem to mind Laura's scars, and within minutes, she was laughing and scratching his chin like Alejandro showed her.

Shirley ignored the gorgeous hunk of human masculinity altogether and concentrated on giving Bob whispered endearments and a good scratch behind his ear.

Sarge and Rocky and Dalton largely ignored one another.

But it all seemed to go well, to KD's relief. None of the horses misbehaved, and most of the humans seemed happy with their new, long-faced friends. And with that, the first session of horse therapy at the Rough Creek Second Chance Rehabilitation Center began.

CHAPTER 18

After almost two months travel over sea and land, the three Afghans arrived in Matamoros, Mexico just after noon. There, they were met by four armed cartel soldiers who searched them for weapons, took the old Afghan's valise, and gave them hoods to put over their heads. It was hot and hard to breathe under the hoods, but the Afghans said nothing.

For an hour, they drove on a bumpy road with many bridges and sharp turns, until the car clattered over a metal barrier and stopped. The driver spoke to someone outside of the car, then they drove on for another distance, slowed, and stopped again. This time, they were taken out of the vehicle and turned over to two other armed men, who allowed them to remove their hoods.

When they did, one of the new cartel soldiers laughed and pointed at the older Afghan's face. "Él tiene una cicatriz también."

The other man snickered, which made the Afghan angry. Although he spoke English well, he did not speak

Spanish, and he did not like the way these Mexican infidels looked at him when they laughed.

But he remained silent. He had other slights to address.

The two soldiers led them into a low metal building painted the color of the foliage around it and screened by brush and dozens of tall palm trees. A sharp breeze that smelled of the sea rattled the palm leaves, but the air was so damp and humid the sweat on their faces from wearing the hoods was slow to dry.

They were searched again, then given water to drink. The valise was returned to the older Afghan, and they were led up a sandy path to another metal structure, this one partially buried into the side of a tall, brushy sand dune. Two men with automatic rifles stood outside, watching their approach. A third man waited in the open doorway: Caracortada—Scarface—the leader of the newly formed and highly ambitious Matamoros Cartel.

"I am Khalil Farid," the old Afghan said in English to Caracortada. He had been told the cartel leader also spoke and understood that language. "I bring to you a gift and a proposition. All I ask in return is a small favor that is well within your powers to grant."

Late Saturday afternoon a week after the attendees had arrived, the Whitcomb sisters—minus Len—and their significant others sat on the veranda, awaiting the call to dinner. Without Mama there, they'd decided to eat on the veranda rather than the formal dining room. With the sunshades down and the misters on and the two water coolers Mama installed every summer blasting away, the outdoor room was as cool as a November Sunday.

Dalton and Raney shared one chaise. KD and Richard shared another, Richard slouched against the backrest, legs straddling the chaise, feet on the floor, while KD half reclined with her back against his chest. Joss stretched out in

the third chaise, Lyric sleeping on her stomach, while
Grady slumped in one of the upholstered chairs, head back,
mouth sagging open, snoring. Apparently, he'd been on
baby duty the previous night.

It had been a long week, getting the horse therapy project
off the ground. Yet KD thought it was going well. Nobody
had been thrown, kicked, or bitten. Horses, either. Shirley's
cooking was getting rave reviews. Tommy TBI hadn't wandered off yet, and Laura had smiled once at Alejandro. Even
Sarge had quit complaining and seemed in strangely high
spirits whenever Shirley was around. Plus Mama was too
busy doing God knows what with the sheriff to interfere.

Suddenly Joss bolted upright on her chaise, almost tum-
bling her sleeping daughter off her lap. "I've got an idea!"

Grady stopped mid-snore, roused himself to look around,
saw nothing unusual, then dropped his head back again.

"She has an idea," KD murmured.

"Should I brace myself?" Richard murmured back.

"Might be wise."

Joss ignored them. "To celebrate KD's and Richard's
soon-to-be-announced engagement, we should go out to
Harley's Roadhouse tonight!"

"Tonight?" KD was already so tired, she could barely
keep her eyes open.

"I have to go out there anyway," Joss went on. "Grady
scheduled me to do a benefit for those people from Gunther
whose house burned down. It'll be fun! Sort of a last hoo-
rah before parenthood claims Raney and Dalton and wedding plans tie up Richard and KD."

"Do we have wedding plans?" Richard asked.

"No!" KD barked, felt Richard tense, and immediately
softened the denial. "Not yet." She was running out of patience trying to convince everybody, including Richard, that
they weren't officially engaged. She wanted it done right, and
at the right time. Which meant telling Mama first, and when
she was ready, and after Richard issued an actual proposal.

"Count me out," Raney said. "Since I can't drink now, and I never could dance, it's a waste of my time. Besides," she added, with a glance at Dalton behind her, "after what happened last year, the place has bad memories for me."

"What happened?" Richard asked.

"Two guys picked a fight with my husband."

Richard grinned at Dalton. "What'd you do to them?"

"Put them in the hospital, that's what!" Joss crowed. "The fat one still limps and the other guy hears bells every time he shakes his head."

Raney wasn't amused. "It was awful. The scariest thing I've ever seen, the way they came at him."

Dalton kissed his wife's head. "Don't get worked up, sweetheart. It wasn't that bad and you'll upset the baby."

"It was definitely bad for those two asshats."

Their cook, Maria, appeared in the hallway to announce that dinner was ready and for them to come into the kitchen and dish up their plates. As if on cue, Alejandro and Hicks came up the veranda steps.

Hearing the two newcomers enter woke Grady. "Time to eat?" He rubbed his hands over his face and yawned. "Sorry. Must have dropped off. Did I hear something about going out to the roadhouse tonight?"

Cradling Lyric in her arms, Joss rose and frowned at her older sister. "Raney won't go."

"Then maybe she can babysit," Grady suggested, falling in behind his wife as they all headed into the kitchen.

It was apparent to KD that the new father needed a break. And equally apparent that Joss hadn't thought about who would babysit her daughter while she was out kicking up her heels, guzzling beer, and charming the locals. Immediately, her frown became a smile. "That's perfect! It'll be great practice for her."

"I don't wanna," Raney whined as she loaded her plate. "I'm tired."

Fearing if Raney bailed, she and Richard would be re-

cruited, KD quickly announced that she and Richard were
going. "He was just saying he wished he could hear you
sing, Joss."

Richard muttered something KD didn't catch.

"Great! Then it's settled! Grady, sweetie, Lyric needs
changing. I'll fill you a plate."

*The two younger Afghans were told to wait while Khalil
Farid and two of the cartel soldiers followed Caracortada
to his office inside the half-buried building. There, Khalil
was given a chair facing a massive carved desk, while
Caracortada sat in a throne-like chair across from him.*

It was difficult for Khalil not to avert his eyes.

*Caracortada was hideously disfigured by a long, jagged
scar that bisected his face from hairline, through his right
eye, and down to the right corner of his mouth. His right
eye was a milky white mass of scar tissue. The wound had
been stitched badly and pulled the Mexican's mouth into a
permanent grimace. Khalil carried his own scar, but his
did not make him look like a monster.*

*"I am listening," the cartel leader said in a mumbling
voice that made Khalil wonder if his tongue had been cut,
as well.*

Khalil put his valise on top of the desk.

*Immediately, the two soldiers stepped closer, guns drawn
and pointed at Khalil's head.*

*"Alejarse," Caracortada said in his soft, slurred voice.
The men stepped back.*

*Khalil opened the valise and turned it around so his
host could see the three kilos of heroin inside. "Have your
men test it, if you wish."*

*At Caracortada's nod, one of the soldiers snapped the
valise closed, picked it up, and left. "What is your proposition?"*

"It has come to my attention," Khalil began, "that you

*seek to expand your drug trade. Sadly, the product avail-
able to you from Mexico and Colombia is not as pure as
the heroin from my country. That makes it less profitable,
which means your expansion is moving slower than you
might wish. I ask that you consider buying from me. I can
attest to the purity of my product since it comes from my
own poppy fields. An agreement between us will make us
both rich men."*

The Mexican said nothing for a long time. Khalil forced
himself to be patient and not look away from that one
milky eye.

*"And what is this favor you ask in return if I agree to
your proposal?"* Caracortada finally asked.

*"My men and I seek vengeance on those who murdered
my son and dishonored my family. To do this, we must
cross in and out of the United States undetected, which I
cannot do without your help. I would also ask that a car, a
map of the state of Texas, American currency, three new
prepaid phones, automatic rifles, and pistols be waiting for
us on the other side. The car and guns will be given back
to you when we return after completing our mission."*
Khalil shrugged and spread his hands wide. *"A simple
thing for a man with your powerful connections."*

Caracortada stood. *"Thank you for your gift, Señor
Farid. I will consider your proposal. If your product is as
good as you say, we will talk again about the favor you ask.
Until then, you and your men will be my guests."*

Harley's Roadhouse was packed, as it usually was on summer Saturday nights, and Richard had a hard time finding
a parking spot big enough for the big crew cab truck. Luckily, management had anticipated the crowd, and the roof-
mounted air conditioners were running full bore, cranking
out cool air.

As soon as they entered, Joss and Grady were engulfed

by fans and groupies. KD was barely able to pull Richard off to the side and out of the worst of the crush. Memories assailed her as she looked around. She hadn't been to the dance hall in several years and felt a charge of exhilaration at the party-like atmosphere.

The nose was deafening. Huge bass speakers pulsed so hard she could feel the vibrations beneath her feet. The smell of the beer flowing constantly from the stainless taps behind the bar, the voices of friends calling to friends, and the thud of bootheels hitting the planks in unison as line dancers circled the giant dance floor all awakened happy memories of her carefree high school days. Everybody was cutting the wolf loose tonight, and the excitement was contagious.

"Ever been to an old-fashioned Texas dance hall?" she shouted to Richard.

He shook his head.

"Then you're in for a treat. Beer first, then a table." Spotting a waitress weaving through the crowd with a tray of Lone Star longnecks held high, KD gave a shrill whistle to get her attention and raised two fingers. "I hope you brought money," she yelled to Richard.

"How much?"

"If you expect her to come around again, ten bucks."

Once they had their longnecks, they looked for a table with a good view of the stage. Luckily there was one on the mezzanine, the raised area on either side of the dance floor where alcohol was allowed. Since the Roadhouse was family friendly in the old Texas dance hall tradition, people of all ages were allowed in, but those under twenty-one were required to wear NO BEER wristbands and were restricted to the main floor of the hall, where alcohol wasn't allowed. Consequently, it wasn't unusual to see preteens and older teenagers dancing alongside grandparents shuffling through the Texas two-step with happy grins on their faces.

It was too loud for easy conversation, so KD and Richard sat side by side at their tiny table and silently watched the dancers circle past. After a while, KD leaned toward him and asked if he danced.

He shrugged and watched a row of line dancers stomp by, hands in the front pockets of their jeans, booted feet doing intricate kicks and cross steps. "As a couple. Not in a line like these guys."

"Want to try one? Some are pretty easy. I think I can remember the steps to the Cowboy Hustle." Seeing his lack of enthusiasm, she smiled. "Or we could try the two-step." She pointed to an elementary-aged couple. "If those little kids can do it, surely you can. Or you can scooch over here and put your arm across my shoulders and we can pretend we're dancing while we drink beer and watch."

"I can do that." And he did.

Later, during a lull in the music, Richard went for another beer, and KD saw Deputy Toby Langers watching him from beside the bar. He had always been a fixture at the roadhouse on weekends. Probably raking in overtime for doing nothing but fantasizing about the younger women. Seeing the way the jerk scowled at Richard made KD wonder if Sheriff Ford had told him that Richard might be thinking to run for his job after he retired.

KD had no doubt Richard would make an excellent sheriff. In addition to being smarter, nearly a foot taller, and way hotter than the deputy, his temperament was better suited to the job. Toby's reputation for pushing his weight around had earned him the nickname *Deputy Dawg*. He was older than KD, so she didn't know him personally, but Raney had told her there was a long history of antagonism between Langers and Dalton that dated back to high school, and it had only become worse after Dalton got out of prison. KD was convinced that with endorsements from the sheriff and the Whitcombs, the job of Gunther County sheriff was Richard's for the taking.

If he wanted it.

She watched Langers track Richard back to the table, then quickly look away when he caught KD scowling at him. He was such a weasel. As soon as Richard sat down, KD waved him closer. "See that guy over there?" She pointed at Langers, who was now looking down the tank top of a high school girl trying to use a fake ID to get beer. KD recognized all of the kid's moves. She'd used them herself. And with as little luck. "That's the guy you'd be up against if you ran for sheriff."

Richard studied the other man. He didn't seem impressed. Turning back to KD, he asked if she wanted him to run.

She shook her head. "Not my call. Just pointing out the competition."

"Sounds like you want me to run."

"I want you to do what you want to do. Running for sheriff is just one option of many."

"If I were elected, we'd be close to your family."

KD made a face. "Not sure if that's good or bad."

"We could spend our evenings with Mama. Maybe play checkers."

"Knit pot holders," KD added, getting into the spirit of it. "Plan high school reunions for the geriatric set."

"Try out recipes and do each other's hair. Babysitting on weekends."

"You win," she conceded with a laugh. "You don't have to run for sheriff."

"Maybe I want to." He thought for a moment. "It wouldn't be a bad life. I like Texas, and your family, and you. If it's a package deal, I'm okay with that."

KD felt a warm tingle. *He was so damn sweet.* "Is this another proposal, Warrant Officer Murdock?"

"It could be. But marriage is a partnership. What do you want?"

You. "Time," she said instead. "Time to get Khalil out

of our lives, to see if the rehab program will work, for you to find something you really want to do."

He studied her for a long time, then smiled and shook his head. "You really know how to work me, don't you, babe?"

"What do you mean?"

"By not forcing a decision that would suit you, you're leading me exactly where you want me to be."

That sounded manipulative. "Which is where?" she asked, trying not to be offended.

"Into making a decision that would suit us both."

"Is that good?"

"Time will tell."

Suddenly, the music started blaring again, and the hall erupted in whistles and cheers.

Joss was at the mic.

"Isn't she great?" KD asked after Joss had finished her third song.

"She is. Definitely star material."

KD's cell phone vibrated. She pulled it out and saw it was Dalton. "Hey," she said, wondering why he would call her here. *It's Dalton*, she mouthed to Richard. "What's up? What? Wait—I can barely hear you. Hold on while I go outside."

Motioning for Richard to follow, she hurried out the exit. Once they were far away from the inside noise, she put the phone on speaker. "Dalton, I've got you on speaker. Richard's here, too. What's going on? Are Raney and Mama okay?"

"Everybody's fine," Dalton assured her. "But the sheriff just called. His contact on the Border Patrol said an informer saw three Middle Eastern guys get off a trawler at the port in Matamoros, Mexico, this afternoon. One of them, an older, heavyset guy, had a long scar across his face. Sound familiar, Richard?"

"Khalil Farid has a scar like that. When?"

"About four hours ago. Probably bribed their way through customs. Or what passes for customs down there."

"Where are they now?"

"Presumed to still be around Matamoros. They drove off with four guys, the informer said. Possibly soldiers in the Matamoros Cartel. No sign of them since."

Richard asked KD where Matamoros was.

"Across from Brownsville."

"Close?"

"Maybe ten hours by car. More with stops. But that's a long drive though some of the state's most congested areas, so it might take longer."

"I doubt they'd take that route," Dalton broke in. "They'd want to stay off the interstates, which are more heavily patrolled, and drive slightly below the speed limit, just to be safe. Back roads, slower speeds."

"That would take a lot longer," KD pointed out. "And since most small towns close early, they'd have fewer chances to eat and get gas if they drove at night. Might take twelve, fourteen hours. Less if they flew."

When Richard asked where the nearest airport was, Raney told him Dallas–Fort Worth made international flights. "But you said he was on the no-fly list."

"Then what about a private airport? Somewhere a small private plane could land unnoticed."

"That'd be Gunther," Dalton said.

"Then it's possible they could fly directly from Brownsville to Gunther on a private plane," Richard said. "How long would that take?"

"A lot less than fourteen hours."

"But why would they?" KD argued. "They'd still need a car to get from Gunther to the ranch. I doubt they have any contacts this far off the beaten path, and we sure as hell don't have Uber around here."

"You're right," Dalton agreed. "They'll have to drive the interstates. Take at least twelve hours, including stops. Possibly longer."

"That assumes everything was prearranged," Richard put in, "and they left as soon as they got off the boat, rather than driving off with four Mexicans. When were they last seen?"

"Six this evening," Dalton answered.

"Then they won't come tonight," Richard decided. "They'll need transportation, weapons, money, a way to get across the border. That'll take time. And they'll need to rest up. Once they cross the border, they'll want to get in and out as fast as they can. I figure, at the earliest, they'll leave Mexico tomorrow. Probably late morning so they'll get here after midnight."

"That gives us a day to get ready," Dalton said. "Should we alert the MPs at Hood?"

"They can't help," Richard said. "It's a civilian matter. We're on our own."

"Don't say anything to the people in Tent City," KD told Dalton. "I'll talk to Dr. Prescott. They're scheduled to leave tomorrow anyway."

"How soon can you get back to the house?"

"Forty minutes. Is Mama home yet?"

"Ford took her to stay with Len in Dallas. Then he's coming to the ranch."

"Good," KD said. "The married workers need to be ready to take their families somewhere safe until this is over. I don't want any kids in danger."

"Alejandro is talking to them now."

"The ranch will cover any expenses," KD added. "I think Raney keeps cash on hand for emergencies. Pass that around if you need to. How's she taking it?"

He made a snorting noise. "She's oiling her Glock."

"That's my big sis. See you soon."

KD pocketed her cell then looked at Richard. "Damn. It's really happening."

They left the roadhouse as soon as they could drag Joss away from her admirers. While they drove, KD told her and Grady about Khalil Farid. As predicted, Joss went ballistic. Not that KD blamed her. She had a daughter to protect. "You need to leave as soon as you can," KD explained after Joss had calmed down enough to listen. "Go stay with Mama at Len's. Tell them I'll keep them posted, but under no circumstances should they come to the ranch until Dalton or Richard says it's okay."

"Is there anything I can do?" Grady asked.

"Just keep Joss and Lyric safe. We knew this might happen, and have everything under control at the ranch."

"You *knew* about this?" Joss yelled from the backseat of the truck. "Why didn't you tell me, KD? Jesus! Lyric could be in danger!"

"I said it *might* happen, Joss. And we still don't know for sure that it will. We're just being cautious."

That didn't do much to calm down her volatile sister, but at least Joss quit yelling for the rest of the way home.

CHAPTER 19

When they drove through the gate thirty-eight minutes later, it looked like every window on the ranch was lit up. Dalton and Harvey stood with the sheriff on the front porch, Harvey with his rifle resting in the crook of his arm. Dalton didn't appear to be armed.

As soon as Richard pulled the truck in beside the sheriff's cruiser in the back parking area, Joss threw open the rear door and hopped out. "You pack our stuff, Grady. I'll get Lyric's."

"Joss, there's no rush," KD told her. "We've got time."

Joss whirled. "You sure about that, KD? Sure enough to guarantee Lyric's safety?"

KD didn't answer.

"I thought so. I can't believe you brought this asshole down on your family! What were you thinking?" Without waiting for an answer, she stomped through the gate toward the veranda.

Unwilling to let her get away with that, Richard called after her, "It's not you he's after, Joss. It's your sister."

Joss called back, "Small comfort if we're caught in the crossfire."

Richard started to set her straight, but KD put her hand on his arm to stop him. "Let her go. She's just worried about Lyric. I can't blame her. If I hadn't—"

"Bullshit!" Richard barked. "This isn't your fault any more than it's mine. Khalil is a fucking lunatic. Period. Now focus on what needs to be done and quit feeling sorry for yourself and making excuses for your sister."

KD wanted to hit him.

Then hug him.

He was right. She couldn't dwell on what she couldn't change. *Hope for the best, plan for the worst.* "What do you want me to do?" she asked him.

He told her to gather all the household handguns, rifles, shotguns, whatever, and put them on the dining room table with what ammo she could find, including the boxes Dalton had just bought. "If you have binocs, bring those, too. I don't suppose you have any game cams or night vision goggles?"

"There might be some in Dad's old stuff," Raney said, coming through the gate toward the truck. "But they'd be pretty outdated." She looked back at Joss as her sister rushed into the house, shouting orders to Grady. "What's up with Joss?"

"She's afraid for Lyric," KD answered before Richard could tee off again. The last thing they needed was a family brawl. She steered Raney toward the house, Richard falling in behind. "What are you doing up this late?"

"Making lists. And talking to Mama. Len's got her hands full keeping her calm. Richard, we may have some traps in the barn."

"What kind of traps?"

"Hog snares, mostly." Stopping when they reached the veranda, she turned to explain. "Rather than shoot them, our workers trap them alive and take them to the processors. Good eating and less disease that way."

"How do the snares work?"

"I've never set one, but I think it's like a noose with a special kind of closure, made of thick cable that can't be broken or chewed through. It can also be anchored so it won't pull loose if the hog thrashes around. Our guys put them on trails where hogs go under the fences or rub up against fence posts."

"Are they lethal?"

"Not supposed to be."

"Would they work on a human?"

She thought for a moment. "Possible, but not probable. If a person tried to crawl under a fence, it might catch him around the arm or foot. But the snares are rigged so they don't close completely, so it probably wouldn't do permanent injury. Without wire cutters or a way to pry open the closure, it would be hard to get loose. Definitely slow him down for a while."

An irritated voice called from upstairs. Raney made a face. "Better go see what Princess Joss wants."

"You think the snares will work?" KD asked Richard as Raney left.

"Worth a try. Maybe we could put some at approach points around the house. I'll go talk to Alejandro and find out how many you have and if they'll work on people. Then I'll go talk to the sheriff."

Thirty minutes later, Richard joined Ford and Dalton and Harvey on the veranda. The lawman didn't look happy. Apparently, the idea of deputizing a bunch of locals didn't sit easy with the sheriff. But the idea of foreign terrorists wiping out the county's most influential family—and the family of the woman he was courting—sat even worse. Even though Ford had already given Dalton and Harvey all his reasons for not deputizing them, Richard had him go through it again without interruption. He'd found that when working through a problem, often the fastest way to reach a solution was to put it in words, step by step, as many times as necessary.

When Ford had finally finished explaining why forming a civilian posse was problematic and inherently dangerous, Richard nodded and said, "Normally, I'd agree with you. All manner of things could go wrong. But if we did it legally, under your supervision as the county's highest-ranking law enforcement authority, there's a much better chance it wouldn't turn into a bloodbath."

Ford winced at the mention of bloodshed.

Richard pushed harder. "We're morally and legally obligated to protect ourselves and those in our care." He motioned to Dalton and Harvey. "The three of us have combat training, and probably more experience than that deputy I saw gawking at underaged tits tonight at Harley's Roadhouse. We can do this, Sheriff. But we'd prefer to do it with your help. What do you say?"

Ford chewed on it for a minute, then gave up. "How many men do you have?"

"Five, and they're not all men. Whoever is left will be on recon."

The sheriff glanced at the rifle slung over Harvey's shoulder. "I only see one firearm here."

"I've got two handguns, Glenn has a hunting rifle, Harvey's got his sniper rifle, KD was an expert marksman in the army, and Alejandro . . ." Richard turned to Dalton. "What about Alejandro?"

Dalton shrugged.

"Right." Richard turned back to Ford. "He's in charge of recon. Plus, Raney has experience with a Glock and her dad's shotguns and hunting rifles."

"Lord help us." Ford let out a weary sigh. "Call them together. I'll get the paperwork started. But I'm only deputizing the five," he added with a sharp look at Dalton. "The other ranch hands better not be shooting."

"They don't need guns," Harvey said, then burst out laughing. The first words Richard had ever heard him speak. He hoped deputizing the old sniper wouldn't prove a bad idea.

Joss and her family left just before the sheriff did. Apparently, she and KD had made up because there was a lot of hugging and crying—at least, on Joss's part—as they climbed into Grady's BMW. Richard didn't know where they were headed and didn't care. He was still pissed that Joss had dumped that load of crap on KD. He wasn't that tolerant of drama queens.

After agreeing they probably had until the following night before Farid and his men could reach the ranch, Ford suggested they all get some rest, then left to do the same. Harvey and his Remington .50 headed to his bunk in the bachelor quarters. Dalton checked all the household doors and locks, then he and Raney went upstairs.

On his way to bed, Richard stopped in the dining room to do a quick check of the guns and ammo KD had laid out on the table. Two rifles, three shotguns, two handguns, not counting his two and Raney's Glock, three sets of binoculars, some outdated game cams, no night vision, and at least two dozen boxes of ammo.

A start.

With a yawn, he headed to bed.

That night, KD had the dream again, except this time, the person shooting at her was a featureless man with a scar across his mannequin-smooth cheek. She tried to scream, but made no sound, and gasped into wakefulness. She lay still, her heart pounding against her ribs, trying not to awaken Richard. But he always seemed to know when she was in trouble.

Before she could catch her breath, his arms came around her and pulled her back against his warm, solid chest.

"You're okay, babe," he murmured in a sleep-roughened

voice. "I've got you. You're safe." After a while, his even breathing by her ear calmed her down and she was able to drift back to sleep.

The next time she opened her eyes, sunlight was streaming into the room and Richard's tall, muscular form was silhouetted against the window. He stood in his boxers, hands braced high on either side of the window opening, looking out over the ranch.

Her bodyguard. Her man.

She must have made a sound. He turned, the light so bright behind him, she couldn't read his expression. But she knew him well enough now to sense his mood. He was worried. As was she. And probably wondering how it was possible that the nightmare they thought they'd left back in Afghanistan was now on its way to sleepy little Rough Creek to haunt them again.

He walked over and sat on the bed beside her. Reaching out, he brushed a tangle of hair off her forehead and gave a lopsided smile. "Get any sleep, babe?"

"I did. Thanks to you."

He leaned down and kissed her, then straightened. "We've got this. Four experienced soldiers against a lard-ass and two camel-humpers."

"I'm not sure that's PC. And don't forget Raney and her Glock."

"Plus we're now fully deputized law enforcement personnel."

"With our very own sheriff," KD added with a smile. "Although I feel sorry for him, the way you bullied him into deputizing us."

"No choice. He's our official face in all this. It'll read better coming from a sheriff, instead of gun-happy ranch folk."

"CYA. I'm familiar." Yawning, she sat up. "I better go talk to Conan. We need to get the therapy group out of here before the fireworks start."

"I think you should shower first, babe."

"What is it about you and showers?"

"I'm just a clean person, I guess. C'mon. I'll help."

After talking to KD, Dr. Prescott was ready to load up the van, then and there, even though she emphasized they didn't know for certain if the man spotted in Matamoros was Khalil Farid. "And if it is," she argued, "unless he has expert intel, which I doubt, he doesn't know where I live. He might go to Fort Hood first to find out, or register a complaint that justice hadn't been done for his son. At which time, he'll be nabbed for being in the country illegally. Either way, we'll have advance warning. There's no need to stress out the patients with a hasty departure."

"We were leaving today anyway. Both Thomas and Laura are in fragile states right now. A situation like this could set them back. Maybe permanently."

KD sighed. Her test run had gone so well up to now. She hated for it to end on such a bad note. "Of course, then, they should go back. We're sending our married families away, too. Although I'm not sure Sarge or Shirley will go willingly."

Conan sighed. "I agree. They're both more likely to run toward trouble than away from it. But I'm only their therapist, not their superior officer, and since they're still on leave, I can't force them to return to Hood. If they insist on staying to help, can you think of a way they could participate on a limited level? Unarmed, of course. Arming our patients is against regulations."

"I think so. But let's see if that's even necessary. They may all be delighted to head back as soon as possible."

Dr. Prescott certainly knew his patients. Laura said she'd leave now if Conan thought she should. "Although I'd like to say goodbye to the horses—and Alejandro—before I go," she added.

Tommy TBI just shrugged. Or twitched. Hard to say.

Sarge and Shirley were less open to the idea of returning to Hood. In fact, as soon as KD explained the possibility of a crazed, heroin-addicted pedophile showing up to attack the ranch, they became almost giddy.

"That's what I'm talking about!" Sarge's grin was positively evil. "No more sitting. Time for *doing*. OO-rah."

"OO-rah," Shirley echoed, reaching up to give him a high five.

These were American army combat soldiers, after all.

"We can't give you guns," KD warned. "But if you stay, we need as many lookouts as we can get. Assuming Farid is headed to the ranch. Which he may not be."

"No matter. I'm staying," Shirley announced. "I didn't get this bionic leg just so I could run from trouble. And I'm a medic. You might need me."

KD hoped not, but asked Shirley to check out their first aid kit, just in case.

"If you on doctor duty," Sarge said, grinning at Shirley, "who be doing our cooking?"

"I can do both."

"I know. But you be fightin' now, Mighty Mouse, not cookin'."

"Damn right!"

KD was so proud, she wanted to hug them. Once a soldier, always a soldier. She felt the same way. "There'll be no fighting." She tried to sound stern.

They both laughed.

The Wounded Warrior van left an hour later, taking Conan, Laura, and Tommy TBI back to Fort Hood. KD was sad to see them go, but glad they would be safe.

The rest of the day was spent making sure the ranch was secure. Gates and outbuildings were locked. Animals were moved to distant pastures—except for the more valuable horses and bulls, which were stalled in the fireproof barn. After the married workers and their families had left to stay with friends and relatives, the ranch began to feel like a ghost town.

Which left ten, plus Sheriff Ford, to protect the ranch.

Eleven to three. Even Richard felt okay with those odds.

Dalton assigned defensive positions should they get word that Khalil was on the move: Glenn Hicks and Chuy would stay in Glenn's house by the road, where they could monitor cars passing by or stopping at the gate. Harvey would watch the driveway and house from the loft of the hay barn. After Alejandro set the snares and placed the game cams around the house and barn, he would begin patrolling the fence lines on horseback.

Not wanting Sarge and Shirley to stay at Tent City without protection, KD insisted the sergeant stay with Alejandro and Harvey in the bachelor quarters over the AI labs, where he could keep watch over the more remote buildings, while Shirley was to move into Len's old room in the main house, which had the best second-story view of the driveway. Since the cooks were gone, the scrappy amputee happily volunteered for kitchen duty, too. But rather than having her do double duty at both the house and the bachelor quarters—and since neither KD nor Raney could cook water—they decided eight of those remaining would take their meals together in the kitchen above the AI lab, while Glenn and Chuy ate at the foreman's house.

Everyone had a position. And everyone vulnerable had been evacuated.

Except Raney.

No matter how many times her husband and KD and Richard pleaded with her to go, or how strenuously Mama insisted during her daily phone calls that she join her and Len and Joss in Dallas, Raney wouldn't budge.

"I'm not leaving!" she argued. "I run this ranch!" Seeing her husband's frown, she added, "We both do. And it's our jobs to see this through."

"You're pregnant," her husband reminded her.

"So?"

Dalton just looked at her.

"Damnit!" Raney yanked off her ball cap and slapped it onto the kitchen counter. "I've already given up working with the stallions and training the cutting horses. I don't drink booze or coffee, or eat rare steaks or undercooked eggs or smoke—"

"You never did," Dalton cut in.

"Didn't even get to paint my baby's nursery. And now you say I can't protect my own home?"

KD knew how devoted Raney was to Four Star. Saw it in the glimmer of tears in her bright blue eyes and heard it in the quaver of her voice. They'd never get her to leave. Especially if she had to stay with Joss and Mama at Len's. Pregnancy hadn't increased her sister's tolerance for hovering or dramatics.

"She's right," she told Dalton. "Raney should be here."

"At least someone's on my side."

KD turned back to her sister. "But if, and when, we get word that Khalil is coming, Raney, you have to promise to do what Dalton says. No arguments."

"I second that," Richard put in.

Raney looked mutinously at the three faces staring back at her. "Okay. But none of you are taking my Glock."

Just before noon, six hundred miles south of their ultimate destination, the three Afghan men and one of the cartel soldiers crossed unnoticed into the United States. Having been warned that beards attracted attention in this godless, beardless country, the two younger men had shaved their faces, and now wore American ball caps and sunglasses. Khalil's black beard was a symbol of his status. He would not give it up. Nor would he wear a silly ball cap. But before leaving Matamoros, he had his beard trimmed and his gray hair cut very short. After the three men changed into westernized clothing, they blended in well with the infidels on the street.

The soldier led them to an older Nissan sedan parked on a back street close to a highway in Brownsville, handed them the keys, then left. As Caracortada had promised, the gas tank was full and the trunk of the vehicle had a false bottom. Under it, they found American currency, a map of the state of Texas, three unpackaged prepaid cell phones, two Kalashnikov pattern AK-47s with 30-round magazines, and three automatic handguns, with fifty rounds of additional ammunition. Satisfied, the men took everything but the guns and ammunition from the hidden compartment, closed the trunk, and climbed into the Nissan. This time, Khalil rode in the passenger seat. The car was dirty and smelled of old food, but he did not complain. He was finally in the country of his son's murderer.

The three men drove one block to Highway 77, turned north, and settled in for the long drive to Rough Creek, Texas, where the woman who killed Asef lived with her family. It would take them many hours to get there and do what they'd come to do, and almost as many hours to return to Brownsville, where Caracortada's men waited to take them back across the border. But Khalil was a patient man, and he knew Allah would keep them safe.

As the Nissan turned onto the highway, in a shadowed doorway behind them, a man pulled a cell phone from his pocket. He punched in a number and said, "They're driving an older blue Nissan four-door. US 77 North." He gave the license plate number, then returned the phone to his pocket and walked away.

CHAPTER 20

That evening, they were finishing a delicious meal prepared by Shirley in the kitchen above the AI offices when Glenn called on Raney's cell. "Sheriff Ford's at the gate. Should I let him in?"

"Of course. Tell him we'll meet him at the house." Leaving the bachelors to help Shirley with cleanup, Raney and Dalton headed back to the house with KD and Richard.

The sheriff was nervously pacing by his car in the parking area when they walked up. He looked frazzled and tired, his normally crisp uniform wrinkled and damp with sweat. "Thought your foreman was going to shoot me when I stopped at the gate."

"Just doing his job," Raney said, leading the way across the lawn toward the veranda. "Watch your step. There may be hog snares in the shrubs."

The sheriff slowed his pace. "Having trouble with pigs, are you?"

"Always. Mama doesn't want them rooting up her azaleas." Pulling a jangling set of keys from her jeans pocket,

Raney unlocked the door leading from the veranda to the kitchen.

"Think they'll get into the house, too?" the sheriff asked.

She smiled back at him as she opened the door. "Hope not. But if they do, we're prepared. Does anyone know how to fix coffee?"

"Or there's beer," Dalton suggested.

He and Richard and KD opted for longnecks. Raney had juice. The sheriff didn't seem to care what he drank, so KD bought him a big glass of sweet tea with ice, two slices of lemon, and a sprig of fresh mint. Exactly how Mama liked it. It seemed to settle him down.

Leaving the men to do a quick walk-through of the house and check that all the windows and exterior doors were still locked, KD and Raney led Ford back to the veranda. KD turned on the misters and overhead fans, but left the shades up, the lights off, and the water coolers on low. She wanted to be able to see and hear if anything, or anyone, crossed the back lawn.

"Place seems quiet," Sheriff Ford observed, settling into the upholstered chair Dalton had brought out from the office, so that all five of them could sit around the ottoman.

KD wondered if he was referring to the absence of her mother or the lack of activity around the ranch buildings.

"We moved everybody out who was at risk," Raney told him as Richard and Dalton walked back in and sat down. "After your last visit, we thought it best to be prepared."

"Good thing you are." Ford removed his hat, leaned forward to set it on the ottoman, then sat back. "Heard from my contact with Border Patrol again. Their informant positively ID'd Khalil Farid as one of three Middle Eastern men in a dark blue 2012 Nissan four-door that left Brownsville this morning."

Raney reached for her husband's hand.

"How'd they cross the border?" Dalton asked.

"Not sure. The Matamoros Cartel has a lot of money to

toss around, which means they have a lot of ways to beat the system."

"That's irrelevant now," Richard said. "They're in the country. So where do they head next?"

"The informant said they turned onto US 77 north." The sheriff went on to outline the route he thought they'd take—north to San Antonio, then up to Austin, and on to Gunther, ending with the forty-five-minute drive from Gunther to the ranch. "I've alerted Texas Highway Patrol to keep an eye out for the Nissan. Unless these guys stay on the back roads, but that would take a lot longer."

"So they're on their way," Dalton said.

Raney muttered something.

KD slumped in her chair, guilt and fear swirling through her mind. *I did this. I brought this madman to my family.*

"If so, we're ready." Without looking at her, Richard reached over and took KD's hand, his long fingers lacing through hers in a tight grip. "We have our positions and we know what to do. We'll be okay."

KD looked over at him, her eyes stinging. It seemed that all her life she'd needed to be the strong one, never showing weakness, making as few mistakes as possible, and depending on no one but herself. But with Richard, she could admit to doubt or fear because she knew if she faltered, he would be there to lend her his strength. It was confusing yet liberating. She depended on him more than anyone in her life. Yet she felt freer than she ever had. *I love you*, she thought. She knew that as surely as she knew he would be there to help her get through this.

"Do you have a guess when they'll get here?" Dalton asked the sheriff.

"Hard to say. It's probably ten, eleven hours from Brownsville to Gunther, plus the forty-five-minute drive to the ranch." Ford looked up at the ceiling fan, as if calculating in his mind. "Add a couple more hours for gas and food and to change drivers. Fourteen hours, give or take."

"Hard to believe Texas is that big," Richard muttered.

"Over eight hundred miles top to bottom. Nearly that wide, too," Ford continued his calculations. "From Brownsville to here is only about six hundred and fifty miles if they take the faster route along the major highways. They'll stay under the speed limit, but not by much. And when they do stop, it'll be at the big truck stops. Places with prepared food, and so busy they won't be noticed." He sighed and looked at Dalton. "Might not notice them anyway. The informant said the two guys with Khalil were wearing ball caps and sunglasses and had shaved their beards. Khalil just trimmed his. He'd be the most recognizable because of the scar across his face, so he probably won't let himself be seen."

"When did they leave Brownsville?"

"After eleven this morning. If they follow the route I think they will, and only make short stops for food and gas and so on, they could be here by one tonight, give or take."

Richard checked his watch. "We have at least four hours. Maybe five."

"I'll call Glenn and have Alejandro tell the others to rest up for now, but to be in their positions by eleven o'clock," Raney said.

"And have someone walk Shirley down here," KD advised.

"I doubt they'll come before midnight," Dalton said, while Raney talked to Glenn. "They'll want the ranch settled in for the night."

"Do we keep all the lights on and make him wait?" Richard asked. "Or go dark, and hope to lure them in?"

They decided to leave lights on at the main gate, the livestock barn and the AI offices, but off in the bachelor quarters upstairs so Sarge didn't make himself a target. Same with the hay barn where Harvey was posted.

"Glenn will keep the lights off at his house," Raney told them after she'd finished her call. "And he said if we keep the house dark, the snares might not be as visible."

"Sounds like you've thought this through," Sheriff Ford said. "If you want, I can have Deputy Langers sit outside Gunther and let us know if he sees the Nissan make the turn toward the ranch."

Dalton snorted. "Better not tell him it's to help us, or he might not do it."

Ford scratched at the stubble under his chin. "How bad do you need me here?"

"Up to you. We appreciate all you've done for us so far."

"Especially getting Mama to safety," KD put in. *And out of our hair.*

"Then how about I head up to Gunther and send Deputy Langers over to Rough Creek? Farid might go there first then double back to the ranch. Probably not, but that would keep Langers busy."

"Sounds like a plan."

The sheriff left for Gunther a few minutes later, after reiterating his instructions to avoid lethal force if possible and for all of them to stay safe. Sounded like a mixed message to KD.

At nine o'clock, Richard left to patrol the perimeter of the house. Dalton checked the dozen flashlights on the kitchen counter, set aside three for the women, two for him and Richard, and took four to distribute among the men.

KD drummed her fingers on the arm of her chair and watched Raney chew her thumbnail. "It might be hours yet, sis. Why don't you go upstairs and stretch out?"

"I'm not tired. Besides, it's almost time for Mama's nightly harassment call."

KD didn't want to be around for that. At a sound, she saw Shirley and Sarge coming across the lawn. "Shirley can sit with you."

"I don't need a babysitter."

KD struggled to curb her temper. Sometimes Raney could be as hardheaded as a rented mule. "And if you doze off down here, you'll be able to hear Shirley call out from Len's room?"

"Why would I call out?" Shirley asked as she came up the veranda steps and Sarge headed back to his post above the AI lab.

"I'd feel better if I knew you and Raney were watching out for each other."

"Where will you be?"

"Patrolling the house."

Shirley looked at Raney. "Makes sense."

With a deep sigh, Raney rose from her chair.

"Before you go up," KD told them, "grab a flashlight off the kitchen counter. Shirley, there's a big coffee urn and coffee in the pantry. Could you make us a pot? I think we'll need it before this night is over."

"I'm on it."

As soon as her sister and Shirley went upstairs, KD walked through the house, checking windows and doors and turning off lights. The silence creeped her out. Grabbing a cup of coffee on her way through the kitchen, she went to stand at the office window. From there, she had a partial view of the road past the gate, and a good view of the driveway leading past the house to the horse barn and AI lab, and on down to the dark, looming shadow of the hay barn, where Henry waited with his rifle.

As she watched, the floodlight at the main gate came on. Then the exterior floodlights at the livestock barn. And finally, the lights in and around the ground floor of the AI building. The upstairs bachelor quarters where Sarge sat remained dark. No lights showed at the hay barn, the married duplex, or Glenn's house near the front gate. With the early moon already down, a stranger wouldn't know those buildings were there.

They were ready.

Satisfied, she stepped into the guest room for a quick

shower since it was early yet and Khalil probably wouldn't get near the ranch for several more hours.

Dalton and Richard agreed it might look too much like a trap if the house were completely dark, so they turned on the front porch light, a lamp in the office, and a lamp in Lyric's bedroom, as well as a yard light on the left side of the house where the cars were parked. Hopefully, that would encourage intruders to approach the house from the right or rear, where snares were set and anchored, or through the darkened veranda, where either he or Dalton would be waiting.

A good plan, considering what they had to work with. Unless the Afghans came in on three sides and sprayed the whole house, dark or not. But Richard doubted that would happen. He was still convinced Khalil was a coward and would send in his two flunkies before he made an appearance. They would use a stealth approach, cruising by the gate several times then parking out of sight and coming through the fence. If so, and they got past the snares along the fence line, Alejandro, Chuy, or Glenn would spot them and call Dalton. Or if they tried to come through the back of the ranch, Harvey would spot them. Or they'd end up in the creek.

Hope for the best, plan for the worst. That's all they could do. That, and wait. Battling impatience, he settled on the veranda with Dalton to do just that.

At nine thirty, Dalton's cell buzzed. When he saw who it was, he put it on speaker. "What's up, Sheriff?"

"Highway patrol just stopped the blue Nissan sedan south of Austin."

Richard sat up, heart pumping. "Farid?"

"Not unless he's a young Caucasian. Said he bought the car off a lot in San Antonio that afternoon. They checked him out. The car, too. He was legit, but the car had a false bottom in the trunk that tested positive for gunpowder and gun oil."

It's them. Richard was sure of it. "Did they check out the dealer who sold him the car?"

"Said an old Hispanic guy brought it in. No arrests or warrants."

Now what? Had the informant lied about the car? Had there been another car waiting outside of Brownsville? Or were they totally on the wrong track?

"What do you want me to do?" Ford prodded. "Do you want me to stay here?"

"How many cars drive through Gunther after midnight?" Dalton asked.

"On Sunday? Not many. Maybe five, six at most."

Dalton asked the sheriff if he could stay in Gunther awhile longer, and let them know if any unfamiliar cars with three men made the turn toward the ranch.

Ford said he could.

After ending the call, Dalton called Glenn, told him to forget the Nissan and watch for any car coming down the road from either direction, and to alert them if he spotted one that seemed suspicious. Then he went upstairs to let the women know what the sheriff had said.

Since neither Harvey nor Sarge had cell phones, Richard jogged down to tell them about the change in plans. After checking the locks and windows at the AI lab and the horse barn, he went back to the house and found Dalton sitting on the veranda, a mug of coffee in his hands. "Heard anything?" Richard asked.

"Nary a peep."

Richard went into the kitchen, filled a mug with coffee, then came back and plopped into the chair beside Cardwell. "How are the women?"

"Raney and Shirley are dozing. KD's about to."

"She look okay? No panic?"

"Not that I could tell. Seemed pretty focused."

Richard felt a surge of pride. His KD was tough. She'd get through this.

His KD? Where'd that come from? Yet the sentiment rolled sweetly through his mind, and the more he thought about it, the righter it felt. KD was his. As much as he was hers. He couldn't imagine a life without her.

"What are you smiling about?" Dalton asked.

"KD." Richard's grin spread. "And what I have to do to get her to marry me."

"Good luck with that. These Whitcomb girls don't fall easy. But when they do, watch out."

"She thinks I care that she might not be able to have kids."

"You don't?"

"We can adopt. Use a surrogate, in vitro, whatever. It's definitely not a problem with me. I just have to convince her of that."

Dalton studied him for a moment, a smile tugging at one corner of his mouth. "I don't think she'll put up much of a fight. The way she looks at you, she's all in."

"Really?" Richard rose from the chair. "Maybe I should go talk to her."

KD stepped out of the shower to find Richard stretched out on the bed, arms folded behind his head, a sexy grin on his face.

"I can't believe you showered without me," he scolded. Then he must have seen something in her face. His grin faded. "What's wrong?"

She gave a broken laugh. "Wrong? You mean other than a psychopathic pederast coming thousands of miles just to kill me?" She tried to sound offhand, but she felt like she was coming apart inside. What if something happened to Richard? What if he died because of her? How could she go on?

"Babe." He patted the bed beside his hip. "Sit down and tell me what I can do to convince you we're going to be okay."

Slumping onto the edge of the bed, she brushed back that fall of dark hair that shadowed his beautiful eyes. "You can live."

"I plan to."

Tears she had held back too long rose in her eyes. "I need you, Richard. I know you can't stay here forever—damn." Her voice gave out as tears rolled down her face. "I hate being so clingy."

"I like clingy." He pulled her down and kissed the tears from her cheek. "And it's okay to need me. I need you, too."

She sat back, losing him in a blur of tears that wouldn't stop coming. His was the voice that calmed her before a storm. The hands that steadied her when she stumbled. His was the body that made hers sing. She needed him like water and air and hope. "I love you, Richard."

He went still. Then, with a deep breath that swept hot across her cheek, he pulled her back down against his chest. "Oh, babe . . ."

Since they had hours yet, he made love to her with slow, gentle hands and coaxing words until KD abandoned herself to sensation, her limbs trembling, the taste and scent of him filling her mind. And when she could bear no more, he took her away from herself and sent her soaring to a place she had never been. It was more than sex. It was a joining on some elemental level she had never known existed. It was bliss and boundless joy and total, unquestionable love. And after she slowly sank back to earth, replete and renewed, she fell into dreamless sleep, safely anchored in his arms.

Just after midnight, Richard's phone buzzed. When he saw who it was, he went instantly alert. "What?"

"Glenn called." Dalton sounded out of breath, like he was running. "Chuy saw the same car twice. First time, driving slow, lights off. Two in front, one in back. Couple of minutes later, they came back by with only two in front. He sent Chuy to see if they parked somewhere up the road by the west pasture. I'm going now to check if Harvey or Sarge have seen anything."

As soon as the call ended, Richard bolted from the bed and began pulling on clothes. "One of them must have gotten out somewhere along the front fence line."

KD was already up, half-dressed and reaching for the belt holding the holster and her S&W .357 revolver, speed loaders, and extra ammo. "He might be coming in early to start a distraction. A fire. Something explosive." Excitement that the waiting was finally over gave her a surge of energy, even as fear for Richard closed like a vise around her heart. "I'll go warn Raney and Shirley."

"Wait!" Before she could leave, Richard pulled her into his arms. His heart was a drumbeat against her chest. His breath rasped in her ear. "I love you, KD," he said in a ragged voice. "I should have told you earlier. I wish I had—"

She stopped him with a hard, fast kiss. "I know. I love you, too." She kissed him again. Softer this time. Salty with tears. Hers. His. Both. It didn't matter. "You said we've got this and I believe you." She swiped a hand across her face and gave him a shaky smile. "Now go do what you need to do."

Richard reached the veranda just as Dalton bounded up the steps after talking to Harvey and Sarge. "They see anything?"

Dalton shook his head. "Nothing's moving out there. Shit! Where is he?"

Using the faint starlight, Richard scanned the back lawn with binoculars, but couldn't see much without night vision. "Anything from Glenn?"

"Nothing. Alejandro's riding the front fence line to see

if there are any breaks. Chuy's still checking for a car parked up the road."

"Call the sheriff," Richard said. "He's wasting his time parked in Gunther."

While Dalton talked to Ford, Richard took the binocs to the parking area and scanned the other buildings. Nothing. Dalton came out with his own binoculars and studied the tree line by the creek. Still nothing.

Forty minutes later, headlights showed at the gate. Richard recognized the roof rack on the sheriff's cruiser. Through the binoculars, he watched Glenn unlock the gate, wave the sheriff through, then lock up again as the cruiser kicked up a cloud of dust down the drive to the house. Richard headed back inside to get the women, but found them already waiting on the porch with mugs of coffee.

Dalton and Ford joined them. When KD handed the sheriff a mug of coffee, Richard noticed his hands were shaky. Maybe age. Maybe not.

After the older man drank, he finally spoke. "Glenn said your wrangler found a man with his foot in a snare just off the front fence. He'd torn himself up pretty bad, trying to get loose. Alejandro disarmed him, had a talk with him, and took him to Glenn's. They left him tied and unconscious in the locked tool shed. Sounds like he won't be going anywhere soon."

Richard felt a surge of relief. Even KD was smiling. "One down, two to go. Progress."

Ford sipped from his mug again. He seemed calmer now, his voice steadier. "I suspect when we get around to collecting the guy, he'll show injuries other than those caused by the snare."

Dalton bit back a smile. "Glenn did say he was torn up."

Raney put on a worried face. "Hopefully the hogs won't find him."

"Mercy, I didn't think about that!" KD made a show of looking around. "Anybody got a hog caller?" It seemed they were all feeling a burst of giddy optimism at this small bit of good news.

The sheriff didn't share their amusement. "I don't need to hear that kind of talk from my deputies," he said without much enthusiasm.

Dalton's cell buzzed again. He put it on speaker. "What's up, Glenn?"

"That car I sent Chuy to find? It's parked up the road. Empty."

They scrambled to fix positions. Ford was to cover the inside of the house. Richard was stationed at the livestock barn, where he could watch the driveway from the front gate, past the house, and down to the barn, while Dalton took the area on the other side of the barn toward the AI lab. Raney and Shirley would keep watch at Len's window, and KD would cover the upstairs hallway and staircase leading down to the kitchen. Harvey and Sarge were to hold their positions in the hay barn and the AI building, but to look for two men instead of three, since the man in Glenn's tool shed was out of commission.

Before leaving for his position, Dalton called Glenn to tell the foreman and Chuy to be ready to move wherever he called, and for Alejandro to shift his patrol to the trees along the creek. "Is the guy in the shed still alive?" he asked.

"When Alejandro left, he was."

Fifteen minutes later, positions were set and everybody was locked and loaded.

Showtime.

CHAPTER 21

Khalil Farid frowned at his fancy new phone. Mohammad called it a smartphone. It was very different from the flip top phones they used in Afghanistan. He was weary from the long drive and found it difficult to remember the codes and how to work the many applications. Muhammad was the one who understood such devices. He even knew how to put aerial maps and photographs on phones. The one Khalil studied now was the most recent satellite image of his enemy's dwelling, taken from hundreds of kilometers above the earth. An amazing thing. But it troubled Khalil that this image was different from the printed one they had studied in Afghanistan.

The house was the same: set back almost three hundred meters from the road. A long drive ran along the left side of the dwelling to a parking area at the back, before it turned left toward the other ranch buildings. None of that had changed.

But what of the new structures that had suddenly appeared on this latest image? A cluster of six, maybe more, half hidden by trees along the small creek. There was no activity around them. Were they abandoned? Muhammad thought they might be temporary shelters for hay or equipment storage, or even transient agricultural workers. But why were they set apart from the other buildings? And why was no one using them? If unoccupied, they might be perfect for their purposes.

With a muttered curse, Khalil punched the button that darkened the image to prolong battery life, and slipped the cell phone into his pocket. He had a charger—a power bank, Muhammad called it—in his other pocket, but Muhammad had warned him to save it for later, when they had the murderous infidel woman and Warrant Officer Murdock in their hands. Filming videos used up a lot of power. Khalil trusted Muhammad. He and Asef had been like brothers, and Muhammad was as intent on vengeance as Khalil.

Impatience churned in his belly as he looked at his watch. Already it was early morning. He was weary of hiding in the trees. Muhammad should have called by now to let them know he had the woman.

Had he not found her? Or had something gone wrong?

He looked with disgust at his nephew, Mostafa, who was looking at lewd images of filthy Western women on his new phone. He was young and foolish, but Khalil's brother had insisted he come. "To make a man of him," he had said. Khalil thought it was too late for that. The boy was too weak to change.

"What are you doing, Mostafa?" he hissed in Dari as he struck his nephew across the back of his head. "You will run down the battery! Muhammad warned us to use the phones only when necessary!"

Mostafa quickly put the phone away. "How much longer do we wait?"

Khalil ignored him.

The silence lengthened.

Khalil checked his watch again. Soon, the darkness

*around them would fade. It was time to act. They could
wait no longer. Turning to Mostafa, he said, "Muhammad
has failed. It is now up to you to get the woman."*

*"Me?" Mostafa's dark eyes showed his fear. "How do a
I find her?"*

*"Infidel women are weak. She will sleep inside the dwell-
ing. Look at the photograph Muhammad put on your phone
so you will know her when you see her. Find her and bring
her to the place Muhammad has chosen. Hurt her if you
must, but do not let her die."*

"What of the soldier? Warrant Officer Murdock?"

*"If you have no choice, kill him. Use your knife and do
it quietly."*

*"How will I know him? Muhammad gave me no photo-
graph."*

*"He is older than the woman and will be wearing the
uniform of the infidel soldiers." Khalil gripped his young
nephew's shoulder in a fatherly way. "Be strong, Mostafa.
Allah calls upon you to be a brave soldier."*

"I will do as you say, Uncle."

*He's an idiot, Khalil thought, turning away to hide his
disappointment. A young, foolish, inept idiot. But after
Muhammad's failure, there was no one else.*

*"With Allah's help, we will be victorious," he said, striv-
ing to put strength into his words. "We will kill the infidels
who dishonored our family and show the world how we re-
pay our enemies. Only then, Mostafa, after we have restored
the good name of Asef Farid, can we go home."*

"Allahu Akbar," Mostafa whispered, fear still in his eyes.

At a quarter to three, a muffled *thump* startled KD as she
rested against the wall at the head of the stairs. She sat up,
head cocked. Small sounds, hardly noticeable. From the veranda? Probably the sheriff, restless from waiting or checking the locks again. But just to be sure, she rose, pulled the

.357 revolver from her holster, and moved silently down the staircase.

The lower landing was empty. No sign of the sheriff in the kitchen, either. Then she heard something odd. Like a groan, coming from the veranda.

Fully alert, she cocked the .357. Staying flat against the wall, she crept past the pantry and along the short hallway off the kitchen. At the doorway onto the darkened veranda, she stopped and listened, gun up and ready.

"Sheriff?" she whispered.

No answer. Then another faint groan.

Reaching past her right shoulder with her left hand, she flipped the switch. Light flooded the porch. Squinting against the sudden brightness, she saw the sheriff lying on the floor just before something slammed into the back of her head.

After an hour of waiting in the dark beside the barn, the rush of adrenalin that had flooded Richard's body earlier had drained away. Fatigue had set in. His gut ached. He felt jittery from too much coffee and not enough sleep. It was a struggle to keep his mind focused. It would be dawn soon. Maybe Khalil had given up. Maybe he'd gone back to the car and left. How much longer could he and the others stay alert without food or sleep?

To stave off boredom, he called KD to see what was happening at the house. But when it went to voice mail, he stared at the phone in confusion. She should have answered. Why hadn't she answered?

Unless she couldn't.

Yanking the SIG 40 from the holster on his belt, he raced toward the house.

Dalton must have seen him from the AI offices. He ran through the lawn gate seconds behind him. "What happened?" he whispered, following him up the steps to the darkened veranda.

"KD didn't answer her cell." Richard stumbled to a stop when he saw the shadowed form of the sheriff lying on the veranda tiles. A second later, he was pounding up the stairs, heart racing, his footsteps loud in the silent house. "KD!"

Raney and Shirley burst out of Len's bedroom. "What's wrong?"

"Ford's hurt. Where's KD?"

"Last we saw, here on the landing."

Dalton yelled from downstairs. "Raney! Shirley! Get the first aid kit! The sheriff's been stabbed!"

The next few minutes were bedlam as Raney ran around the house, collecting the things Shirley needed to stop the blood seeping from the wound in Ford's chest. Richard knelt beside him, applying pressure while Dalton talked to 911, then called Glenn to tell him what had happened.

Panic sucked the air from Richard's lungs. *I can't do this. I have to find her. If she's hurt*—He couldn't finish the thought.

As soon as Dalton got off his cell, Richard shot to his feet and let Raney help Shirley bandage the sheriff's chest. "Did they see anything?"

"Nothing. Chuy's covering the car, in case they take her there. Glenn's checking on the one in the shed."

Richard felt his stomach roll. "You think they took her?"

"She wouldn't have wandered off on her own."

"Oh, damn . . ."

Dalton gripped his shoulder, gave him a rough shake. "Get it together, Richard! We'll find her."

Richard swallowed hard and nodded. "When will the ambulance get here?"

"It's coming from Gunther. If we're lucky, thirty minutes."

"I can't wait that long."

"Then go. We've got this."

Richard pulled his backup Beretta M9 from his pocket and thrust it toward Dalton. "Take it. I don't give a damn what Ford says."

Dalton slipped it into his belt. "Raney and I will cover the house. Go do what you have to do."

When Richard cut through the parked cars, he saw Glenn running down the drive toward the house. "He's gone!" the foreman yelled as he approached. "Somehow the sonofabitch got out of the shed!"

"Tell Dalton, then go back and cover Chuy! They took KD! We can't let them leave with her. Go!" Half sick with dread, Richard raced on to the AI lab.

As Mostafa struggled to carry the woman across the creek, he heard yelling behind him. Fear sent him stumbling forward at a faster pace.

They must have found the soldier he'd stabbed. He hoped the cursed infidel was dead. He would have made certain of it, but he heard the woman on the stairs and had been forced to hide. When he saw her creep past his hiding place, he had almost wept with joy. It was the same woman in the photograph on his phone. The one who had murdered Asef. The one he had been sent to find. Allah had surely blessed him to put both the woman and the uniformed soldier in his path.

He hoped she wasn't dead. He had tried not to hit her too hard. He shifted her weight in his arms, wondering how one so small could feel so heavy. His legs wobbled with the strain of carrying her. Every breath burned in his throat. His heart drummed so loud, he could hear nothing but the beat of it. Stopping to catch his breath, he looked around, trying to remember the path in the image his uncle had shown him. Then he saw a faint glow ahead and knew he was almost there.

Suddenly a form appeared beside him. Big. Bloody. Teeth bared.

Mostafa cried out, almost dropping the woman.

"Be silent!" the figure hissed in Dari, and Mostafa realized it was Muhammad, come back from the dead.

* * *

Sarge saw Richard coming and ran down the stairs to meet him at the door of the AI offices.

Richard told him about KD and the man escaping the shed. "Tell Harvey with KD out there to watch his shots. But if he sees the Afghans, to blow their damn heads off."

"Fuck, yeah! Now we talkin'!"

After Sarge went to tell Harvey what had happened, Richard wasn't sure where he should go. He listened for voices or movement but couldn't hear anything over his own labored breathing.

KD would put up a fight. Make noise. Do something. Unless she couldn't and was being carried. If that was the case, whoever had her wouldn't be able to move fast or far. Where would he take her? They'd covered all the logical places.

Except Tent City.

He started running.

And almost ran into Alejandro and his horse in the trees.

Richard repeated everything he'd told Sarge. When Alejandro heard that KD had been taken and the man he'd left in the shed had escaped, he let loose a string of hissed curses, both Spanish and English.

"We don't have time for that!" Richard warned in a whisper. "You see or hear anything by the creek?"

With effort, Alejandro calmed himself. "Before you came, I was tracking something I heard moving through the trees. Clumsy. Too noisy to be deer. Maybe hogs."

"Moving where?"

Alejandro pointed in the direction Richard had been running. "Toward the tents."

Sudden elation almost sent Richard charging through the brush. Instead, he forced himself to stop and think. A rushed frontal assault would probably get KD killed. But if they could think of a diversion, something to draw the Afghans out . . .

He pulled out his phone. While he waited for Dalton to

answer, he told Alejandro to go tell Sarge to come to the
tents. "No noise. Tell Harvey to stay where he is in case one
of them tries to run—Hey, Dalton," he said in a low voice
when Cardwell answered. "She's at Tent City. I'm sure of it.
Here's what I need you to do."

By the time he'd finished the call, Alejandro was riding
back through the trees. Richard told him to unsaddle his
horse, but leave on the bridle, then bring the horse and follow him as quietly as he could.

KD rose out of the blackness in fits and starts. Pain. In her
head, her neck, even her hands and feet. Dimly, she heard
voices whispering and wondered if she was back in the hospital in Germany. But the voices weren't speaking English.

Dari!

Panic engulfed her. She tried to move, couldn't, and
forced open her eyes. When she saw her wrists and ankles
zip-tied to a camp chair, terror exploded. Before she could
scream, a hand clamped over her mouth, fingers digging
into her cheeks and jaw.

"Be silent!"

A face appeared before hers, backlit by the light above
his head. Bearded, scarred. Khalil Farid.

Her mind reeled.

A rough jerk brought her back. "If you bring them, I will
kill them. Like I killed the traitor, Samira, and Warrant
Officer Murdock, and will soon kill you."

Richard was dead? She started to spiral.

He shook her again, nails digging into her jaw. "Be silent! Do you understand?"

With his hand over her mouth, she couldn't answer or
nod. All she could do was stare up at him in helpless terror,
knowing what was to come but no way to stop it. *Richard . . .
oh God . . . I'm so sorry.*

With a shove that sent her head spinning again, he released her and walked a few feet away to where two men were arguing and punching on their cell phones. Beside them stood a small table with several automatic handguns and knives on top and two AK-47s leaning against it.

She fought to bring her thoughts into focus. When had he killed Richard? They would have heard or seen something. Were the others still alive? She looked around, recognized the plank floor and canvas walls, and realized she was in one of the therapy tents. She couldn't have been there long. It was still dark outside.

Think!

She needed a weapon. Something to cut the zip ties binding her to the chair. But other than the guns and knives on the table, she saw nothing she could use to protect herself . . . or even take her own life if it came to that.

No! Don't give up! He'll come! Khalil must have confused Richard with the sheriff. *God . . . let him be alive.*

Time. That's all she had. If she could buy enough of it, Richard would find her. Even if it cost her a beating, she had to keep the Afghans distracted until he came. "Khalil Farid," she said in a hoarse voice. "You're wrong."

The three men looked up.

One was very young, despite the dark stubble on his jaw. A true believer. She saw fear on his face and guessed he was also the weakest link.

The one trying to work the phone was a mess. Dirty, his face battered, one pantleg soaked with blood. The one caught in the snare? When they argued, Farid called him Mohammad. His eyes were cold and hard and showed no fear. Apparently he was resourceful enough to free himself, but not smart enough to work a smartphone.

Next to him, Khalil looked fat and old. But seeing the way the injured one—Muhammad—deferred to him told KD he was the leader. A fucking lunatic, Richard had called him. He looked it. Maybe he was high on drugs. He was definitely the most dangerous of the three.

"The man you killed was a lawman," she told him. "A sheriff. Not an army officer. Not Murdock."

With a look of fury, Khalil rounded on the youngest man. He said something in Dari. When the panicked kid shook his head, Khalil hit him across the face.

Realizing it was probably the young one who had hurt the sheriff and taken her from the house, KD saw a way to add to their confusion. "Murdock is still alive," she said loudly, regaining Khalil's attention. "And he's coming for you."

"You lie!" Farid lunged toward her, fist rising.

She tried to duck, but the blow hit her head and knocked her and the chair over onto its side. She lay stunned, while above her, a tense, whispered argument went on until the one with the bloody leg pulled Farid away.

She tried to listen as they argued. Over the ringing in her ears, all she could make out was the Dari word for *wait*. But when she saw Muhammad point at his phone then at her and make a slashing motion across his neck, she knew what they had planned, had seen it on the news over and over. Was she to be another videoed assassination?

Bile burned in her throat. Her lungs seized. She began to shake. It took all of her strength to block the images flashing through her mind. *God . . . don't let them . . . please . . . help me.*

The three men bent over the phones again.

Numbly, she watched them from where she lay, her stomach churning with fear. From what she could make out, their three phones were identical except for the security codes. They either didn't have facial recognition or couldn't remember which code opened which phone or couldn't figure out how to work the apps. Not surprising, since technical expertise wasn't a priority in Afghanistan.

The young one came over and struggled to pull her chair back on its feet. As soon as he got KD upright, Farid came over and thrust a paper in her face. "Read!" he ordered.

It was written in Arabic. KD couldn't tell which dialect.

"Do you have one in English?" she mumbled through swollen lips, wincing at the throb in her head.

He slapped her. Started to draw back his arm again.

Then the one named Muhammad turned off the overhead light.

In the sudden dimness, KD heard him hiss for silence. As her eyes adjusted, she saw him point to the side of the tent as he snatched up one of the AKs. Flipping the safety to full auto, he worked the bolt, then put his ear close to the canvas wall.

All KD heard was an odd, snuffling noise. Like an animal's snort.

The kid rushed over and grabbed the other AK. Khalil took a pistol, racked the slide, then they both flattened against the tent wall, guns up and ready.

Another snorting nose. Something big moving nearby.

KD couldn't see what was happening. One eye didn't open all the way and her head wouldn't stop spinning long enough for her to focus. The three men argued in tense whispers. She didn't understand their words but guessed they thought someone was outside the tent.

God, let it be Richard. She tried to listen, but all she heard was the rush of blood past her ear and moths batting against the darkened light above her head.

When nothing happened, Khalil muttered instructions to the young Afghan, then shoved him out of the tent. KD prayed for a gunshot, a scream, the sound of a body falling. But all that broke the silence was the distant wail of a siren.

Seconds later, the kid called back something that sounded like "*aspa*" or "*asp*," which might have been Dari for "horse."

A horse? Why was a horse running loose?

Khalil eased the flap open a few inches and looked outside. Through the gap, KD could see the dark silhouettes of tree branches against the sky and knew it was nearing dawn. Richard would find her soon.

After a short, whispered conversation with the kid,

Khalil drew back inside with obvious relief. Muhammad propped his AK against the table and went back to the cell phones. They didn't turn on the light. Khalil stuck his handgun into his belt and stood beside Muhammad, arguing and pointing to the screen. KD wished the bullet he'd left in the chamber of his automatic would discharge and blow his balls off.

Minutes passed. When the kid didn't return, Khalil stepped close to the canvas and called in a soft voice, "Mostafa?"

No answer.

He called again, louder.

When there was still no answer, the two Afghans looked at each other. KD watched confusion turn to fear, then panic. Muhammad snatched up the AK. Khalil grabbed a knife and rushed toward KD.

With a cry, she wrenched away, expecting to feel the blade slice into her throat. When nothing happened, she saw Khalil waiting tensely beside her and Muhammad edging toward the gap in the opening of the tent. With the barrel of his AK, he eased back the flap. One inch. Two. Stepping closer, he peered out.

A deafening blast. He flew backward, clutching at his throat, then fell to the floor and lay still.

With a cry, Khalil dropped to his knees behind KD, using her for cover.

She twisted and bucked, trying to tip the chair on its side so she would be out of the line of fire, but Khalil grabbed her hair, yanked her head back, and pressed the knife against her throat.

KD froze, her breath coming in short, shallow gasps.

A second later, Richard stepped over Muhammad's body and into the tent.

He wore an expression KD had never seen. Teeth bared. Eyes so focused, he hardly blinked. Muscles taut in the arms and hands that held his big automatic in a two-handed shooter's grip. "Put down the knife, Farid," he ordered.

"Stay back!" Khalil warned, pushing the blade harder against KD's neck.

She felt a warm trickle but didn't dare move. Khalil panted behind her, his hot breath against the back of her head.

Shoot him! Shoot him now!

Richard took a step forward. He didn't look at KD. The barrel of his gun never wavered. "Now, Farid."

Dalton stepped into the tent, his pistol up and ready. Alejandro came in behind him, holding a knife. Then Sarge, smiling and flexing his hands.

"Stop! Or I will kill her!" The Afghan cried out in a high, thin voice.

"Let her go and we'll let you go," Dalton said. He stepped off to Richard's side, forcing Farid to shift on his knees so KD would screen him from both men.

The Afghan's breathing turned into a whimper and he shifted back when Alejandro and Sarge stepped nearer on his other side. "Come no closer!"

"We don't want to hurt you," Dalton said in his calm, even voice. "Put down the knife. And the gun in your belt. We won't shoot."

The man behind her didn't move. KD could smell his sweat, feel the tremble in the knife against her neck. Afraid Khalil's terror would drive him to do something stupid, KD said in a strained voice, "You've done nothing wrong, Khalil."

"Be silent!" he hissed, his breath rancid with fear.

"It was Mostafa who killed the sheriff," she insisted, hoping she was wrong and Ford was still alive. "Not you. By our laws, you've done nothing wrong. They'll have to let you go."

"It's true," Dalton cut in. "If you release her, we have to let you go. That's the law. But if you hurt her, we'll kill you."

KD sensed the man's terror and indecision. Felt the knife waver.

Shoot him! her mind screamed.

"Last chance," Dalton said. "Drop it now."

Alejandro and Sarge edged closer.

Richard didn't move. Never looked away from Khalil.

One second. Two. The blade left KD's neck. Khalil let go of her hair. When KD heard the *thump* of the knife hitting the floor, she sagged forward in relief.

"Good choice, Khalil," Dalton said. "Stand up."

Grunting with the effort, Khalil staggered to his feet.

"Now step back."

Khalil stepped back. But KD could still feel him looming behind her and shrank away, terrified he might try to grab her again.

"Take out the gun and put it on the floor," Dalton ordered.

KD watched Dalton's eyes as he tracked Khalil's hand down to his belt. Heard the rustle of cloth as Farid pulled the gun free. Then she flinched in startled terror when Richard's gun went off with an earsplitting *boom*, and Khalil fell to the floor behind her.

The next few minutes were chaos—Richard kneeling by her chair to cut the ties—Dalton calling Raney to bring the Expedition but to keep the EMTs there until they brought KD to the house—Alejandro and Sarge crowding close, faces worried, asking if she was okay.

She couldn't answer. Couldn't think. Hoarse sobs rose in her throat.

As soon as she was free, she threw herself at Richard, desperate to feel his arms around her, to know she was safe and he was alive. She couldn't get close enough. Couldn't stop shaking. Couldn't believe they had survived. "He said you were dead," she cried against his neck. "I didn't believe it. I knew you would come. You always come when I need you."

She could feel the tremble in his arms, the thud of his heart against hers, hot tears falling into her hair. "I'm here, babe. You're safe. I'm safe. It's over."

CHAPTER 22

After telling the men not to touch anything and to leave the tent, Richard took KD out to a bench beside the fire ring. Alejandro found a blanket in one of the other tents, brought it to Richard, murmured something in Spanish to KD, then left to find his horse and take it back to the livestock barn.

After wrapping the blanket around KD's shaking body, Richard pulled her onto his lap and held her tight against his body, not knowing if her shivering was from fear, or shock or because she was cold. Closing his eyes against an onslaught of emotion, he began to rock, the same thoughts circling his mind in an unending loop: *She's alive. She's safe. Thank you, God.*

A few minutes later, Raney drove up with good news. Sheriff Ford was alive and had a good chance of pulling through. Hearing that after such a long, terrible night, boosted everyone's sagging spirits.

While Richard gently loaded KD into the second row of seats in the Expedition then climbed in beside her, Sarge showed Dalton where he'd come across the third Afghan—

facedown in the creek. No obvious wounds, but the angle of the head might indicate a broken neck. No one asked Sarge how he'd discovered the body. No one wanted to know.

After returning Richard's backup gun, Dalton took the wheel of the Expedition; Raney, the passenger seat; and Sarge crowded into the rear. Then they headed slowly back to the house.

Richard couldn't tell how badly KD was hurt. She seemed lucid and was able to talk, although she was shaking so much, he had trouble understanding her. He was shaky, too, still caught between fear and rage whenever he thought of Khalil's knife at her throat. He tried to stay calm, knowing the day wasn't over and there would be questions to answer, but he had little energy left to think. All he could do was look down at the woman in his arms and wonder what he would have done if he'd lost her.

In the front seat, Raney chattered nonstop, as strung out on adrenalin as the rest of them were. She told them that without Shirley's quick intervention, Ford might have bled to death, but now he was stable and ready for transport as soon as the EMTs checked out KD. "He was even able to talk to Mama on the phone, which was kind of sweet."

But there was troubling news, too.

Someone in either the Border Patrol, the Texas Highway Patrol, or the army's MP Division had alerted the Department of Homeland Security about the three Afghans crossing the border, and DHS had called in the FBI. "They're already showing up," Raney warned.

Richard envisioned a long day ahead and was determined that, if charges were brought, none of these guys went down with him. "Listen up," he said, loud enough to be heard over the noise of the motor. "Let me talk to the FBI. Dalton, if either you or Sarge are questioned, I want you to say you weren't inside the tent when Farid or the other man were shot."

"Muhammad," KD said weakly. "He was the one in the snare. The young one . . . Mostafa . . . took me from the house."

Richard filed that away, then continued his instructions. "Say you didn't see anything. Period. Sarge, make sure Alejandro knows. KD will back you up, right, babe?"

She gave a shaky nod. "I only remember seeing you come in, then hearing gunfire."

The words sounded convincing, but Richard knew they weren't true. He'd seen the fear and horror on her poor battered face. She'd been aware of everything going on around her.

"Why you trying to cover for us?" Sarge asked from the rear seat.

"I'm not covering. I'm simplifying. My SIG 40 was the only gun fired. Which means I'm the only shooter. Got it?"

Sarge laughed. "I don't need no fucking gun to kill a terrorist," he said, giving Richard another reason to keep him as far away from the feds as possible.

"Look, guys." Richard needed to get this settled before they reached the house. "I know what I'm doing. I was interrogated dozens of times as part of my PsyOps training, and I conducted double that number as a CID agent. I know how to protect myself, so let me handle it, Okay?"

Richard knew there would be questions. No witnesses to Mostafa's death—and only Richard's account of how Muhammad and Farid died. The FBI would question KD, but she would tell them the same thing Richard did, or fall back on a memory lapse after her attack. Either way, forensics would back them up. As long as Dalton, Alejandro, and Sarge said they came into the tent *after* the shooting, everything would be okay.

Granted, there might be lingering doubts about the cuts and contusions on Muhammad. Or questions about how three Afghans on the national watch list could have gotten into the country undetected. Or why the State Department had issued an entry visa to a known Taliban sympathizer in the first place. But the answers to most of those questions were classified, and since there was no one to corroborate or refute Richard's and KD's accounts of what happened in the tent, Richard was confident they could all walk away clean from this nightmare.

It took some discussion, but by the time they'd arrived at the house, they were all agreed: Richard had the only gun; no one saw Mostafa after he left to follow the horse; only KD and Richard had been in the tent when Farid and Muhammad were shot. And most important—Richard would be the one to talk to the feds.

As long as he could stay awake.

It wouldn't be easy. The constant need to stay vigilant and ready to act on an instant's notice, coupled with his unrelenting fear for KD, had sucked all the energy out of him. The adrenalin crash left him feeling numb, sluggish, his thoughts scattered. All he wanted to do was sleep. But he knew he had to stay focused if he hoped to convince the FBI that the shootings in Tent City were warranted. He might not like what he'd had to do, but he certainly wouldn't lose sleep over killing two terrorists. Some actions were justified, no matter how brutal and ugly they were, and using lethal force against two terrorists was one of them.

An EMT was waiting on the veranda when Dalton pulled into the parking area—as were four stern-faced people wearing FBI ball caps and windbreakers. When the medic took KD into the guest room to check her over, an FBI tech with a black bag and a camera around her neck went with them.

Richard pulled Raney aside and told her to go with them. "Make sure they get samples of Khalil's blood in KD's hair and on the back of her shirt." As soon as the door had closed behind her, he went back to the three agents on the veranda and said, "There are three dead bodies out past the creek. Cardwell can show you where."

Immediately, the female special agent in charge—SAIC Remmert—sent an agent back to the crime scene with Dal-

ton. Then she and Agent Brouwer, a young man with less
cynicism in his eyes than the SAIC, took Richard into the
office for a private interview. Remmert motioned for Richard to take one of the leather chairs flanking the fireplace.
She moved to the other. Agent Brouwer pulled up the desk
chair. Smiles all around. Nothing threatening or official
here, folks. Just a friendly, cozy chat.

Yeah, right.

As soon as he'd sat down, Richard asked for something
to drink and eat.

The junior agent went back to the kitchen. Remmert
took a small recorder from her pocket and set it on the table
between their chairs. With an apologetic smile, she explained that it was agency policy to record all interviews.

"Good idea," Richard said, and pulled out his cell phone,
set it to record, and put it on the table beside the FBI recorder. Remmert didn't look happy, but she didn't ask Richard to remove it.

By the time they'd covered the basics—Richard's full
name, DOB, etc., Brouwer was back with coffee, water, and
a PB&J wrapped in a paper towel.

While he ate, Richard told them he had shot Khalil
Farid and the man KD had identified as Muhammad—last
name unknown. The younger Afghan, Mostafa—also
last name unknown—had died of either a broken neck or
drowning. Possibly from a fall, since they'd found him at
the bottom of a six-foot drop, facedown, in the creek. Then
the questions began, growing less friendly and more direct
as they went along, carefully timed to keep the person being questioned off balance. A common interrogation tech-
nique. Richard was familiar with it. But unlike most of the
people he had interviewed, he knew to keep his answers
short and on point.

Once they'd covered background—Richard's previous
employment in the army and why he'd left, his relationship
with the Whitcombs, KD in particular, his time spent in

Afghanistan, and his thoughts about Middle Eastern people in general—they moved on to what he knew of KD's abduction, which was nothing, since he'd been at the barn when it happened.

Undeterred, they asked him to explain the purpose of the tent compound and why Richard thought the Afghans had taken KD out there.

He told them about the horse therapy project, adding that the tents were currently unoccupied, and since all the other ranch buildings were being watched, he figured if KD was still at the ranch, Tent City was where she would be.

By then, they'd been at it for almost two hours. The SAIC called a short break, which Richard took to mean the agent sent to the crime scene had probably returned and they wanted to compare notes with him.

As soon as Remmert and Brouwer had left, Raney came in.

Richard pointed to the recorder on the table, to his ear, then in the direction the agents had gone. When he saw that she understood they were being recorded, he asked what the EMTs had said about KD.

Raney reported she had a mild concussion, contusions, a few cuts that didn't need stitching, and no broken bones. "Mostly bruised and battered. They took Ford on to University Medical in Lubbock," she added. "Mama's meeting them there. They wanted KD to go in for observation, but you can guess how that went."

"What's she doing now?"

"Resting. After everybody cleared out, we made her take a shower and eat some scrambled eggs and toast. She's in bed, but I doubt she's asleep. Seems pretty worried about you."

"If she's still awake, tell her I'm fine and I'll be in as soon as I'm finished here. How're you and Dalton holding up?"

"He's less concerned about me than how this will affect the baby. He's such a worrier," said the family worrier. "He and the other guys are moving the horses and bulls back to their paddocks and taking care of ranch business. As for me, I'm heading up for a long, long nap. You need anything, Shirley's on kitchen duty."

She surprised Richard by bending down to give him a hug and whisper in his ear, "Hang in there, we've got your back." Then she straightened, patted his shoulder and left. Like he was already part of the family. Richard appreciated that.

As soon as she'd walked out, the agents came back in. Almost as if they'd heard she was about to leave. After returning to their seats, Remmert pretended to turn the recorder back on, and got down to business. "Tell us about your connection to Khalil Farid."

"There is no connection," Richard answered.

"Then why did he come here all the way from Afghanistan?"

"To kill me and KD Whitcomb."

"To kill you? Why?"

"Because of our involvement in an incident in Afghanistan."

"Describe this incident."

"I can't. It's classified."

Richard sensed their frustration, but instead of giving up, they shifted the questions back to Tent City.

"When you arrived at the compound," Brouwer said, "were you armed?"

"I had a SIG 40 and a backup Beretta M9."

"Why did you feel you needed two weapons?"

"Same reason you carry a backup. In case my primary firearm jammed." *Why else?*

"You expected trouble?"

"I expected to get KD away from her abductors, whatever it took."

"How did you know for certain they were inside the tent?" Brouwer asked.

"I heard voices and recognized Khalil Farid's from earlier threats he'd made."

"Threats made in Afghanistan?"

"That's classified." Richard could almost hear Remmert's teeth grinding.

"When you approached the tent, did you call out, or fire a warning shot?"

And alert them that we were there? What kind of a fucktard did they think he was? "We didn't want to risk anything happening to KD."

"Who is the 'we' you're referring to?" Remmert asked.

Richard gave them Dalton's, Alejandro's, and Sergeant Rayfield's names.

"Were they armed, too?"

"No." He explained that Alejandro didn't own a gun, Dalton had been in prison and wasn't allowed to use a gun, and Sarge was a therapy patient.

"Why did they accompany you to the compound if they weren't armed?"

Richard felt a headache build. "It wasn't a planned thing. We were all out looking for KD and ran into each other near the tents."

For the next hour it was all about his guns—where Richard got them, how long he'd had them, were they registered, did he have a carry permit, what kind of training had he had, and so on. Richard's answers started to get muddled as they went over each question several times. Finally, he lost what patience he had left and asked for something to drink.

Remmert and Brouwer both left. But they were probably watching him through a keyhole or something, because as soon as Richard had tipped back his head and closed his eyes, they came back in with a small glass of water and started grilling him again, the questions coming hard and fast.

"Let's go back to the tent compound," Remmert said after Richard had put the empty glass on the table. "How did you know where she was?"

Richard stretched and yawned. "I heard voices inside one of the tents. Didn't I already tell you that?"

"We're just getting it straight in our minds," Brouwer said. "When you realized you'd found her, what did you do next?"

Richard thought for a moment, trying to remember the sequence. "We decided we needed a diversion. Something to draw the Afghans out. So we sent a horse into the clearing."

"We?" Brouwer paused to consult his notes. "You mean you, Dalton, Alejandro, and Sergeant Rayfield?"

"Actually, Alejandro sent it in. It's his horse."

"Okay, so it's Alejandro's horse," Remmert snapped. Seems she didn't like being fucked with, either. "What did the other two men do when Alejandro sent in his horse?"

Richard rubbed his bleary eyes. "Since I was the only one with a gun, I told them to find cover."

"Why?"

"In case the Afghans came out to investigate or started shooting."

"And did they?"

Come out shooting? Or take cover? Things were starting to scramble in Richard's head. They'd been questioning him for hours now, and it was wearing him down. He couldn't let it go on much longer. "Dalton and Sarge ducked behind the porta-potties. Alejandro went into the trees. I watched from behind another tent to see what would happen."

"And what did happen?" the SAIC prodded impatiently.

"A man came out of the tent to investigate and saw the horse."

"The one who drowned in the creek? Mostafa?"

Richard nodded, then winced when it made the pounding in his head worse. "I didn't know he drowned until later."

"Was he armed?"

"Yes. An AK-47."

"Did you confront him?"

With a handgun? He would have laughed if he'd had the energy. "No. I was more worried about the two still in the tent with KD. Is there any coffee left?"

There was. Barely warm. Richard drank it anyway and tried to ignore the burn of acid in his stomach. After he set the empty cup aside, the SAIC asked what happened when Mostafa came out to investigate.

"He saw the horse. Whispered something to the Afghans still in the tent, then followed the horse around the back toward the creek." Richard didn't mention that he might have seen Sarge head that way, too. "That's the last we saw of him until later, when we found his body in the creek."

"What did you do after Mostafa left to follow the horse?"

"I drew my handgun and approached the tent." Hadn't he already told them that? He wasn't sure. "I need to use the head."

"If you can wait just a—"

"Now."

He took his time, splashed his face with cold water, took a couple of antacids and an ibuprofen from the medicine cabinet, then went back to the office to find Shirley passing out sandwiches, fruit, and tall glasses of iced tea. Was it lunch already? Or was this supper?

As he sat down, he asked the corporal how KD was doing.

"Resting, but she seems okay," Shirley answered, giving Richard an encouraging smile. "You should do the same," she added with a meaningful look at the feds as she left the room.

Relief for KD boosted Richard's energy. He ate all he could, drank two glasses of tea, then peeled a banana. The antacids started to calm his stomach and he felt like he might be getting a second wind.

Then they started in again. Same song and dance, second—or maybe third—verse.

"Let's go back for a moment, Richard," Remmert said. "After Mostafa followed the horse toward the creek, did you see or hear anything? Tell us step-by-step what happened."

"I saw movement by the opening of the tent. The barrel of a rifle pushing the flap aside. A man looked out. I didn't recognize him, but I knew he wasn't Farid. When he saw me, he swung the AK toward me. I fired first."

"Then what?"

"The man I shot fell backward, and I entered the tent."

Saying the words aloud put all those terrible moments back into Richard's head. Stepping over the body, seeing KD's battered, swollen face, smelling the dead man's blood, the sound of footsteps coming up behind him.

He began to sweat. A sour taste rose in his mouth. His heart pounded so hard and fast he felt a little dizzy. It took all his strength to push the panic down and calm his breathing. Someone handed him a glass of water. He gulped it down. It astonished him how quickly it had come on, how close he had come to totally coming unhinged. Was this what KD felt when she had a panic attack?

He looked up to see SAIC Remmert staring at him. "You okay, Richard?"

"Not really." Richard rubbed his face, realized his fingers were shaking, and dropped his hand to his thigh. "We about done? I haven't slept in almost forty hours." And why was it so hot? Had they turned off the AC?

Don't let them get comfortable. Turn the heat up or the air-conditioning off. Keep them distracted. One of the first lessons he'd been taught in training.

"Only a few more questions, then we'll call it a day." Remmert shuffled through her notes. "Tell us what happened when you entered the tent."

Richard struggled to stay focused. "I saw KD zip-tied to a chair. Farid was crouched on his knees behind her, using her for cover, pulling her head back by her hair. He had a knife at her throat."

"Any other weapons?"

"A pistol tucked in his belt."

"Did you say or do anything?"

"I told him to drop the knife and put the gun on the floor. He pushed the blade harder against her neck. She started bleeding."

"And then what?"

"When I saw blood, I knew if I didn't stop him, he would kill her. I told him if he let her go, I would let him go. All he had to do was let go of her hair, stand up, and walk out."

"What did he do?"

"He let go of her hair and stood up." Richard dragged a hand over his face, trying to wipe away the memory of KD slumping forward, blood dripping from her neck, and the rage he'd felt when he shifted his gaze to Khalil's face.

"What happened next?"

"He reached for the gun in his belt."

"What did you do?"

"I shot him in the face."

"Maybe he was surrendering."

"I doubt it." And it wouldn't have mattered to Richard if he was.

"Anyone else in the tent?"

Lifting the tail of his shirt, Richard wiped sweat from his face. "Not then. The other men came in after." He rose on wobbly legs. "That's it for now. I need to lie down before I puke." And without waiting for permission, he walked out.

It was the longest day KD had ever suffered through. And suffer she did. Her head wouldn't stop pounding, her body was so sore, it hurt to roll over, her stomach was queasy from all the anti-anxiety meds she'd taken, and every time she looked in the mirror, she started to cry again. On top of all that pain and misery, she'd had a half-dozen calls from Mama, who had flown from Dallas to Lubbock to be there when Sheriff Ford came out of surgery.

KD knew Mama was worried and trying to be supportive, but she didn't need long-distance hovering when there
were plenty of people in the house already doing it. Nothing
seemed to help. Even after two showers, she still couldn't rid
herself of the stink of Khalil's unwashed body and the reek
of blood. She couldn't eat, couldn't sleep, and every time she
shut her eyes, it all played out in her head again, or the door
would open, or her phone would buzz, or a noise from some
other part of the house would jar her awake. She didn't want
company, or soup, or tea, or a back rub, or to talk about what
happened. She just wanted Richard.

And on top of all that misery and her worry about him,
there were lingering feelings of fear and anger she couldn't
seem to shake. She wanted to cry, hit something, scream in
rage. But she hadn't the will or energy to do anything but
curl up under the covers, shivering and fearful, and wait for
Richard to come take her into his arms and tell her again
that she was safe, he was safe, it was over, and everything
would be right again tomorrow.

At some point, she must have finally dozed off. Or
maybe she only imagined she slept. Either way, the next
time she opened her eyes, the sun hung low in the sky outside her window, there was a plate of food on the bedside
table, and Richard sat dozing in the chair.

She lurched upright, wincing at the pull of bruised muscles. "Richard?"

His eyes fluttered open. He lifted his head, saw her looking at him, and gave a weary smile. "Babe. How you feel?"

Seeing him sitting there, safe and whole, flooded her
with overwhelming relief. Emotion swelled in her chest.
Her eyes burned and words couldn't get past the clog in her
throat. All she could do was let the tears fall and hold out
her arms.

He climbed in beside her and put his arms around her.
"It's okay, babe," he murmured in a hoarse voice. "I'm here.
I won't leave you. I promise."

He must have showered, too. He smelled of soap and her strawberry shampoo and beneath it, the masculine scent that was uniquely his.

He held her until she ran out of tears. Then he carefully dried her sore face, gently kissed her swollen lips, and said, "It over, KD. Done. So no more excuses. You damn well better marry me or I'll never let you out of this bed."

She wanted to smile but was afraid her lip would start bleeding again. "That's not much of a threat."

"I'm serious, KD. I've never been more serious about anything in my life. When I walked into that tent and saw what they'd done to you . . ." His voice started to shake. He stopped, cleared his throat and said, "I love you, KD. I didn't realize how much until I thought I'd lost you. I almost went crazy . . ." Again, his voice faltered. "Just tell me you love me and you'll marry me. I need to hear you say it."

Taking his face in her hands, she looked directly into his weary blue eyes. "Of course I'll marry you, Richard. And I'll love you like you've never been loved in your life, until we're both so old and gray and don't remember who we are, then I'll fall in love with you all over again." Leaning up, she gently pressed her lips to his, then drew back. "You're my man."

Blinking hard, he pulled her so tight against his chest, she could hardly breathe. "Always."

KD slowly improved. After interviewing everyone a second time, the FBI left and the media descended. The ranch phone rang continuously. TV news vans with forests of antennas sprouting from their rooftops crowded the county road outside the main gate. Without actual footage, news anchors wallowed in speculation, happily tossing out unfounded tidbits to keep viewers tuned in. Even with Chuy and Hicks posted at the gate to keep intruders out, KD felt like she had become a prisoner in her own home.

Now that Khalil Farid was no longer a threat and the horse therapy program was at a temporary standstill, she didn't have much to do except worry. Mostly she worried about Richard. She sensed a distance growing between them but didn't know the cause. He seemed to become more distracted every day. Possibly a reaction to the shootings. Or worry about what the FBI was doing. Or maybe he was trying to figure out what he wanted to do with the rest of his life, and whether to stay or leave. That uncertainty carved a hollow place inside her. She felt like worry was eating her from the inside out, devouring hope and leaving in its wake regret and despair.

Killing Asef Farid had changed her. She no longer fully trusted her instincts. She was less decisive, more hesitant, and her indecision often made her doubt her own feelings. A new thing for KD.

And what about Richard? To protect her, he had killed two men. That had to have affected him. Maybe being at the ranch and seeing her every day was a constant reminder of that.

Maybe. If only. What if.

Unable to tolerate the lack of resolution, KD did what she always did when pressure built—she stepped back and quietly began to armor herself against the heartache she was afraid might be coming her way.

It all came to a head the night Richard's father called. It was after nine. KD was in the bathroom, towel drying her hair, and Richard was stretched out on the bed, scrolling through e-mails. The door into the bedroom stood open, so she heard the call come through, and could tell by the tone of his voice during the one-sided conversation that it wasn't good news. That hollow space inside expanded when she heard him say, "I'll be there as soon as I can."

She moved to the doorway. "What?" she asked when he ended the call.

He looked up, a worried expression on his face. "My mother had a heart attack."

KD pressed a hand to her throat. "Will she be okay?"

"It was mild. Minor damage." As he spoke, he rose from the bed, pulled his duffle out of the closet, and carried it to the bureau. "She's scheduled tomorrow afternoon for angioplasty and a stent," he went on as he tossed clothes into the duffle. "She wants to see me before she goes into surgery."

"Is the procedure risky?"

"Not usually. But she's in her sixties and she's put on weight."

She's afraid, KD thought. *She wants to reconcile in case something goes wrong.* Mama had shown similar fears before she'd had her appendix removed.

Richard zipped the duffle closed and looked around, as if checking to see what he might have forgotten. Then he pulled up a map on his phone.

"You're not leaving now, are you?" KD asked in alarm. "It's almost ten."

"She goes in at one." He slipped the phone into his pocket. "It's a twelve-hour drive to Tucson. I can take a two-hour stop if I need to and still get there before the procedure." He began loading his pockets with his wallet, his sunglasses, spare bills, and change.

"Do you want me to go with you?" KD offered.

"Not necessary. You've been through enough without stumbling into the middle of a family crisis." He must have seen her growing panic. "Hey, stop worrying. I'll only be gone four or five days at most."

"I'm not worried," she lied. Not about him leaving. But what if he never came back?

"Come here." He held out his arms. As soon as she stepped close enough, he pulled her in for a long, tight hug.

She drew him in—his warmth, his scent, the steady drum of his heart beneath her cheek. If he didn't come back to her, it would break her.

"This might be a good thing, babe," he said against her hair, the vibration of his low voice rumbling through her

ear. "Give me a chance to figure out what I want to do. I
can't freeload at the ranch forever."

She kept her head tucked and tried to keep her voice
light. "We could always put you to work."

"You already have."

"We could do it again."

He chuckled. "I don't doubt it." Loosening his arms, he
kissed her forehead, trailed his lips down her cheek, settled
in for a longer kiss on her mouth. When he lifted his head,
he was smiling. "Maybe while I'm trying to figure out what
I want to do, you can figure out what you want to do. Other
than the usual, of course. We'll compare notes. Winner gets
to sleep with the loser." He bent to pick up his duffle. As he
slung the strap over his shoulder, KD watched his smile soften
into something tender, and sweet, and maybe a little sad. It
brought an ache to her heart. "I'll miss you, babe. Call if
you need me."

Then he was gone.

The days dragged on. Dalton and Raney did their best to
keep the ranch running, and with the return of the married
workers and help from Sarge and Shirley, who showed no
interest in returning to Hood, they muddled through.

Sheriff Ford moved out of the ICU and was scheduled to
leave the hospital in a few days. Once Raney gave assurances that everything was under control at the ranch, Mama
decided that when "poor Lewis" was released, she would
stay with him at his house in Gunther to make sure he continued to improve. She'd even hired one of Maria's nieces
to help out and chaperone. Yeah, right.

Richard only called once, letting her know the procedure had gone well and his mother was back home. He'd
had several long talks with his parents, and things were
better. He was beginning to understand that their anger
over Kenny's death was mostly directed at themselves,

rather than at him. "We'd all failed him in one way or another," he said in a regretful tone. "But ultimately, Kenny's death was because of his choices, not ours. It doesn't lessen the grief, but does help ease some of the guilt."

He asked about Ford and how things were going at the ranch and when the therapy program would start up again. She told him hopefully soon. Conan had several vets who were interested, and Dalton was replacing the tent where the shootings had occurred. "I've already convinced Sarge and Shirley to stay on to help run future sessions. I think they're hot for each other," she added with a smile. "I've never seen Sarge so mellow."

"Sounds like you've got it all under control."

"We're trying."

They talked for a few more minutes. When she asked how long he was staying in Tucson, he said he'd be heading back in a few days. "Got people to see and plans to make." He sounded hopeful and impatient at the same time. Ready to get on with his life. He ended with, "Gotta go. Miss you, babe. See you soon."

Short and sweet and somewhat impersonal. It felt like a knife in KD's heart.

Two days later, KD was walking back from Tent City when she saw a familiar blue pickup heading toward the house.

She stopped, breath caught. *Richard!* An explosion of joy almost sent her racing toward him shrieking and laughing. She had to force herself to continue at a normal pace as he climbed out of the truck, then stood beside it, watching her. After a moment, he started toward her with long, purposeful strides.

"You're back," she said when he drew near.

Instead of answering, he took two more steps, then swept her up in his arms and held her against his chest. "God, I missed you," he breathed in her ear.

KD buried her face against his throat, arms tight around his neck, not wanting him to see the emotion she couldn't hide. He felt so good. So solid. So perfect against her.

After a moment, he loosened his hold just enough that she could slide back to the ground, but not enough to let her go completely.

"You've lost weight," he said, smiling down at her, his beautiful blue eyes alight with a familiar fire.

"You were only gone four days," she reminded him.

"Too long." Loosening his hold but keeping one arm around her shoulders so he could anchor her to his side, he steered her toward the house.

Slipping an arm around his lean waist, she matched her stride to his. "So what are you going to do?" she asked.

"About what?"

"Before you left, you said you were going to figure out what you wanted to do. Did you?"

"Mostly. A lot of it depends on you."

She stopped and looked up at him. "How so?"

He hesitated, then said, "It's complicated."

She almost hit him. After all her worry and doubt, she couldn't let him get away with that. Letting go of his waist, she crossed her arms over her chest. "Then let me simplify it for you. Do you love me?"

He blinked, taken aback. "Of course."

"Do you want to marry me?"

"Absolutely. But—"

"But what? You have exceptions? Reservations? Stipulations?"

"Well—"

She threw a hand up. "No! There is no room in this discussion for *buts* and *wells*. It's a simple yes or no question. Do you want to marry me?"

He gave an emphatic nod, his eyes dancing. "Yes. I want to marry you. I'm desperate to marry you. Darling."

"But . . . ?"

He let out a deep breath. "But I don't want to live at the ranch."

KD blinked in astonishment. *That's what this is about?*

Apparently misreading her stunned expression, he quickly said, "I love the ranch and your family. But I think we should go our own way. Not far. I wouldn't take you away from the horse therapy program. But how about Gunther?" Before she could respond, he hurried on. "I stopped there on my way back. Had a long talk with the sheriff. And your mother, of course. A very encouraging woman," he added with a weak smile.

"If you mean manipulative, I agree. Go on."

"He—they—convinced me to run for sheriff. If I win, maybe we could get a place somewhere between town and the ranch so you could still have time with your family and run Tent City. What do you think?"

KD had to laugh. Throwing her arms around him, she gave him a long, hard kiss, then laughed again. "I think it's perfect!"

EPILOGUE

Whitcomb Four Star Ranch
Rough Creek, Texas
Two months later

Needing a break from all the guests milling about the house, Coralee Whitcomb hurried down the hallway off the kitchen, ducked into the quiet dimness of the office and closed the door.

Blessed silence.

She stood for a moment, eyes closed, as the past whispered around her. The lingering scent of the cigars Charlie smoked at his desk, thinking she didn't know. The rumble of men's voices when he talked strategy with his business and political cronies. The lonely days after his death when she had come here, hoping to find solace in the room that had always been uniquely his.

With a sigh, she opened her eyes. "We had some good times in here, didn't we, Charlie?"

Smiling faintly, she drifted through the memories, imprinting on her mind every scent and sound and detail of the room that had been the hub of the ranch she had helped nurture over the last three-and-a-half decades. The girls' laughter as they'd played with their dolls and horses on the rug by his chair. The bookcases filled with awards, memorabilia, photographs, and well-worn law books. The gallery of animal heads she'd never grown accustomed to—she'd always hated those glass eyes staring down at her. But this had been Charlie's domain, and even after his death, she hadn't been able to alter a thing. Perhaps Raney would. This was her office now. She and Dalton would fill it with memories of their own.

As she moved past his desk, Coralee paused to open the scrapbook of newspaper clippings that Raney had put together during the last month of her pregnancy.

DRUG CARTEL INVADES GUNTHER COUNTY, the first headline read, followed by a totally fictional account of three men attempting to run a heroin pipeline through Gunther County. It amazed Coralee that anyone would believe such a thing. No mention of Afghan terrorists targeting American soldiers. Or KD's abduction. Or the DOD's controversial policy that had set these events in motion in the first place. The powers that be had decided on this absurd explanation, so here it was.

On the opposite page was another headline: GUNTHER COUNTY SHERIFF INJURED IN BRUTAL ATTACK. Coralee didn't read that article. Simply thinking about those harrowing days she'd spent at Lewis's bedside made her stomach knot. That he had made such a full and remarkable recovery was a miracle.

She scanned other pages, pausing on a headline that read, GOVERNOR HONORS LOCAL HEROES. She smiled, remembering how nervous they'd been that day. *"Sheriff Lewis Ford, along with sheriff-elect Richard M. Murdock, former special agent with the Army's Criminal Investigation Division, and Dalton Cardwell, quarter horse trainer and facilities manager of the sprawling Whitcomb Four Star Ranch, were honored this week by the governor of Texas for their bravery and courage in defending the county against members of a violent drug cartel."* Thankfully, no mention of the FBI's long investigation into the deaths of those "cartel" members, which ended with no charges being filed against the heroes owing to a lack of witnesses or evidence of criminality.

She flipped through write-ups about Lewis's retirement, the special election to fill his position, Richard's landslide win. She especially liked the one describing Lewis's retirement party and the crush of people who had come out to the ranch to wish him well. *"The outpouring of support for retiring Sheriff Ford is a reflection of the high esteem and affection the citizens of Gunther County hold for the man who has served and protected them for over three decades."* He had been so happy and humbled by the huge turnout.

But her favorite clippings filled the last two pages and were the most recent. The first was dated two weeks ago. No bold headline. No fanfare. Just the picture of a tiny baby and, below it, an announcement of the birth of Charles Whitcomb Cardwell to Raney and Dalton Cardwell of Rough Creek. After Len's son, the second male born in Coralee's family since her father's birth over ninety years ago.

"You always wanted a son, Charlie," she murmured aloud. "Now you have four and two grandsons. How I wish you could have known them."

The last clipping was more elaborate, with a quarter-page photograph of KD and Richard, standing stiffly in formal attire, announcing their upcoming marriage at the ranch on the last Saturday in October. Today.

Coralee was a little miffed that although Richard was featured prominently as the new county sheriff, there was barely mention of the Rough Creek Second Chance Rehabilitation and Horse Therapy Center that KD, Shirley, and Sarge were planning to build at the ranch. Perhaps once they completed construction, they could have the reporter out to see the results.

All in all, it had been a rough year, but one that had ended well.

Closing the scrapbook, she sighed and looked around again. These walls had seen so many changes. Mostly happy, joyful changes, with more on the way. A new baby, another marriage, Joss scheduled to headline her own tour, Len and Ryan growing closer as they watched their own babies circle the nest on fragile wings. And now dear KD, the youngest and strongest of them all, rising above the horrors she had suffered to find love and hope with a man strong enough to stand beside her. They were blessed in so many ways.

"You would have been proud of our girls, Charlie," she whispered to the silent room. "Such beautiful, strong, loving women. The best of both of us."

She walked slowly past the bookcases, trailing her fingertips over this frame or that trinket or any of the many special treasures collected over the years. "I know you've been watching over us, Charlie. I've felt your presence when I've needed you. God bless you for that. And for the beautiful babies you gave me."

She felt tears form but resolutely blinked them away. She didn't want to dampen KD's wedding day with tears. This wasn't a sad goodbye. It was a new beginning. Another step in the journey of her life.

And what a wonderful, fulfilling life it had been.

Through blurred eyes, she smiled up at the portrait above the fireplace mantle that showed Charlie as she would always remember him—forever young, vital, a man in his prime. Sitting proudly beside him, a much younger version of herself, while gathered at their feet sat their four precious daughters all prettied up in their Sunday best.

"We made a beautiful family, didn't we, Charlie?" Her smile faltered on a wistful sigh. "But now our babies are all grown. Younger, stronger backs are needed to carry the legacy we've built." She swiped a hand over her stinging eyes as her heart ached with a familiar sense of loss. "Dear Charlie, how I've missed you. You were the rock I leaned on. The presence that gave me the strength to go on after you were taken from us. I will always treasure the years we had together. But . . . as hard as it will be, dearest, it's time for me to let you go."

"Who are you talking to?"

Startled, she turned to see Lewis standing in the doorway, a worried frown on his handsome face. He looked so much better than he had two months ago. She had been so afraid she was losing him. But now he looked as sturdy and strong as ever.

"Charlie," she said, walking toward him.

"Telling him about me?"

"About us."

When she stopped before him, he rested his hands on her shoulders. "Think he approves?" He said it with a smile, but she saw the doubt in his gray eyes.

"Absolutely. Charlie always liked you." She slid her arms around his waist, still not believing she had been granted the gift of a second chance to love and be loved. "He would have wanted me to have someone like you in my life."

With his thumb, he wiped away the last tear. "Then I hope he knows how grateful I am." He leaned down and kissed her, then straightened when raised voices drifted down the hall from the veranda. "They're about to toast the new bride and groom. Ready to make your announcement? You'll have to make it quick," he added in warning. "Or we'll miss our flight. Without the cruiser, we won't be able to run the lights and speed."

She laughed and patted his cheek. *Dear, sweet man. So honest and dependable.* Hopefully, by the time their honeymoon ended, she would have shown him that some rules were sweeter when broken.

"I've changed my mind," she told him. "I've written down everything I wanted to say and sealed it in an envelope, along with the deed to the west pasture so KD will have a place to build a permanent horse therapy camp. I also included several sizable donations I rounded up to help get them started."

"You don't even want to tell them goodbye?"

"I don't want to intrude on KD's and Richard's day. I've left the letter with Raney and asked her to give it to KD when all the guests have left and it's only the girls and their husbands. I've got it all figured out."

He chuckled. "I'm sure you do. But please tell me that you won't supervise me as relentlessly as you do them. I've been a bachelor too long to be easily managed."

"Don't be silly. You're perfect as you are." She gave him a scolding look. "And stop listening to the girls. If I hadn't been such a relentless manager, they wouldn't be where they are now."

"I'm not complaining, honey. Just warning you it'll take a lot of effort to bring me to heel."

"Oh . . . I like the sound of that."

"Don't be sassy."

Poor Lewis. If he only knew how sassy she could be.

His smile faded. "Think they'll be upset you're marrying again?"

"Not at all. They love you, too. And now that they're grown women with husbands of their own, they want me to have someone, too."

"Good. Because I've chased after you for too many years to let you get away now."

Not wanting to argue about who had pursued whom, Coralee simply smiled. Slipping her hand into the crook of his arm, she led him to the side door. "Come along, my darling. A world of happiness awaits us, and I can't wait to get there."

Don't miss

Rough Creek

Available now from Berkley Jove!

With grim determination, Coralee Lennox Whitcomb sat at her dressing table and set to work transforming a sixty-year-old grandmother into a confident woman in her prime. Her later prime.

In truth, she was tired. Tired of trying so hard. Tired of pretending sixty was the new thirty-nine. Tired of being tired. It was that empty, unsettled kind of weariness that came to those fortunate enough to have once lived full, useful lives, but who now had nothing to do. She didn't like the feeling.

She tried to convince herself that the face staring back at her wasn't truly old, but even she could see it lacked the vitality it once had. The top lip was a little longer and the smile lines sagged a little more. Her hair was still thick and shiny, but there was more gray than brown now, and the hair coloring never seemed to cover it all. But if she looked hard enough into the slightly faded blue eyes, she could still see the dynamic, energetic young woman she had once been. There was still time to make a change and hopefully find that woman again. But what change?

"What are you frowning about?" a voice asked.

Coralee turned to see her second daughter, Raney, come up behind her. "Do I look older to you?"

"Older than what?"

"Don't equivocate. I'm serious." Coralee turned back to the mirror. "I think I look old."

"Some days I do, too."

"You're not yet thirty, dear."

"Near enough." A pause, then: "Is this about your birthday?"

"My sixtieth birthday," Coralee reminded her. "That's over half a century."

"But not yet two-thirds of one. I hear that's when the real aging starts."

"You're not helping."

"Then stop fishing for compliments. You know you're beautiful." Raney stood at Coralee's shoulder and studied her in the mirror. "I thought you'd be happy, Mama, with all your chicks flocking back home to toast yet another year in your amazingly long life. Plus, you still have all your teeth."

Coralee smiled into eyes the same bright, electric blue hers once were. "Still not helping."

Despite her tendency toward sarcasm and a disinterest in anything not having to do with the ranch, Raney was the daughter most like her. She got things done. And with as little fuss or drama as possible.

Coralee had always considered herself the driving force behind the ranch—and her husband, if truth be told—but Raney was its heart and soul. She was the one who had stepped into her father's boots after his death, and in the nine years since, had given up everything—college, marriage, a family of her own—to keep Charlie's legacy going. Other than one ghastly near-marriage, Raney had never even made an attempt to build a life apart from the ranch. Perhaps she was as stuck as Coralee was.

"I am happy," Coralee insisted now. "But I think I might need a change." And with those words, an idea formed. Why shouldn't she try something new?

Dating was out of the question. Not in a town as small as Rough Creek. Pickings were too slim and gossip too rampant. She'd learned that after her "date" with Walter Esterbrook, a man she'd known for two decades and who faithfully attended her church every Sunday. At least, she'd thought she knew him.

She could start a business, or manage something. If Rough Creek had a zoo or museum or even a hospital, she could do volunteer work, other than her weekly afternoon at the food bank. But the only thing around worth managing was the ranch, and Raney already did an excellent job of that.

Despite her sometimes-frivolous facade, Coralee considered herself an astute manager. She always had been, whether it was finding ways to double the size of the Lennox family farm or helping guide her husband through the backwaters of Texas politics toward a lucrative career in the oil and gas industry, or ensuring that she and her daughters were well protected and financially independent after his death. If she was relentless, she'd had to be. And it had paid off. By the time of Charlie's passing, the Lennox farm had doubled yet again, been renamed the Whitcomb Four Star Ranch in honor of their four lovely daughters, and was known for breeding prize-winning Angus cattle. But what had she done lately?

"You're scheming again, aren't you?" With a sigh, Raney sank down onto the edge of Coralee's bed. "What is it this time? A parade of acceptable marriage prospects for your unweddable daughter?"

"If you're unmarried, dear, it's by your own choice."

"Exactly. So, stay out of it. Please."

Ignoring that, Coralee picked up her tray of shadows and went to work on her eyes. Her slightly wrinkled, aging

eyes. "I'm not scheming. I'm planning. With KD starting
Officer Training School soon, it might be months—years,
even—before the five of us can be at the ranch at the same
time." She paused to dab a spot of turquoise to the outside
corners of her upper lids to bring out the blue of her eyes.
"I thought we might make a festive occasion of it."

"Such as?" Raney gave her a wary look.

"We could start with a nice chat to catch up on all the
news, then dinner, followed by wine on the back veranda.
What do you think?" She checked her eyes, thought they
looked trashy, and wiped the color off.

"I think it'll be cold out there," Raney said.

"We can light a fire." Coralee tried basic, unimaginative
taupe. Boring, but better. "And drop the shades if it's windy."
Which it invariably was in spring in northwest Texas. And
when they were all comfy and mellowed by wine, she would
make her announcement. Hopefully, by then, she would know
what that announcement would be. At this point, all that was
certain was she needed to do something different. Refocus.
Make herself her next project. If she explained whatever it was
clearly and calmly, maybe they could avoid the drama that
characterized most of their family gatherings.

"You said 'change.' What kind of change? Nothing involving me, I hope."

Where had her daughter gotten such a suspicious nature?

"I haven't decided." A faint ding from her watch saved
Coralee from further explanation. "Mercy! KD's plane has
landed and you haven't even left yet."

"That's what I came in to tell you." Raney rose from the
bed. "Len and Joss are picking her up on their way from
Dallas."

"Wonderful!" A last fluff of her hair and Coralee rose
from the dressing table. "I'd best help Maria get the hors
d'oeuvres ready." She paused to scan Raney's outfit—her
usual baseball cap and ponytail, jeans, boots, and plaid

shirt over a tank top. Why did she insist on downplaying her fine figure and beauty by dressing like a lumberjack? She would never attract a man dressed like that, unless he was as horse-crazy as she was. "You are planning to change your clothes, aren't you?"

"They're my sisters. What do they care?"

"I care. Please, dear. It's my birthday. And hurry along. They'll be here soon."

Later that afternoon, Dalton Cardwell stepped off the bus at the crossroads in Rough Creek. It was as if nothing had changed in his eighteen-month absence. Same dusty store-fronts, same beat-up trucks in front of the Roughneck Bar, same galvanized water troughs and cattle feeders stacked outside the feed store. The only things different were the weather and the plants in the baskets hanging outside Mellie's Diner. It had been September when he'd left. Now it was early spring and Mellie's flowers were just starting to bud. That sense of sameness was both comforting and disturbing. He liked the constancy of things that had been part of his life for all of his thirty-two years. But he was surprised that nothing had changed in a year and a half. He certainly had.

His stomach rumbled, reminding him that other than a vending machine snack when he'd changed buses in Dallas, his last meal had been almost fourteen hours earlier. Since he hadn't told his parents when he would arrive and it didn't seem right to show up and expect to be fed right off, he crossed to the diner. He figured he'd earned a last unhurried meal before facing his old life and reassessing the burdens it represented. If he'd learned anything while he was in prison, it was that he was done taking orders and having every move dictated by the schedules of others. He'd been doing that for most of his life, from working beside his father on their small cattle ranch, to his stint in the army, to the regimented directives of his time in prison. He was ready for a change.

Other than a waitress refilling ketchup bottles, and a couple of Hispanic ranch hands at the counter talking to the cook through the serving window into the kitchen, the diner was empty. He recognized the waitress, not the workers. Crossing to a booth next to the back window, he slid into the bench against the wall when the waitress walked toward him armed with a coffeepot and mug.

"Dalton? That you?"

Warily, Dalton looked up, not sure what to expect.

Like most small towns, there were few secrets in Rough Creek. His arrest had been big news, and he wasn't sure how many friends he had left. He had known Suze Anderson for most of his life and had even taken her out a couple of times back in high school. But he was an ex-con now, and that had a way of killing friendships.

Her friendly smile said otherwise. "When'd you get out?" she asked.

"This morning."

"Well, welcome home, stranger." She set the mug down in front of him and filled it with coffee. There was an awkward silence, then she said, "I never thought you did it, you know."

He looked up at her.

She made an offhand movement with her free hand. "Yeah, I know. You confessed. But I always figured there was more to it than what the papers said." She leaned closer and dropped her voice. "Heard the commissioner's nephew had been drinking. If you hadn't waived a trial, that might have gotten you off."

He poured a packet of sugar into his cup. "Water under the bridge." To change the subject, he added, "You look good, Suze." And she did. Hair the color of ripe wheat, skin like clover honey, and eyes as brown as dark, rich coffee.

Hell. He must be hungry if he looked at a pretty face and thought of food.

She grinned and patted her flat stomach. "Not bad for two kids. Buddy wants to try for two more. Girls, this time. But I don't know. That's a lot of kids."

Buddy was Suze's husband, and through school, had been Dalton's closest friend. A country boy in the best sense of the words, and a good match for Suze. Solid farm folks and hard workers, totally content to stay in Rough Creek forever. At one time, Dalton had thought that would be enough for him, too.

She gave him an assessing look, her gaze flicking from his scuffed prison shoes to his overlong dark brown hair and the too-tight shirt he'd been issued on discharge. "Gotten even bigger than when you got home from Iraq, I see. Bet nobody calls you Beanpole now."

"Not lately." Not after months of daily two-hour workouts. Another thing he'd learned in prison. If you don't want to fight, look like you can.

"I like it. Even with that god-awful haircut, you're still handsome enough to turn a girl's head." She winked. "Even one that's happily married."

He waved the comment aside, embarrassed, yet gratified that after being locked away with nothing but men for eighteen months, he still had enough polish left that a pretty woman would give him a second look. "Watch out, Suze. I don't want Buddy gunning for me."

The door opened and a couple came in. Tourists, by the look of them. Suze told them to sit anywhere they liked, then took Dalton's order—bacon cheeseburger with extra onions, fries, iced tea, and a piece of Mellie's lemon meringue pie for desert. She started toward the kitchen, hesitated, then turned back, a flush rising up her cheeks. "Look, I'm not sure if you heard, but Karla left. Moved to Fort Worth just after Christmas."

"I know. She wrote to me."

Suze looked relieved. "She talked about leaving Rough Creek all her life. The only reason she stayed so long was because of you."

Dalton had no response to that. He hadn't been surprised that Karla had cut and run after he was sent to Huntsville. Not many women as smart as she was would want to pin their futures on an ex-con. Still, he missed her. She'd been fun to hang with, even though he'd known from the beginning that she'd eventually move on.

His meal came in record time and was every bit as good as he remembered.

By the time he finished, the place was filling up with late diners, probably heading home after a local high school sports event. Spring football practice, or maybe soccer or baseball, judging by the uniforms. He recognized a few of the customers, but despite some curious looks pointed his way, no one approached him.

"How was it?" Suze asked when he went to the register to pay his tab.

"Best meal I've had in a long time. Especially that pie." Seeing how busy the place was, he didn't linger, told Suze to tell Buddy "hi," then stepped outside.

A sense of hope spread through him. Maybe this wouldn't be so bad. Maybe he really could put it all behind him and make a fresh start.

"Heard those idiots on the parole board let you out early," a familiar taunting voice said behind him.

Or maybe not.

Dalton turned to see Deputy Langers coming from the direction of the sheriff's office down the street. He and Toby Langers hadn't gotten along since high school, when Dalton, a fourteen-year-old freshman, had taken over the older, smaller boy's position on the football team. After Dalton's arrest and while he'd been in county lockup awaiting sentencing, the taunting had only gotten worse. Not surprising, since Toby was the county commissioner's local toady, and it was Commissioner Adkins's nephew that Dalton was supposed to have killed. He had hoped the animosity between him and Toby might have cooled during his absence, but Dalton could see it hadn't.

"Thought you'd have sense enough not to come back to Rough Creek," Langers said. "'Specially now that Karla's gone." At one time, Toby had had his eye on Karla, himself.

"It's my home, Toby."

"Maybe not for long. And it's Deputy Langers to you." Puffing out his chest, Langers hooked his thumbs in a duty belt that boasted more paraphernalia than Dalton had ever carried as a grunt in Sandland. "I'm guessing you haven't been out to the ranch yet," he went on, rocking back on his heels so he wouldn't have to tip his head back so far to smirk up at Dalton.

"Heading there now."

"How?" Langers made a show of looking around. "You got a car? Oh, that's right. You're not allowed to drive, are you?"

Not strictly true, since his suspension was for only a year. But Dalton didn't want to get into a discussion about it. "Thought I'd walk."

"Probably wise. Hard for ex-cons to get rides nowadays. Best start now, if you plan to get there before midnight."

Dalton turned and started walking, his jaw clamped on a rush of angry words best left unsaid.

"You be careful," Langers called after him. "Lot of bad things happen on that road. But then, you already know that, don't you? Be sure to give my best to your folks, in case I don't see them before they go."

Go where? But Dalton didn't prolong the conversation by asking.

Luckily, he didn't have to walk more than two miles before he heard a truck rattling up behind him. Spinning a one-eighty, he walked backward, facing the oncoming vehicle, his thumb out.

The truck slowed, tailpipe popping out a barrage of backfire that jittered along Dalton's nerves and made him think of Iraq. He recognized the driver. Harve Henswick, an elderly man who lived two miles past his parents' place and just over the county line.

With a belch of black exhaust, the truck rolled to a stop. The driver sat for a moment, studying him through the dust-and-bug-smeared windshield, then nodded.

"Thanks." Dalton climbed in. Not sure if the old man remembered who he was, he stuck out his hand and was about to introduce himself when Henswick turned and gave him a hard stare.

"When'd you get out?" he asked.

Dalton let his hand drop to his thigh. "This morning."

"Thought you were in for two years."

"I got six months off for good behavior."

"Well, then." Henswick shifted into gear and gave the engine enough gas to make it shudder forward in fits and starts.

And that was the extent of their conversation for the next eighteen minutes.

Dalton watched ten miles of barbed wire fence roll by, broken by the occasional metal gate leading to wooden holding pens with loading chutes. In the middle distance, windmills slowly churned, their grit-scoured blades flashing orange in the lowering sun, while here and there, rusted pump jacks sat silent, their walking beams tilted down, heads to the ground like grazing horses.

The pickup began to slow. When it finally rolled to a stop, Dalton climbed out and shut the door. "Thanks for the ride," he said through the open window.

"Tell your pa I'm still waiting for that ratchet he borrowed. I'd prefer he didn't leave town with it." Without waiting for a response, Henswick pulled out slow enough that Dalton was only mildly peppered with pebbles and black soot.

He stood listening to the rumble and pop of the truck's exhaust until it faded and all that broke the silence was the rustle of the gentle breeze through new grass, the distant hum and whir of big irrigation sprinklers in nearby hay fields, and the *skree* of a hawk floating past on rising thermals. After a year and a half living in close quarters with almost two thousand restless convicts and shouting guards, the still openness was a balm to his battered senses. Even the air felt better.

Dalton closed his eyes and breathed deep.

Gradually the stink of sweat, disinfectant, rancid cooking oils, and harsh cleaners gave way to the familiar smells of alfalfa, cow and horse manure, and good old Texas dust, all underlaid with the faint scent of petroleum rising out of the abandoned wellheads.

It was good to be home.

He turned and walked up the drive toward the sagging gate with the familiar plank sign that read CARDWELL in faded gray letters. But as he drew closer, he slowed to a stop and stared.

On the tilting post that anchored the gate was another sign. Smaller. Not familiar. Made of cardboard and carrying a single word in bold back script.

SOLD.

Ready to find
your next great read?

Let us help.

Visit prh.com/nextread

Penguin
Random
House